31

M
OR

Lonely Teardrops

FREDA LIGHTFOOT

Lonely Teardrops

HODDER &
STOUGHTON

First published in Great Britain in 2008 by Hodder & Stoughton
An Hachette Livre UK company

I

A CIP catalogue record for this title is available from the British Library

ISBN 978 0 340 89744 7

Typeset in Plantin Light by
Palimpsest Book Production Limited,
Grangemouth, Stirlingshire

Printed and bound in the UK by CPI Mackays, Chatham ME5 8TD

Hodder & Stoughton policy is to use papers that are natural, renewable and
recyclable products and made from wood grown in sustainable forests. The
logging and manufacturing processes are expected to conform to the
environmental regulations of the country of origin.

Hodder & Stoughton Ltd
338 Euston Road
London NW1 3BH

www.hodder.co.uk

1959

I

Harriet

'I need to tell you summat, lass. Summat you should've been told years ago. I reckon now's as good a time as any. I know you think Joyce is yer mam, but she isn't.'

Rain was sheeting down, bubbling on the pavements, gurgling and washing the rubbish along the gutters and into the open grates on Champion Street Market, bringing a blessed relief from the early summer heat. The canvas awnings over the market stalls sagged and bellied under the weight of trapped water. It was still only late morning but many of the traders had already begun to pack up and call it a day, giving up on the struggle to keep their stalls erect against the deluge.

Harriet Ashton, standing at the sink as she washed up a few dishes from a late breakfast in the flat above her mother's hairdresser's shop, could see none of this, nothing but water running down the window. Or were they her own tears?

She blinked, rubbing them away with the back of one wet hand, but the image remained blurred as her slate-grey eyes once more filled with a rush of tears. Why did it always have to rain at a funeral? It just made the whole occasion even worse than it already was.

She certainly wasn't concentrating on what her grandmother was saying.

This was a day Harriet had been dreading for years. She could scarcely believe he was gone. For as long as she could remember Dad had been there for her, a vital and essential part of her life. He'd acted as a buffer against the harsh reality of her world, despite his being confined to a wheelchair. He'd spent much of his life restricted to one room downstairs behind her mother's hairdressing salon, with friends often popping in for a chat. On fine days he'd sit at the front door which gave him a good view of the market, chatting to customers despite his wife's complaint that he got under everyone's feet. Harriet had cared for him and loved him, poured out her troubles to his sympathetic ear and endlessly listened to his wise advice.

Now he was gone and she felt so alone.

The voice of her mother shouting up the stairs brought Harriet sharply out of her reverie, so that she almost dropped the plate she was idly washing.

'Have you not finished that washing up yet? Stop day-dreaming, girl, we haven't got all day. The hearse will be here any minute.'

Harriet's heart sank at the sound of her mother's voice. 'How will I manage?' She hadn't realised she'd spoken the words out loud until her grandmother answered.

'You'll manage, chuck, because you've no choice. Don't rely on that madam to be there for you.' Rose took the plate from her granddaughter's shaking fingers, swiftly dried it then pulled the plug, watching as the soapy water swirled away down the sink. 'Did you hear what I just said, lass? About that secret which has been deliberately kept from you.'

Harriet was mopping tears from her eyes, splashing her face with cold water in an effort to look more presentable. 'Sorry, what did you say?'

She stopped patting her face dry on the roller towel that hung behind the kitchen door to look at the small, round woman beside her, uncharacteristically smart in her black coat and veiled felt hat. A slight frown creased Harriet's brow just above a small straight nose flushed red with weeping.

'What was that you said about Mam?'

The old woman sighed, whistling slightly through her dentures. 'To tell the truth, which you should've been told years ago, and would've been if I'd had my way . . . well . . . it were all a cover-up.'

The light was dim in the shabby kitchen as the rain beat

relentlessly against the window, seeming to reverberate through the ancient building and shake it to its foundations, but the girl made not a sound as she stared at her grandmother.

'You'll have to start again, I'm not following this. I think I must be going mad, Nan, because I thought you just said Mam wasn't really me mother.'

'Eeh, love, it breaks me heart to have to tell you, but it's true right enough. Neither of 'em wanted to come clean, through shame, I dare say, but it were a bad mistake to my mind. Weren't right, weren't right at all.'

The older woman gathered Harriet to her plump bosom, holding her so fiercely, and pressing her face into the fortified wall of her corseted chest, that the young girl felt suffocated by the combined smells of lavender and moth balls emanating from the coat, kept only for best and for days such as today.

Harriet pulled herself free of the cloying embrace. 'Tell me again, slowly.'

'Well, there's nowt much else to say. That's about the sum of it. She's not yer *real* mam. By rights, I suppose, you'd have to call her yer stepmother.'

Harriet stared at Rose, dumb-founded, unable to think of a sensible response as a confused rush of emotions whirled through her head. Not her mother? Joyce, the shrewd-eyed, sharp-tongued woman who'd brought her up with such casual efficiency, was actually her *stepmother*? She shook her head in bewilderment.

'I don't understand.'

As if on cue her mother's voice again called from below. 'Will you get a move on you two, the hearse is here at last.'

Quick as a flash, Rose snatched up her granddaughter's coat and gloves, pinching the girl's cheeks to bring some colour into them and started to push her downstairs.

'Let's not upset her today any more than she already is. We can talk later.'

Harriet's alleged mother and brother were impatiently standing by the front door of the hairdressing salon, and, despite the relentless rain, a growing crowd gathered round the hearse waiting outside. Joyce considered the girl with a disapproving glare. 'Is that the best you can do? You look like summat the cat's dragged in.'

Harriet glanced rather vaguely at her old green raincoat and tie shoes. 'I don't have anything darker to wear, nor anything smarter.'

'You do look a bit of a tuckle,' Grant said, a self-satisfied smirk twisting his tightly pursed mouth. His broad shoulders seemed to strain the dark navy suit he wore, newly purchased from Burton's Tailors.

Joyce herself was clothed from head to toe in unrelieved black: black suit, a tiny feathered black hat, black handbag and gloves, and glossy black patent court shoes. She looked very much the part of the grieving widow, and as smart and stylish as ever with her dark brown, softly waved hair which she painstakingly teased into fashionable kiss curls, the pencilled brows lending a slightly surprised expression to her pale, oval face. But there was evidence of discontent to the slash of crimson mouth and a few fine lines drawn from each down-turned corner to the small pointed chin.

'What's wrong with your navy school skirt?'

'You must be joking. I haven't worn that since I left over two years ago. It's far too small.'

'Why didn't you mention it sooner that you'd nowt decent to wear?'

'I didn't think about it. Anyway, what does it matter what I wear?'

'You always do like to show me up,' Joyce snapped. 'And you can stop that crying, girl. Tears won't bring your precious father back, so try to show a bit of dignity. Now get in that car before you make an exhibition of us all.'

Standing by the graveside less than an hour later, her hands bunched in the pockets of the old raincoat, strawberry-blond hair tucked into a drab headscarf and protected by a large black umbrella held by her brother, dignity was the last thing on Harriet's mind. She longed simply to slip into the open wound of the sodden ground, hammer on the coffin lid and force her dad to wake up and come back to her.

How dare he leave her alone like this? How was she ever going to cope without him? And now there was all this other stuff thrust at her, which she really needed to ask him about. Her grandmother's words were still spinning round and round in her head, like sharp black needles of pain attempting to stab through the mists of her grief. Could it really be true what Nan had said, that this woman, Joyce Ashton, whom she'd always believed to be her mother wasn't her mam at all? It didn't seem possible. But if it *were* true, then it would explain why she'd always treated Harriet with barely disguised contempt.

A more frightening thought pierced her pain. What if Stan Ashton weren't her real father? Oh, no, that would be unbearable.

She glanced about at the many friends come to pay their last respects. There was Belle Garside, looking as voluptuous and flashy as ever in a too-tight black skirt and high heels that were rapidly sinking into the mud. Winnie and Barry Holmes, Big Molly Poulson weeping quietly into her handkerchief, Jimmy Ramsay, the big red-cheeked butcher, Alec Hall and Sam Beckett, both ex-servicemen, together with several members of the Bertalone clan.

Did these people also know the truth about her birth? Were they in on this so-called secret which had been so carefully kept from her? And what was the truth? Who was her mother, if it wasn't Joyce? Fear gnawed at her, chilling her soul.

Harriet felt a gentle hand squeeze her arm and looked into her grandmother's sympathetic brown eyes.

'Are you all right, chuck?' Rose whispered, and Harriet nodded, although it was a lie. She felt ill, sick to her stomach, as if there were a great weight on her heart. Her head throbbed with the effort of not crying when all she wanted to do was fall to her knees and sob. What was happening to her? Why did her life seem to be unravelling before her very eyes?

She swallowed her tears, knowing her mother hated any display of emotion in public and had given her strict orders to keep a stiff upper lip throughout, no matter what she might feel inside. Harriet's lip, however, was trembling, and she gratefully accepted the clean handkerchief her grandmother handed her to surreptitiously wipe her eyes and blow her dripping nose.

Somehow she got through the short funeral service, barely hearing the priest talk about Stan Ashton, the war hero, who had nearly died for his country. Seriously wounded in 1944, he'd endured a number of operations till finally he'd lost a leg and been confined to a wheelchair ever since. He was offered a prosthesis but couldn't tolerate the pain and problems that went with it.

Harriet had looked after him with loving care and attention throughout her young life, running to fetch whatever he needed and couldn't reach for himself, reading her favourite *William* stories to him, entertaining him with market gossip and the jokes she collected from her *Dandy* and *Beano* comics to make him laugh.

'Yer a right little tomboy, you,' he would say, chuckling as she leapt about in a pretend sword fight or galloped round the kitchen on her imaginary horse wearing a Roy Roger's cowboy hat and gun holster. She'd always liked to hear her dad laugh.

As she got older, Harriet had been the one to cope with his frequent black moods when he was in pain, while her mother did only what duty demanded, devoting herself to her hairdressing business. Joyce argued that if she hadn't done that they would all have starved, which Harriet supposed must be true. It just hurt that she'd showed so little compassion or love for the man she'd married.

As a child, Harriet had never understood why her mother always seemed so angry with him, and with her too, as if by association. She'd been aware that she and Joyce were not close, and that her brother Grant, at nineteen older than her by not quite two years, was her favourite. Why that should be Harriet had never understood, assuming that for some reason Joyce preferred boys. Following Nan's revelation though, if what she said was true, then it would explain everything.

Joyce nudged Harriet in the side with a sharp elbow. 'Get a move on, girl. Show's over, and I suppose we'll have to ask folk back for a brew. Did you get any food in like I asked you to?'

'Yes, Mother, I did.'

'Go on ahead then and put t'kettle on. And start cutting them ham sandwiches, I'm fair clemmed.'

Her mother was an attractive woman, still winning admiring, lingering glances from men, for all she was almost forty. But once she opened her mouth she sounded dead rough. Except when she was working in her hair salon, that is, when she put on airs something shocking. It almost made Harriet laugh at times to hear her mam trying to sound so posh when they all knew she'd been born and brought up in the Dardanelles, one of the roughest parts of Ancoats.

But Harriet knew better than to argue and quickened her pace to do as she was bid. She'd always hated the fact that her mother seemed to look upon her as little more than a skivvy, useful only to put on the dinner, do the shopping, wash up and generally mind the flat while Joyce herself spent every waking moment either with her customers in the salon, or down at the Dog and Duck with her men friends. And it wasn't as if Harriet didn't have better things she could be doing, like learning her short forms and studying for her Pitman's exams.

Wanting to please her mother, Harriet had agreed to attend secretarial college which Joyce was quite certain was the best way for her to secure a good job, but even that wasn't right. She either complained that her daughter never had her head out of a book, or else wasn't putting in enough effort, depending on her mood on any particular day. Even when Harriet had saved up to buy herself a second-hand typewriter to give herself more time to practise, she complained about the constant tap-tap-tapping of the keys. She never seemed to stop criticising whatever her daughter did.

Today, if she hurried, Harriet thought she might at least have a few blessed moments alone to mull over her loss before the other mourners arrived, and to think about what she'd just learned on this miserable day. Though perhaps it was best not to think at all.

Oh, if only she'd been told all of this before Dad died, then she could have asked him for a proper explanation. For some reason he'd chosen to keep it a secret but she had to know more. Why would he do that to her? Why would he lie? And could she now rely on her mother to tell her the truth? Harriet was determined to drag the whole story out of her grandmother, since she was the one who had opened up this particular Pandora's box. She wanted, *needed*, to hear every last detail. Joyce not her mother? Lord, what a mess!

2

Joyce

The day Joyce met Stan Ashton seemed to mark the start of a perfect summer. It was July 1939 and she'd been instantly bowled over by his charm, and by his rugged good looks. She met him quite by accident while she was standing in a queue, the first of many during that long, endless war. Later, Joyce couldn't even remember what she had been queuing for, sausages perhaps for her dad's breakfast, but one minute she'd been standing in line, the next she was sprawling in the gutter. Some great bulk of a woman had elbowed her way to the front, sending Joyce flying.

'Hey, I know I'm irresistible to women, but they don't usually fall at my feet.'

Heads swivelled to see who this rich male voice belonged to as the young man helped her to her feet. Joyce could see their glances of pure envy as he dusted down her skirt and picked up her shopping basket.

He was smartly dressed, polite, and utterly gorgeous, and just looking into those slate-grey eyes made Joyce go all weak at the knees and almost made her collapse again. He wasn't too tall. Joyce didn't care for tall gangly men. Stan was of medium build, broad shouldered, with a shock of red-gold hair and a teasing smile on his freckled face. Warm, easy going, he filled her with a strange, pulsing excitement, as if she knew she'd met her destiny.

Champion Street Market was humming with activity that morning. As always, women's heads were bobbing anxiously together as they discussed the looming spectre of war. People had long since lost faith in any attempt at appeasement made by the Prime Minister Neville Chamberlain. He appeared now as a rather foolish old man with his rolled-up umbrella and bit of paper he thought could solve everything. No one had any doubt that war would come. But not yet, Joyce thought, smiling cheekily back at the stranger, please not yet.

It was a summer for love, for dreaming and hoping everything might turn out right after all. The sun never seemed to stop shining and each evening Joyce would dash home from the market where she worked on Molly Poulson's cheese stall, to meet this handsome young man. They'd walk arm in arm out into a warm, summer's evening, not caring where they went, with eyes only for each other.

They were young, and naïve, Joyce just turned eighteen and Stan barely a year older. They felt as if they could conquer the world, instead of facing the grumbling warnings of a world war.

He proved to be the perfect gentleman, never trying anything on that he shouldn't. They kissed a great deal, mainly in the back row at the flicks, and talked endlessly.

He told her all about his family, who lived in Macclesfield. His father ran a wholesale ironmongery business and Joyce got the feeling they were quite comfortably off. This made her nervous and she was reluctant to tell him about her own father, who was a mere dustman, surely the lowest of the low. Joyce had always felt a bit ashamed of her family, living as they did in a pretty rough part of Ancoats. It was a relief for her to escape each day even to Castlefield, which was marginally, although not much, better. But she had hopes and dreams of a better future. Joyce intended to make something of her life. She told him simply that her dad worked for the council.

As July and August slipped rapidly by, the atmosphere gradually changed. Hitler signed a pact with the Soviet Union and even Neville Chamberlain was saying, 'We are now confronted with the imminent peril of war.' Joyce began to feel as if she were on a roller-coaster, one minute high with excitement, the next plunging into an abyss she couldn't even imagine. The world was changing and she could do nothing to stop it.

Then one evening as they strolled on the towpath by the Bridgewater Canal, Stan gave her a lingering kiss, holding her tighter than usual in his arms.

'There's something I need to tell you.'

Joyce's heart skipped a beat. Was he going to say that he loved her?

He fidgeted a little then destroyed her dreams with just a few simple words. 'I've volunteered to join the navy.'

'What?' In a way she'd been half expecting this, dreading it in fact as mobilisation had already started. But she'd shut the thought out of her head, not caring to face the inevitable. Now she swallowed the ball of fear that tightened her throat. 'When do you leave?'

'I'm expecting to be called up for training any day soon.'

She nodded, too uncertain of him to express all the thoughts that were crowding in her head. Perhaps he was similarly affected for even now he didn't declare himself. Joyce had believed him to be quite keen, as taken with her as she was with him, yet he didn't even ask her to write.

It cast a shadow over their last few days together, but did nothing to prevent her from falling head over heels in love. It was far too late anyway to stop that from happening. She'd hoped he might feel the same way.

On 1 September 1939, Hitler marched his troops into Poland and two days later war was declared. There was a surge of panic, with people lifting their eyes to the skies as if half expecting it to turn black with German bombers, as Goering had promised.

Two days after that Joyce was standing on the platform at London Road Station, saying goodbye. 'It's been a great summer,' Stan said, taking her gently into his arms. 'You're a great girl, Joyce, I'm glad I met you.'

'I'm glad I met you too,' she told him, going all misty eyed with unshed tears.

All around them were other young couples weeping and saying their goodbyes. There were women as well as men dressed in khaki and navy blue, some of them looking quite skittish with blonde curls and lipstick, which surely was against regulations. Not that Joyce blamed them for this small show of defiance; they'd need all the courage they could muster where they were going. She felt her own surge of pride to be standing with this handsome young sailor who was holding her so tightly in his arms.

'I don't suppose you'll miss me,' he jokily remarked, as he stepped away and swung his kitbag on to his shoulder.

'I don't suppose I will,' she jauntily replied, afraid of seeming needy.

She ached for him to tell her that he loved her, to ask her to wait for him, and to write to him every day. He paused, uncertain for a moment, as if he might be about to say something more, but then a rowdy group of laughing sailors suddenly surged all round them.

He had time only to give her one last kiss on the tip of her nose before climbing into a carriage with them. As the train started to move he leant out of the carriage window shouting something to her which might have been, 'I'll write,' but she couldn't be certain. Then he was steaming out of her life, and far too late Joyce remembered that as she'd never allowed him to come to her home, he didn't even know her address. She didn't expect ever to see Stan Ashton again.

Thinking about that day now, twenty years later, made Joyce's heart bleed. She and Stan had started out with such high hopes. He an idealistic, eager young man setting off on the adventure of war. She a silly young girl with romance filling her head. They hadn't the first idea what they were facing. It had all seemed so unreal, like something out of a Hollywood movie. Yet when reality had struck, they'd both sadly come down to earth with a bump.

Now he was dead, praise the Lord, and Joyce did not encourage the mourners to linger. Once everyone was fed, courtesy of her daughter, she made it very clear that she had a more pressing engagement.

'I must open the salon in time for my three o'clock appointment,' she informed her guests in her carefully enunciated diction. 'The lady in question is one of my regulars.'

'Show some respect,' Rose hissed, under her breath. Even though she'd had little affection for her son-in-law when he was alive, it didn't seem quite proper to shuffle everyone off in order to rush the next person under the hairdryer before they'd decently disposed of the body.

Joyce, however, had no such sensitivities. 'It's all right for you, Mother, but I've my living to earn. Haven't I always had to fend for myself?'

Even the priest winced at this blatant reference to her late husband's incapacity in that direction. People took the hint and one by one began to set down their cups and saucers and drift away, some of them to adjourn to the saloon bar of the Dog and Duck.

'If you'll excuse me, I must change,' Joyce coldly announced, her smile frosty as she walked away. 'Please show people out, Harriet, and thank them for coming and giving your father such a good send off.' Just as if he were going on some long sea voyage and not into the hereafter.

Harriet did as she was told, appalled by her mother's blatant lack of tact. The prospect of life in this claustrophobic little flat over the hairdressing salon without Dad to keep the peace between the three women filled her with sudden fear. There'd be blue murder done before the week was out.

After the guests had gone, Harriet followed her mother downstairs. 'Could I just have a quick word, Mam, before you start your three o'clock?' Her pale, heart-shaped face was etched with anxiety.

'Not now. Haven't I just said that I'm busy?'

Really, that girl had never been anything but a trial to her. Always ready to voice some opinion of her own and never prepared simply to do as she was told. Arrogant little madam and stubborn as a mule, just like her father. Joyce felt bitterness sear her soul, as always when Harriet approached with what should have been a perfectly reasonable request. She'd done her best by her though, she really had, more than most would have been willing to do in the circumstances. It was simply asking too much to expect her to feel the same way about this child as she did about her own darling Grant.

She'd loved her son from the moment he'd been put into her arms despite a long-drawn-out labour and a painful, difficult birth. As he'd grown older she'd seen him as compensation for rushing into a hasty and unsatisfactory marriage.

But then life never turned out quite as you expected. Nor people either. Stan Ashton certainly hadn't been the strong, dependable husband she'd hoped for. In Joyce's opinion he was a lazy, good-for-nothing lout who couldn't keep his hands off other women. He'd always hotly denied this, save for landing her with Harriet whom he could hardly deny was his child. But Joyce was convinced there'd been any number of other women, one in every port. Weren't sailors always like that? She'd accused him of such time and time again but he would just look at her sadly and sigh.

'There was just the one, Joyce, as you well know. More's the pity,' he would say, treating her as if she were stupid.

Then they would sink to petty point scoring yet again. 'The pity is that I ever married you in the first place,' she would fire right back, which seemed to amuse him, much to her irritation.

'Or that I believed your own eagerness to wed me was a result of true love.'

She'd refused to answer that charge, simply insisting that no woman in their right mind would love such a useless imbecile, great lazy lump that he was. Stan would agree that, trapped by their own folly, each had indeed made the other's life a complete misery, destroying something beautiful between them. Joyce hated such remarks and would accuse him of making no effort to rebuild his life after the war, and of using his disability as a means of avoiding family responsibilities.

'The only time you ever make use of your crutches is to stagger down to the pub, which is no doubt where you pick up your women.'

'Whereas I'd be better off using them to knock some sense into your daft head. I ask you, what woman would take me on, eh? Long John Silver would have more luck.'

Sometimes he would mock her for acting above herself, for her airs and graces and her grand ideas when she left Poulson's Pie and Cheese stall to train as a hairdresser and later opened her own shop. He teased her for her love of frills and furbelows on her cushions and curtains and dressing-table skirts, her fastidiousness, even for sleeping in a hairnet and plastering her face with Pond's cold cream before retiring alone to her single twin bed. The funny and tender man she'd fallen in love with could be bitingly cruel at times, and the fact this was often as a result of the pain he suffered, was no excuse in Joyce's eyes.

Having suffered from the ignominious shame of what she considered to be a poverty-stricken childhood, for all Rose might insist she'd lacked for nothing she really needed, Joyce had made up her mind quite early on that she was going to make something of herself. If Stan Ashton couldn't provide it, then she'd get it for herself. She certainly had no intention of turning into a slob like him.

He was right about one thing though, their marriage had been a complete shambles, doomed from the start. He simply wasn't the man she'd fallen in love with.

After Harriet had been born in November 1941, almost two years to the day since they married, the shame of this unexpected and unwanted child had set her on a course of action, the consequences of which she was feeling to this day. And who else could be blamed for the outcome of that long-running battle between them, but her cheating husband?

Oh, yes, Joyce was glad that he was dead, and the endless war of attrition between them was finally at an end.

'Will you be wanting a little trim, Mrs Gregson?' Joyce brightly enquired of her customer, combing her fingers through the woman's hennaed locks. 'When did you last have it cut? Was it four weeks ago or five?'

'I wouldn't know, dear, but I rely entirely upon your opinion, and your skill with those scissors.'

On this occasion Joyce used a razor, efficiently cutting the hair into graduated lengths from two inches to five to suit the latest pixie style. She was just putting in the last of the rollers, wound smoothly in place from right to left, starting at the crown and then down each side, when Harriet stuck her head around the door once again.

'Hello, Mrs Gregson, would you like a coffee?'

'Oh, what a dear girl you are. That would be lovely. Two sugars please. You are so fortunate in your daughter, Joyce. What a treasure she is.'

'Indeed,' Joyce agreed with a tight smile, starting on a row of pin curls to frame her client's face. *She's no daughter of mine,* Joyce longed to say but kept her lip buttoned, as she had for nearly eighteen years. If fate had decreed that she be the one left holding the baby, it failed to make her love the child, try as she might.

There had been a time when she'd been desperate for another child, had dreamed of adopting this one so that Harriet would indeed be her own, but that was when Joyce had still held hopes of saving her marriage. They'd proved to be false hopes. Later, after all that happened, she'd been driven by duty, and a certain sense of responsibility, reinforced by pressure from her own mother. Nevertheless, Joyce had fully intended to escape her disastrous marriage the very moment peace was declared, and reclaim her precious freedom.

Unfortunately, by the end of the war everything had changed yet again. Stan had come home crippled, both physically and emotionally. Deeply bitter and mentally scarred, he'd been quite unable to fend for himself. Like it or not they were tied to each other, trapped, and, as a consequence, succeeded only in making each other's lives a misery. What's more, she fully expected Harriet to make an equal mess of her own life. *Nature will run its course, no matter what, and there was bad blood in that girl.*

Joyce did feel that at least she'd made a success of her little hairdressing business, of which, quite rightly, she was immensely proud.

She most certainly intended things to change for the better now that her useless husband was gone. There had to be a limit to any woman's patience and generosity, and no matter what Rose might say to the contrary, she'd certainly reached hers. With the girl's father no longer around to hold her to that reluctant promise, she was now free to do as she pleased.

'Could I have five minutes before your next customer then?' Harriet persisted.

The smile did not leave Joyce's crimson mouth, despite the clipped quality of her tone. 'I'm busy right up to seven o'clock, as I always am, so whatever it is, Harriet, will have to wait.'

Once the client was tucked under the dryer with a cup of coffee and the latest copy of *My Weekly*, Joyce marched upstairs and accosted her daughter.

'What do you mean by keeping on interrupting me when I've already told you I'm busy? What's so important that it can't wait?'

Harriet took a breath. 'Nan told me something today that shocked me. I can't quite take it in, so I need to ask you if it's true.'

Joyce cast a swift glance across at her mother's chair only to find it empty. She rightly guessed that Rose had finally let the proverbial cat out of the bag, as she had threatened to do many times. The old woman evidently meant to stay well clear until the matter had been dealt with, a skill at which she was past master. So be it. Joyce felt more than ready to tell the girl the truth, except that she would do so in her own good time, duly edited, naturally. Joyce glanced at her watch and let out an impatient sigh. 'I've already explained that whatever it is will have to wait until later.'

'But it's important, and you might be going out later.'

'I certainly will be going out. When have you ever found me lazing about the house as your father used to do?'

Cheeks bright, Harriet said, 'He didn't have much choice, did he?'

'He wasn't always crippled, but he never did find much time

to take his wife out on the town, being far more interested in his other women. And after all these years stuck in this house like a prisoner, why shouldn't I enjoy meself a bit and get some pleasure out of life?'

'Don't exaggerate, Mam. You've never been a prisoner, not like Dad was, so don't start. Not today of all days. Dad's gone, isn't that enough? Let him rest in peace at least.'

Joyce bit down hard on her lip to stop the vitriol which threatened to erupt. What devil inside drove her to say such harsh and cruel things? Rose insisted they'd each been equally responsible for destroying their marriage, but then she hadn't been the one compelled to live with him, or suffer his moods and fits of temper in more recent years. As for Harriet, the girl had seen him only through the eyes of an adoring daughter, not that of a betrayed wife.

'You just remember who you're talking to. This is still *my* house, *my* business that pays the bills, so see my dinner's ready sharp on seven-thirty. Joe Southworth has offered to buy me a rum and coke this evening, and I reckon I deserve it after what I've been through today. I'll talk to you when I'm good and ready.'

On these words Joyce stalked off to comb out her client and fluff out the soft pixie curls all over her head.

3

Harriet

'No, it wouldn't matter to me who your mother was. Why would it, it's you I love.'

Harriet was sitting down by the River Irwell, cuddled up on a bench with Steve Blackstock, weeping into his shoulder. The Spam sandwich she'd bought for her lunch was quite forgotten.

Steve had been a part of her life for as long as she could remember, ever since they were in primary school together. For the last year they'd been going steady and Harriet simply adored him. She loved the teasing expression in his dark brown eyes which were looking at her even now with absolute love. She adored his heavy straight brows, somewhat flattened nose and wide nostrils set above a firm square chin, his dark hair cut to less than half an inch all over his head. Steve was a solid sort of guy, both in character and physique, and she was nuts about him.

'It matters to me. How would you feel if you'd just been told your mam wasn't really your mam, and that you were illegitimate? It's all a bit of a shock,' she ruefully admitted, blowing her nose and dabbing at her eyes. For her entire life Harriet had thought of Joyce as her mother. How could she suddenly stop thinking of her as such? 'I can't even get Mam – Joyce – I suppose I should call her now, to talk about it. Even Nan is avoiding me, and won't say another word.'

Steve snorted with laughter. 'Rose is very good at tossing down a grenade and then running for cover.'

'Oh, I wish Dad were here.' Slate-grey eyes swam with tears yet again as Steve put his arm about Harriet to draw her close.

If only she could turn back the clock so that things could be exactly as they once were. A week ago she'd been going along quite happily, caring for her dad, seeing Steve most evenings, if only for a chat, a kiss and a cuddle up some back alley or a walk by the river.

Harriet wanted her father to be alive still, so she could tell him off for keeping such important information from her. Harriet wished she could ask him to explain about this unknown woman who had given birth to her. She wanted to talk it all through with him, to learn more about her real mother and how much he'd loved her. But she couldn't, he was gone.

'He must've been in on the secret too though, mustn't he? Why was that, I wonder? Why did he never tell you?' Steve asked, echoing her thoughts.

For the first time in her young life Harriet felt as if her father had let her down. He should have been open and honest and told her the truth, given her the chance to understand and ask questions.

'I don't know, do I? But that's obviously why Mam and me never did get on. I suppose he thought if I ever found out she wasn't my *real* mother, then that would finish it for us completely.'

Harriet had often dreamed about how she would like a mother to be. Not like Joyce, all cold and distant. She'd once or twice been over to the Bertalones' house and been mesmerised by the way Carlotta fussed over her brood. She was constantly hugging and kissing them, tucking them into woolly hats and scarves if it was cold, cooking pasta for them, playing games with them, or just listening to their troubles. The kind of things Joyce never did. Would her real mother have been like that? Would she have loved Harriet more?

'But why don't you get on?'

Harriet tucked a stray blond curl behind her ear. 'Because no one can compete with the wonderful Grant, I suppose. She always picks fault with everything I do, never will find the time to talk to me, nor even take the trouble to get to know me properly.'

'*I* know you,' Steve said, rubbing his nose against hers. 'I know that you like the coconut sweets best in a box of Liquorice Allsorts, that you're afraid of spiders, have a little mole above your left breast, and hate doing your shorthand homework.'

'Who wouldn't?' Harriet giggled, almost forgetting for a moment how miserable and unhappy she was. She wrapped her arms about his sturdy waist and leaned into him, breathing in his familiar scent. Steve had recently started working for Barry Holmes on his fruit and vegetable stall as a summer job before he went off to Teacher Training College in the autumn, and he always smelled deliciously of apples, earthy potatoes and crisp lettuce.

'Anyway, my doing that secretarial course was her idea, not mine. I mean, can you see me as a secretary?'

'Ooh, yes,' Steve said, flicking his eyebrows up and down in comic fashion. 'In a short black skirt, white blouse and dark-framed glasses. You'd look real sexy.'

'Stop it,' she laughed, playfully slapping him so that he had to kiss her again to make her stop.

Where was the point in pretending to enjoy that dratted secretarial course, simply in order to win Joyce's approval when it would never be forthcoming, not now. Did this mean that she was free of Joyce's tyranny and could please herself what she did in future? The thought brought little comfort, for Harriet had no idea what she wanted to do with this new-found freedom, if that's what it was. She was a home bird, no doubt about that. Her life revolved around a familiar and unvaried daily routine, blown apart now by the revelation of this long-kept secret, and new sensations were stirring in her. Anger and resentment and rebellion.

In the distance they could hear the sound of ships' hooters, the shunt of trains in the goods yard, the hum of traffic. But hidden by hawthorn and cow parsley down at the bottom of these stone steps, sitting on the bench as they watched the water slide sluggishly beneath the old lock, they could be deep in the countryside and not in the heart of the city at all.

'So what do you intend to do about it?' Steve asked.

'What can I do? I'm still convinced there's more to it than they've told me so far, and I want to hear the whole story. Surely that's not too much to ask?'

Two more agonising days passed and Harriet was still waiting to hear the full tale, growing increasingly impatient. She was preparing the evening meal, with Grant being more of a hindrance than a help, as usual. Heading for the living room to lay the table she found him lounging in the doorway, her passage blocked. 'Do you mind getting out of the way, some of us have work to do.'

Her brother was tall, a great, broad bully of a lad with short greasy brown hair that sprouted out at odd angles all over his head, as if he'd just climbed out of bed and not bothered to brush it. He had a habit of hunching his shoulders up into his thick neck, which he was doing now as he leaned against the door-jamb, watching her with a narrowed, probing gaze.

'I'm not stopping you.' Smirking nastily, he stepped to one side but just as she was about to slip past, side-stepped back again so that she almost collided with him. Snaking out his hands he latched on to her, his fingers digging into her shoulders as he hissed his next words right in her face.

'It's time you started to be nice to me. Particularly now that you can no longer run to Daddy for protection.'

Harriet gave him a scathing look. 'I can manage, so long as folk keep out of my way.' Thrusting him to one side she carried a plate of bread and butter to the table and began to set out knives and soup spoons for the chicken broth she'd made. Grant stood watching, breathing noisily through his open mouth. Irritated, Harriet asked him to fetch the cruet, and the plate of cheese she'd left on the kitchen dresser. He made no move to do so and her patience snapped. 'For goodness' sake, can't you find something useful to do with your life instead of getting under my feet?'

Grant spent a great deal of time in the local pub, largely spending money provided by Joyce, and somehow managing to avoid the necessity of working himself. He might claim to 'have a few irons in the fire' but they rarely came to fruition. Nevertheless, money was his god.

'Don't imagine that when it's Mam's turn to follow our beloved father to the cemetery, or even Nan's, you'll be left so much as a brass farthing. You're not the favourite now, I am. You'll get nowt. You're a nobody.'

Harriet looked up at him coldly as she went back to stirring the broth. 'You think I care about money? Even if Mam had any, which she doesn't, I wouldn't touch a penny of it, not now.'

Grant's smirk vanished as he was thrown off balance by this response. 'Why wouldn't you? What do you mean, *not now*? What's happened?'

'None of your business. Go and call Mam.'

Ignoring her instruction, and deciding she was only making an argument for the sake of it, he gave a little self-satisfied chuckle. 'Oh, there's money all right. There's the hair salon for one thing. Mam owns that outright, you know. She doesn't pay rent. And Nan must have some life savings stashed away in her Post Office Savings Account.'

'You disgust me. Get out of my way.' Pushing him to one side she went to the head of the stairs and shouted down to Joyce to tell her supper was ready.

With supper over, Joyce finally consented to tell the tale of how Harriet's mother, her real mother, had died in an air raid. Harriet herself had apparently been rescued from among the rubble. The story was swiftly told, the bare details only given, and there was something like triumph in the gleam of the older woman's eyes, which brought a sour taste to Harriet's mouth.

Joyce seemed to be implying that this poor girl, whoever she might be, had deserved her fate for having been so careless as to bring an unwanted child into the world.

Harriet felt stunned by this information, which wasn't at all what she'd expected to hear. Her head teemed with questions yet she couldn't find her voice in order to ask any of them. Given the choice, she would have preferred this discussion to have taken place in private, without her brother listening to all these juicy details as he slurped tea from his saucer.

Surprisingly, Joyce snapped at her son in an unusual chastisement. 'Use the cup, Grant, like everyone else.'

Harriet remained silent for some long moments while she digested the story of her mother's tragic end. 'And she wasn't married?'

'No.'

'So, it's true then, I am illegitimate?'

'If we're being strictly accurate, yes, you are.'

Grant gave a loud guffaw of laughter. 'You mean Dad's wonderful little princess isn't so perfect after all? She's just a little bastard.'

Rose smacked his face, as only a grandmother dare. 'I'll wash yer mouth out with carbolic soap if you use such words in my presence again.'

Unfazed by her anger he shook the slap off as if batting away a fly, and carried on eating his fish supper. Grant had refused the chicken broth and bought himself haddock and chips instead from Frankie Morris's shop across the road. Even the greasy smell of them was making Harriet feel queasy.

She again addressed the woman she'd always believed to be her mother, her heart beating slowly and painfully in her breast. 'Why did you keep me then?'

'It were a miracle you survived that bomb,' Rose said, rushing into the ensuing silence and rubbing a comforting hand up and down Harriet's arm. 'You've been a survivor ever since, eh?'

Harriet tried to smile at her grandmother but her face felt all stiff and unresponsive. She turned back to Joyce. 'Well, why did you, when you clearly never have liked me very much, let alone loved me as a mother should?'

'Nay,' Rose gasped. 'What a thing to say!'

'It's true enough, isn't it? I love you, of course. You're my mam, so why wouldn't I love you. But I've never felt loved in return.'

Joyce looked at her, not troubling to deny the accusation.

'I could've insisted you were adopted, I suppose, instead of keeping you.'

'So why didn't you? For all the interest and affection you've shown towards me over the years, it's a pity you didn't. I might've found someone prepared to love me properly.' Harriet's lovely face seemed to have shrunk, it looked so pinched and diminished, with twin spots of feverish pink on each pale cheek.

'Your dad and I thought it best to keep you. It seemed the right thing to do. There was a war on, remember.'

'That's right,' Rose said, directing fierce glances at her daughter. 'Rules change in a war. We all have to pull together.'

'Aw, give over, you'll be going on about the Dunkirk spirit next. Why would you be so generous when your husband has just cheated on you? At least, I'm assuming that's what happened, unless of course there's something you aren't telling me? Was Stan really my father?'

There was a long, telling silence as Harriet looked from one woman to the other. She could feel her breath balled tight in her chest as she waited for the answer.

Joyce fluffed out her dark curls with one careless hand. 'Course he was your father. No doubt about that. Stan never minded who he slept with, so why not some chit of a girl whose name he didn't even know?'

A deep sense of relief flooded through Harriet, as if the world had tilted from its axis for a moment and had now righted itself again. What did it matter who her mother was, so long as Stan Ashton was still her lovely dad? She supposed she should feel a nudge of sympathy for Joyce being faced with clear evidence of her husband's infidelity, but it wasn't easy. She was such a cold fish, so hard and brittle that Harriet couldn't entirely blame her father for looking elsewhere. Maybe the girl had been kind to him. But something was puzzling her, something about this story didn't ring quite true.

'You say Dad didn't even know her name, but *you* must've known it, or how else would you have been aware she had a child by him, or that she'd died in a bomb raid?'

Joyce glanced across at Rose, a glare which clearly said see what a mess you've got us all into now. Rose didn't meet her daughter's gaze but kept her eyes on her empty soup bowl.

'Well, of course he knew her name, in the end we all did. I meant he probably didn't bother to ask it before he did the business. Typical!'

'So what was it?'

'I beg your pardon?'

'Her name. What was her name?'

Joyce drew in a sharp breath. 'Good lord, I can't remember her flaming name, not after all these years. I'm sure there were any number of women your wonderful father went out with. He wasn't too fussy.'

Harriet lifted her chin. 'Yet he always denied that.'

'Huh, and you'd be a fool to believe him.'

'He must have stuck by her all those months though, otherwise how would you know she'd been killed?'

Again that chilling silence before Joyce bit back. 'Doesn't that just prove what a lout he was to keep on seeing her, despite having a wife and son. Now do you see what I had to put up with?'

Desperate to discover all that she could, Harriet persisted with her interrogation. 'So, what was she like then, this girl who was my real mother?'

'She were a bitch,' Grant put in, momentarily taking his eyes from his fish supper to turn his amused gaze upon Harriet.

'How would you know, you were nobbut a babby?' Rose snapped at him, quick as a lash.

Joyce got up from the table, smoothing her hands over her linen skirt as if to brush the matter away. 'Grant is right, Mother. The daft girl slept with my husband, so don't expect me to say owt nice about her, even if she was a – a friend of sorts.'

'A friend?' Harriet queried, but no one was listening to her.

'She was a whore, nothing less.'

'Nay, that's coming a bit rich, even from you,' Rose protested, her cheeks pink.

With a freezing glare Joyce looked down upon her mother where she sat all tight-lipped with one protective arm about her granddaughter. 'When I want your opinion, I'll ask for it.'

'I've nowt to say save the truth,' Rose shouted right back. 'All right, the lass were mebbe no saint, but that doesn't mean she was what you've just called her. And if your husband turned to . . . well . . . to another woman, we know he wasn't entirely blameless, don't we? I'll admit that I never really took to Stan Ashton. He were a Catholic for one thing, and a Yorkshireman for another. Wrong religion and wrong side of the Pennines, and then for what he did . . . But then, he must've been soft in the head to wed you. I said from the start it were a bad mistake, but would you listen?'

'He was a good dad to me,' Harriet stoutly declared.

Grant grumbled, 'Huh, he allus made it very clear you were his favourite.'

Ignoring the boy, Rose smiled and gently patted her arm. 'Aye, he were a good dad to you, and to you too, Grant, though you might not have appreciated it. No one could say otherwise.'

'Oh, spare me the hearts and flowers,' Joyce snapped. 'Stan Ashton betrayed me and then forced me to take on his by-blow but—'

'Forced?' Rose interrupted.

'Obliged then. But now he's gone, thank God, so let the sinner rest in peace.'

'And what about me?' Harriet asked, getting to her feet to meet the hard, unforgiving eyes of her stepmother with a furious glare of her own. 'I suppose you want me to go an' all. Do you want me to leave now Dad is dead?'

Rose was gabbling a protest, clutching her hands to her chest in some distress over the direction the family argument had taken, but it was Grant who answered before anyone else had the chance. 'Aye, go, why don't you? See if we care. You're a selfish little bitch you, just like yer mam, whoever the tart was.'

'Leave it, Grant,' Joyce said. 'This discussion is closed. I'm off out, in search of a bit of peace and relaxation. You can start clearing this table, girl, and look sharp about it. And see you get to bed early, you've work to do in the morning.'

Harriet's cheeks flamed with temper. 'Oh, so you're quite happy for me to carry on being your skivvy then, even if I am the daughter of a tart?'

'You can go to hell in a basket for all I care.' And without so much as a backward glance Joyce stalked off.

In that moment Harriet felt utterly bereft, as if she were alone in the entire world.

4

Rose

There was nothing Rose liked better than a bit of a crack with her mates from the market. On this occasion they were all moaning about the poor state of trade due to the heavy rain which had been falling since the day of Stan's funeral. Belle Garside was insisting they needed to call an extraordinary general meeting of the committee to address the latest rumour that Champion Street Market was once more under threat of demolition.

Joe Southworth, who used to be the market superintendent before Belle was elected to replace him, was resisting the idea, saying that's all it was: a rumour. 'Why would anyone want to demolish our lovely old Victorian market hall when we've only just finished building on the new fish-market extension? Where did you hear such nonsense?'

'From an impeccable source.'

'Who, Sam Beckett?' Joe sneered.

'No, as a matter of fact, it wasn't Sam. Ask Alec, he's heard the same rumour. The city's house-building schemes are making rapid progress. I heard that Kersal, Regent Road and the Hanky Park slums will come down this year. There's no stopping them. Both Salford and Manchester City Council are voting in favour of demolition all over the shop. It's inevitable.'

'I'll believe it when it happens,' Joe scoffed, reaching for his pint of bitter.

'Oh, so we do nowt till it's too late, do we? Is that the way you're thinking?' Belle challenged him, violet eyes flashing with anger. 'Good job you're not in charge any more then, isn't it?'

Rose was sitting with her best mate, Winnie Holmes, a glass of lemonade on the mahogany table in front of her, only half listening to the argument as it ebbed and flowed about her. Having decently disposed of the deceased a few days ago, they were now dissecting his life and character.

'He were a quiet man, were Stan, very private. Patient, you know, but then he'd need to be married to my Joyce. Save for when he were in pain, then he could really let rip. I can't say we were ever bosom pals but I used to feel sorry for the poor chap at times. Never complained. Kept things close to his chest, as I mentioned earlier. Secretive like.'

'But now it's all out in the open, eh, all that stuff you told me after the funeral? It may be none of my business, but how did your Harriet take it?' Winnie asked, avid for every gory detail, as always.

'Like a trouper. I dare say she's still champing at the bit for more, but I'll leave that to Joyce.'

Winnie took a sip of her Guinness, then wiped the froth from her upper lip with the edge of one finger. 'Is that wise? I mean, Joyce won't make it easy for the lass, if you don't mind my saying so.'

'How could I mind, when it's true? But I've decided it's nowt to do wi' me. Not my job to interfere,' said Rose, somewhat self-righteously, as if she hadn't done so already.

Winnie considered her friend with a wry shrewdness. 'Aye, I reckon it's best to leave 'em to it, in the circumstances. So who was she then, this flighty piece Stan knocked up, and what happened to her?'

There was a slight tightening of Rose's mouth but Winnie didn't notice. 'She was killed in an air raid in nineteen forty-one. Harriet were nobbut a couple of months old.'

'Eeh, that were a bit of bad luck. And Stan were away at sea at the time, eh?'

Rose agreed, the long earrings she always wore clicking noisily as she briskly nodded. 'Aye, as luck would have it. We were still living in Ancoats at the time. Anyroad, by a miracle the babby survived, found half buried beneath the rubble and he weren't for letting her go, not Stan, for all she'd be a cuckoo in the nest.'

'Oh, aye, soft as butter that lad, not like your Joyce who's hard as nails.'

'You might say that,' Rose drily commented. 'Though life has played some cruel tricks on her, so softness isn't summat she can afford.' Quietly sipping her drink Rose was beginning to wish she'd never started on this conversation. Joyce was very particular about not being shown up in front of folk and she'd go for the jugular if she thought her mother had been talking out of turn. Fortunately, Rose had only related their agreed version of the tale, although even that might be too much.

Eyes stretched wide with curiosity, Winnie was saying, 'Eeh, it were a miracle that babby were found alive. The good Lord must've been watching over the little lass on that day.'

'As He has been watching over her ever since.' Rose smiled softly, knowing she too had kept a watchful eye on the girl, just in case the good Lord forgot. The reason she'd broken her word to her daughter after all these years was because of Harriet. She couldn't bear to see the child go on being blamed for a situation that was none of her making, and it would be sure to get worse, now that her father was no longer around to protect her. Anyroad, it was long past time the matter was brought out into the open, and to hang with the consequences. They surely couldn't be any worse than they were already.

'Even so she has my profound sympathy. Joyce never struck me as a woman who'd generously overlook her husband's fall from grace and take in a poor illegitimate infant. She must've been mad as blazes to have such trouble land on her own doorstep. It's a miracle she forgave him.'

Rose pondered this for a moment. 'I'm not sure she ever did. No one could say they enjoyed a happy marriage, more like world war three.'

'Still, there's allus a silver lining, eh? She's a treasure is young Harriet. Though I must say I were surprised when you told me all of this. I never thought that the lass weren't Joyce's real daughter, not for a minute, and I shall look on Joyce with more compassion in future. She's a real trouper, bless her heart. A saint, no less to accept the lass as her own.'

Rose swallowed the last of her lemonade in a single gulp and stood up. She'd said more than enough. Too much. 'I reckon I'll be off to me bed. It's been a long day one way or another and I'm fair beat. See you tomorrow, Winnie.'

'Aye, chuck, take care. And don't worry, it'll all come out in the wash.'

'Yes,' Rose wryly agreed. 'Dirty laundry generally does.'

An hour or two later, Rose was sterilising the scissors and combs and wiping down the counter tops as she usually did at the end of a working day. Once the salon was all neat and tidy, with every scrap of hair swept up off the linoleum-covered floor, they'd go upstairs and she would put the kettle on for a brew before supper.

Joyce took off her pink overall and hung it behind the door, then touching up her make-up and teasing her dark curls into place with a damp finger, she told her mother not to bother making a cup for her as she was going straight out to meet Joe in the Dog and Duck, as usual.

Rose muttered something under her breath but her daughter's response was swift. 'If you've something on your mind, Mother, come right out and say it. Don't chunner to yerself like some old witch.'

Rose, ever the puritan, for once decided not to take issue on the perils of demon drink and instead mildly enquired, 'I only wondered if you'd seen our Harriet recently?'

'No, I haven't.'

'It's just that I haven't seen much of her today and I wondered if happen you'd found time to have another little chat with her.'

'No, why should I?'

'Well you were a bit blunt the other day, the way you told the tale, and you left quite a bit out, didn't you?'

Joyce stabbed at her thin mouth with a bright fuchsia pink lipstick. 'I told her all she needed to know. Anyroad, how would

I know where she is, I'm not her keeper? No doubt she's off sulking somewhere, still nursing her supposed wounds.'

Rose leaned on the brush and considered her daughter. 'So you aren't going to tell her the rest?'

'No, I'm not.'

'No names, no places, no further details, nothing more.'

'No, and don't you say owt neither or you'll be sorry. You've said too much already. Why can't you keep your big trap shut and leave these matters to me?'

'I were only trying to help, in my way,' Rose protested.

'Well you didn't help, not one bit. You just made matters worse.' Joyce pencilled a smooth brown line along each thinly clipped brow.

Rose pursed her lips. 'And what about our Grant? What are you going to tell him? Were you thinking of ever getting round to telling your son about *his* correct parentage? That Stan was no more his father than you were Harriet's mother, that the pair of you based that sham of a marriage on a lie. No wonder it ended up mired in secrets as dark and nasty as a muck-cart.'

Joyce whirled about before even her mother had finished speaking, her face draining of all colour so that the pink lips looked lurid against the grey pallor of her skin.

'Shut your bleeding mouth. I've told you a thousand times to keep your nose out of my business and not interfere.'

'Right then, I'll shut up,' Rose announced, slamming down the brush. 'My lips are sealed. Not another word. I'll just have to conveniently lose my memory, then, won't I? As you say, it's none of my business. But don't blame me if the lass keeps on probing. She's not stupid isn't our Harriet.'

Rose stalked off upstairs to put on the kettle for that much-needed cup of tea, and Joyce left the salon in a huff to meet up with Joe in the Dog and Duck, so neither of them saw Grant emerge from the little kitchenette just behind the salon. He'd been in there helping himself to a few quid from the stash of notes his mother kept in a small safe in the wall. He'd acquired the combination some months ago but was always careful not to take too much at a time, and to make sure he never touched the money on a Saturday when she counted it carefully and audited her accounts before depositing the cash in the bank on a Monday morning.

This evening, apart from being anxious for the two women not to discover this little habit he'd acquired of furnishing his own back pocket with a bit extra, he'd been riveted by the conversation between the two of them. He hadn't been able to believe his own ears. Now he walked out into the darkened, empty salon rather as a sleep-walker might.

He was shocked, stunned to the core. Stan not his real father? Then who the hell was, and why had his mother never bothered to inform him of this important fact? He felt betrayed, cheated, and deeply angry.

Grant presumed that Joyce must have been pregnant when she married Stan, a fact she'd obviously omitted to mention to her unsuspecting husband. That would be what his grandmother had meant when she said the marriage had been based on a lie.

The little minx! Although it was entirely typical of her, Grant had to admit. Never own up to the truth if there's any danger of it causing you problems, that was Joyce's motto. And his dearly beloved mother was nothing if not creative, which was perhaps a skill he'd inherited from her. Poor old Stan probably hadn't even been aware of what was going on until it was too late.

But he hated the fact that his mam had lied to *him* just as she had to Harriet. Not that it made him feel any more sympathetic towards his half-sister. Grant cared about nobody but himself.

Deep down he blamed Harriet entirely. He certainly didn't blame his mother. If Joyce hadn't been compelled by Stan to keep his stupid love-child, then he might well have paid more attention to his son, albeit one who wasn't of his own flesh and blood. And if Nan hadn't taken it into her daft noddle to spill the beans in an effort to protect her precious granddaughter from his mam's so-called bullying, none of this would've come out at all, and he'd have been none the wiser. So any way you looked at it, Harriet was the one to blame.

But what did this mean for him? Grant had no regrets about not having Stan's blood run through his veins. He'd hated the man for years, sensing there was some problem between them which had blocked all hope of a normal relationship, rather as Joyce had felt towards Harriet. He laughed, a bitter mirthless sound.

'What a flaming mess! What a family!'

It wasn't really a laughing matter though. He'd been happily seeing himself as better than Harriet, a cut above, as it were, since he'd been born in wedlock. Now it seemed they were tarred by the same brush, both by-blows of somebody or other in this farce of a marriage. All that mocking he'd done, calling Harriet a bastard, and now he'd discovered he was one himself, although he had still been born in wedlock, so maybe he wasn't.

Grant glowered, his agile brain clicking over like tumblers unlocking a door. It might be worth finding out who his father really was though. If he'd been a married man, which was likely since the pair of them had obviously been unable to marry, the chap might be none too pleased to find a forgotten son emerging out of the woodwork. And he might well be willing to pay to keep his mouth shut on the matter. Grant made a mental note to try to find out the names of some of his mother's war-time friends from Nan. Rose would be bound to know. But he'd do it without arousing suspicion if he could, at least at first until he knew a bit more. Such information could prove to be very useful. Money, after all, was far more important than whose blood ran in your veins.

What this revelation also meant, of course, was that he and Harriet were not related at all. They didn't share a single parent so she wasn't even his half-sister. A part of him almost regretted this. He'd always rather fancied her in a funny sort of way. Grant had little time for taboos but he supposed he could savour that feeling to the full now. It would be all the more fascinating because Harriet wouldn't know anything of what he'd just learned. She would continue to think they were related, which would be all the more fun for him.

He chuckled softly at the thought.

Neither were his mother and grandmother aware that he'd overheard their conversation. So really he was free to do as he pleased with this fascinating piece of information, and perhaps use it one day to his advantage, if only with this so-called half-sister of his.

5

Harriet

Harriet couldn't stop herself from thinking about the poor girl who'd given birth to her. How old had she been? What on earth did it feel like to find yourself pregnant and with no chance of putting things right by marrying the man responsible? She shivered at the thought. Even more dreadful was to die like that under a pile of rubble, or burned to death in the fire that always followed such bombing raids.

And what amazing luck that she herself had survived. Where had they found her, that little baby? Harriet wondered. How come she too hadn't been killed by the bomb? Didn't people usually hide under the stairs during an air raid, or in an Anderson shelter in the back yard? Maybe she'd been flung clear by the blast. Harriet decided she must ask Nan for more details, just as soon as she felt strong enough to cope with the answers.

Once her afternoon shift at the salon was over Harriet had walked down to her favourite place by the river, this time quite alone, needing time to think. She was still struggling to come to terms with all that had happened to her, and somehow, knowing that her friend Patsy was about to get married on Saturday seemed to emphasise the precariousness of her own situation. Patsy had found a place for herself at last, a man to love, a family to belong to, something Harriet had always taken for granted. Now she couldn't, not any longer.

Harriet thought about her mother, her *real* mother, and wondered what she'd been like, wishing she had a picture of her. Had she been a strawberry blonde with the same stormy grey eyes as her own? No, she got those from her dad. Had she too been afraid of spiders, hated rhubarb and loved to walk by the river so she could smell the new grass and pretend she was in the country?

Had she intended to keep this unexpected baby, dreamed of a good future for the two of them before she died in that terrible bomb raid? Or was the poor girl upset at finding herself in such a predicament, at a loss to know how to cope?

And what about her own future? Would Joyce even want her around now? Did *she* herself wish to stay?

Harriet glanced about her, at the rickety old footbridge that straddled the lock, the cracked paving stones beneath her feet that looked like a map of the world, and began, very softly, to weep. A part of her wanted to run away from this miserable situation and escape into a different world, to a place where no one knew her, where she could start afresh as someone new.

Yet the thought of leaving home, leaving Champion Street and all her friends, filled her with fear. She loved the market and the people who worked on it. Most of all she couldn't bear the thought of leaving her nan. Harriet loved that old woman, and, whether they were blood related or not, would always think of Rose as her grandmother.

Something rustled in the undergrowth and Harriet jerked round in her seat, dashing the tears from her eyes as she listened for the sound of a footfall. Was this Steve coming to look for her? She could do with a comforting hug right now. 'Hello, is there anyone there?'

When no answer came she sank back into her gloom, her face cupped in her hands, her thoughts and grief utterly consuming.

She'd tried all her life to be a good daughter. She'd always done what she could to help in a practical way, for Nan's sake, if nothing else. She put a good meal on the table each night, kept the small flat clean while Joyce worked in the salon below, and Rose helped with the washing and ironing.

They both saw this as their contribution, their share of the chores, which was fair enough. Harriet had sometimes felt as if she did more than her fair share, often being required to work in the salon in between attending the dreaded shorthand and typing course. She would have liked to see her brother making an offer to do the dishes once in a while, but mentioning this complaint to Joyce brought no response at all. Favourite sons, apparently, were spared such mundane tasks.

She'd tried to be loving and affectionate, although having been ignored or pushed away so often Harriet had largely given up the effort where her mother – stepmother as she should now call her – was concerned. She'd grown used to coping with Joyce's ill temper, to her sharp tongue and the way she veered from total indifference to bitter criticism.

But so long as she'd still had Dad Harriet had learned not to let her mother's coldness bother her too much. Now this behaviour had taken on a whole new significance.

As the sun dropped lower in the sky she plucked a few daisies and began to thread them into a chain. Dad used to make daisy chains for her when she'd pushed him out in his wheelchair. He had indeed called her his little princess, worthy of a crown, even if it was only made of daisies. Oh, how she missed him.

And this poor girl, her *mother*, must've loved him too, or why would they have stayed in touch, as they surely must have done throughout her pregnancy? He must have cared for the girl or else he wouldn't have insisted that Joyce adopt the child, despite the difficult circumstances.

Harriet chewed on a piece of grass and thought about this for a while.

Could anyone have coped any better than Joyce had? Could *she* accept a child in similar circumstances, if it were Steve's, for instance? Harriet shuddered even at the thought of Steve being with another girl, let alone getting her pregnant and producing a child. Was it any wonder if Joyce had been cold and lacking in affection towards Harriet throughout her childhood? Maybe it was time to stop blaming her adopted mother for being all frozen and bitter, now that she understood the reason. Maybe they could at last be friends.

But Harriet knew in her heart that it was far too late for them ever to be close. Joyce would never love her, however much Harriet might long for her to do so. Life had changed. Stan was dead, and Nan had finally revealed some uncomfortable facts about her birth. Nothing would ever be the same again.

Oh, but she loved her nan. She loved Steve. She loved Champion Street Market. So the most important question was, could they all make a fresh start and be a family again, despite everything? Somehow, Harriet very much doubted it.

Again there came the sound of rustling in the hedgerow and Harriet abruptly sat up, staring round with wide eyes, quite certain that she had heard something this time. She really should be getting home, making a start on the evening meal and her chores. This wasn't deep in the country at all, even though she liked to think it was. It was a pretty rough area, right in the heart of the city. There might be rats, the two-legged kind as well as those that scurried about in muck heaps in dank riverbanks.

Harriet suddenly realised that it must be quite late as the sun was setting, slipping down below the horizon, looking very like the ball of fire that must have destroyed her mother. Hooking her red-gold hair behind her ears she was about to get up and head for home when she heard a snort of laughter, and then a loud thump as a male figure dropped on to the path ahead of her.

'Grant, what on earth . . . You scared the life out of me, for goodness' sake. Have you been following me?'

Her half-brother snorted with laughter, as he always did when he'd taken her by surprise or played some nasty joke on her. 'I've come to walk you home, since your weedy boy-friend doesn't seem to be around.' He put a hand on her arm and Harriet shook it off.

'I can walk myself home, ta very much.'

'No need,' he said, taking her arm again and tucking it firmly into his. 'You'll never be alone while I'm around.'

Harriet pulled away, angry now. 'Keep your hands off me. I want to be alone, right? And I certainly don't need your help. Anyway, I thought you wanted rid of me.'

Grant chuckled softly, but it wasn't a comforting sound. 'Maybe I'm changing my mind. Maybe you and I might find we have more in common than we might think. Like I say, there's nothing for you now from the Ashton family, except what I'd be prepared to allow you. You no longer belong.'

'That's where you're wrong. Stan is still my dad.'

'Unfortunately your beloved father is dead and gone, so can do little to help. Mam is hardly likely to be on your side and Nan's getting on, just an old lady who probably hasn't got long for this world. So your only option is to be *very* nice to me in future, if you don't want to find yourself cast out and penniless.'

'Don't be ridiculous,' Harriet snapped, and marched off ahead of him on the path.

Grant wouldn't allow her to escape. Having trailed after her all the way home he was still being a pest when supper was over, still wearing that strange smirking smile on his face. Harriet ignored him and got on with the washing up. But once again he took up his favourite position, leaning against the doorjamb to watch her work.

'I should've guessed all along that you were a cuckoo in the nest. Yer not a bit like Mam and me.'

'Praise the Lord for that,' Harriet smartly responded. 'I take after Dad. I've got his grey eyes, and the red-blond hair he had before it turned grey. As a matter of fact, I'd like to think that I take after him in other ways too: his gentleness and courage, his determination not to let things get him down, even when he was in pain. His sense of fun.'

'You've got his bloody-mindedness, I'll give you that.'

Harriet lifted her chin. 'I hope so. You're such an evil little toad, Grant, God knows who *you* take after. You're one on your own.'

'You say the sweetest things, sister dear. Oops, I keep forgetting, you're only my half-sister, aren't you? Poor little bastard!'

'I assume it gives you a kick to keep saying that.'

He grinned at her. 'Oh, it does, it does indeed.'

Grant came closer to station himself right beside her, his breath
fanning her face so that she could smell the beer he'd recently
consumed in the Dog and Duck. Harriet edged away and set the
tap running to fill the sink with hot soapy water.

'It's nowt, is it, half-brother? Hardly any relation at all.'

Harriet rewarded him with a scathing glance. 'It certainly
explains a lot.'

His mean little mouth twisted into a mocking smile then he
ran the back of one finger down her cheek. 'No wonder I've
always felt this magnetic attraction towards you, even though I
loathe the sight of you.'

She slapped his hand away, sending soap suds flying. 'Magnetic
attraction? What rubbish are you talking now?'

'I've allus felt it, and I know you have, that's why we argue all
the time. You simply can't resist me. Admit it, it's compulsive,
this love-hate thing we have going between us.'

'Love-hate?' A shudder rippled down her spine as Harriet
snorted her derision. 'Get out of my way.' Plunging the dirty
dishes in the hot soapy water she turned her back on him, then
felt the heat of his bulky body press hard against her, trapping
her against the sink.

'Aw, come on, admit it. You like me really, half-brother or not.
You find me utterly fascinating.'

Harriet was struggling to free herself, feeling completely
powerless as she used the only means available to fight him
with, slapping hot soap suds in his laughing face. 'Utterly
revolting, you mean.'

'Of course, and totally compelling. We're chalk and cheese, oil
and water, Beauty and the Beast, you and me. But you can't
resist my fatal charm.'

Finally, she slapped him in the face with the hot dish cloth
and he quickly backed off, rubbing his face dry on the roller
towel as he tried to regain his dignity.

'For God's sake, stop messing about, you stupid fool. I've had
enough of your nastiness. I can see you think it's all some sort
of huge joke, but to me it's really rather upsetting.'

'Ooh, dear, really rather upsetting, is it? I'm weeping for you. Poor little bastard!'

Harriet swallowed her fury and got on with the washing up, determined to ignore him, but even then he wasn't done. As she moved back and forth in the small confines of the back kitchen, drying dishes and putting them away, Grant constantly blocked her path, teasing and mocking her till her temper flared to boiling point and she almost felt like cracking a plate over his head.

'For heaven's sake get from under my feet or you'll feel the back of my hand, even if you are bigger than me.'

'Now that I would like to see. Could be fun though, a real David and Goliath battle, and who do you reckon would win? Of course, if my attentions are so unwelcome—'

'Obscene,' she spat at him.

'. . . then the solution is in your own hands. All you have to do is pack your bags and leave.'

'This is my *home*. I've as much right to be here as—'

'. . . as me? I don't think so. What was it Mam called you? A by-blow, but I call you nowt but a bit of muck from the gutter found on the heel of someone's shoe.' His dark eyes glittered with menace and Harriet shivered, despite the heat in the small kitchen.

Yet she said nothing more, simply revealing in her glare all the loathing that had built up inside her towards this alleged brother of hers over the years. She remembered all the times he'd bullied her, when he'd torn up her books, spoiled her jigsaws, knocked over the water jar when she was painting in her colouring book, or broken her favourite doll. He even once tied a tin can to the tail of her cat who had run off and never returned. Now she no longer needed to feel guilty about hating him so much. Now she understood.

Head high, Harriet stormed past him to go to her room, the sound of his cruel laughter echoing chillingly in her ears. And for some reason she couldn't rightly explain, she stuck a chair under the door handle of her room that night and slept not a wink.

6

Joyce

It was the following day and every chair in the salon was occupied, with all the ladies of Champion Street Market in a fever of preparation for Patsy Bowman's wedding. Dena Dobson had her head in the sink while Harriet rubbed it vigorously with lemon-scented shampoo. Belle Garside and Clara Higginson were both tucked under the dryers, thankful that the noise meant they didn't have to engage in conversation with each other. Joyce herself was trimming Winnie Holmes's grey locks, more usually tucked inside an old woolly bobble hat.

Winnie, who ran the fabric stall, knew everything that was going on around the market. 'Anyroad, she's pregnant again is young Amy George, and Chris is walking around like a dog wi' two tails.'

Joyce tutted. 'What unfortunate timing. I thought she was to be a bridesmaid at the wedding on Saturday?'

'Oh, she don't show much yet, allus was a skinny little mite. It'll be a Christmas baby, I reckon. I should think you'll be looking forward to being a grandma yerself soon, Joyce, now your Harriet is walking out.'

'Walking out?' Joyce glanced sharply across at Harriet who, blushing furiously, was rinsing off the shampoo, pretending not to hear.

'Aye, isn't she doing a bit of courting wi' that Steve Blackstock who works for my Barry? Lovely lad, I couldn't have chosen better meself. And it may be none of my business but Joe Southworth and his wife Irma look like they're coming to the end of the line at last. But then he's never been backward at coming forward where other women are concerned, has he? Madam over there were quite cosy with him once.' She indicated Belle Garside, who was blithely unaware she was being talked about beneath the noisy hum of the dryer. 'Eeh, poor Irma. It's a miracle she hasn't done him in before now.'

Pursing her lips, Joyce tugged at the curly grey locks as she rapidly snipped. 'It certainly isn't any of your business. You're a vicious old gossip, Winnie Holmes.'

'Eeh, don't I know it, but what else is there to do to keep meself amused round here? And how are you holding up, Joyce love? I were talking to your mam last night about your dear departed. A lovely man, though none of us saw much of him since he were cut down by the war, just like my Donald. Bit of a rogue in his day, eh, which my dear husband never were, bless him. Anyroad, you have my deepest sympathies.'

'Do you want me to wash and set it on rollers or not, Winnie?' Joyce snapped, without any pretence at politeness.

'Nay, don't waste yer time. Who'd notice?'

'We all would, if you're going to attend this wedding on Saturday. Come on, stick your head in the sink. I'm sure you can afford a proper shampoo and set for once, and you don't want folk talking about *you*, now do you?'

Winnie groaned but did as she was told, knowing you didn't argue with Joyce Ashton. Moments later while pink sponge rollers were wound into place the old woman again glanced across at Harriet, and, raising her voice against the general din of gossip and machines, shouted across to her, 'Are you working here now, chuck? I thought you were training to be a secretary.'

'She is,' Joyce answered before Harriet had time to speak for herself. 'I mean her to do well, come what may, but I'm a bit hard pressed at the moment, what with the wedding and everything, so she's helping out. She has to earn her keep somehow or other.'

'Course she does.'

Harriet sat Dena back in the big leather chair and began to towel dry her hair. 'Actually, I'm thinking of giving up on the secretarial course. I don't think it's quite me.'

'Eeh, now there's a turn-up for the book. So what have you got in mind instead, chuck?' Winnie asked.

'Well, I could go and work for Lizzie Pringle selling chocolates, or perhaps on Bertalones' ice-cream stall. Or I could always go and join Maureen down by the arches. I'm sure she could find me a bit of business that'd make me much more money than being a secretary. My *mother* reckons that's just about where I belong. What do you think, Winnie?'

Winnie looked into Joyce's livid gaze through the mirror set above the sink before her. 'I think your mam is going to make me look a right bobby-dazzler.'

Later that same morning while Harriet shampooed Joan Chapman, Joyce slipped out and made a beeline for Barry Holmes's fruit and vegetable stall.

'One pound of Granny Smiths, and don't give me no bruised ones.'

Steve grinned up at Joyce as he dropped the apples one at a time into a brown paper bag resting on the big iron weighing scales. 'I'd never do that to you, Mrs Ashton. Anyroad, I know you'd only fetch 'em back.'

'Quite right too. And I'll take three pounds of Jersey potatoes too please, and half a cabbage,' she asked, in the clipped, over-polite tones she generally used when she was trying to sound all proper and rather grand. 'Not too big mind, there's only the four of us remember. And an onion or two.'

'The onions are big too. Are you sure you don't want me to cut one of them in half as well?'

'Don't get smart with me, lad, I'm by far the sharpest knife in the drawer.'

'I'm sure you are, Mrs Ashton.' Secretly pleased that he'd ruffled her out of her self-imposed posturing, Steve calmly weighed the onions and dropped them into her bag, then decided to risk a question. 'How's Harriet? Is she feeling any better? I know she's been really cut up over her dad's death.'

'I should think you've had ample opportunity to ask her

that yourself, since you and she are walking out. Or so rumour has it.'

Joyce gave him a tight little smile, watching with interest as a hot tide of colour stained the young man's neck. It was true then what Winnie had told her. The lad was soft on the girl. It irked her considerably to imagine the pair of them in love. Not that it would do the lass much good. Being in love certainly hadn't led to a happy-ever-after ending for Joyce, so what right did Harriet have to be happy? No right at all after the way her father had behaved.

'We always were close and I suppose we do see quite a lot of each other, that's true,' Steve was saying, fidgeting with discomfort as he weighed the potatoes. 'I'm not sure you'd call it walking out exactly.'

'What would you call it then? Getting yer leg over?'

He drew in a sharp, surprised breath, his sensitive young skin now draining of all colour. 'It's not like that, not at all. I respect Harriet too much to try anything on. We're just good friends. Anyway, we're a bit young to start getting too serious. You can trust me, Mrs Ashton.'

Joyce laughed, a harsh, brittle sound that chilled him. 'I wouldn't trust owt in a pair of trousers, which is where most men keep their brains.'

Then setting aside any attempt at polite interest, she allowed the intrinsic bitterness that was so much a part of her character to bubble to the surface as she leaned closer, hissing like a snake in his ear. 'You'll stay away from her, do you understand? I don't want Harriet bringing no trouble home. There's bad blood in that girl. Mark my words she'll come to a sticky end if she's not careful. Anyroad, aren't you off to college in the autumn?'

'I hope to train as a teacher, yes.'

'Well then, it wouldn't please your parents, would it, to see you getting yourself mixed up with some cheap guttersnipe.'

Steve drew himself up straight on a sharp, indrawn breath of fury. 'I'd rather you didn't call Harriet such names, if you don't mind, Mrs Ashton. And I do assure you, my parents aren't snobs.'

Joyce smirked. 'That's not what I heard. Well-brought-up lad like you with a father who's summat important in the bank. Your mother would have fifty fits at the very idea of joining her one and only son with a bastard. She'll have you lined up for a conservative with a double-barrelled name, I shouldn't wonder. If I were you, I'd find some other girl to dangle on your arm in future.' And slamming the coins down on the stall in front of him, Joyce spun on her heels and walked away. Steve watched her go with eyes clouded with worry.

Joyce didn't go straight back to the salon. She lit up a cigarette and scanned the market for the person most on her mind, Joe Southworth, with whom she was also anxious to have a word following Winnie's gossip. She caught sight of him up by the market hall wrestling with some trestle tables. Glancing quickly about to make sure she wasn't being watched, Joyce hurried over, and wasting no time came straight to the point.

'Is it true that you and Irma are finally splitting up?'

Joe looked up, startled to find himself so unexpectedly accosted about his private life while in the middle of this steady job. 'Hello, Joyce, and how are you this fine morning?' he pointedly enquired.

She sucked hard on her cigarette. 'Don't mess me about. *Are* you?'

Joe scratched behind one ear with the screwdriver he'd been using to fix the trestles, and frowned. 'Someone's been talking, have they?'

'Winnie, who else?' Joyce had been engaged in an affair with Joe Southworth for the better part of six months. Not that Irma, his wife, knew anything of this, any more than Stan had, or so Joyce believed. 'You've told her then?'

'Not yet,' Joe informed the legs of the trestle table as he again applied the screwdriver to the task in hand, just as if the question she was asking was of no concern to him at all.

'So when do you intend to?'

Joe knew Joyce wasn't one to let go till she had her answer and stood up, easing the stiff muscles in his aching back. 'Oh, pretty soon, but not today. She's put a lot of work into this wedding. Let's get that out of the way first, shall we? Anyroad, what's the big hurry? Your Stan is barely cold in his grave.'

'He never was *my* Stan, and you were happy enough to enjoy my favours while the warm blood was still flowing through his veins so why not now he's dead and gone?'

'Respect, Joyce. We need to show a bit of respect. Let some water flow under the proverbial bridge before we push the boat out.' He grinned at her, as if he'd made some sort of joke.

'You still haven't answered my question.' Joyce felt closer to losing control than ever in her life before. Everything was going wrong. She'd felt nothing but relief when she'd found Stan dead in his bed the other morning. All she'd been able to think was that her sentence, her long term of punishment, was finally over.

If she'd wept, it had surely been out of nostalgia for lost dreams, for the romantic young fool she'd once been, certainly not from grief. Even her mother spilling the beans over the big family secret hadn't greatly troubled her. She'd have told Harriet the truth herself pretty soon anyway, although not quite the whole of it, naturally.

But if Stan's death didn't make it any easier for her and Joe to spend a bit more time together, where was the point in being free?

Joyce cast him her most beguiling glance. 'You'll tell her soon though?'

'All in the fullness of time, Joyce, all in the fullness of time.'

'Make it soon, I don't care to be made a fool of.'

And as she rushed back to the salon, tossing the half-smoked cigarette aside in a show of temper, Joe twirled the screwdriver in his hand with a thoughtful frown. He had the strangest feeling he was getting in over his head with this one.

It was Joyce's friend, Eileen, who'd invited her to the party. It was the end of September, right at the start of the war, three weeks after Stan had departed for his naval training, and she'd heard not a word since. Not that she'd expected him to write.

Joyce's foolish pride had prevented her from revealing her address, so how could he?

All she'd done since he left was to listen to the wireless, waiting for news. If this was how she was going to be spending the months or years of war, Joyce didn't much care for it.

Probably he wasn't in the least bothered about her. If Stan Ashton wanted to see her again, or if he'd been keen for her to write to him, he would surely have said so. Obviously, their little love affair had been nothing more than a summer flirtation. She'd helped him to while away a few weeks in the sun before going off to war, that was all.

There was tension in the air now, and anxiety, a devil-may-care attitude creeping in, and a great deal of beer being drunk as many of the boys Eileen had invited to her impromptu party were expecting to be called up too, any day now.

Joyce hadn't touched a drop so far, as always afraid of losing control and making a fool of herself. People thought her quite confident because of the way she dressed and the airs and graces she gave herself to prove she wasn't a nobody. But she was really quite unsure of herself underneath, with this great big chip on her shoulder over her background, nervous of making a mistake in this lovely home which belonged to Eileen's parents.

Her father was an accountant, her mother a housewife, never having needed to work outside the home, and Eileen was training to be some sort of clerk in the bank. She was dark and pretty, with a mischievous grin, and had always been top of the class for all she could act like a complete scatterbrain at times. The pair of them had been friends for years, although what she saw in a girl who worked on a cheese stall on Champion Street Market, Joyce couldn't rightly say.

Again someone offered her a drink but she refused. Even beer made her feel quite light headed. Joyce longed for a glass of orangeade or Tizer, but couldn't find any. Not that it mattered as she was enjoying herself too much, dancing with one young man after another, laughing and joking and having such a good time she'd almost forgotten about one handsome sailor. Almost.

'How is he then, lover-boy? I assume he's written you sack-loads of passionate love letters?' Eileen teased, coming to hook her arm in Joyce's.

Joyce shrugged, trying to appear unconcerned. 'I expect he's busy.' She'd no wish to reveal that she'd foolishly forgotten to give him her address, nor had he given her his.

'Busy? Lord, not in the first weeks surely? It's a laugh that initial training. My Bill writes to me every day. Actually he's in France now, did I tell you? The sun is shining and he says it's just like being on holiday.' Eileen giggled but Joyce wasn't amused.

All this talk of war was very scary. People were saying that the British Army was totally unfit to fight, but Joyce didn't believe that. The Navy would certainly be strong, if only because Stan was part of it, and she was quite certain the army would be too. In any case weren't our boys in France behind the impregnable Maginot Line? Even so, they were facing great danger.

'They could be killed or wounded any day. You really do say the most stupid things, Eileen.'

'Ooh, pardon me for breathing. Who do you think you are, Miss Uppity? At least Bill writes every day. *Your* man, if that's what he is, can't even be bothered to write at all.'

'And if yours is having such a good time, maybe he's found himself a French sweetheart to keep him amused. What else will there be for him to do in this Phoney War?'

Eileen didn't much care for this comment, and, as on so many occasions in the past, their friendship rocked a little as a result and the argument got a bit heated after that. Then Joyce stuck her chin in the air, told her so-called friend that she was going upstairs to fetch her coat, and then going home.

'Suit yourself.'

The coats were heaped on top of the big double bed in Eileen's parents' room, and it took Joyce some time to rummage through and drag out her own from the bottom of the pile. She'd hardly snatched it up when the door flew open and a young sailor, very much the worse for drink, staggered in.

'Whoops!' Joyce said, laughing as she tried to help him to his feet. 'I think you've had a skinful. Take it easy, lad, you'll do yourself a mischief if you fall down those stairs.'

He looked at her, all bleary eyed, and blinked. 'By heck, you're pretty. I like brunettes, especially when they have long sexy legs like yours. What's your name, chuck?'

He was rather plump with wiry dark hair, wearing a big silly grin on his round face. Joyce didn't fancy him at all but his words made her blush, perhaps because she didn't get many compliments, not even from drunks. She saw no reason not to tell him her name. 'I'm Joyce, and you are?'

He didn't answer, just hiccupped loudly then lurched forward once more, only this time as he fell against her, his arms fastened about her waist as if for support, knocking her backwards into the jumble of coats and scarves and hats. Joyce found herself pinioned beneath him and simply couldn't move.

'Get off me, you idiot,' she cried, laughing despite her predicament.

'Hey, who you calling an idiot?'

'Move, you great clod!'

Afterwards she could never remember why, or when, it turned nasty. One minute they were both lying in a tangle of coats laughing, the lad demanding a kiss by way of an apology and Joyce trying to tell him that she had a sailor boyfriend already, thanks very much. But foolishly, she gave in and allowed him one quick kiss. It would do no harm and might pacify him, she thought. Only it fired his blood for more. The next instant he was holding her down, pressing one arm tight against her throat.

Joyce tried to protest but nothing came out of her mouth except a squeak. She felt sure he was about to throttle her, yet that was as nothing compared to what he was doing with his other hand. He was tugging up her skirt, sliding his hands between her legs and squeezing her, tugging at her panties and then fumbling with his trousers. By this time Joyce was in a state of panic, wriggling and kicking and squirming, but there was no escape.

He might be drunk but he was big and heavy, and seemed to have the strength of ten men. She couldn't even catch a choking breath or cry out, let alone prevent what happened next. Fear flooded through as he ripped open her blouse and sucked at her breast, then suddenly he was inside her, plunging and bucking like a mad thing. If she managed anything more than a strangled squeal nobody heard her above the pounding jazz music being played downstairs on Eileen's parents' posh radiogram.

When it was over he carefully buttoned his trousers then threw up all over the bedroom carpet. Joyce grabbed her coat to her bare breasts and fled, rushing down the stairs and dashing out of the house before anyone could witness her shame.

7

Rose

The day on which Patsy Bowman and Marc Bertalone were at last to tie the knot thankfully dawned bright and sunny after all the recent rain. A beautiful hot day in early July, with only a few lacy clouds streaking a sky as blue as a robin's egg. Each stall was trimmed with streamers and paper roses and everyone from Champion Street Market was invited to the wedding.

Irma Southworth, Joe's wife, and perhaps soon to be his ex-wife if Joyce got her way, had been responsible for baking a beautiful three-tiered wedding cake for the happy couple. The smallest tier was to be sealed in an airtight tin after the event to save as a christening cake for the first baby, as tradition dictated. Not that Patsy was in any hurry to take up motherhood, as she kept reminding Marc and his large Italian Catholic family.

Catering for the event had been a community affair. Big Molly Poulson had made the sausage rolls and pork pies, using the finest ingredients Jimmy Ramsay could supply, and Chris George had baked the fancy cakes and bread for the ham sandwiches, which Rose had helped cut and make up. Barry Holmes had volunteered to provide strawberries for everyone, and Papa Bertalone the ice cream to go with them. At intervals along the centre of the tables were trays of chocolates supplied by Lizzie Pringle's Chocolate Cabin. And there was plenty of sparkling wine for the many guests, shipped in at a discount by Leo Catlow.

Everyone declared that it was the finest spread anyone had ever seen. It was indeed a feast to gladden the eye, all set out on trestle tables that ran the length of Champion Street, while Terry Hall's skiffle group entertained the guests with Lonnie Donegan and Buddy Holly hits.

A day to celebrate and for everyone to share in the young couple's happiness.

Rose could see that her daughter was glad of a few hours off. The last few days had been hectic with all the cutting and styling required for this special day, not to mention a full hour that morning making the bride look beautiful, along with her two bridesmaids, Lizzie Pringle and Amy George. But she'd made a good job of them, as always. No one could deny that her Joyce wasn't gifted with her hands, even if her tongue was as sharp as a razor.

Betty Hemley had done the flowers, of course, sweetly fragrant bouquets of freesia and lily of the valley, signifying a return to happiness which surely the bride and groom deserved.

The church was crowded to the doors with not a spare seat in the house, little attention being paid to which side one should sit. Just as well since Patsy had no family. She'd come to the market as a starving orphan, having run away from her foster parents as she searched for her mother, but had been fortunate enough to not only be taken in by Clara and Annie Higginson who ran the millinery stall, but also right to the hearts of all the market folk, once she'd got over her initial defiance and rebellion, that is.

Annie had died some months ago but Clara was standing beside Patsy today, pink cheeked and proud as punch, as loyal as any mother could be, real or not.

As Rose watched Patsy glide down the aisle in her flowing white silk gown, designed and stitched by her Italian mother-in-law, she couldn't help worrying how her own granddaughter would cope with a similar problem. At least Harriet knew who her dad was, which was something, but not knowing who your mother was must be a heavy cross to bear. Yet Patsy had survived, so why shouldn't Harriet?

★

Once the service was over, Rose stood with her arm linked in Harriet's, watching as folk clicked their little box brownies to snap pictures of the happy bride and groom. There was a frown on her pale, heart-shaped face, the poor girl not looking half so joyful as the occasion demanded. Feeling the need to ease her worries, Rose squeezed her granddaughter's arm and whispered in her ear. 'Stop thinking about it. Put it behind you. Look at Patsy, she's fine.'

'I know, and I'm still *me* inside.'

'Course you are, chuck. Yer a real little gem, and allus will be. Just remember, it's our Joyce's problem, not yours. Only the future matters for you now, not the past.'

Easy said, Harriet thought, but she understood what her grandmother was trying to say and nodded bleakly, doing her best to smile.

Rose was very fond of weddings and surreptitiously wiped a tear from her eye. It reminded her of her own to Ronnie Ibbetson, a lovely man if ever there was one. Rose considered that she'd been blessed with a good marriage, to a man who'd come into her life if not exactly like a knight on a white charger, but at least willing to work hard so they could eventually escape the slums of Ancoats.

She'd endured a poverty-stricken childhood, far worse than the one her daughter claimed to have suffered. Back before the Great War when Rose was growing up you thought yourself lucky if you had a pair of shoes to put on your feet, and managed to get your grubby fist round a dripping butty at some point in a day.

Joyce might complain bitterly about what she'd lacked as a child in the way of material goods, but she'd never gone hungry, nor ever went short of love. Yet she remained ashamed of her roots, and didn't take kindly to being reminded of her humble origins, not even by her own mother. She'd rather lie than admit she'd once been a scruffy little tyke with a father who was a dustman. As if that mattered! It was what sort of a person you were inside that counted, not how much money you had.

Something her daughter couldn't quite get her fancy head round.

Rose freely admitted to being a bit frugal herself where money was concerned, some might say to the point of meanness, so she could understand her daughter's obsession to a degree, although she was doing very nicely in that salon of hers and wasn't short of a bob or two.

But then young Grant was every bit as greedy, the little tyke. Pity he didn't have his mother's work ethic.

Rose watched with resignation as the boy sidled up to her now, beady black eyes as sharp as a ferret's, breathing noisily, as he'd always suffered sinus problems ever since he was a lad.

'I'm bored with this wedding. Lend us a quid, Nan, then I can go to the dogs.'

'Nay, tha went to the dogs years ago, lad,' Rose said, in chortling good humour.

'Very funny. Go on, you can spare me ten bob at least.'

'Want, want, want! Do you reckon money grows on trees?' She gave him five shillings. 'Don't spend it all at once.'

He didn't trouble to thank her, just slipped away into the crowd, off to the greyhound track or about his own nefarious business.

Rose didn't rightly care. Too used to handing out cash when he asked for it, Rose instantly forgot about him, and glanced over to where Joyce was openly flirting with Joe Southworth, making it very plain what was going on there to anyone who cared to look. Done up like a dog's dinner she was too, in a cream shantung two piece with a box jacket and tight skirt, almost like a bride herself.

Rose was wearing a frock she'd had since the thirties. It was magenta silk, a bit faded admittedly but Ron had bought it for her and Rose had always kept it for best so it hardly looked worn. She'd never need to replace it, that was for sure, and why should she? It reminded her so much of him, and his loving, tender generosity towards her. She'd dressed it up with a pair of dangly pink earrings and a sparkly brooch. Ron had been fond of buying her the odd trinket, once he could afford to spoil her a bit.

She could buy her own bits and bobs now, she supposed, should she wish to do so, but liked to be a bit careful with her brass. You were bound to end up that way when you'd never had much in the first place.

'How much do you reckon all this lot cost?' Rose asked of her granddaughter. There was nothing Rose loved more than trying to assess what someone might have paid for a dress, necklace, house, or whatever. 'A pretty penny, I should imagine.'

Rose had quite a bit put by herself, as he'd always been prudent had Ron, opening a post office savings account, putting money aside in the Oddfellows Friendly Society for their old age, and in case any of them should need to see a doctor. It'd built up nicely over the years as they'd all been pretty healthy. The dear man had even shown considerable sensitivity by dropping dead of a heart attack, thereby not requiring any funds to be spent on his own medical care.

He'd also been a bit of a gambler, not on the dogs or the gee-gees, but in something called the stock market.

'Nothing ventured, nothing gained,' had been Ron's motto, along with, 'We're right at the bottom of the heap, you and me, lass, so we can only go up. What have we got to lose?'

Rose hadn't understood any of it, but it seemed he didn't lose, at least not too often or too much, and had left her surprisingly well provided for.

Not that Joyce was aware of quite how much her dustman father had left. Oh, no, Rose kept that very close to her chest. The silly lass had looked down on Ron when he was alive, so she didn't deserve to benefit from his death. Ruined the silly mare's life, in a way, that snobby streak she had.

Anyroad, just as well if she didn't inherit, since that madam went through money like water. No, when Rose went to meet her maker, she meant to leave whatever remained of her savings to Harriet, not selfish, silly Joyce. Not that she'd informed her daughter of these intentions, not yet.

Harriet was saying, 'Much of this celebration has been given to Patsy as a gift by the other traders, since she has no mum and dad of her own. Rather like me.'

'Nay,' Rose demurred. 'Not at all like you. You have me. I'm still yer nan, and you had a father, don't forget.'

'I'll never forget Dad. But I'm sad he didn't tell me the truth. Why didn't he?'

'He did what he thought was best,' Rose prevaricated, for once defending her son-in-law. 'Your Mam . . . Joyce . . . did too. It might've turned out all wrong but they did it for the best of reasons, at least, we have to assume so.'

Why Joyce felt so bitter about the blows that life had dealt her, was quite beyond Rose. She would never have taken her personal grievances out on Harriet, even if she was the child of a straying husband. Why Joyce persisted in doing so, and had got herself so churned up with revenge, Rose would never understand, not if she lived to be a hundred. Some good had come out of it, she supposed, in that they still had Harriet, but quite a bit of bad too.

She again wiped a tear from her eye, one of sadness this time.

'What about your mum, she died young, didn't she?' Harriet had heard this story before but still loved to have it repeated. She needed to hear it now to prove that she still had a place in the Ashton and Ibbetson family tree. She felt so alone, as if the world had shifted and she was about to fall off the end of it. Even though she'd never felt close to Joyce, she still thought of her as her mother. It was hard not to, since that's what she'd been for Harriet's entire life.

Rose nodded. 'Aye, my mam were sickly with TB, and died young leaving six childer. Me Dad were a docker working on the wharves, and a right bully. He'd beat the living daylights out of you soon as look at you. A Yorkshireman no less, so no wonder I never had no time for that son-in-law of mine, since he came from the same neck of the woods.'

'Dad wasn't violent,' Harriet protested. 'He never laid a finger on Mam, though he'd sometimes land Grant a clip round the ear.'

'Aye, and the stupid lad probably deserved it.'

Harriet half smiled, glancing about as if expecting to see Grant emerge out of the crowd. She'd deliberately avoided him today, since she still felt uneasy over the fact he'd followed her down to the river the other day. Whatever little game he was playing, she didn't find it in the least amusing.

Rose was saying, 'Anyroad, when my mother died, Dad said he could only cope with me two brothers. Me and my three younger sisters were farmed out, split up around the family, and never managed to keep in touch. Iris and Daisy are in London somewhere, I think, although it's that long ago I can't quite remember. But to this day I've no idea where our Violet lives, or even if she's alive or dead.' Rose frowned. 'Though I might've forgotten that too, I suppose.'

'Oh, Nan, that's so sad.'

'Well, my memory isn't what it was, not by a long chalk.'

'No, I mean about losing touch with your sister.'

'It happens, sometimes, in a big family. Aye well, that's enough about me, eh? Doesn't Patsy look pretty, and all flushed and happy. Things turned out all right for her in the end.'

Rose often stopped the story at this point, not wanting to remember too closely how she herself had been brought up by an elderly great aunt who claimed not to like children and was living on a penurious pension. She'd seemed to think that having a youngster around would be useful for running errands, cooking her meals and helping to care for her in her old age.

When the doctor had called one day to find the house fetid, the old woman almost comatose and eight-year-old Rose near starving to death, they were both finally taken into the work-house. At least there someone remembered to feed and clothe her, although Rose never properly recovered from her ordeal, feeling rejected and spurned by her father, and neglected by the rest of the family.

Trust, love and affection were not words that had held much meaning for Rose as a young girl, not until she'd met Ron Ibbetson. He'd walked into the laundry where she worked to ask what it would cost to have his shirts done every week. In the end she'd married him and washed them for nothing, but he was a wonderful husband to her and although he was only a dustman and hadn't two beans to rub together in the early years of their marriage, they'd never gone short of love. They'd had a good life together and Rose still missed him badly.

Now she squeezed her granddaughter's hand. 'Happen it weren't the brightest decision our Joyce ever made to keep this all from you, but it wasn't easy for her to discover her husband were a cheat, and then to be made homeless, bombed out like she was, and landed with a little bundle of joy.'

'Mam and Dad were bombed out too? I never knew that.' Harriet's eyes stretched wide, instantly wondering why they'd never even bothered to tell her something so important. Could the two incidents be linked in some way? If so, she couldn't for the life of her think how. 'Was it in the Christmas Blitz, or around the same time as the young girl, my mother, was killed?'

'Er, one or t'other, I don't remember,' Rose said, sounding flustered. 'You were only a babby, I know that.'

'Where were you all living?'

'Ancoats.'

'I mean where in Ancoats? What street?'

Rose's expression became dead-pan, as it sometimes would when she'd walked into the kitchen and forgotten what she'd come in for. 'Nay, don't ask, you know how confused I get.'

'You surely must remember your own address, Nan?'

'Nay, we was allus flitting. You did in them days. First we were in the Dardanelles, then moved on to Ducie Street and, eeh I don't know . . . we never seemed to stop in one place for very long, what with the war and everything. It were summat fanciful or flowery, I seem to recall. I think there were a pub on the corner with a Scottish-sounding name, although it might be gone now. I can't say for certain. Eeh, will you look at them flowers Betty Hemley is setting out on the tables. If she ever sends Patsy a bill for that lot, the poor lass'll have to declare herself bankrupt.'

Something like panic had come into the old woman's eyes and

Harriet was instantly filled with compassion and worry for her grandmother. She was getting very forgetful all of a sudden. Surely she wasn't going senile? Oh, she did hope not.

'Come on, chuck, I'm starving hungry, let's get stuck in.'

Harriet laughed. 'At least you haven't lost your appetite.'

'Oh, no, I can still remember where me mouth is.'

8

Harriet

Curiosity got the better of Harriet and she decided to do a bit of snooping on her own account. The next day, being a Sunday, she persuaded Steve to go with her to Ancoats and see what she could find out. He wasn't too keen at first, warning her that delving into the past sometimes made things worse, not better.

'You don't understand,' she argued, ruffled that he couldn't see how angry she felt inside at being so badly let down by her parents. She was beginning to feel quite rebellious for having been lied to so heartlessly all these years. 'I have to know who I am, and what happened. But then it's my life, not yours, so how could you possibly understand?'

'I'm trying to understand, Harriet. I want only to protect you.'

'I don't need protecting, not by you, not by anyone. I just need the truth, something which everyone seems determined to keep from me.'

'OK, OK, we'll go.'

So here they were, walking along Great Ancoats Street. It was hard to imagine that this had once been green countryside where farmers had cultivated their land, and grand mansions once graced meadows that sloped down to the River Medlock. The industrialisation of the eighteenth and nineteenth centuries had put paid to all of that rural idyll but now change was again in the air. The ramshackle cottages and unsanitary terraced houses were being cleared away, as were the bombed-out houses left by the war.

'Where did they live?' Steve asked.

Letting him take her hand, even though she still felt cross with him, Harriet matched her stride easily to his. 'According to Nan you go along Great Ancoats Street, up Union Street, and their house was near some mill or other.'

'Oh, that's helpful. There are any number of mills in Ancoats, and were probably even more then.'

'She's also mentioned warehouses, when she's talked before about living in Ancoats.'

'Which warehouses? There are plenty of those too.'

'I don't know, do I? I'm doing my best to remember.'

Now Harriet was wishing she'd asked more questions, found out more details which were admittedly vague before embarking on this exercise. 'Nan couldn't seem to remember the address as they were constantly flitting, because of the war or whatever. But she thought it might be something fanciful, maybe like Paradise Street, but then she started talking about flowers. Oh, and there could well have been a pub on the corner with a Scottish-sounding name, although that might be gone now.'

'Great! Something fanciful, or possibly flowery, and a Scottish pub that might or might not still be there. Fat chance after all this time.'

'You could try to sound a bit more optimistic.'

'I am trying, but we don't have much to go on.' Then seeing Harriet's gloomy expression, he gave her hand a little squeeze. 'Why don't you admit this is a complete waste of time, love? Like I say, it probably wouldn't do you any good in the long run.'

'No, I absolutely refuse to give up so easily. We can ask someone. I mean to find out what happened.'

Steve sighed. 'Think hard then. Your nan must have dropped some other clues in all the times she's talked about her child-hood, and yer mam's. Did she ever tell you anything really useful, like an address?'

Harriet felt filled with frustration, and irritated with him for finding the obvious flaws in her quest. 'Nan's so vague these days, getting quite forgetful.' She frowned, then brightened as a memory stirred. 'It must have been near the market, not far from Smithfield. I remember her once saying that her uncle and aunt had a stall on the market, selling fish. And they could hear the trains shunting in the goods yard.'

'Right, well we know where that is. Let's go and look for a flowery or fanciful street not too far from Smithfield and the railway. But if we haven't found it in a hour, we're going home, right?'

'OK.'

It took them less than twenty minutes. 'This must be it, Blossom Street,' Harriet cried excitedly. 'And here's the pub, look: the Edinburgh Castle. You can't get more Scottish than that, and it's still here. Oh, but I expected the street to be little more than a pile of rubble yet it looks perfectly all right, as if it's never been troubled by war at all.'

They stopped to ask a woman pushing a pram if she remembered a house being bombed in this street during the war but, laughing, she shook her head. 'I was only a toddler, love, at the time. You'll have to ask someone a lot older. Try Mrs Marsh at the bottom house. She's lived here for years.'

Mrs Marsh at the bottom house must have been out, or deaf, because she didn't answer when they knocked, but an old man next door came out to see who was making all the racket.

'Are you talking about the Christmas Blitz?' he asked, in answer to their question.

'When was that exactly?' Harriet wanted to know.

'Christmas,' the old man drily remarked.

Harriet smiled, used to dry Lancashire wit. 'I mean what year?'

'Nineteen forty. Manchester was ablaze. Plenty of folk were killed in the blitz.'

She shook her head. 'No, this must have happened the following year, nineteen forty-one, the year I was born.'

The old man frowned and scratched his head. 'I weren't around then, I were away fighting in Africa at the time, but me wife were here, and me daughter. I'm trying to remember if they ever mentioned a bomb. Are you looking for someone, love?'

Harriet swallowed. 'My mother. I've been told she was living in this street and was killed during an air raid. I just wanted to find the house.'

'Eeh, I'm right sorry to hear that. I wish I could be more helpful but my wife's dead too, and me daughter is living in Cheshire now.' The old man peered short-sightedly along the street. 'Course, stray bombs did fall from time to time, long after the blitz, and the Jerries were fond of dropping 'em here in Manchester because they were aiming for the factories as well as the Ship Canal. I suppose there could well have been one dropped around these parts, but I can't say for certain.'

It wasn't a very satisfactory result but, despite asking a couple of other people, they managed to elicit no further information.

'I shall have to try asking Nan again for the full address. Make her put her thinking cap on.'

'Or ask your mother. Joyce, I mean.'

'No thanks. She'd never tell me, anyroad. She's declared the subject closed. Definitely off-limits. I can understand her attitude, in a way. I don't like thinking about it much either.'

'Then don't. What does it matter anyway? No one will know you're illegitimate if you don't say anything. Just forget it,' Steve said, giving a casual shrug of his shoulders. Harriet instantly saw red and stopped in her tracks to stare at him.

'*Forget it?* That's easy for you to say but I can't simply dismiss it out of hand. You think it isn't important to me who my mother was, where I was born and where I nearly died? Don't you realise that I hate the thought of being illegitimate? It's awful, dreadful. I feel dirty in some way, besmirched, and as if I've been cast adrift from the life I once knew. I *have* to investigate further. I *must!*'

'OK, OK, I get the picture.'

Harriet didn't even hear his apology. 'I need to know if my mother, my *real* mother, loved me. If she meant to keep me, and what sort of person she was. I need to find that house, the exact place where that little baby, *me*, was discovered. Which heap of rubble saved me from an almost certain death? Did I have something on me to say who I was? How did Joyce know I was that girl's baby? Why won't she tell me her name? She and Nan are still keeping something from me, I'm sure of it, and I mean to get to the bottom of this and find out exactly what happened, and who I *am*!'

She stopped at last, short of breath, heart pounding, her cheeks wet with tears although Harriet hadn't even realised she was crying.

Steve pulled her close to awkwardly pat her on the back. 'I do understand how you feel, love, really I do. But just remember that you're still *you*, the girl I love.'

'And what about that poor girl, my mother, having a baby she didn't want, and then being killed in an air raid? That's *tragic*!'

Steve kissed her nose. 'But *you're* still here. And what a lovely baby you were. She'd be pleased about that, this tragic mother of yours. I know I am. So come on, love, calm down and give me one of your lovely smiles.'

Harriet managed a shy smile for him through her tears. He was so patient with her, so kind and loving, and all she did was bicker and be irritable. He was at least here with her, wasn't he, trying to help?

'Let me just check out the next street, then we'll do something much more fun, shall we? The pictures are closed today, being Sunday, but we could go home by way of the canal and do a bit of necking under the bridge. How about that?'

Steve grinned. 'I thought you'd never ask.'

Later, flushed and happy from their short interlude under the arches by the Bridgewater Canal, they sat down to lunch with Steve's parents, as they often did on a Sunday. Harriet liked Mr and Mrs Blackstock. Steve's father was always jolly and friendly, cracking little jokes and making silly remarks about popping in to the salon for a new hairdo as he stroked his bald pate, or claiming the sun was about to come out any minute, even when it was raining stair rods.

Mrs Blackstock was less easy-going but still pleasant and friendly enough. She was a small, round, no-nonsense sort of woman, heavily involved in the WVS during the war and even now seemed to be on any number of committees, whose task was to raise money for worthy causes. She spent every Sunday morning at the Baptist chapel, once she'd put on the roast for lunch, and which they'd be eating up cold until at least Tuesday. Her one extravagance seemed to be to come in to the salon once a month for a blue rinse on her short grey hair and she always asked for camomile tea and a cream wafer.

Steve was an only child and in all the years Harriet had known him and his family she'd always felt welcome in their house. She loved to be invited as the atmosphere was so much more relaxed than at home. But today, she noticed at once that something had changed. Mr Blackstock seemed unusually quiet, never quite meeting her eye, while Steve's mother was practically monosyllabic.

'Can I help?' Harriet offered, jumping to her feet as she noticed dishes being set on the table. She usually helped lay it, make the gravy or pick flowers with Mrs Blackstock in the tiny back garden behind the tall terraced house, and watch admiringly as she deftly created a charming display for the table.

'No thanks,' was the cool response today.

'Shall I make the mint sauce?'

'It's done.'

Harriet politely took her seat. Mrs Blackstock set a plate of roast lamb before each of them, vegetable dishes were handed round, the gravy boat passed from hand to hand and then, without a word, everyone began to eat. There was no lively chatter, no questions about how Harriet's secretarial course was progressing, as she usually took pains to enquire. She didn't ask how Joyce was, or if they'd been busy in the salon. Not even a word about the excitement of Patsy's wedding. Nothing.

Harriet stole a sideways glance at Steve but he had his eyes firmly fixed on his plate. After a while Mr Blackstock told his wife that the meat was 'done to a turn' and, looking pleased, she at last addressed a question to Harriet.

'So what have you two been up to this morning?'

Harriet tried to quickly swallow a mouthful of lamb but before she had time to speak, Steve answered for her.

'Nothing much. Just went for a walk by the canal, since it was such a nice day.'

Harriet shot him a questioning look, one which clearly asked why they couldn't be entirely open and truthful and admit they'd been investigating her family's past. But his eyes warned her otherwise as he gave an infinitesimal shake of the head.

'That's nice,' Margaret Blackstock agreed. 'You should enjoy what free time you have left together, before Stephen goes off to college in September.' She smiled at Harriet then, though it seemed cooler than usual, more distant. 'We're so pleased that all his hard work has paid off. I'm quite sure he'll do well at college so long as he doesn't have too many distractions. We want only the best for him. But then he's a bright lad who will go far.'

'Mother!'

She patted his hand. 'Don't be modest, dear, it's true. Once you're qualified, you'll be a headmaster in no time, I'm quite sure of it. Then you'll be able to afford to buy a nice semi-detached house in a good area of Manchester, find yourself a nice middle-class girl to marry and provide us with a couple of lovely grandchildren. Won't that be nice, dear?'

There was a small silence while Harriet digested this comment.

Nice was one of Mrs Blackstock's favourite words. She liked everything to be nice, from the way she set her dining-room table to her neatly tended back garden. Her home was liberally decorated with flowery prints, tapestry cushions, embroidered fire screens and other pretty things which she'd no doubt stitched herself. There were Persian rugs and Royal Dalton figurines in crinolines; Toby jugs and a good deal of polished brass. It was the kind of house Joyce would have given her soul for. To Harriet, it seemed like another world here in St John's Place, far from the everyday hustle and bustle of Champion Street.

Not even glancing at Harriet's stunned face Steve gave an

awkward little laugh. 'One thing at a time, Mother, I've two years hard graft at Teacher Training College first. Besides, Harriet doesn't want to hear all of this stuff.'

'I'm sure she's very interested in how you plan to spend your future, aren't you, dear? And I should think she understands perfectly that since we've all had such a struggle recovering from the war years, we wouldn't want our only son stuck in this seedy part of Manchester for the rest of his life. Not when he has the chance to better himself.'

'I quite like Castlefield, actually,' Harriet stoutly responded. 'And Champion Street will always be my home.'

'But you weren't born there, were you, dear? Or so I've been led to believe.'

Again that small taut silence, in which all knives and forks stopped moving as eyes swivelled to the woman's bland, enquiring smile.

Mr Blackstock cleared his throat. 'I reckon I'll have a few more of those lovely crunchy roast potatoes. Would you like one, Harriet?'

'No, thanks, Mr Blackstock. You're quite right, I wasn't born in Champion Street. Fancy your knowing that when I've only just found out myself.'

The older woman delicately dabbed her mouth with an embroidered napkin. 'Oh dear, I do hope I haven't upset you. Word gets around so quickly in these parts, doesn't it? Full of old gossips that market is, which is another reason why we want our Stephen to make his life elsewhere. I'm sure you're ready to move on too, dear, following these recent traumas you've been obliged to endure. Losing your poor dear father and discovering that your mother wasn't who you thought she was.'

'Margaret,' Mr Blackstock said on a warning note, but his wife pressed on as if he hadn't spoken.

'And no one could blame you if you did up sticks and leave. For our part we look forward to moving to the Fylde Coast once Ralph retires from the bank. By then, of course, Stephen will be long off our hands and nicely settled.'

Living in a *nice* semi-detached house and married to a *nice* middle-class girl, Harriet thought, unshed tears smarting at the backs of her eyes as she struggled to focus on her roast lamb. Unfortunately her throat had closed up tight and she'd quite lost her appetite. She judged it wise not to say anything more on the subject, hoping perhaps that Steve might refute his mother's plans for him.

He said nothing, simply kept his head down and concentrated on eating his Sunday lunch, which galled her somewhat.

Margaret Blackstock, however, was well into her stride. 'And of course, none of us can be held responsible for where, or how, or to whom we were born, can we, even if it does prove to be a blight on our lives?'

Harriet looked at her, her stormy grey gaze steady. 'No, we can't, although some people might insist on apportioning blame on the innocent.'

Margaret Blackstock blinked. 'I'm sure no one would do any such thing.'

Harriet smiled. 'And would you still describe *me* as a *nice* girl, Mrs Blackstock?'

Still Steve said nothing, although he shot her a furious glare which Harriet did not miss. His father too seemed strangely silent, concentrating entirely upon his meal.

'You always were very direct, dear.'

'I see no disgrace in speaking the truth.'

Harriet's heart had started to beat very slowly and painfully in her breast. She laid her knife and fork neatly together in the centre of her plate, as Mrs Blackstock liked her to do. 'Well, that was lovely, thank you, but for some reason I seem to have lost my appetite. I won't bother with a sweet, if you don't mind. I think I'd best be going.'

'As you wish, dear. I'm sure you must feel more comfortable at home. It's bound to take time for you to adjust to your new status.'

Like being a bastard you mean, Harriet thought, but managed not to say so. And when Steve made no effort to come to her defence, she pushed back her chair and headed for the door. She'd deal with him later.

Her acceptance by the Blackstocks into their son's life seemed to be entirely dependent upon the quality of her pedigree, which was now apparently beyond redemption.

9

Rose

Summer was coming to an end and the mornings were fresher now with that first hint of autumn in the air. The Committee should have been making their plans for Christmas, which they liked to do in good time, organising the fairy lights and the tree in order to make the market look festive. Instead they were holding an emergency meeting to discuss the new threat to the market.

The half-derelict houses at the bottom of the street had long been in need of demolition, and everyone would welcome something more modern and pleasant in their place. The problem was that since the right to develop this section of the street had been acquired, the rest of it now seemed to be under threat too, even though those houses were still in perfectly good order. And the developers wanted the market to move out of the street altogether.

It had become apparent that several people who lived at the top of the street and owned their own houses had already been offered a great deal of money to sell their property, and their pitch. The proposal had come via a firm of solicitors who represented the development company.

Winnie Holmes had received such an offer for her old house, now rented out to Dena Dobson, and her new husband Barry a similar one for his. Both Clara Higginson and Big Molly Poulson were also under pressure to sell. This meeting was an attempt to discover how far the problem had spread.

There were one or two notable absentees. One was Alex Hall, who hadn't been seen around the market since Stan's funeral in

late July, and whose music shop was now being run by his son
Terry. Rumour had it that he'd returned to Korea where he apparently still had a wife. Judy Beckett, who usually ran a little stall
to sell her own artwork, was hiding away somewhere, a fact which
nobody quite liked to mention since her husband Sam, the cause
of her flight, was present at the meeting.

The committee, plus a number of long-established stallholders
co-opted for this extraordinary general meeting, were gathered
round the market superintendent's desk, a position still occupied
by Belle Garside, and she had asked for a show of hands.

'From what I can ascertain, that makes ten or twelve offers
for property so far, would you agree with my figures?' She
glanced briefly at the assembled company but continued without
waiting for an answer. 'So, the question is, what are we going
to do about it?'

Rose had agreed to do her bit in this fight to save the market.
She sat on the back row, a neat trim figure in a startlingly red
and yellow flowered linen dress, circa nineteen-thirties, complete
with matching dangly earrings, listening quietly as folk began to
put forward suggestions, some of which were not even legal.

She listened as Papa Bertalone likened the developers to the
Gestapo; smiled as Big Molly nudged her husband Ozzy in the
ribs, and, having failed to bully him into speaking, shouted out
that her son Robert depended on Champion Street being around
for some time to come if he was to take over the pie business.

'We should march on the council offices and demand their full
support,' Jimmy Ramsay insisted, shaking a powerful fist more
used to slicing up meat carcasses. 'Let them know we refuse to
be bullied.'

'Aye, that's right. No one is going to walk all over us,' cried
one stallholder.

'And we'll punch anyone who tries,' yelled another.

There was a noisy chorus of agreement, and several other
suggestions about what folk would like to do to any councillors
who refused to stand by them. Clara Higginson cleared her throat
to quietly point out that these kind of threats weren't getting them

anywhere, and gradually the grumbles subsided as they listened to her sound common sense.

'From what I understand, this generous offer will stand for only a limited period and then will be reduced. There may be some people present who would be willing to accept it, so should we perhaps take a vote before we proceed any further?'

A small silence ensued while people digested this uncomfortable truth. Glances flicked all around as everyone attempted to assess which of those present might be seduced by such blackmail.

'Who would admit to it?' Sam Beckett scoffed. 'Although I'm sure some of us may well be considering retirement, or a possible move anyway, we're hardly likely to risk damaging our business by saying so.'

Everyone looked at him, and wondered.

Belle, in her usual forthright way, said, 'Well, let's find out. Is there anyone here willing to accept this undoubtedly generous offer, bearing in mind, as Clara points out, that it has a limited life-span?'

No one volunteered a reply to this question although whether that was because they had no intention of ever accepting, or were keeping their intentions close to their chest, as Sam suggested, wasn't clear.

Chris George said, 'We should also remember that not everyone on Champion Street owns their own property. Many houses are rented so it will be the landlord who decides, over whom we have no control. My own father owns our baker's shop, for instance.'

This was a sobering thought.

'Can't we persuade them to draw up a new agreement to spare those houses in good condition, and allow the market to stay, even if they do demolish the older ones?' Barry Holmes wanted to know.

'We've tried, so far with little success,' Belle told him.

'Would they agree to meet us on site, to come and view our properties and discuss the matter more fully? Do we know what kind of flats they intend to build, and when they hope to start? Do you have the answer to any of those questions, Belle?'

Belle didn't.

Rose, who had other plans for her day besides being cooped up in a stuffy meeting room, finally made up her mind to speak. 'Seems to me, what we need is someone to investigate the matter further. We need to gather more information, to find out exactly who this company is and what they intend to do with Champion Street, if and when they've bought up everyone's property.'

'By heck, she's right,' Jimmy Ramsay agreed, slapping one huge thigh with the flat of his hand. 'We need to form a special committee to investigate the matter. And if they should discover that this development company means to destroy everything, the market and *all* the houses in Champion Street, then our task must be to start a campaign to save it.'

This proposal was put to the meeting and voted upon almost unanimously. A group of stalwarts was quickly selected for the task, Rose included. She did notice, however, that Sam Beckett, and the Georges, abstained, which she found rather interesting.

The sprawl of the market was spreading. The number of barrows in the surrounding area from Tonman Street to Deansgate, as well as all along Champion Street itself, was steadily increasing, adding to the liveliness and popularity of the place. One side of the market hall now had an extension, hygienically enclosing the new meat and fish market beneath a glass roof.

Irma Southworth, tilting her biscuit tins at just the right angle for her customers to make a selection as she did every morning, felt compelled, much against her better judgement, to admit that this was one improvement at least that Belle Garside had achieved. It was something her own husband Joe had failed to do when he was market superintendent. It grieved her to have to concede this fact as Belle had at one time enjoyed what she termed 'a little fling' with Irma's husband. And despite her having known Belle for years, Irma could still barely speak a civil word to the woman.

Nevertheless, as a consequence of the recent improvements she'd made, people now came from far and wide to explore the market to taste Bertalones' ice cream, buy Lizzie Pringle's chocolate mints, savour Big Molly Poulson's meat and potato pies and Jimmy Ramsay's pork sausages. They loved to listen to the stallholders' banter, watch plates being juggled, take part in a mock auction and buy something they never wanted at a knock-down price they simply couldn't resist.

It was a tragedy that, if the rumours were true, all of this would soon have to go, swept away in a thorough cleansing of everything that was old and Victorian in the city's relentless quest for progress.

Irma loved the market. Her family had been involved with markets and fairs for generations. She could remember a time when the stallholders used a language all their own. They'd turn a word upside down so that one became eno, and ten turned into net. She couldn't remember why. She also recalled the flower gazers that used to cluster along Piccadilly. They'd carry huge baskets hung on a strap round their neck and would have to stand in the gutter to do their selling, not allowed to even set foot on the pavement or they'd be fined.

The flower gazers were all gone now in this rapidly changing, modern world, so it was a real treat to see Betty Hemley setting out her flower buckets, still trying to hang on to the old ways. There wasn't much Betty missed seated there amongst her flowers. She not only knew the language of flowers, she understood people and what made them tick. Betty liked tradition, for things to stay the way they always had, and Irma felt exactly the same.

She rather thought it was because she, like Betty Hemley, was so set in her ways, a bit old fashioned she supposed, that Joe had grown bored with her. Belle Garside had been only one of several women over the years who had fired his blood, encouraging him to grasp at a youth long gone. He had one on the go at the moment. Though Irma had her suspicions, she couldn't quite make up her mind who it was. It couldn't be Betty's daughter Lynda, because she was having an on-off affair with Terry Hall. Besides, she was far too young.

Nor could it be Judy Beckett because she was embroiled in a bitter divorce with her husband Sam who ran the ironmongery stall, not to mention a fierce custody battle over their two children. What a mess that marriage was in. It was always worse where children were involved.

As things had turned out, Irma was thankful that she had only the one son. Ian was thirty now, and seemed to be very happily married, thank God. She also had two delightful grandchildren who were the light of her life.

There had been a time when Irma had wanted more babies but none had come along, and then once Ian had left home, and because of her husband's philandering, she and Joe had moved into separate bedrooms not simply separate beds. After nearly thirty-two years it was a sterile marriage, no sort of a life at all really.

He'd seemed such a harmless sort of chap when she'd wed him, but he'd never been the same since he came back from Italy after the war. Irma knew she should have booted Joe out long since but he was such a wet lettuce she felt sorry for him, she did really. She was too soft, that was her trouble, far too easy-going. She probably only let him stay for the sake of appearances. She'd seen her young romantic dreams fade away one by one, till now the only thing they had in common was the market stall – the biscuit business they'd built up together over the years.

Betty Hemley herself was suffering from an ex-husband having returned to the marital home uninvited, and causing any amount of grief. Word had it he was something of a violent bully. Poor Betty. Irma felt sorry for her old friend. She supposed she should be grateful that although Joe might be a bit useless on the romance front, he wouldn't hurt a fly. He wasn't a bit of bother to look after, and his high jinks could easily be ignored.

A customer interrupted her musings, wanting a pound of mixed biscuits.

'How about a few Garibaldi?' Irma suggested, instantly adopting the bright smile she always used with her customers.

Irma Southworth was a large woman. The wrap-over apron she always wore was so Persil-white it made you blink and it strained over her ample bosom and hips. Her button-bright blue eyes were alert and kind, and her silver-grey hair was shiny and bouncy about a round, smiling face. She was well liked on the market: for her friendly cheerfulness, her helpful manner and the care she took over the cakes she made to suit those special moments in a person's life. She would certainly never be known for her stunning beauty, her rosy cheeks being somewhat flabby and her chin having long since given up any pretence of being firm.

But, unlike these new-fangled supermarkets they were bringing in with girls who yawned at their cash desks and looked right through you, Irma cared about her customers, and knew most of them by name.

'Custard creams for you, eh, Mrs Cartwright? Ginger snaps and fig rolls for your two girls? And one or two delicious Bourbons perhaps?'

'Aye, and put in half a dozen fruit shortcakes. My Phil loves them.'

When the woman had gone, a half pound of broken biscuits at a special discounted price also added to her basket, Irma couldn't help pondering on how nice it must be to care about a man so much you made a point of picking out his favourite biscuits.

But then not every man was a selfish womaniser like Joe. You'd've thought he would have developed a bit of sense now that he was past the fifty mark, but he showed no sign of doing so.

A queue had formed by this time, and Irma concentrated on serving her biscuits. Highland Shortbread. Homewheat Chocolate Digestive. Syrup and Oat Cookies. Was it any wonder she'd lost her figure, with a straying husband to contend with and surrounded by all these riches? Which came first, she wondered, the fat on her hips or the affairs? She didn't care to consider and, really, did it matter? There were more important things in life than daft husbands who couldn't keep their trousers buttoned.

He should be here by rights, helping her, but then when had he ever pulled his weight? If he wasn't warming some woman's

bed he was pontificating his opinions at meetings of the market
committee. Even though he was no longer market superintendent,
he couldn't keep his nose out. All summer he'd been fretting
about this talk of yet another threat to Champion Street Market,
of developers wanting to move in and bulldoze the area clean to
build yet more blocks of flats.

The rumour had seriously alarmed Joe, although while considering it a tragic shame, Irma was more philosophical. If they lost
the biscuit stall she still had her wedding-cake business, and her
other little sidelines. She made and decorated cakes for all occasions, in fact, not simply weddings. For birthdays, anniversaries,
christenings, you name it. Events, very often, that she herself had
predicted thanks to her skill with the cards, reading tea leaves or
palms, whatever seemed appropriate for the client. She'd never
been asked to make a cake to celebrate a divorce though, but
there was always a first time for everything. Maybe she'd make
one for her own.

Or maybe she'd hang on to him, just to be awkward. If they
lost the stall happen she could force Joe to go out and get a
proper job, make him pay for what he'd done to her. Serve him
right for all the suffering he'd caused her over the years. And she
would stay at home for a bit and indulge her hobbies. Maybe it
was time for the shoe to be on the other foot.

And then she saw him, heading for the office at the back of
the market hall. She noticed how he glanced back over his shoulder
then pause as Joyce Ashton approached. There was something
in the way the pair glanced cautiously about them before putting
their faces up close to whisper to each other, as if they were
entirely alone, or wanted to be.

'So that's how the land lies, is it?' Irma thought, not realising
she'd spoken aloud until she heard Winnie Holmes's soft chuckle.

'Hasta only just noticed? Nay, she's been your Joe's latest fancy
piece for months now. Daft article that he is. There's one man
who doesn't know what side his bread is buttered.'

Irma froze. 'And what can I get for you, Winnie?'

'Eeh, don't come over all hoity-toity wi' me, lass. We've been friends too many years. Anyroad, there isn't a soul on this market doesn't know how it is with your Joe. But if it's any comfort to you, Irma love, everyone's on your side, and I reckon he might've met his match this time round. Trust me, that woman will make his life hell.'

Irma smiled, making her rosy cheeks puff out and glow with pleasure. 'I do hope you're right, Winnie. I shall enjoy watching him burn.'

Before returning to the hair salon, Rose called at Irma Southworth's biscuit stall, not to make a purchase, but to set an appointment for a reading, palm or cards, she really didn't mind. Rose felt that she had some very important decisions to make and if anyone could help her see into the future, Irma could. Anything which helped her to make up her mind would be most welcome.

Having done that, she got on a bus bound for Ancoats. Rose had an important errand to do there too, and so long as she was quick Joyce wouldn't even notice she was gone. Her daughter would simply assume that she was in the Dog and Duck chewing over the results of the meeting. But then she'd got away with this particular little trip many times before, so she was an expert.

I O

Harriet

Harriet was writing a letter. She was sitting on her bed with her legs tucked beneath her trying to think what she could say to a woman she'd never known, who was probably dead, but who she'd just discovered was her mother. She didn't even have a Christian name, yet felt this great urge to put her thoughts and feelings down on paper.

The Blackstocks' change of attitude towards her had shaken Harriet to the core. Until that moment she'd believed she could weather this storm, that all she had to do was persuade Joyce, and her nan, to be a bit more forthcoming with the facts. Now, following that difficult Sunday lunch, she saw that indeed everything had changed, and that from now on people would view her differently. It wasn't a comfortable feeling.

She'd tackled Steve on the subject the very next day, and he'd been strangely defensive.

'I agree that my parents have taken an old-fashioned, somewhat puritan stand on this, but then they're from a different generation.'

'Which means you have to blindly accept everything they say and not speak up for me? I haven't grown two heads just because I no longer know who my mother is.'

'I can't be seen to take sides in this,' he demurred.

'Why not?'

'They're my parents. They have a right to their viewpoint.'

'And I thought I was the girl you were going to settle down with and marry one day, and not necessarily in a nice semi-detached house in some garden suburb either.'

He'd reached for her then and laughed. 'You mustn't take everything Mother says so seriously.'

Harriet had pushed his hands away, not yet ready to forgive. 'Why wouldn't I? *You* obviously do. Isn't it time you stood up to her? She seems to have your entire life mapped out.'

'Don't be daft. They had a hard time of it during the war and Mother likes to dream, that's all. When the time comes, I shall do as I please.'

'Meanwhile I'm to sit back and allow her to insult me, is that it?'

'Now you're being over-sensitive.'

'Over-sensitive? She tells me it will take time for me to grow accustomed to my new *status*, by which I assume she means the fact I'm *illegitimate*, and you think I should sit and take it, without saying a word in my own defence?'

Steve's jaw tightened. 'There's no necessity for you to defend yourself, but she is my mother. You have to show her some respect.'

'Why? She showed none to me. She can go stuff herself.'

And that's how it had ended, the most terrible row they'd ever had.

Now, acknowledging to herself that she really didn't know what it felt like to have a loving mother who watched out for you all the time, or put you first before everyone and everything else, Harriet had decided to write the letter. Maybe if she put her feelings down on paper, she would understand exactly what changes might evolve from this so-called *change of status*. But she wasn't finding it easy. And what she would do with the letter, once it was written, was anyone's guess.

A week went by with no sign of Steve. Feeling increasingly annoyed and rebellious, Harriet gave in her notice on the secretarial course. She had no intention of allowing Joyce to dictate what she did with her life any longer. She never had wanted to spend her days filing, docketing, answering the phone, or any of the other numerous office-type tasks which she loathed. She'd no idea what the future held for her, but being a secretary wasn't part of it.

In the meantime she'd got herself a job helping Lizzie Pringle make chocolates in her rapidly expanding business, a delicious task if ever there was one. And if Joyce considered Harriet to be an educational failure as a consequence of her low ambitions, so be it. See if she cared! Harriet loved the market, and was proud to be a part of its hustle and bustle.

Harriet finished writing the letter to her mother, which in fact had been most therapeutic, if a bit pointless. She could hardly address it to her in heaven, could she? Secretly, Harriet felt a bit silly having written a letter to a dead woman, so had simply written *Mother* on the envelope and stuffed it behind the lamp on the bedside table in her room, trying not to think about it too much.

She couldn't even make up her mind whether it had helped her to adjust to this so-called *new status*. Harriet was hoping that Steve might be able to help her with that one, when next she saw him.

So far, she hadn't clapped eyes on him for days and was trying not to be too downcast about this. He was probably busy buying gear for Teacher Training College, studying, or whatever students did, as he was due to start his course any day now. She would miss him, Harriet thought bleakly.

They had planned to go to the Friday night dance together, as usual, and Harriet duly got ready for the evening out with fast-beating heart. She often felt a bit fluttery inside whenever she was seeing Steve, but tonight she had real butterflies. Would he still be mad with her for disagreeing with his parents? Would they be able to make up after their quarrel? Oh, she did hope everything was back to normal between them. The last thing she needed right now was to fall out with Steve. He was her lifeline, the one person she could rely on, other than Nan, of course.

She chose to wear a pretty blue polished-cotton daisy skirt, bought from Dena Dobson's stall, and a tight-fitting, off-the-shoulder black sweater which would surely wow him. Harriet thought she had rather good shoulders, and not a bad cleavage, though she said so herself. And this was a night when she needed to make the best use of her assets. She wanted Steve to fall in love with her all over again so they could patch up this silly quarrel and carry on being the best of friends, as they always had been.

Harriet was standing on the corner of Champion Street, her dancing shoes in the small vanity case in her hand, waiting for Steve. She never liked him to call for her at the house as she feared sarcastic remarks from Joyce, so they'd got into the habit of meeting at the door of the school hall where the dances were held. But tonight he was late. She'd been trying to deny this fact and making excuses to herself for over half an hour as hordes of young people passed by and hurried inside to enjoy the dance.

Harriet could hear the music thumping. 'Lonely Teardrops' sung by Jackie Wilson was playing, which seemed entirely appropriate for she was having great difficulty stopping uncharacteristic tears of self-pity from spilling over and running down her cheeks. Her life seemed to be falling apart and she with it.

With an increasing sense of desperation she scanned the length of the street, empty now as all would-be revellers were already inside bopping and jiving to the music. All except for her.

Harriet rummaged in the little red plastic vanity case, looking for a hanky to wipe her eyes and blow her nose. Drat, she'd forgotten to put one in and angrily tried to scrub the tears away with her fingers, which only made her cry all the more, and her mascara run, so she'd look a real sight when he did get here. Where was he? Why hadn't he come? Did this mean they were finished, or was he just making a point? Was he trying to make her sorry for not having shown proper respect to his mother?

She began to desperately search her pockets for a hanky.

Whatever the reason, it wasn't fair to leave her hanging around like this. And what should she do about it? She'd lost track of most of her friends in the fifteen months she and Steve had been seriously dating. Many of them were going steady themselves now, and she really had no wish to play gooseberry, nor to go home with her tail between her legs.

'Here you are, love, have mine.' Harriet found a clean white handkerchief was being thrust into her hand.

'Thank you,' she mumbled, without even looking up.

'You been stood up, babe? Pretty chick like you shouldn't be standing around waiting for some lout who can't be bothered to arrive on time.'

'My sentiment entirely,' she hiccupped, almost losing control.

'Come on, mop up, or you'll have us all at it,' he teased, and taking the hanky from her began to dab gently at her eyes.

She looked at him then and knew instantly who he was. Local bad boy Vinny Turner, slightly older than Harriet at about twenty, she guessed. She was surprised to see him on his own, as he usually hung around with a group of lads who were generally up to no good. Everyone knew Vinny's gang drank too much and racketed about the streets long into the small hours.

She believed he lived in the yard behind the new fish market. What family he had, Harriet wasn't sure, but rather thought he had a couple of younger brothers and a sister, at least. There was nothing new or agreeable about those houses, despite the fish market itself having been done up. They were little better than slums. No one on Champion Street would object to a bulldozer razing those properties to the ground.

Nevertheless, despite these disadvantages, Vinny was really quite good looking, and on a summer's evening like this he was looking particularly suave.

A Saint Christopher medal glimmered in the open neck of the pale blue shirt he wore, and the tight blue denim jeans were fastened with a thick leather belt that emphasised the lean muscled length of his hips and thighs. He wore winkle-pickers and his hair was a rich dark brown with a quiff that fell over a wide brow. Not exactly a Teddy Boy, but not far off.

He was smiling down at her, a lop-sided, cynical sort of grin and she noticed that his hazel eyes were rimmed with gold, an entrancing combination. There was just one snag. Attractive though he might be, and kind to offer her his hanky, he wasn't Steve.

'Thanks, I'm all right now,' she said, about to offer him his handkerchief back until she realised she'd used it, then shoved it in her pocket. 'I'll return it when I've washed it,' she said.

'Don't worry about that. I assume it's wonderboy Steve Blackstock you're waiting for. I've seen you hanging around with him.'

Harriet looked at him in surprise. Why would Vinny Turner notice who she was with? But the comment reminded her again about Steve, and she glanced up and down the length of the street wishing he would materialise out of the growing dusk. But the street was still empty and she lifted her chin, doing her best to appear unconcerned. 'I'm sure he'll be here soon.'

'And like a fool, you're going to go on waiting for him, are you, and miss all the fun?' He shrugged, then hooking his thumbs in his thick leather belt started to stroll away. 'Suit yourself, no skin off my nose. I'll be inside, if you change your mind.'

A spurt of rebellion burst inside her. 'I'm no fool, so don't call me one.'

'Course you are. Do you need me to draw a picture? Any bird who can't read the writing on the wall when a guy doesn't turn up has got to be stupid. He's chucked you, love. Dumped you. Dropped you. Is probably right at this moment trying to get inside some other chick's knickers.'

The door banged shut behind him and an unexpected chill touched her spine, making her shiver. Harriet remembered how Steve had kept his gaze firmly fixed on his plate throughout his mother's caustic comments; how he'd made no effort to stand by her during that attack, and then had defended his *mother*, not Harriet, when later she'd taken him to task over the issue. Maybe he too considered her beneath contempt, now that he knew she was illegitimate. A part of her shrivelled inside with shame, as if she felt suddenly unclean, and Harriet felt less sure of what had once been a certainty in her life: Steve's love for her.

'Drat you, Steve Blackstock! See if I care.' And fired with rebellion, Harriet lifted her chin and walked into the dance hall in Vinny's wake.

*

Harriet had to admit that she was having a great time. Vinny was fun, although his mates when they turned up later were a bit of a pain, rather loud and raucous, embarrassing her a bit in front of all her friends. Terry Hall's skiffle group had been playing for over an hour, beating out several popular numbers including two of her favourites, 'Bird Dog', and 'Stagger Lee'.

When Terry stepped down from the stage, Vinny and his mates gathered up their guitars and climbed up to take their place. They weren't very good, being far too loud and slightly out of tune but everyone clapped and cheered and bopped like crazy. What they lacked in skill they more than made up for in the energy they exerted by throwing themselves about the stage. It was a real laugh.

Lizzie Pringle came over to say hello, mentioning how pleased she was that Harriet was working with her. She was still called by this name, because of the business, even though she'd married her beloved Charlie. 'Steve not here tonight?' she asked.

Harriet shook her head, not trusting herself to answer.

Lizzie glanced across at Vinny, standing at the door as he sank a pint of bitter. Alcohol wasn't allowed on the premises but he was old enough to buy it elsewhere.

'You can sit with us, if you're on your own,' Lizzie said, indicating the group of friends she was with, which, besides Charlie, included Lynda Hemley who was always around when Terry was doing a turn with his group; Dena Dobson with her new doctor friend; and Gina Bertalone and Luc.

Harriet decided she'd feel out of place as the only single. Besides, she told herself firmly, she'd stopped looking for Steve after the third or fourth dance. If he was no longer interested in her, why should she care about him? He wasn't the only boy in the world.

'I'm OK, thanks.'

'You don't look it, to be honest.' Lizzie peered closely into her face and glanced across at Vinny as if she disapproved. Then Terry Hall put on a slow record, 'It's All in the Game', sung by Tommy Edwards, and before Harriet could think of a suitable reply Vinny came right over and pulled her into his arms for a smooch without even asking.

Harriet laughed as he pressed her close against him, running his hands up and down her back. 'As you can see, I'm having a great time and I'm fine,' she called out to her friend as they moved away.

'If you're sure . . .' Lizzie looked unconvinced but shrugged her shoulders and left them to it. It was then that Harriet saw him. Steve had arrived. He was standing at the door glaring right across at her. Determined to show that she really didn't care about being stood up, she slid her arms tighter about Vinny's neck and ignored him. If he wanted her, let him show it. Let him make the first move.

The next instant he was standing beside her. He tapped Vinny on the shoulder. 'You can leave now, mate.'

'Excuse me?' Vinny blinked at him, as if he were looking at some worm that had just crawled up through the floorboards.

'That's my girl you're dancing with, so I'd be obliged if you'd hand her over and sling your hook.'

Vinny's hazel eyes widened in mock surprise. 'Hand her over? What is she, a parcel? Anyway, who says she's your girl?'

'I do.'

'Is that right?'

'Yeah, that's right! So beat it.'

'Aren't you even going to apologise for abandoning her, for leaving her standing out in the street all on her own for an hour?'

'I might apologise to her, not to you, buster. Move.'

Harriet finally found her voice. 'Excuse me, but would you mind not speaking about me as if I'm not even here. Vinny's right, you did abandon me, quite without warning. You stood me up, so what gives you the right to march in and ask him to hand me over, just as if I were a bit of baggage you forgot to pick up?'

Steve looked surprised by her attitude. 'I can explain.'

'I'm not sure I want to listen to your excuses.'

'They aren't excuses. I thought you'd wait for me, Harriet, not go off with someone else. You're my girl, so of course you belong to me.'

Vinny stifled a guffaw of laughter, and, still holding Harriet firmly in his arms, quietly remarked, 'Is that right, babe, do you belong to him? And there's me thinking you were a free and independent-minded young woman.'

'So I am,' Harriet hotly protested, inflamed by Steve's assumption that she'd still be hanging around waiting for him, all pathetic and needy. 'Sorry, Steve. I'm dancing with Vinny right now. Would you mind getting out of the way as you're causing a scene. You can ask me again later, when I'm free,' and resting her cheek against Vinny's, she let him sway her in his arms, in time to the music.

Tight lipped, Steve whirled on his heels and strode away without another word. When the dance was over Harriet could see no sign of him. Her stomach gave an uncomfortable lurch. She'd obviously upset him by not rushing straight into his arms, as she might eagerly have done only a week ago. But she really didn't care. He'd let her down by not supporting her against his parents' disapproval. How things had changed. Oh, but she didn't want to lose him.

'Take no notice of wonderboy,' Vinny was saying as he nibbled her ear lobe. 'Doesn't know how to treat a girl. Say what you like about me, I do know how to give a chick a good time.'

Harriet gave Vinny a vague smile, but her mind was on Steve. She couldn't instantly stop loving him simply because he was in a sulk, or didn't quite know how to handle this complicated situation. Maybe she was being a bit hard on him. He was confused about it all, and so was she. Then Harriet caught sight of him across the dance floor, and, politely excusing herself to Vinny, began to make her way towards him, unable to resist allowing her beloved Steve one last chance to apologise.

Before she reached him the music started up again and, after casting a furious glare in her direction, he turned away and asked a blonde to dance. The girl almost fell into his arms, obviously delighted to be asked, and Steve eagerly wrapped his arms about her.

Harriet stopped dead, hugely embarrassed that she should be left standing in the middle of the dance floor, so obviously snubbed. Vinny saw her dilemma and was back at her elbow in a second. 'Come on, babe, let's get some fresh air.'

Feeling weak, and shaken by Steve's rebuff, Harriet allowed Vinny to lead her outside. He pressed her up against a wall and started to kiss her with the same kind of energy and single-mindedness that he'd demonstrated on stage earlier. Harriet offered no resistance. At any other time she might have slapped him away, but tonight her self-esteem was at an all-time low.

Harriet was hurting badly, feeling let down by Steve's thoughtless arrogance. Not only had he failed to support her against his mother's sarcasm then ignored her all week, but he'd turned up at the dance over an hour late, and taken it for granted she'd still be hanging around waiting for him. What cheek! And to add insult to injury, he now had his arms wrapped round that blonde.

Maybe *she* was the kind of *nice* girl his mother would approve of. Perhaps he agreed with his parents' sudden change of attitude towards her, and didn't feel the need to show Harriet any respect either, now that she wasn't quite what he thought. She felt a deep sense of shame, as if she'd committed some sin or other, instantly quenched by a stir of hot fury that roared through her veins. How dare Steve treat her with such contempt!

The unexpected anger at least helped to offset the pain that was clenching her heart, and she put her arms around Vinny's neck and began to kiss him with renewed fervour.

Steve Blackstock could go take a long walk off a short pier, as Nan would say. He'd had his chance and lost it.

I I

Joyce

Joyce had been dreadfully upset by what had happened at her friend Eileen's party. She felt unclean, dirty and despoiled. The first thing she did when she got home that night was to run a bath, far more than the regulatory few inches, and she soaped herself all over, inside and out. Joyce was appalled by what had happened to her, and, once the first shock passed, had sobbed her heart out.

Who would want to marry her now? No respectable man, that was for sure. Certainly not a handsome sailor. She was ruined, desecrated, violated. Her hopes and dreams for a better future were now quite gone. She'd end up under the arches with the other prossies.

Joyce spent the next hour or two in self-chastisement, berating herself for being all kinds of a fool, telling herself she should have made a run for it the minute she'd seen what state the young man was in. But then the lad had seemed quite merry, really quite jolly at first, and non-threatening. How was she to know he'd turn nasty?

After a while she dried her tears, pushed back her hair and started to think more clearly. Who knew about this? No one. It became very clear to her in a moment of complete lucidity, that the least said, soonest mended. She didn't even know his name, and he was so drunk she doubted he would recognise her even if he did ever see her again. The chances were he wouldn't remember anything about it. With luck, their paths would never cross and this whole unpleasant episode could be swept aside and forgotten.

Joyce made up her mind not to tell a soul, certainly not her own mother who was a strong Methodist and didn't believe in hanky-panky before marriage, nor strong liquor at any time. Rose would be sure to accuse her of drinking, even though she hadn't touched a drop. Her mother would castigate her for even being at a party where strong drink was being served, and no doubt blame *Joyce* for things getting out of hand.

She could almost hear her saying it. 'You should have had more sense. Boys will be boys. You shouldn't have even been at a party where there were drunks.'

It simply wasn't worth risking the arguments that would surely follow simply for a bit of sympathy. Nor had Joyce any wish to lose her reputation, which was very important to her.

Silence, that was the answer. Joyce had no intention of allowing one drunken sailor to ruin her life. Who would believe in her innocence? What was she supposed to do, for goodness' sake, report this silly young man, whose name she didn't even know, to the police? And what would they do? Nothing! They'd tell her off for being so stupid as to let him. Men always stuck together, didn't they?

Besides, they'd hardly be likely to blame a young serviceman for wanting a bit of fun before he went off to fight for his country. They'd remind her there was a war on, that tensions were running high, that whisky and fear can do funny things to a bloke, and that the young man might be dead next week.

Joyce made up her mind. If her friends didn't know, if *no one* knew, then no one could ever turn round and accuse her of behaving like a tart.

A week or two later, to her great surprise and delight, she did get a letter from Stan, and Joyce knew instantly that she'd made the right decision. She ripped open the envelope and read the letter with fast-beating heart. He was apologising for not having written sooner, explaining that he'd had a hard job finding out her address, and weren't they a pair of daft clucks for not having thought of that. He'd been granted a few days' leave following his initial training, and could they please meet up?

Joyce wrote back at once to say, yes please.

★

On the Saturday morning following her committee meeting, Rose asked, 'Can we have us tea early tonight? Only I'm off round to Irma's, having me cards read.'

Harriet didn't seem to hear as she placed a plate of scrambled eggs on toast before her grandmother. She kept endlessly going over what had happened at the dance the previous night, wondering what became of Steve after he'd waltzed off with that blonde. She hadn't seen him again all evening. But then she'd spent rather a long time outside getting some 'fresh air' with Vinny Turner.

Oh, she did hope Steve didn't see her necking with him. That would be too embarrassing. Harriet was feeling just a little ashamed of her reckless behaviour, already having second thoughts over accepting an invitation to see Vinny again tonight. That had come about as a moment of rebellion because she suspected Steve had gone off with his blonde.

Joyce's voice intruded sharply upon her thoughts. 'I asked for salt and pepper. You can't even set a breakfast table properly.'

Harriet brought the cruet set without comment, then turning to her grandmother, finally answered her question. 'Course we can have supper early, Nan, no problem. Just tell me what you'd like to eat.'

'Nay, chuck, I don't mind. Whatever you cook is allus delicious. Summat I can chew easy with these new false teeth of mine.'

'An early tea would suit me too as I'm going out myself, as a matter of fact, to the pictures with a friend.'

'It might not suit me,' Grant complained, in his habitual whine.

Both Harriet and Rose ignored him.

'You off out with young Steve?' Rose queried with a teasing wink, but to her surprise, Harriet shook her head.

'No, not tonight.'

'Eeh, that's a turn up for the book, I thought you and him were like that,' Nan said, crossing her fingers, which wasn't easy with a piece of toast clutched in them.

'So who are you going with?' Joyce sharply enquired.

'Anyone I know?' Grant added.

Harriet cast him a vague smile. 'I do hope not.'

Rose smacked her grandson's hand as he reached for the last slice of toast. 'You keep yer nose out, you. Leave the poor lass alone. If her and Steve are having problems it's nowt to do wi' you. Anyroad, I'm going to solve all our problems tonight with a throw of them cards. Irma's ability at fortune telling is unsurpassed.'

Joyce snorted her derision. 'Lot of superstitious nonsense.'

'Course it is, and I believe every word.'

'There's a fool born every minute.'

Rose laughed. 'Well, I can't help how I were born. At least I haven't made a life-time's career of being one, like some folk I could mention.'

Joyce glared at her mother, but said nothing further.

Grant simply grinned, thinking that he might make it his business to find out exactly who it was Harriet was seeing tonight. It could well prove interesting.

Joyce endured a long, tiring day at the salon and when finally she shut up for the day, was delighted to discover that everyone, including her mother, had gone out for the evening. Harriet had left supper for her under a plate in the oven to keep warm. She turned it off, hungry for something other than food.

Joyce loved it when she and Joe were able to enjoy a little privacy, making the most of these few hours alone to slip into bed together. It never took him long to get out of his working togs and between the sheets. Joe liked his bit of fun and was a generous lover, always making sure that Joyce was happy too.

And he made a point of remembering to keep her well provided with rum and coke, Joyce's favourite tipple. They were soon cuddled up against the pillows, sipping their drinks contentedly together.

'So poor Irma's on her own again this evening?'

'I'm afraid so.'

'Do you reckon she suspects?'

'I've no idea. She wouldn't dream of telling me what she thinks.'

'Why, because she's used to you and your women?'

'Nay, Joyce love, you're the only one for me.'

'But not the first.' It was not a question.

Joe took a long swallow of his drink. He was more a beer man himself, but went through with this little ritual of sipping a rum and coke after their love-making session for Joyce's benefit. It made him feel as if he were pleasing her. But where was the point in pretending she was the first? It was no secret that he had many notches on his belt, something of which he was really quite proud. 'Well, that might be true, love, but it's best to be the last, isn't it, rather than the first?'

'Ooh, Joe, what a smarmy old softy you are. I bet you say that to all the girls,' Joyce giggled, giving him a smacking kiss on his bristled cheek. 'I could really fancy you, if I weren't taken,' she teased. 'Ooh, silly me, what am I saying? I'm not taken, am I? I'm free as air, at last, which you seem to have failed to notice.'

'Aye, course I've noticed. All the better for me that you are free.' Almost as soon as the words were out of his mouth Joe regretted them. He didn't care to acknowledge how free Joyce was following her husband's demise. Irma never complained about his little peccadilloes, and they rubbed along surprisingly well. She was a first-rate cook, and he doubted Joyce would take such care of him. He couldn't quite see her keeping his overalls so dazzling white, important on a food stall, or darning his favourite socks. So whatever had possessed him to say such a stupid thing? He was perfectly happy with the way things were, and had no wish to change the situation.

Joyce, however, took quite the opposite view. Now that her husband Stan had died, she was beginning to realise that maybe she wanted more than a quick tumble between the sheets. She had her future to think of, after all, and much as she enjoyed her little hairdressing business, she thought it was about time she relaxed a little more and let someone else look after her for a change.

'All the better for me too,' Joyce agreed. 'You wouldn't believe what I had to put up with, fetching and carrying for that man, suffering his black moods, trapped in this house.'

'Eeh, I don't know about trapped exactly, you and me seemed to get together quite regular, though of course nowhere near often enough,' Joe hastily added, noting the glint in her glare.

'Not to mention putting up with . . . other things which Stan foisted on me.'

Joe considered pretending not to understand, but then Joyce had dropped enough hints over these last months to give him a good picture of how things stood between herself and Harriet, so quietly remarked, 'Well, at least the lass was able to share the load, once she got older.'

'Huh, lot of use *she* was.'

Joyce genuinely believed that she'd sacrificed her life to Stan, that she'd spent much of it caring for a crippled husband, tied to the house in case he should need something. She conveniently ignored the fact that once Harriet was old enough, she had indeed been the one who'd done the lion's share of caring for her father.

Now, Joyce was entranced by the prospect of having the freedom to enjoy herself, to go out and about more and have a man take care of her for a change. It was an intoxicating thought, something she'd never been lucky enough to have. Joe Southworth featured largely in these plans for the future. He had a good business, wasn't in bad shape for a man his age, and she was really quite fond of him.

'So you will tell Irma soon then, now that we're going to be spending more time together? In fact, I was wondering if you'd like to move in.'

'Move in? What, here, with you?' Joe's eyes widened with shock.

'That was the general idea. Then when the divorce comes through, we can tie the knot all legal and above board. What do you say?'

Joe was too stunned to speak for a moment. This was the last thing he'd expected. 'Nay, I could never do that.'

'Why not?'

He floundered a little, wondering what he could possibly say to avoid this looming hazard. 'Live o'er t'brush together, you mean? Nay, what would folk think? And Irma would never stand for it.'

Joyce chuckled. 'Irma would have no say in the matter, and folk would only think what a laddo you are. A real man!' She slid her hands between his legs and fondled the hot hardness of him. 'I've ample proof of that, haven't I?'

Joe loved it when she made him out to be a real lothario, as it was rather how he saw himself. 'Yeah, but aren't you a bit over-crowded here already, what with your mother, and Grant, and that young lass, of course. Harriet, for one, wouldn't care to have me take her father's place.'

'She'll do as she's told,' Joyce snapped, pulling his trousers off him just as he'd started to pull them on.

Joe certainly had no difficulty in performing an encore which brought great pleasure to them both, but whether he wished to make these little overtures into a life-long symphony, he couldn't quite decide. He avoided further discussion by taking Joyce off to the Dog and Duck for her second rum and coke, where conversation could move along less dangerous lines.

What he didn't appreciate was that once Joyce Ashton had set her mind on something, she generally got her way. Although if she were honest, that trait hadn't always served her well in the past.

12

Joyce

Joyce had been so excited that Stan had got back in touch that this time she agreed he may call for her at the house. She even introduced him to Rose, who managed to behave herself for once. Her mother didn't bring out any old baby photographs of Joyce, nor did she make any embarrassing jokes or tell boring little anecdotes about her as a little girl. She just sat smiling as she watched her daughter with her young man, clearly pleased to see her happy.

Oh, and they were happy. Joyce was in love, no doubt about that. After a while they left the small house in Ducie Street and walked down by the canal, watching the barges carry cotton and other goods down to the docks. Joyce thought Stan looked so handsome in his sailor's uniform. Then they sat on a bench and talked all evening, about nothing in particular, and of course kissed a good deal.

'Can I see you again?' he asked. 'You know you're very special to me, don't you, Joyce?'

'Am I?'

'I've been going frantic trying to find you. I didn't even know your last name. I was asking all the chaps if they knew you, and nobody did.'

Joyce was incensed. 'I should hope not, I'm a decent girl.' She tried not to think of what had happened at the party.

'You know what I mean. I needed to find you. I was growing desperate.'

She wanted to believe this was true, but couldn't quite.

He was so wonderful, so handsome. What on earth did he see in her?

'In the end I asked Bill, and he asked Eileen and there you have it. I found you. She's a star is Eileen. What would we do without her?'

This was a comment that would return to haunt Joyce in later years.

She let him kiss her a great deal more, but Stan was careful to stop before passion overwhelmed him and took them too far. Joyce appreciated the fact that he respected her, even though she would quite happily have let things go a little further, if not all the way. She was anxious to give the impression that she was still a virgin, having successfully blocked that unpleasant incident at Eileen's party from her mind.

This time when Stan returned to his ship, which was still in dock awaiting orders, he wrote to her regularly, at least three times a week, and Joyce wrote back every bit as assiduously. She was deeply in love, and heady with happiness.

That is, until it occurred to her that she hadn't seen her period for a while. The next morning she threw up in the sink and Joyce realised with dread that she was pregnant.

Grant enjoyed a gamble but he wasn't one to rely on chance, whether they be cards, palm readings, tea leaves or the crystal ball. He preferred a more hands-on approach. Besides which he was far more interested in the past rather than any future his nan might discover from Irma's fortune telling. In particular, his mother's early life.

Over these last few days he'd been asking rather a lot of questions of the various stallholders on the market, enquiring if they remembered Joyce when she was young.

'I was wondering what friends me mam had during the war, if she had a boyfriend before she married me dad.' He'd tried making his request sound casual, as if he were only mildly curious.

Some, like Winnie Holmes, told him sharply that she didn't

poke her nose in other folk's business, which was so blatantly untrue it almost made him laugh out loud. 'You must know something.'

'I know nowt, and even if I did, my lips are sealed.' Which was the kind of enigmatic remark that didn't help him in the slightest.

With others it had been hard to get them to stop. Once they started reminiscing, they'd go on for ages. They'd rant on about the home guard and rationing, a son or some other loved one they'd lost in the war, even recalling Stan when he'd been young and virile, which Grant had no wish to hear about at all.

Many of the men, like Sam Beckett and Jimmy Ramsay, hadn't been around, since they'd been in the forces doing their stint. Marco Bertalone had been in an aliens' camp on the Isle of Man as he was Italian. Barry Holmes had been living in Blackpool, Clara Higginson in Paris of all places for much of the war, and several others had only come to the market in recent years.

Worn out from listening to these boring old yarns, Grant was beginning to despair of ever discovering anything useful. He wondered if it was worth even bothering to try this evening. Maybe he'd give it one more bash, but first he needed to check up on Harriet, and was intrigued to discover that her latest date was Vinny Turner.

Grant watched the couple stroll into the Salford Cinema arm in arm, then left them to it. A right loser he was. It gave him enormous satisfaction to think that Vinny would bring her nothing but misery as he sauntered off to pursue more interesting prospects.

Having left off stalking his half-sister and her latest boyfriend, Grant decided to treat himself to a hamburger and frothy coffee at Belle's café, despite having just enjoyed the steak and onions Harriet had made. And while he was enjoying this second supper, he thought he might as well ask if Belle had known his mother during the war.

'I might've done,' Belle told him, with a casual shrug. 'Your mam did use to work on this market during the war, for Poulson's

Pies I seem to remember. That was before she took up hair-dressing. Why do you ask?'

Grant was pleased and surprised by this snippet of information, the most he'd got so far, though how much it would help him he wasn't quite sure. 'Er, I'm planning a party to cheer her up,' he improvised, saying the first thing that came into his head. 'And I wanted to invite some of her old friends.'

Frowning, Belle set the hamburger before him, watching as he liberally dowsed it in tomato ketchup. 'Is it her birthday or something?'

'Not really, it's just that she's been a bit down lately, what with losing Dad and everything.' Grant took a huge bite of the juicy beef, so that ketchup oozed out of his mouth and dripped down his hands. He licked it up, pleased with the tale he was devising, quite off the top of his head. 'So, do you know of any? Old friends, I mean.'

Belle smiled. 'Now that'd be telling, wouldn't it?'

He felt a spurt of hope. 'So you do know summat? Go on then, tell all, who were her special friends during the war? I'd really appreciate it, and I'm sure Mam would too. She likes a good party.' Grant thought this bit of fiction so inspired he might even go through with it. It would be worth the effort to actually meet some of the old flames in her life. And his real father might turn out to be one of them.

'I'm not so sure about that. We all have our secrets from when we were young, don't we? And your mam is no exception,' Belle darkly reminded him, handing Grant a paper napkin, which he ignored. 'But I'll give it some thought.' She began to walk away, quietly chuckling, then half turned to cast him a teasing glance over her shoulder. 'Of course, you could always ask Frankie Morris, over at the chip shop. He might be able to point you in the right direction.'

Grant sighed, grinding his teeth in frustration. Frankie Morris indeed. That big, blubbery man in a soiled apron whose bald head gleamed as if greased from the fat on his own hands? He'd be the last person in the world his mother would hang out with, war or no war. He was getting nowhere, nowhere at all.

Nevertheless, on his way home he did call in at the fish and chip shop, and risked the question. 'Did you know my mam during the war when she was young?' Grant asked.

Frankie paused in his labours of battering the fish, wiped his sticky hands on his greasy apron and waddled over to glower at the lad. 'What's it to you?'

'I – I just wondered.'

'If I did, that's my business, not yours. Buzz off!'

'So you did know her?'

'That's not what I said.'

'But you knew some of her friends?' Again Grant spun his yarn about a party he was planning, but something about the expression on Frankie's face made him wonder if he'd pushed the explanation too far. 'Well?'

'What makes you think your mam likes parties?'

'Everyone likes parties.'

'Not your mam.'

'Why?'

'Would you like to see how it feels to be battered like a wet fish?'

Grant fled.

When he got back home he was surprised to find his mother sitting alone in the kitchen, sipping a rum and coke and looking very sorry for herself. It wasn't like Joyce to drink alone and he wanted to ask where Joe was, but hadn't got round to plucking up the courage to do so when she came right out with it and told him.

'Before you ask, Joe has gone home early. Apparently Irma has a wedding cake to deliver first thing in the morning, and Joe has to be up early to drive her there.'

'Oh, right!' Grant didn't dare risk commenting further, knowing it would only inflame her disappointment over the apparent short-comings of her lover still further. Instead, wanting to please her, he told her the gossip he'd picked up about Harriet.

'Hey, what do you think? You'll never guess who our Harriet

is out with tonight? Vinny Turner, no less. What do you reckon to that?'

'Vinny Turner?'

'Aye, he has a police record as long as your arm. Been up for shop lifting, drunkenness and assault, you name it. Lives round the back of the fish market with—'

'I know who Vinny Turner is, and the whole rapscallion crew that makes up that no-good Irish family. Why on earth would our Harriet be seeing him? He's not in Steve Blackstock's league.'

Grant was startled by how concerned and angry she sounded, but pleased that he'd obviously got Harriet into yet more trouble. 'I reckon it must be what you might call teenage rebellion.'

Joyce glowered at him. 'Teenage rebellion my left foot. I'll give that little madam what for when I catch her.'

And for the second time in the space of one evening, Grant thought it best to beat a hasty retreat.

Harriet returned home from the pictures later than usual, her cheeks glowing bright pink from all the kisses Vinny had given her. She knew in her heart that she was playing a dangerous game by going out with him when he had such a tarnished reputation, but rebellion was strong in her. She had this urge to do something really wicked, to make people sit up and take notice, to have them see her as a real person with feelings and needs, albeit one damaged and hurt from all the revelations that had been thrust at her.

Maybe she was behaving badly because she *was* illegitimate, losing her moral standards or whatever it was; her decency or proper status in the community, exactly as people predicted. Certainly as Steve's parents expected. But deep in her heart she didn't want that to happen. It was Steve she wanted, Steve she loved not Vinny Turner, only she didn't quite have the courage to confront him and resolve their quarrel.

In the meantime Vinny was making her feel good about herself, something she needed after having been so badly let down.

Harriet went to the kitchen to get herself a cup of cocoa and found Joyce sitting in her dressing-gown sipping a small whisky and more than a little the worse for drink. Apparently, she was waiting up for Harriet.

'What's all this?' Harriet asked on a laugh, almost tripping over something blocking her way as she walked in. She glanced down at the suitcase, all packed, ready and waiting, in surprise. 'Are you off on a trip somewhere?'

'No, *you* are. I've put you up some sandwiches, and there's money in the purse to buy yourself a train ticket to wherever you want to go.'

'Go? What are you talking about? Go where?'

'Wherever you like. A new beginning, a new job, whatever you fancy, only you're not stopping here. I've done my duty by you, much against my better judgement, and despite your being no relation. Now it's over. Joe will be moving in soon, and we reckon it would be best for all concerned if you weren't around when he did. It's time for you to leave, so you can go first thing in the morning.' Joyce's eyes were half closed and her voice sounded slurred, so that Harriet could hardly believe what she was hearing.

'You can't be serious. Where am I supposed to go?'

'Why don't you ask them new friends of yours for some ideas? That rabble-rousing lot you hung out with last night at the dance, Vinny Turner and his mates.'

'I – I don't understand.'

'You don't have to understand. You've lost the right to stop here, that's all there is to it.'

'Why? I wasn't doing any harm going out with Vinny.'

'You were showing yourself up, showing *me* up, which is worse, and you're not even my responsibility any more.'

'Mam . . .'

'Don't call me that,' Joyce snapped. 'I never was your mother, and you never saw me as such, not really. It was always your dad, dad, dad, who came first, second and third. He was the one you always ran to, not me. So now he's gone, you can go too.'

'Mam, I never came to you because you always shoved me

away, but I still love you. I didn't know how to please you, how to make you happy. Don't you care about me at all?'

Joyce looked at her erstwhile daughter for a long moment. 'Why would I? I don't even know who you are.' Then picking up her glass, she refilled it with whisky and went upstairs to bed without another word.

13

Rose

Rose spent the evening with Irma, as agreed, having her cards read. She'd been worrying a good deal about Harriet lately, about how much it was safe to tell her, and the idea had come to her that a bit of insight into the future might help her to decide the best way to tackle the problem.

Irma shuffled a pack of cards and spread it out on the table. 'Choose three, please, then place them face down in a row.'

Rose did so. Picking up the first card Irma revealed a two of spades. She considered this in silence for a moment and then, smiling at Rose to reassure her, said, 'This simply tells me that you are torn between two choices. Would you say that's how you feel?'

'Oh, yes.'

Irma picked up the second card, and the smile faded.

Rose gulped. 'Go on, tell me what it says.'

'It's the five of hearts which means that this choice, this problem, is bringing you great sorrow. Is that true?'

'Oh, aye, that's true,' Rose agreed. 'I'm at me wits' end. That's why I'm here. I were hoping you could help me decide what's best to be done.'

Again Irma smiled at her kindly. 'I can't help at all, only the cards can do that. But I shall do my best to interpret what they have to say correctly. Now, let's look at the third card. Ah, a ten of diamonds. Something to do with a letter?'

Rose frowned, looking puzzled. 'Not that I know of. I know nowt about no letter. Is that it? Is that all you can tell me?'

'This was but a first and very basic reading. Let's try for a little more detail.'

This time when she shuffled and spread the deck, she asked Rose to choose ten cards, then Irma laid them out in the shape of a pyramid. 'This top card tells us the major influence upon your problem. Ah, the six of hearts. Something to do with the past, something you're holding on to. It could be a memory, a person you miss, or a secret, perhaps. Only you can work out the answer to that.'

Rose nodded, but said nothing, waiting for whatever came next.

Irma's hand hovered over the next card. 'This second row concerns the choices you have to make. Two of diamonds and a two of spades.' Irma frowned. 'These suits do not sit well together. The cards seem to suggest a difficult union is at the heart of the problem, and that there may be a parting of ways in the offing. Does that make any sense? Is someone in the family planning to leave?'

'Eeh, I do hope not.'

Irma looked into Rose's pale face and patted the other woman's hand. 'Let's not worry too much till we've read the rest.'

The next row did indeed give some encouragement as Irma turned up a Jack between numbered cards. 'This seems to indicate that a young person is getting support from two close companions.'

'That'll be our Harriet,' Rose burst out, relieved that not all the news was bad. 'She's had a bit of a shock recently – but I'm certainly doing what I can for the lass, and so is young Steve, I'm sure.' She pointed to the rest of the cards. 'And this last row, what's that all about?'

'This may offer us some advice on how to resolve your dilemma, whatever it is. But I have to say that if this is a problem of Harriet's you're concerned with, then she will need to come for a separate reading. I can't help without her being present. The cards are speaking only to you, remember.'

'Right, yes, I understand. I'll tell her. But I still need to know what *I* should do for the best. Go on.'

'It's not an exact science,' Irma warned. 'You may not get too precise an answer but I shall interpret what they say as well as I can, to help you decide.'

'I'm listening.'

Irma turned over the next card. 'The nine of spades. I'm afraid that seems to indicate a loss of health, or possibly money.' She tapped one finger on the card. 'It may simply mean too much worry, of course, imagined health problems, or a feeling of depression, so don't start writing your will quite yet.'

Rose frowned. 'I've done that already.'

'The two of clubs next, which urges you to trust in your own intuition. That makes good sense. Now let's see what the two remaining cards have to say,' Irma said, hurrying on. It always troubled her when the run of cards was not good, and this wasn't exactly a happy reading, not by anybody's standards. As she turned up the penultimate card, she smiled with relief.

'The six of diamonds. This gives us good news in that there may well be a successful outcome if help is given at the appropriate time. Ah, and this last card, the ace of hearts is one to treasure. This represents new love. Something or someone wonderful is to come into your life.' Irma glanced up at Rose with a beaming smile. 'Maybe you'll find yourself a new fella who might solve all your problems.'

'Don't talk daft. I'm too old for all of that nonsense.'

'No one is ever too old for love.'

Rose felt all hot and bothered by what she'd learned, and more confused than ever. 'All this talk of choices, sorrow, partings and bad health. It don't sound too good, do it? I'm not sure I'm any nearer solving my problem.'

'It's not easy to take everything in all at once. Give yourself time to think about it. I'm sure all will be revealed in the fullness of time.' Irma began to collect up the cards, shuffled them, then put them back in their box.

'Can't we do it again?' Rose asked, still looking troubled.

'I'm afraid not. Take heart, Rose, that a good outcome was forecast so long as you remember what the cards said. You must use your intuition as the two of clubs recommends, of which you have plenty. That will help you make the right choices.'

'But what about all this talk of partings, and a letter, and great sorrow. Is someone going to die?' The old woman pressed one hand to her breast in sudden panic. 'Not our Harriet?'

'No, no, I've told you this isn't about Harriet, it's about you.'

Rose went white. 'Then I'm going to die?'

'No one's going to die. The cards said nothing about death. It could be a loss of money, as I said, and not health at all. You'll just have to wait and see, but at least you are prepared now, and hopefully will be better able to deal with whatever happens.'

Rose wasn't too sure about that, but didn't like to say so.

Irma led her to the door. 'Come and see me again in a few weeks' time if things haven't improved. We could perhaps try the crystal and see what that can tell us. And don't forget that ace of hearts for new love. That should give you real hope.'

Rose went home to her bed and spent a restless night going over and over what the cards had said, which didn't give her any hope at all of resolving her dilemma. She'd promised Joyce that she'd keep her lip buttoned, but what if this continuing silence harmed her lovely Harriet, what then? Which of them, Harriet or Joyce, did she have the most duty to protect in the long run? On this point, the cards hadn't helped one bit.

The next morning Rose woke early, headed straight for the kitchen as she generally did to make a pot of tea. There was nothing like the freshness of that first brew of the day. She'd take a cup up to Harriet, see if she'd enjoyed her night out and try to get to the bottom of what had gone wrong between her and Steve.

Getting no reply as she knocked softly on the girl's bedroom door, Rose crept into Harriet's room only to find it empty. She started to straighten the covers of her granddaughter's bed, smoothing her pillow, thinking she must have gone into the bathroom while she'd been downstairs making the tea. Rose was worried about the lass and the old woman's eyes filled with tears at the recollection of how shocked and hurt Harriet had been when she'd first learned the truth about her birth.

She half regretted having been the one to tell her about her mother, and in quite such a blunt manner. Yet she knew Joyce had only been waiting for Stan's death to deal the blow herself, and would have done it with far less tact, making sure she bullied the girl quite a bit first, which had been Rose's deepest concern.

But despite Rose's desire to bring honesty and openness, she still felt mired in secrets. There was still much to worry over, and Rose's faith in the cards had slipped a little, due to the confusion in the readings.

Her hands paused in their smoothing of the pillow slip upon which she herself had embroidered her granddaughter's initials as it occurred to her that the bed was already made – in fact it didn't look as if it had even been slept in.

Her hands flew to her face in horror. Where was she then? Where had the lass spent the night? Surely not with her new boyfriend!

'Don't be daft,' she scolded herself. 'She's probably made her bed and is right at this minute enjoying a leisurely bath in peace.'

Rose decided to investigate her theory, but as she picked up the cup and saucer and turned to leave, she noticed the letter, exactly as the cards had predicted, half hidden behind the bedside lamp. The small white envelope bore a single name: *Mother*. Rose stared at it in dismay.

Turning it over to examine it she saw that it was sealed and felt quite bulky, but she realised at once what it was. The poor lass had poured her heart out on paper, in a letter to a long-dead mother she'd only recently learned existed. And having written it, she'd nowhere to send it. How upsetting for the child!

But if Joyce should see it there'd be hell to pay. She'd think Rose had been talking again. Tucking the letter into her apron pocket Rose again turned to leave, half shaking her head in amazement. The cards had been right after all. There was indeed a letter. Now she'd have to think carefully about what else they'd told her. She'd need all her wits about her if she was to take Joyce on.

It was then that she noticed the note which Harriet had left on the bedside table addressed with her own name: Nan. Puzzled, Rose unfolded the paper and read the few words scribbled inside. She felt as if all the blood was draining from her face and she came over all light headed.

Frantic with anxiety, she searched drawers and cupboards, only to discover her worst fears were realised. Her granddaughter had gone. The girl's bedroom was empty of all her possessions.

Rose rushed straight to her daughter, who was by this time in the kitchen making toast under the grill, and demanded to know what was going on.

'Where's our Harriet?'

Joyce's lip curled with distaste. 'Gone.'

'What d'you mean gone? Gone where?'

'I neither know nor care. She's spread her wings and flown the nest. It was long past time for her to start living her own life.' Joyce gave an airy shrug as she spilled cornflakes into a bowl, then looked vaguely round for the milk bottle as if she hadn't an idea where it was kept.

For the first time in a great number of years she was obliged to make her own breakfast, which was a downside to the situation, admittedly. She just fancied a bacon sarnie this morning, which might have helped this terrible hangover she was suffering. Joyce wondered if she could coax her mother into operating the frying pan, even though Rose had sworn never to touch it again after the complaints she'd received the last time she cooked her daughter breakfast. Then in the next breath Joyce was making the excuse that Joe would be moving in soon. 'Harriet would have been sure to object.'

'I might object myself,' Rose bluntly remarked. 'Has Joe actually promised to move in or is this merely hope on your part?'

Judging by the way her daughter's face tightened in response to this question, Rose rather thought she might have hit the nail on the head, as it were.

'Joe will do as I say,' Joyce snapped, rubbing at her pounding forehead with the tips of her fingers. 'I've already explained Joe and I *need* to be together.'

'And what about his wife? Does she have any say in the matter? What right have you to rob another woman of her husband?'

'If Irma had anything about her, Joe wouldn't want to leave.'

'What Joe Southworth needs is a boot up the backside. He doesn't know when he's well off. Irma's a treasure, an absolute saint to put up with that man.'

Sorry as Rose was for Irma, she felt a hundred times sorrier for herself. The cards had been right yet again. Hadn't they warned of a parting, and a great deal of sorrow? Not for one moment though had she imagined they meant Harriet would leave home. Hadn't Irma assured her the cards were telling Rose's fortune, not her granddaughter's? She'd feared that she might be the one about to turn up her toes, what with all that stuff about losing her health or her money. But losing Harriet was far worse, and it was all Joyce's fault. Rose could feel herself going all hot and cold in pure panic, prickling all over as if she were on fire. How dare Joyce be so cruel as to turn the girl out on to the streets!

'Perhaps saints don't make good bedfellows. A man has needs, after all,' Joyce muttered.

'Men and booze, that's all you ever think about. You've a one-track mind, you. You disgust me. I'm going to find our Harriet, and when I do, I'm leaving with her, do you understand, you great brainless moron? From the moment that child first drew breath you've set out to ruin her life. That's the reason I stopped on, for her, not for you. Well, you've ruined your own life, that's for sure, with this desperate need you have for revenge, but I'm damned if I'll let you succeed in ruining our Harriet's. She's an innocent in all of this, remember that, madam, an innocent.'

14

Harriet

Harriet had left the house before dawn, as Rose had surmised, without even bothering to go to bed. She shed a few tears at the prospect of being forced to leave her home, however unwelcome Joyce had made her feel in it, and hated the prospect of leaving her nan. But there seemed little point in waking the old woman just to cause her more upset by saying goodbye, so Harriet left the short note instead.

Harriet would also have liked to say goodbye to Steve, had things not gone so badly wrong between them. In any case, he'd be off to college soon, so he probably wouldn't even notice she was gone.

After the confrontation with her stepmother, Harriet dried her eyes, washed her face and dressed in more practical clothes, jeans and a shirt and sweater. She then packed a few more items which Joyce had forgotten: a photo of her dad, the tiny teddy bear he'd brought her back from the war, and slipped quietly out into a cool grey dawn with not the first idea where she was going.

It was so early that even Champion Street was looking strangely bereft without the usual bustle of market crowds. Not even the stallholders, always early risers, had begun to get their pitch ready for the day.

And for all it was only early September, a chill wind blew along the empty street, scattering dry leaves from the churchyard, paper bags and cigarette ends, sending a shudder down Harriet's spine. Dustbin lids rattled and one clattered to the ground as a lone tabby cat streaked across in front of her, startled by her sudden presence. Harriet was even more unnerved by the noise, almost jumping out of her skin. What on earth was she doing? Where was she supposed to go?

She stopped walking to look in the purse which Joyce had left with the suitcase, quickly counting the notes inside. It contained twenty-five pounds, quite a sum of money, Harriet supposed. Yet it was still a cheap way of ridding herself of a troublesome step-daughter. She tucked the purse carefully back into her pocket, then picking up the suitcase she set off down the street. She'd go to London Road Station and get on the first train which came in, she decided. That seemed as good a way as any to decide what to do with the rest of her life.

It was as she turned into Grove Street that she realised she was no longer alone. The sound was little more than a whisper, but close, too close, and Harriet glanced anxiously over her shoulder. There was no one there, the street completely empty. She carried on walking, then heard what sounded like a snort of laughter. This time she felt the small hairs rise on the back of her neck and Harriet increased her pace as she heard footsteps. Someone was following her, she was sure of it.

By the time she reached the end of Grove Street she had started to run but then, feeling foolish, slowed her pace as she turned into Gartside Street. Who else would be around at this time in the morning? It was barely four o' clock.

The thought had hardly registered in her head when she found herself surrounded by a group of jeering youths. Her heart gave a frightening lurch as she realised at once who they were. Vinny Turner's mates. She'd seen them at the dance the other night. Now they were behaving as if they'd been out drinking all night. Perhaps they had. They certainly looked the worse for wear.

'Come on, chuck, hand it over,' one of them instructed. He was big, with a large beer belly which made him look as if he were nine months pregnant.

Harriet swallowed. 'Hand what over? I doubt my clothes would fit you,' indicating the small brown suitcase in her hand. Harriet was amazed by how normal her voice sounded. How was that possible when fear was pulsing through her, fizzing in her brain so that she could barely think?

'Don't play games with me,' said Beer Belly. 'We know you've got a nice fat purse. We saw you looking at it just now. Don't make life difficult for yourself. Be a good girl and hand it over.'

She thought about running but they were all round her, a tight-knit, hostile group of at least four or five lads, all mocking and taunting her. A skinny one gave her a hefty shove and Harriet would have fallen over had not another propped her up from behind. Then they were all doing it, pushing and shoving her, bouncing her between them like a rubber ball. She fell to the ground and one kicked her in the back. Harriet let out a whimper of fear and they laughed all the more, another yelling, 'Get her, Jimmy. Let her have it.'

Skinny Jimmy grabbed her by the hair and dragged her to her feet. Suddenly enraged by her own terror, Harriet took a swing at him with the suitcase, still clutched tight in her hand. Laughing, he ducked, then snatching it from her, snapped it open and tossed her things out on to the mucky pavement.

'*Get off!*' she screamed, hating to see his dirty hands rummaging through her night clothes, and her pretty skirts and blouses, as he searched for anything valuable.

Harriet couldn't believe this was happening to her, and practically on her own doorstep too. How was she ever going to manage out in the big brave world on her own if she couldn't even look after herself a mere step away from Champion Street?

'Give me the bloody purse,' Beer Belly repeated. 'I won't ask a third time.'

Harriet could tell by the way he was flexing his fat fists that he'd beat her to a pulp if she didn't comply, and no doubt still get the twenty-five quid. It certainly wasn't worth dying for. Even so, it was all she had in the world . . .

She reached down to the suitcase as if about to pluck the purse from a pocket inside, then kicked the skinny one in the ankle, making him yelp, while digging an elbow in Beer Belly. By a miracle she managed to take them both by surprise sufficiently to break free, then ran for her life. But not for long. Seconds later Harriet could hear feet pounding behind her.

She didn't think about where she was running to but twisted and turned, ducking and weaving down back streets and alleys in an effort to confuse them as she searched frantically for a hiding place. She certainly couldn't keep up this pace for long, and they had much longer legs than her.

Finding herself out on Water Street she hurriedly climbed over a gate into the yard behind the Old Botany Warehouses, thanking her lucky stars that she'd always been agile, having been something of a tomboy in her youth. Then she flung herself behind a pile of crates, quite out of breath and with a tearing stitch in her side.

How long she lay there, fear still coursing through her veins as she heard the gang banging about looking for her, Harriet had no idea. Maybe as little as five minutes, or as long as an hour. It certainly felt more like the latter. She thought of her lost belongings, her precious clothes, her toothbrush and face flannel, more importantly the photo of her father and even her much-loved teddy bear, and tears sprang to her eyes. Now what was she going to do? She clasped the purse tight in her pocket. At least she still had the money.

'Ah, there you are!' a voice said, and Harriet looked up, knowing she was lost.

Grant had hardly slept a wink since the conversation with his mother, determined to keep an eye out for what might happen next. He'd been curious to know what she was doing in Harriet's room, and then delighted to overhear Joyce order his hated half-sister to leave. He'd rejoiced still more when in the early hours he'd heard Harriet slip out of her room, creep down the stairs and let herself out of the house.

Grant had followed, a safe distance behind, wanting to see where she went, how she intended to handle this disaster.

He'd followed her along Champion Street, fearful of being seen, and struggled to keep pace at one stage when she actually began to run. But even he'd been shocked to see the gang of youths suddenly pounce upon her like feral wolves, while secretly relishing her predicament. Didn't the daft mare deserve a going-over, for all the trouble she'd caused him through the years?

Somehow Harriet broke free and was off again, running like a hare with baying hounds on her trail. Grant quickened his own pace and scuttled after them, not wanting to miss the capture when they would surely tear her apart.

He ran along Grove Street, then down Gartside Street but it was as he turned along Hardman Street heading for the river that one of the youths suddenly leapt out in front of him. To his utter horror, Grant was the one now to find himself surrounded by the gang of youths, every one of them furious at having lost their quarry and eager to take out that anger on anyone who chanced along.

Unfortunately for Grant, this just happened to be him. As they set about him with their fists and their boots, with stones and cudgels, he had time only to consider that this was one more debt Harriet owed him, one more reason for revenge.

Harriet had never felt more alone. She was hurting so much the pain felt like an iron band squeezing her heart. What the hell was she doing sitting in this dark, damp tunnel by the river watching the dawn come up all pink and gold over Prince's Bridge? The purse, with its roll of notes, was still a warm, solid pressure in her jeans pocket but what would happen now?

She'd been lucky that Vinny had been the one to find her and not his mates. And that he seemed willing to help rescue her from her pursuers.

'Don't make a sound,' he'd told her when he'd come across her hiding behind the broken old crates. 'I have you now. You're quite safe.'

'How did you know I was here?'

'I heard you scream. Ssh, they might hear you.'

The next instant they were creeping along by the river, the sluggish Irwell even more dark and gloomy in the eerie pre-dawn light. Vinny had held her firmly by the hand and for some reason she'd no longer felt afraid. Maybe because Harriet was so relieved it hadn't been Beer Belly or Skinny Jimmy who'd chanced upon her instead.

When they'd reached the bridge, he'd pulled her down this narrow tunnel that cut into the rock under the railway lines. And here they were hiding amongst the filth and the damp, the rubble and the broken bricks, tangled bits of wire and no doubt the odd rat. The narrow tunnel dripped with water and stank of cat pee but Vinny had found some reasonably dry cardboard boxes and broken these up for them to sit on.

When it was almost light he volunteered to go and look for her stuff. 'You stay here,' he ordered, and reaching forward, gave her a quick kiss. 'I'll be back in a jiffy.'

Harriet grasped his arm. 'How do I know you won't bring that lot back with you? They're your mates, after all. Why would I trust you?'

Vinny grinned, and somehow the smile softened the hard lines of his handsome face. 'Because I'm sick of that daft lot, I'd much rather be with you. If you want to know the honest truth, I was wanting rid of them anyway. Terry has got me a job in a rock band. I'm going places, babe, and you can come along with me. You and me were meant to be together, I knew it from the first moment I clapped eyes on you. We're free spirits you and me.'

'Are we?' Harriet stared at him, bemused.

'Course we are, why else would we both be here at not much after five in the morning, with our life's possessions in our pockets, well almost. I need to pop back home for me guitar, and a few other bits and bobs. I'll pick up your stuff too. Keep yer head down, I'll be back in two shakes.'

And then he was gone, leaving Harriet all alone in the semi-darkness. She pulled up the collar of her shirt to stop drips of water sliding down her neck and sat shivering, arms tightly wrapped about her knees while she watched the clouds roll away and a limpid sun peep through.

Vinny said she could trust him, but would she be wise to do so?

Harriet was quite sure he must have a police record. Hadn't he been done for shoplifting not so long ago? She was certainly aware that he smoked and drank a lot, that he'd drawn graffiti on the end walls of the terraced houses, tied dustbin lids to door handles and nicked milk bottles from people's doorsteps. He and his gang liked nothing better, in fact, than to create havoc in Champion Street. But how far did his crimes reach? What were his limits? Did he have any moral core at all?

Ever since his family had moved into the smelly old flats behind the new fish market just a few months ago, they'd been the talk of the district. But what other choice did she have but to wait for him? Who else cared where she went or what she did?

Certainly not Joyce, the woman who had half-heartedly carried out the role of mother throughout her life and had now abandoned her almost the moment her father had died. Admittedly the two of them had endured a difficult and complicated relationship but, strangely, Harriet still loved her. Joyce had been the only mother she'd ever known, so why wouldn't she? It hurt so badly that Joyce should reject her in this way.

Harriet had also believed she'd found love with Steve. Yet even he didn't seem interested now that she was no longer the respectable girl his mother had fondly imagined her to be.

She still had Nan, of course, but what could one old woman do? Rose didn't have the clout to stand up to Joyce. Nobody did. Or to deal with Grant, who was a real chip off the old block, cold and condemning, exactly like his mother in so many ways.

Harriet felt as if she were all alone in the world. Whatever she'd taken for granted in the past, was now gone. Love was a commodity not to be trusted. Far too dangerous an emotion to risk since it hurt too much when it was withdrawn for no apparent reason.

How long she waited for Vinny to return Harriet couldn't quite decide, but it felt like an age. The sun was high in the sky and she was beginning to despair he would ever come back when suddenly there he was, loaded down with gear. He was carrying a guitar and a large knapsack on his back, and in his other hand he held her suitcase.

'I'm not sure I've got everything. Some of it might have blown away, but I did my best.'

'Oh, Vinny, thank you so much. I can't tell you how grateful I am.' In that moment she made her decision. To hell with her so-called family. To hell with Steve. He could go off to college and marry a *nice* girl and live in a *nice* semi-detached house in a *nice* garden suburb if that's what he wanted, exactly as his mother expected. He could go out with the blonde he'd been dancing with the other night. Harriet would tag up with Vinny Turner. Vinny would look after her, which was surely better than trying to cope alone.

15

Rose

It was a week now since Harriet had walked out and Rose was frantic with worry, becoming increasingly obsessed with searching for her lost granddaughter. Every single day she went all round the stallholders on the market, asking if they'd seen her, if they knew where Harriet was.

'The lass can't have gone far. She doesn't have any money, and she knows no one but us. Where would she go? She hasn't even got a job.'

The stallholders were most sympathetic. Everyone liked Harriet as she was a lovely girl. But sadly, nobody had seen her around.

Despair set in. Rose was at a loss over what to do next, feeling as if she no longer had any real purpose to her day. The thought of never seeing her lovely granddaughter's cheery smile again was almost unbearable. She felt as if she were in deep mourning, worse in a way than when her lovely Ron had died. But then he'd enjoyed a good long life, after all, while Harriet was still only a young girl, with all her life before her.

'She's not *dead*,' Joyce yelled at her mother, when Rose started worrying along these lines in front of her.

'She might well be for all *we* know. She could've fallen in the canal, jumped off a bridge or under a train, been attacked by hooligans, owt could've happend to the poor lass, and do you care? I bet you didn't even give her any money.'

'Well, that's where you'd be wrong. I gave her twenty-five quid.'

'God,' said Grant. 'You've never given me that much cash in me life. I'd run away too if someone would give me that sort of money.'

'Don't tempt me,' his grandmother retorted. 'Twenty-five quid won't last long if she's rent to pay, has to buy food and so on. How will she manage? You didn't even give her time to find herself a job, or somewhere decent to live. What sort of a mother are you?'

Joyce was only just hanging on to her patience as Joe still hadn't agreed to move in, despite her best efforts to persuade him to take the plunge. She certainly wasn't in the mood to concern herself over a silly young girl. 'That's just it, I'm not her mother at all, am I?'

At this Rose really saw red and she banged her fist on the table. 'You should be ashamed of yourself for saying such a wicked thing. You're the only mother that child's ever known, and all you do is callously chuck her out the door at the first opportunity. All because you're on heat and itching to replace your recently demised husband, that poor girl's *father*, with another chap. You turn my stomach, you do really. Can't you see you've lost a precious daughter, and I a beloved grandchild?'

'I can see that I'm free of a great liability at last.'

'You've still got me, Nan,' Grant simpered. 'In fact, if you've a bit of money going begging, I could find a home for a few bob meself.' Whereupon Rose snorted her derision before storming out of the room, orange earrings bobbing angrily against her tightly clenched jaw.

Joyce's stentorian voice bawled after her. 'Don't you go losing your temper, Mother, it won't do your blood pressure any good at all.'

Over the coming week Rose did everything she possibly could to find her lost granddaughter. She continued to search for Harriet, and constantly asked round the market in case anyone had seen her, all to no avail. No one had seen her or heard any word of her whereabouts. In the end, Rose was forced to conclude that there was nothing more she could do. Her only hope was that Harriet would have the good sense to come home eventually, knowing her nan at least would be worried about her.

Meanwhile, Rose felt she had no choice but to press on with the campaign to save the market.

It was generally agreed they should start a petition and Rose went round all the houses, shops and market stalls, asking people to sign if they wanted the market to stay. This did at least allow her the opportunity to keep on asking about Harriet, although the response was always in the negative.

Where had the girl gone, and why wasn't she keeping in touch? That was what broke Rose's heart. There'd been one measly post-card in those first few days, which at least proved she was alive and well, but there'd been nothing since.

Rose was so worried she felt ill the whole time, sick to her stomach, hardly able to eat because of her distress. Not only that but Joyce made little effort to take over Harriet's chores in the house, and Grant certainly did nothing to help, so the task of making breakfast, dinner and tea each day fell to the old woman.

She was also responsible for all the washing and ironing, the cleaning, and hundreds of other chores like sewing on buttons or darning Grant's smelly socks. And she was still expected to clean up the salon each and every night as she'd always done. Rose felt like a slave and could see now why Harriet may not have protested too much at being thrown out. Maybe she'd gone willingly, and with some relief.

'Mother, is that food not ready yet?' became a constant cry.

'I've only one pair of hands,' Rose would yell right back.

'Well then put them to better purpose than writing letters for that flaming committee. I'm hungry.'

'So why don't you cook summat for yerself for a change? You've got a pair of hands too, and I'm getting on, tha knows. I can't do as much as I used to. You'll have to sweep the back yard today, my back's giving me gip. Or get that lazy article to do summat useful for a change.'

Grant would only smirk and slip quietly away, knowing he was safe from being forced to do anything by his mother.

Rose went on feeling proper poorly, though she didn't let on just how bad she was. Where was the point in expecting sympathy from Joyce when none would be forthcoming. She gave up arguing in the end and just got on with the job, and in the evenings would escape to chat with her friend Winnie Holmes in the Dog and Duck over a glass of stout.

'I don't know how you're coping,' Winnie would say. 'It might be none of my business but I'd walk out if I were you.'

'And go where, to the workhouse? They don't have them any more, do they? Thank the lord for that, or Joyce would book me a bed in one for sure. Nothing would give her greater pleasure than for me to leave too. Then her and her fancy man would have the place practically to themselves.'

Sometimes Rose would call in on Irma to see if she was yet ready to give her a second reading. Her friend was most sympathetic over her concern for Harriet, but didn't seem to think the time was yet right.

'We must see how things pan out first,' Irma explained. 'We can't rush fate along, it must progress at its own rate.'

'Them cards have been right on two counts so far,' Rose told her. 'There was a letter, just as you predicted, one which our Harriet wrote to her real mother, only the poor lass didn't know where to send it. And now a parting, with her being chucked out on to the streets. You could call it three things they got right since they predicted a great deal of sorrow and there's certainly been that. It's heartbreaking.'

'Don't take this situation too much to heart, Rose. Remember the cards also stated that there would be a successful outcome in the end; that you must trust in your own intuition and try to offer help at the appropriate time.'

'And when might that be, I wonder?'

'You won't know till it happens,' Irma consoled her. 'It's a pity your Harriet didn't come round for a reading, like I suggested, but I'm sure your instincts won't let you down when it comes to the crunch.'

'I think we've reached that already and I haven't a sensible idea in me head of what I can do to find her! I feel gutted, I do really.'

'There's still that ace of hearts, remember. I've every faith some newcomer will bring love into your life.'

Rose remained sceptical but said no more. Nor did the two women ever mention Joe, or the fact he might be moving from his wife's house into Joyce's any time soon. The subject never came up and Rose was certainly not going to be the one to raise it.

Belle Garside, the incumbent market superintendent was busy giving any number of interviews to the local press about the threatened demolition works on Champion Street, and continuing to hold an endless round of meetings.

Joe never missed a single one, though he spent most of each meeting disagreeing and arguing with her. They were like a couple of kids having a slanging match in the playground. He took great pleasure in rubbing Belle up the wrong way at the slightest opportunity, somehow managing to imply how much better he could do the job if he were still in charge.

'Yes, well you're not any longer, I am, so bite your tongue, Joe Southworth, before you open that stupid gob of yours once too often.'

'Who are you calling stupid?'

'You must be, the way you're carrying on with that hussy.'

'Oh, so you're jealous, is that it?'

'Don't be ridiculous!'

'Sounds very much like it to me. Well, I'm sorry, Belle, you and I had a good innings, but I called time, if you remember?'

'To my great and profound relief . . .'

Then Jimmy Ramsay would hold up his great big dinner-plate hands and call for silence, rather like a teacher would with a pair of errant pupils. There was an unspoken acceptance that Belle was furious Joe had dumped her in favour of Joyce Ashton, but the danger of losing the market, he tactfully reminded everybody, was far more important than personal feelings.

Every morning as Steve started work on Barry Holmes's fruit and veg stall, he kept a weather eye out in case Harriet should come strolling by, but she never did. He was beginning to feel worried in case she might be ill, or some accident had befallen her. Steve was desperate to talk to her, to explain what had gone wrong the other Friday night, and was beginning to think that she might be avoiding him. He only had one week left before he went up to college. Admittedly it was only in Lancaster and he could come home most weekends, but he wanted everything put right between them before he left. This morning, as luck would have it, he spotted Rose coming out of George's bakery.

'Mrs Ibbotson, could I have a word?'

Rose looked at the lad blankly for a moment and then, realising who he was, hurried over to him filled with hope and excitement. 'What is it, lad, have you seen our Harriet?'

Steve looked stunned. 'That's just what I was going to ask you. I haven't seen her since the Friday we fell out at the dance. She's been avoiding me, I expect, because she thinks I deliberately stood her up. I want you to know, Mrs Ibbotson . . . I want to tell Harriet . . . that I didn't mean to stand her up at all. I was only late for the dance because I was involved in a great big row with my parents. For some reason they've taken against her and—'

'I wonder why that is,' Rose interrupted, her tone ripe with sarcasm.

The boy let out a heavy sigh. 'It's true they objected to the fact that I intended to go on seeing her, despite – well, every-thing – you know, and they tried to stop me going to the dance. But unlike Sunday lunch when I failed to stand up to them, this time I did. I know they're my parents but I pointed out to them, begging your pardon, Mrs Ibbotson, that Harriet can't be blamed for the stupid or wicked things her parents did.'

'You're absolutely right, lad.'

'So will you tell her that our quarrel was just a silly misunder-standing. I hadn't stood her up at all, I was delayed because I was defending her. Unfortunately, I then got all jealous when I saw her dancing with that Vinny Turner which made things worse. Will you tell her I'm sorry, that I still love her, and I want to see her before I go away to college.'

'Aye, lad, course I will,' Rose told him, her faded old eyes warm with pity. 'There's just one small snag. I haven't the first idea where she is.'

Across at the bakery Chris George was showing his wife a letter. It had come from the developers' solicitors and said they were offering him a tidy sum of money to sell up and move out.

'Think what this could mean,' he said to Amy, as she sat feeding their small son toast soldiers dipped in egg yolk. She was also pregnant with their second child and, Chris thought, looking a little strained and tired.

'Why, what would it mean? We're fine as we are, now that your mother and father have retired and left us the bakery business, and we've moved into the flat above.'

Chris sat down next to her at the table. 'Yes, but we could do so much more with the kind of money they're offering. Dad has indicated he might accept, then give us a share of the profit so that we could buy a much better, bigger business in a busier street. It would mean more money in the long run, and a more secure future.'

'And where would we live?'

'Either over whatever shop we bought, as we do here, or we could happen take on a mortgage and buy ourselves a proper house as well.'

Amy looked at him, aghast. 'A mortgage! But that would mean more debt, wouldn't it? I don't like the sound of that at all. Anyway, I like it here, in Champion Street.'

'There are other streets, every bit as good.'

'But we don't know anyone who lives in them.'

'We could get to know them, love, and you can't deny it isn't tempting. It's more money than we've ever dreamed of. Dad could do with a bit extra cash for his retirement too. It's a generous offer.'

Amy looked at him askance. 'Those solicitors also offered Mam and Dad way over the top for Poulson's Pies, but *she* refused.'

Chris looked sceptical. 'That's not what I heard. Your mother was bragging the other night in the Dog and Duck that she'd tossed their offer back at them because it was nowhere near as much as they'd offered Sam Beckett. She admitted that she might accept if they offered more.'

'Rubbish, she never would,' Amy protested. 'Our Robert is going to take over the business, so Mam wants Poulson's to keep on going, then he can afford to pay her a pension from the profits.'

'Huh, I can't see your brother being very reliable on the pension front.'

Amy's cheeks went bright pink. 'What are you suggesting, that he's feckless, a bad manager or too selfish to care about his parents? What?'

'Nothing, I didn't mean anything by it.'

'Yes, you did.'

'Look, didn't we agree not to quarrel any more about our respective families, and here we are going down that same old road.'

'You started it,' Amy said, turning her back on him to show that she wouldn't easily forgive him.

'I'm only asking you to seriously consider this offer.'

Amy slammed down the egg spoon, making little Danny jump, and again swivelled round to face her husband, her small face all pinched and fierce. 'How can you even think of accepting? I thought you loved this market. We both do. Haven't we lived here all our lives?'

'Times change. Remember that awful house we lived in when we first got married? Doesn't that need razing to the ground? Weren't you the one who claimed half the street should be declared derelict, that Manchester should do something to improve its housing stock? That was when you were involved in all that Peace Movement stuff, or have you forgotten?'

Amy had the grace to look a bit shame faced because joining the Peace Movement had created a few problems for herself and Chris, but then so had his mother. She cast him a sheepish smile.

'All right, so I might have said something of the sort, and

maybe some of these old houses should be pulled own. But not all of them, and not *this* house, not *this* shop. And not the entire market and market hall. That would be criminal. Besides, if they pulled down the market I'd lose all my friends, so not another word, Chris George. You write back and tell them the answer's no.'

Chris sighed, tucked the letter into his pocket and went off to make the next batch of bread, privately promising himself that he'd think about it a bit longer before doing anything definite. He was quite sure he'd be able to win Amy round, in the end.

He certainly had little faith in this campaign the committee were waging. Only last week The Church of All Saints in Weaste closed its doors for the last time, The Cromwell Cinema had closed, as had the Alexandra and the Empire. The new maisonettes in Ordsall were all ready for occupation and The Hare and Hounds on Broad Street was to be demolished shortly. What hope did they have of saving Champion Street Market in the light of such determined progress?

One morning towards the end of September, Joyce staggered into the kitchen after yet another late night out with Joe in the Dog and Duck, in search of something to ease her parched throat and dry-as-dust mouth. Her head was thumping from all the rum and cokes she'd consumed the night before, and she was still inwardly seething over the fact that much of the evening had been spent in yet another argument over her proposal that they move in together. Joe still obstinately refused to make up his mind. So when she found the kitchen empty with no sign of any breakfast being made, she reacted badly, instantly awash with self-pity and rage.

Banging open the door at the bottom of the stairs Joyce shouted up to her mother who slept in one of the attic bedrooms, next to Grant's, and to Harriet's, when she'd still lived here.

Joyce was almost beginning to regret having kicked the girl out, since she'd been useful round the house. Yet in other respects she was thankful to be rid of the disapproving looks whenever she came home the worse for wear, as she'd done last night. Not to mention the constant reminder of how the girl had blighted her life, simply by her very existence.

Even so, nothing now got done on time.

'*Mother*! Do I have to do everything meself? I work all hours God sends to keep you lot in comfort, and I shouldn't be expected to put the flamin' kettle on and cook me own breakfast an' all.' She knew this for a slight exaggeration, but the old bat was growing idle in her old age. '*Mother*, are you listening to me? Grant, where the hell are you?'

Joyce marched up the stairs and along the landing, flinging open bedroom doors as she went. Grant lay flat on his stomach, snoring loud enough to wake the dead following yet another hard drinking session the night before, but Rose was still neatly tucked into her own bed, flat on her back, staring blankly up at the ceiling.

Joyce stood in the doorway, hands on hips like a sergeant-major. 'Well, are you going to get off yer fat backside and make me breakfast, or do I have to do everything meself?'

Rose didn't move.

'I'm waiting. Get up, you lazy mare.'

When still her mother made no effort to move, Joyce marched right into the room, and discovered, on closer inspection, that Rose couldn't get up, or do as she was asked because she was quite incapable of moving at all. The old woman attempted to explain this fact to her daughter but her mouth was all skewed to one side and not a sensible word came out of it. Rose had suffered a stroke.

16

Joyce

Joyce was feeling decidedly put upon. She'd already spent years caring for a sick husband, at least in her own eyes, and now, just when she was free to go her own way, her mother goes and has a stroke. She felt trapped. It was so unfair to have yet another sick person dependent upon her. Joyce most certainly had no intention of allowing her life to be ruined by one sad old woman. Didn't she have enough to do looking after her hairdressing business without waiting hand, foot and finger on her mother?

Joyce had called the ambulance the moment she'd found Rose lying in her bed quite unable to move, apparently paralysed from top to toe. She'd been taken to hospital and was making, as the doctors informed her with great tact and gentleness, steady improvement, really rather remarkable progress considering her age. But a full recovery was not anticipated. Nor could they keep her in hospital for too long as they didn't have the beds. In a few weeks, they said, Mother would feel much more comfortable at home, although someone would need to provide constant care for the old lady on a daily basis for some time.

Joyce couldn't believe her bad luck, far more concerned about the impact of the stroke upon her own life rather than Rose's. She was furious, and deeply regretted having given Harriet the order of the boot. The girl could easily have taken care of her grandmother, as she did her father, instead of which the whole caboodle was going to fall on Joyce's own fair shoulders.

Not if she had any say in the matter. Something would have to be done. There were plenty of old folk's homes, after all.

Rose could go into one of those. Or stay in the hospital for all she cared. Where was it written that you had to sacrifice your entire life to caring for flaming invalids, even if they were related?

And why was it, Joyce asked herself, that so many things over which she had no control had changed the direction of her life? In fact, if she'd ever had any say over what happened to her, the moment must have passed her by. Fate seemed to have it in for her at every turn. The moment something good happened, bad news followed almost at once. It had been exactly that way with Stan.

Joyce had fallen in love with Stan at first sight, dreamed of him being a part of her life, but the discovery that she was pregnant was a massive blow to her hopes. She was mortified. It was far too late to confess to the rape which had happened weeks before, so how could she now own up to being pregnant? It was dreadful. Appalling! There seemed to be no way out. She almost wished that Stan had been a bit more pushy in his love making, and then hated herself for such a thought.

It would surely be utterly wicked to put the blame on to Stan for this baby, when he wasn't the one responsible?

A day or two later Joyce received yet another of his regular letters, and she made up her mind to act. She couldn't do this to him, she really couldn't. Such a bare-faced lie would surely ruin both their lives.

She spent hours working out what she should say, chewing on the end of her pen, crossing out, crumpling up sheets of paper she could ill afford. She was in tears by the time she was done, devastated by what had happened, but it seemed the only way.

In the end, the letter was quite short, simply saying that she thought it best if they didn't see each other again. Joyce gave no explanation, no reason at all for her change of heart. She didn't even claim to have found a new love, so it wasn't really a Dear John letter. And it was very final.

She walked round the block twice before plucking up the courage to actually shove it into the letter-box. Then she ran home, shut herself in her room and sobbed her heart out, knowing she'd just destroyed her one chance of happiness.

All she had to do now was get rid of the baby.

Stan turned up at her house within days of receiving that letter. She'd been surprised to see him, shocked even, and how he'd got leave she never dared ask but he wanted to know what the hell it was all about.

'I thought you were keen. I thought you loved me.'

'I do love you,' Joyce told him, before stopping to think what she was saying.

'Well then, that settles it. I've been granted compassionate leave before going overseas, and if it's just that you're worried I might not be serious about you, then I have the proof right here.'

From his pocket he drew out a slip of paper which turned out to be a special licence.

'I invited my parents to attend, but my father is a strict Catholic and doesn't approve of hasty marriages, so they declined. Nevertheless, I'm up for it, if you are?'

Unable to resist, Joyce flung herself into his arms in delight. They were married the very next day, and spent two wonderful days of unrestrained passion, quite unable to keep their hands off each other for more than five minutes at a time. It seemed to signify the end of all her problems, when in reality they were only just beginning.

Now, years later, Joyce was towelling Belle Garside's hair when Grant sauntered in, pretending an interest in the hair-do before blithely enquiring if his mother intended going out with Belle this evening, perhaps taking up with some of her old friends again, now that she was fancy free and a widow. Grant thought this rather a clever ploy in his quest to discover as much infor-mation about Joyce's past as he possibly could. His mother, however, saw through it in seconds and gave him short shrift for being too inquisitive.

'What are you on about? You've got nosy all of a sudden.'

Belle chuckled. 'You don't know the half of it. He was asking me the other day if I knew any of your old flames. Not that I was able to help him, as I was at pains to explain.'

Joyce gave her customer a wavering smile through the mirror, even as she wondered what the hell was going on. She really had no wish to be reminded of her past, full as it was of uncomfortable truths she'd rather not examine too closely. Dear me no. Besides, Joyce was far more interested in the future, and nothing seemed to be going right for her at present.

Apart from the problem of needing someone to care for her mother, she was still desperately trying to urge Joe to divorce his wife and move in with her. Yet she was getting nowhere fast.

The silly man was far too cautious, still obstinately refusing to make up his mind. He gave any number of excuses for the delay from being too busy on the stall, to Joyce needing more time to adjust to Stan's recent demise, to Irma not yet being ready to cope on her own. He even cited the weather, which often created problems one way or another on a market. A right load of old bunkum, in Joyce's opinion. If he really cared for her, he'd tell Irma to her face that he was leaving and that would be that. Joyce fully intended to keep on at him, and to get her own way as she always did in the end.

Although it hadn't quite worked out that way with Stan, had it? For all his confession of undying love for her when they'd first married, and the undoubted passion they'd enjoyed in those first few nights of connubial bliss, he'd betrayed her within months of putting a ring on her finger.

Nevertheless, Joyce meant to have better luck this time.

As she wound Belle Garside's long brunette tresses on to the largest rollers she possessed, she met her customer's curious gaze with a resigned expression of motherly tolerance. 'What has it to do with my son who I went round with when I was a young lass, eh?'

Belle smiled her artificial smile while keeping a keen eye on

Joyce's expression, determined to get to the bottom of this little mystery. 'That's precisely what I told him.'

'Why would he want to know, anyroad?'

Belle glanced through the mirror and caught the panic in Grant's eyes. Had he been genuine, she wondered, with his tale of planning a party? Best not to mention that, just in case. Belle would hate to be the one to spoil a surprise. 'Nay, don't expect me to understand sons. Both of mine have been the bane of my life, a great disappointment to me for all I adored them both and gave my heart and soul to caring for them. That's kids for you. But do you think Grant's sudden interest in the past might have summat to do with your Harriet?'

Whirling about to glare at the unfortunate son in question, Joyce snapped, 'Has it? Because if so . . .'

'Naw, I never said it had owt to do with our Harriet. Why would it?' Grant demurred.

'I should hope not. She might still be family, in a way, but . . .'

'Is she? Are you sure?' There was an unmistakable bitterness in the tone of his voice.

'She is if I say she is,' Joyce bit back. 'Anyroad, she's gone, taken herself off some place, so let's forget her. She can make her own way now, as I'm sure she will.'

'You haven't heard from her then?' Belle smoothly enquired, never one to miss an opportunity for a bit of gossip. Nor had she missed that little slip which seemed to cast doubt on the relationship of the erstwhile siblings. Even Grant didn't seem convinced. What was going on? she wondered. Belle waited patiently for her old rival's response, but Joyce had paused in her labours, and was looking somewhat put out.

Joyce was wondering what line to take. Should she aim to play the concerned mother of a girl who'd run off because she was up to no good, or be honest and admit she threw her out and was glad to see the back of her? But then she'd have to give a good reason, which might be tricky as Joyce didn't rightly know herself what that was. The lass just got on her wick but she could hardly say as much, could she?

She shrugged her shoulders and continued winding the big pink sponge rollers. 'When did kids ever tell you where they were or what they are up to? Never, in my experience. No doubt she'll come home when she's good and ready, when she's tasted the big bad world, and not before.' Ignorance, she decided, was the best policy.

'Perhaps Grant knows where she is,' Belle teased, not yet prepared to accept defeat on this fascinating discussion.

Joyce turned on the hapless Grant once more, where he lounged against the door, hands in pockets. 'You don't know where she is, do you?'

Grant shook his head, honestly assuring his mother that he hadn't the first idea where she might be, although privately wishing that this was not the case. He was far from pleased that he couldn't locate Harriet as he most certainly had a score to settle. He'd even devised an interesting plan over how he meant to achieve this, feeling he deserved to take out his revenge for the way she'd so comprehensively messed up his life simply by her very existence. If it hadn't been for her sucking up to her father, Stan might have taken more of an interest in his adopted son.

And now he had an even greater reason to despise her, as a consequence of all the bruises he'd suffered when he'd followed her the night she ran away. He despised and loathed his half-sister for that attack alone. How dare she escape and leave those brutes to turn on him?

Determined to find her, the morning after she disappeared he'd explored the area around the River Irwell, and, after much persistence and several hours of searching, had found the crushed cardboard which had obviously formed a bed for someone.

Then he'd spotted two pairs of footprints in the mud by Prince's Bridge, one small, possibly Harriet's, and a larger pair of boots, clearly belonging to a bloke. She didn't even have the bottle to leave on her own, the dozy mare. Grant followed both sets of footprints, deciding in the end that they'd crossed the bridge and headed for Salford, most likely the docks.

The fact that she wasn't alone didn't trouble him in the slightest. Whoever her helper might be he couldn't keep watch over her every minute of the day. Satisfied with his morning's work, Grant had finally gone home, but that's where he'd look for her next, on Salford Docks. He'd find her sure enough, and then he'd have some real fun.

Since then he had indeed crossed Prince's Bridge, on several occasions. He'd walked as far as Salford Docks and searched every nook and cranny along the way, yet still found no sign of her. He'd been forced to give up in the end.

Grant hated the thought that he was no better than his half-sister when he'd been quite certain he was a cut above, if only because he was at least legitimate. But who was his real father and why hadn't he married his mother? That's what he wanted to know – facts which were proving incredibly difficult to root out. He needed more names and since Joyce wasn't willing to cough up, Nan had been his only chance. Now it was too late. The stupid old woman was ill in hospital, hardly able to speak a word.

Quite out of the blue, it occurred to him that this meant his grandmother's room was standing empty, and the evidence he needed may well be lying around in diaries, letters, or notebooks. It might take only a matter of moments to discover what he needed, while his mother was thus engaged doing Belle Garside's hair.

'I'll fetch you both a pot of tea, shall I?' he generously offered, making his escape.

'By heck,' Belle said. 'There must be summat up. I've never heard the lad make such an offer before.'

'Nor me neither,' Joyce agreed, watching with curiosity as her great lump of a son boiled the kettle in the little kitchenette behind the salon. He then carefully carried in a tray of tea and biscuits with some trepidation, clearly demonstrating that he'd never done such a thing in his life before.

Much as she adored him, he was a lazy article, and a constant source of worry to her. Could her past really be coming back to haunt her? she wondered. Joyce rather thought it might be.

And how much could her son uncover, if he really tried? She shuddered to think.

What his mother would think had she seen him, moments later, rummaging through Rose's things, Grant didn't trouble to consider. Sadly, he found nothing of any interest, but hadn't by any means given up hope. If there was something to find, he'd discover it sooner or later. In the meantime he helped himself to a few fivers from his nan's secret hoard. She hardly needed money when she was in hospital, did she?

Rose was brought home a couple of weeks later, and Joyce still hadn't found anyone willing to look after her. She'd tried Aunty Dot, the one all the stallholders turned to when they were in trouble. But she was fostering even more children than usual at the moment, as well as being heavily involved in making sweets and chocolates for Lizzie Pringle's shop, so couldn't help.

Molly Poulson, when asked if she could spare the odd hour in her day, said, 'You must be joking. I barely have time to wash me own face, let alone somebody else's.'

Amy George was pregnant, so pointed out she wouldn't be able to lift Rose, or turn her over. Clara Higginson, although she claimed to be semi-retired, seemed busier than ever, not only helping Patsy on the hat stall but involved in many committees at the church, and various charities. Everyone else was too busy earning their living. Joyce was in despair. But here she was, her dearly beloved mother sitting up in bed looking as spry as ever and demanding her tea.

'Look sharp. I'm . . .' the old woman paused, as if searching for the right word. 'Fair clemmed.'

'You've got your voice back then, I see,' Joyce drily remarked.

'Me tongue gets in a – knot. Not good.' She indicated her legs, which she still couldn't move, then demonstrated that she couldn't lift her right arm. 'Floppy. Doctor says – exercises. Every day. You help.'

'Me?' Joyce was horrified. She was thinking, over my dead

body. 'When will I have time to do exercises with you? I've got to get back downstairs now, for me two o'clock.'

'Cooee, can I come up?'

'Now who the hecky-thump is that?'

Seconds later Irma came sailing in, blindingly bright in her wrap-over white overall worn over a warm jumper and skirt against the chill autumn breeze that whooshed through the door with her. A great smile wreathed her round face as she looked on her old friend. 'I heard you were home. How are you, chuck? I've only got a minute but I thought I'd just pop over to welcome you home like. I've fetched you some of me best ginger snaps.'

Rose struggled to communicate but gave up and simply said, 'Ta.'

'By heck, it's a bit chilly in here. Shall I switch the electric fire on?' and she did so, without even a by-your-leave. Then Irma gathered the frail old lady into a warm hug, telling her not to fret if she couldn't get the words out. 'I just popped in to say I'll be delighted to call in regular like for a chat, or happen do a bit more, if you want me to? I could help you have a wash or summat. I don't mind, since you're a good mate.'

Tears stood proud in the old woman's eyes as she glanced up at her daughter, hating her own dependence on Joyce's charity.

'Unless you have some objection to having me here?' Irma pointedly asked.

Joyce ground her teeth together but managed, nonetheless, to see the advantage of Irma's presence, despite its obvious complications. 'It's true that I could do with a bit of help. I have me hands full already with the salon, as you know, and I'm not good on the nursing front.'

'Why does that not surprise me?' Irma drily commented, and sat herself down on the chair next to the bed without even being asked.

Rose smiled at her daughter, a crooked, twisted sort of grimace, but the nearest she could manage to a smile. 'Two cups – love.' She indicated that she and Irma wished to be alone as they had things to talk over.

Joyce too seemed lost for words.

So it was that Joyce found herself not only obliged to make tea for her lover's wife, but also accept Irma's help in caring for her mother. Fate had played its cruel trick, yet again.

17

Harriet

They slept on make-shift cardboard beds for several more nights, although not in the same dank little tunnel. She moved on with Vinny from place to place, sometimes sleeping under the railway arches, sometimes down by the canal, once in a bus shelter. But apart from the first night they were never alone. They were always part of a crowd of other waifs and strays who were likewise sleeping rough amongst the detritus of rubbish, the smell of rotting leaves and sewage, with beetles crawling over them and a litter of used cigarette packets and French johnnies scattered all around.

Harriet learned where to find the best cardboard and discovered the surprising benefits of newspaper. It could double as a bed, form a blanket, and even line the soles of your worn-out shoes. She hadn't quite reached such a sorry state as some of her fellow homeless, her shoes still being in one piece, but she made a mental note of how they coped. Cigarettes were their main luxury, and they could make one last for half a day by continually docking it out and relighting it. In fact, searching for fag ends was a favourite pastime of many of the old lags.

She saw how they always wore mittens, usually gloves with the tips of the fingers removed, how they kept careful watch when people were eating their lunches or picnics in the park or at the bus station, and were ready to swiftly dip in the litter bin should they spot a half-eaten sandwich or pork pie being thrown away. Harriet shuddered at the thought of being driven to such lengths, yet could sympathise totally with their plight.

Many had stories to tell very much like her own. They too had been thrown out on to the street and abandoned, or worse, abused, by a parent. Or they'd suffered some sort of breakdown, perhaps losing a wife, a child, or even a job. They weren't all alcoholics and deadbeats, not by any means.

The nights were drawing in as autumn approached, and the days were growing cooler and Harriet worried about how they would manage when winter really set in. Looking at these unfortunates made her feel uncomfortable, as if she were seeing herself five years from now.

But then Vinny would crack a joke, or find a sixpence someone had dropped and Harriet would shake these fears away. She was young, after all, still with money in her pocket.

The band which Terry Hall had set up for him hadn't materialised, but Vinny had got together a group of optimistic, like-minded musicians and they were working hard rehearsing. Vinny and Bruno played the guitar. Duffy was on double bass, which was nothing more than a tea-chest and broom handle with a single string attached, and Al played the drums. In fact he was the most talented of the four, which sometimes created a few tensions when he was doing a drum solo.

But Vinny meant to go places with his new band. Hadn't he promised her as much?

They found an old deserted warehouse down by the docks where they could sleep out of the wind and rain, which was a relief. It was still cold and dirty, but far better than being out on the streets. The lads were also able to practise in there, pounding out music without fear of disturbing anyone. The trouble was they still weren't earning any money, but nursed high hopes of being spotted by a talent scout one day. Right now, were it not for Harriet's twenty-five pounds, they'd all be starving.

Amazingly, they did have one or two gigs lined up in late October which Vinny had secured by trailing around all the dance halls of Manchester and Salford asking to be given a chance, but these were still a few weeks off. If those went well, then the boys were quite convinced that other bookings, and fame, would surely follow. They'd put out the word that they were still in need of a singer, and were even now in the process of holding auditions to choose one.

Harriet sat on an old upturned orange box watching a stream of hopefuls stand up to sing, then dribble away again one by one. Vinny, she'd discovered, was most particular about what sort of singer he wanted, and very rude to anyone who didn't come up to his standard.

'You sound like a cat on heat,' he told one girl.

'Have you got a hernia or something?' he asked another.

Or, 'Stick to the bath, love, nobody would pay good money to hear you strangle a song.'

Harriet sighed. She rather thought that by October they might all have perished for lack of nourishment, judging by the speed at which her small nest egg was disappearing. She hadn't reckoned on being obliged to feed four big lads as well as herself, although Vinny insisted it would be unfriendly not to. They too had put their own money into the pot, after all, little though it might be, so it was only fair that she did the same.

'All for one and one for all,' he informed her, not giving her any choice in the matter. And she'd be ready enough to enjoy a share in their success when it came, wouldn't she?

'The lads might have to find themselves a job in the end, if we run out of cash,' she warned Vinny when he strolled over to again ask her to rustle up some food for them all.

He blinked at her. 'You are joking! A job? They've got a job, working in this band. How can they make their way in the music world if they don't have time to practise?'

She felt a spurt of resentment, wondering how they would ever have managed if she hadn't been there with Joyce's twenty-five quid, but all she said was, 'So, aren't you going to get a job either?' and laughing, Vinny handed her a cigarette.

'Have a puff of this, love, it'll make you relax and feel much better.' The slight lilt of his Irish accent always sounded much more pronounced when he was laughing at her.

The cigarette had the weirdest smell imaginable and an even stranger taste which Harriet didn't much care for. But, surprisingly, it did make her feel much, much better, really quite light headed. And then so drowsy that she had to lie down and close her eyes for a little rest. Two hours later she woke to find that the band had at last found the girl singer they needed.

She was called Shelley and was a skinny-looking waif with short dark hair and great big blue eyes. Watching the way Vinny hovered over her, Harriet thought it fortunate that she wasn't in the least bit in love with him, or she'd be jealous.

Once the auditions were over, Harriet went to buy them all fish and chips, and a bottle of beer each. Naturally they complained about the puny ration so far as the alcohol was concerned, but on this point she was adamant. No money, no more beer. After they'd eaten, they passed round the funny-smelling cigarettes again, which she accepted. Harriet had no idea what they were but the one she'd tried earlier had left her feeling a bit muzzy but oddly happy.

'Who needs all that nine-to-five shit, anyway?' Vinny was saying with a vacant smile on his face. He had one arm hung round the shoulders of the new girl singer who likewise seemed to be having trouble staying awake after smoking half of one of these funny cigarettes.

They all became rather silly and giddy, telling stupid jokes and having a riotous time. Harriet revelled in the silly banter, and, now that she'd grown used to sleeping rough, had discovered life could be fun. She enjoyed humming along to the band's music while they practised, and could quite see Vinny's point of view.

She'd fully intended to get a job herself, of course, but now it occurred to Harriet that really there was no rush. A spark of rebellion had been lit in her as a result of the rejection she'd suffered. Where did duty and love ever get you, anyway? Nowhere. Her dad was dead, her mother wasn't her mother after all, and had thrown her out. Her boyfriend, who had once claimed to adore her, refused to defend her against his snobbish parents, and had stood her up at the first opportunity and gone off with another girl. So what did it matter where she went or what she did? No one cared a jot about her.

Harriet was filled with a wash of guilt as she remembered this wasn't strictly true. Nan cared for her, deeply. She'd meant to buy a pad of paper and envelopes and write to her grandmother but there'd been too much to think about, too much worry involved in finding somewhere to sleep.

Even when they'd found the deserted warehouse, there'd been the auditions and bookings to arrange. Now, to her shame, Harriet realised that she'd been having such a good time that she'd forgotten all about her poor nan, save for the postcard which she'd sent soon after she'd left home. She made a private promise to buy some paper and write her a long letter first thing in the morning; a loving, apologetic note.

In the meantime she slipped out to find a phone box. Harriet intended to explain that she was fine and that Nan mustn't worry, that she would make her own way in the world with Vinny and his group. Who cared about love anyway? She dialled the number for the salon but it was Joyce who answered.

'Hello, it's me. Can I speak to Nan?'

'She isn't in,' Joyce snapped, and without giving any further explanation, she put down the phone.

Harriet felt bitterly disappointed, let down yet again. She didn't believe for a minute that her grandmother wasn't at home, this was Joyce being difficult. She'd write to Nan tomorrow. She hurried straight back to the warehouse and sucked on the cigarette some more, not quite getting it right, her head spinning giddily. This was great, much better than being bossed and bullied by Joyce, or harassed and stalked by Grant.

She was free, at last.

Harriet found Vinny to be a conflicting mixture of opposites. Tough, almost brutal when it came to defending himself, as demonstrated by the way he'd tackled his old gang single handed when they'd attacked her. Yet he could be as soft as butter if the mood took him, warm and gentle and caring. He was ruthlessly ambitious and yet careless of any sort of commitment when it came to making plans for the future. He would quite happily work for a twelve- or eighteen-hour stretch without complaint, but then stay in bed for the next several days, showing no interest whatsoever in rehearsing.

He could be lively and funny one day, and barely speak to her the next.

Despite these contradictions in his character, and regardless of all common sense, Harriet really rather liked him. She was utterly in his thrall. Maybe this was because he was the only person to have shown her any kindness since her dad died.

One night as they sat on the canal bank beneath a canopy of stars in a velvet-blue sky, alone for once as the others were fast asleep, he began to talk about his childhood. This surprised her because he didn't take kindly to being questioned. It came about quite naturally, with very little prompting. Harriet simply asked him if he remembered his mother, and out it all poured.

She was Irish, he told her, probably with some Romany blood in her. She was unmarried when Vinny's older brother Dermot, and then himself, a couple of years later, had been born in Dublin before the war. 'She was called Maggie, what else? Suited her perfectly. She had red-gold hair, typically Irish, not like mine all brown and mousy.'

'Yours isn't in the least mousy. I'm sure I can see red lights in it, a sort of auburn.'

Vinny grimaced.

'What do you remember most about her as a child?'

'That hair, and her red lips. Her soft smile and skin as pale as silk. And I remember her screams when me da beat the living daylights out of her.' He gave a cynical laugh. 'I bet you never thought you'd be getting involved with the scum of the Irish?'

'You aren't scum. It wasn't your fault. So what happened to your father? Did they get married in the end?'

'When the next little accident came along, or maybe it was the one after that. Anyway, didn't she persuade him to do the deed eventually, more's the pity? I've two younger brothers as well as

Dermot, and me little sister, Sally. Da went in the navy and we never saw him again.'

'You mean he got killed in the war?'

'I mean – we never saw him again. God knows where he is, and I care even less. I hope he rots in hell, so I do.'

Harriet fell silent. It was beginning to dawn on her that she wasn't the only one with family problems.

'We came over to England, to Manchester, some time during the war. Ma got a job in a munitions factory and turned yellow as a result. They called them canaries. It was the gunpowder, I expect. She had to change into special clothing: white coat and brown leather shoes with WD – that's War Department – written on it. No glass buttons or metal as they could create friction with gunpowder. Everything had to be tied with ribbons and she'd be frisked before she went in, for cigarettes or matches. She loved to smoke did my mam. Her job was putting washers on detonators, and any that didn't work she put in a can and a man would come round and squirt oil on the rejects and take them away. She once told me that her friend had worked on filling bombs and shells, using a sort of hopper, and one day did something wrong and got blown up right next to Ma standing at the bench.'

'Oh, my God, how dreadful!'

Vinny offered her a packet of Black Cat cigarettes, but Harriet shook her head. He offered to share with her one of the funny smelly ones instead, which she laughingly agreed to do. She guessed they were even worse for her but really didn't care. They made her feel so much better about herself even if they did leave her feeling muzzy headed and sleepy. And she craved oblivion in order not to think too much about Steve. Vinny lit it for her and they shared the cigarette, drag for drag. It seemed such an intimate thing to do.

'I remember we were constantly packing up and moving on to the next place. It certainly wasn't all treacle toffee and Noddy stories. She never had much time for us, or the energy, always working on two jobs at least, one during the day, and one at night, which we won't go into too closely. Me and my brothers spent our time throwing stones at dogs, pissing up walls, or starting fires. Anything for a laugh, something to do, you know.'

Harriet didn't know, not entirely, but she remained silent, riveted by his tale.

'We were constantly hungry because she'd forget to feed us, daft cow, and then . . .'

Harriet leaned her chin against his shoulder, sensing his pain. 'And then?'

'Then after coming unscathed out of that blasted factory, she fell off the bleeding ferry boat that goes up the Manchester Canal to Liverpool, didn't she, the silly cow? And we were sent to the orphanage.'

'Fell off . . . Oh, my God . . .' Harriet was shocked. 'But I thought you still lived with your mother, behind the fish market.'

Vinny glowered and shook his head. 'Dermot and his girl-friend Jo are supposedly responsible for us now, at least that's what they claim. He's another such as me da, a real bully. The only thing you can say in his favour is that he provides a roof over the kids' heads by paying the rent, and Jo is good with our Sally. But he's not easy to live with, a real chip off the old block. An Irish rogue of the worst kind, through and through. I couldn't take any more. I tell you I was glad to get away.'

Which somehow explained everything. Harriet had tears in her eyes by the time he was done. 'You know what I think?'

He scowled at her. 'What?'

'I think you were right when you said it was fate that brought us together. We have so much in common, you and me, with our messy family lives.'

His expression softened, the way it often did when he relaxed enough to set aside the bitterness and reveal his true nature. 'That means we can help each other, right?'

'Right.'

He began to kiss her, gently pushing Harriet down in the grass beside the canal.

Her head was spinning from the cigarette, but it felt so good to have someone hold and love her like this, to stroke her face and softly kiss her mouth, and then with increasing passion, exploring it with his tongue, stirring a need in her. She rather liked it when he slipped his hand beneath her blouse and fondled her breast, kissed her throat and told her how lovely she was. Harriet made no protest as he unhooked her bra and caressed her naked breasts while he kissed her. She felt so daring, so marvellously free. He unzipped her jeans, and she helped him to tug them down, groaning with delighted shock as he slid his fingers inside her.

She knew it was wrong but a part of her wanted to be bad, to prove she had some control over her own life.

Harriet welcomed him with eagerness and passion when he entered her, not even bothering to remember what Nan had told her about how to make a boy stop, as she'd related the facts of life to her all those years ago, looking all pink cheeked and embarrassed. Harriet didn't care what she *should* be doing, how she *should* be behaving. Who was to tell her now what was right and wrong? What sort of an example had Joyce set her, anyway, or even her own father who'd kept a mistress and a dark secret about her birth for years?

She liked Vinny, even if she had absolutely no intention of falling in love with him, or with anyone in fact. Harriet felt she'd lost everything in the world that mattered to her, so what more did she have to lose?

18

Irma

Gossip was the life blood of Champion Street Market, and the topic on everybody's lips today, as it had been for many mornings in the last few weeks, was the uncertain future of the stallholders. Their livelihoods were under serious threat.

'I really don't know what we'll do,' Amy was saying to Irma, as she chose a selection of biscuits from her stall. 'I think I'd like some of those coconut crunch, please. Chris has a fancy to accept the developers' offer, I'm ashamed to admit, and nothing I say seems to change his mind.'

Irma slipped two or three extra Shrewsbury biscuits into the bag she was weighing to give it good measure before skilfully spinning it between her fingers to secure it.

'It'll be a fair sum of money I reckon?'

'Suspiciously generous,' Amy agreed. 'And of course his dad owns the property so Chris doesn't have total say.'

'You have to look after number one in this world,' Irma said. She was about to hand over the bag of biscuits when a young boy dashed by, knocking a tin of biscuits to the ground.

'Sorry, missus,' he said as he put it back in place, then cheekily added, 'I'll buy them off you, if you like. Me brother and me likes a few broken biscuits.'

'Gerroff, you little monkey. Go and break somebody else's biscuits and leave mine alone. You're getting nowt cheap off me.'

For a moment it looked as if the lad might argue the toss but then he saw how Irma pushed up her overall sleeves to reveal sizeable forearms, and did a runner instead.

'I need eyes in the back of my head to watch them little tykes,' Irma grumbled.

Amy was deeply sympathetic. 'They're just as bad with us over at the bakery. They hang around every morning waiting for Chris to throw away the stale bread so they can pinch it. Anyone would think they were starving.'

Irma frowned. 'I reckon some of 'em are, even though that Harold Macmillan keeps telling us we've never had it so good. People assume it's badness or lack of morals which drives a kid to steal, but it could be out of love for his family, because they're hungry. Why would he care about stupid laws made by folk better off than himself? It's been going on for years. Nabbing, skimming, nicking, whatever you like to call it.'

'Yer right there, Irma,' Winnie Holmes put in, as she sidled up to join in the gossip. 'You have to watch them little blighters. I see 'em run in the market hall for a bottle of Vimto or a tin of condensed milk, then slip summat in their pocket when the stallholder's back is turned. I reckon their parents put 'em up to it.'

'That's just it, this lot don't have no parents,' Irma said. 'I know them Turner kids, and that little tyke was one of them. They've had a bad time of it with no mam and a bully for a big brother. Young Vinny used to stand up for them, not that he's any knight in shining armour, but he made sure they were at least fed. Yet even he's vanished now.'

'And we know who he's vanished with, don't we?' Amy added. 'I can't believe Harriet would do such a stupid thing. What can she see in him?'

'It's none of my business but I put it all down to trouble at home. I can say no more,' Winnie darkly commented, tapping the side of her nose.

The school bell rang somewhere in the distance, and while one group of kids ran hell for leather, scared of being late and made to stand in the school yard until the headmaster saw them, others didn't move a muscle, but just went on messing about in the dirt, playing marbles and swapping cigarette cards.

'Get off to school, you lazy hounds,' Winnie shouted at them.

'Go on, or you'll get a clip round the ear.' As the old woman moved towards them they didn't need telling twice but ran, though whether in the direction of their school classroom was another matter. 'That truant chap isn't doing his job proper, that's what I say,' Winnie said in disgust. 'The world is going to the dogs.'

'Aye it is, when perfectly good houses and more and more markets like this one are being closed down to make way for yet more barracks of high-rise flats,' Irma agreed. 'What will them kids do when Champion Street has been flattened? If their families are in difficulties now, how much worse will their lives get? Their parents barely manage to pay their way here, often doing a moonlight flit when the rent arrears pile up. And they won't all be given posh new council flats in Ordsall.'

Amy was looking thoughtful at her words. 'Maybe they do need something better though than the damp-riddled houses on this street. I've had personal experience of how bad those can be. Happen we do need a clean sweep and a fresh start somewhere decent for our kids to grow up.'

Steve was beginning to see that not only had he been unfortunate in getting embroiled in a quarrel with his parents when he should have been meeting Harriet at the dance, but he'd badly over-reacted when finding her dancing in the arms of another bloke. He'd been stupidly jealous and rather pompous and arrogant, instead of being instantly apologetic for letting her down by being late. No wonder she'd gone off in a huff. She was clearly angry with him.

Everyone was saying that she'd run away with Vinny Turner, but why would she do that? Why would she choose Vinny Turner over him?

But then why had he deliberately asked that blonde for a dance when he'd spotted Harriet walking over to him? Had he just wanted to be perverse, trying to show he didn't care? Well, he'd proved that all right, hadn't he? What a mess he'd made of everything. He missed her so much. He could hardly concentrate on his studies for thinking about how stupid he'd been.

At the first opportunity, once he'd settled in to the college routine, he came home on a weekend visit and went straight to the hair salon to see her. He was horrified to learn that the rumours were true. Harriet had indeed left home. He demanded to know why, and where she'd gone.

'How would I know?' Joyce airily remarked. 'She's a grown woman and pleases herself what she does. Nothing to do with me. Not my responsibility any more. If she wants to hang around with no-good layabouts, that's her decision. You should thank your lucky stars, lad, that you've had such a lucky escape. She's not the girl for you.'

Steve was appalled by the woman's callousness, and yet wondered if perhaps Joyce was in fact riddled with guilt, trying to convince herself she didn't care when deep down she was as concerned as he was. Though if that was the case he had to admit she was disguising her feelings well.

He understood perfectly what had happened. Whatever mischief Rose had caused by revealing those unpalatable facts about Harriet's birth, Joyce had obviously wasted no time in taking advantage of them by showing her the door. But why? Because she disapproved of Vinny Turner, and who could blame her for that, or out of some twisted desire for revenge on the dead father?

Whatever the reason, he felt desperately sorry for Harriet. But where the hell was she? And was she safe?

'Can I speak to Rose?' he asked, thinking he might get more sense out of the grandmother, but Joyce shrugged her shoulders.

'Sure, if you like. She's upstairs in bed, but you'll get no sense out of her. My mother has had a stroke and can barely string two words together.'

'Oh, Christ, I'm so sorry.' Steve was appalled. Everywhere he turned doors seemed to be slammed in his face. His own parents, predictably enough, had offered no support either when Steve turned to them for help.

'What has the fate of one foolish girl got to do with us?' his mother had asked.

'Maybe because I love her? I thought that might count for

something?' Steve told them, anger over their complete indifference making it hard for him to control himself. He had a sudden image of Harriet's face when he'd stupidly retaliated by asking that blonde to dance. She'd looked utterly stricken. If only he could turn back the clock and do it all differently. 'What's more, I believe she still loves me.'

'I don't think so. She's run off with that Vinny Turner,' his mother sharply reminded him. 'That doesn't sound like the action of a girl in love with you, dear boy. Stop behaving like a sentimental fool. What could you do in any case?'

'I have to find her. Couldn't we report her missing to the police or something?'

'Don't be foolish. She left of her own free will, so far as I'm aware. Girls leave home every day. The police aren't going to send out a search party to look for a silly runaway. She's made her choice, leave her to it. You have more important things to think about now. You've a new life to lead, a career to build.'

But as Steve sat through endless hours of lectures, churned out half-hearted attempts at essays, he couldn't get Harriet out of his mind. She was his girl, lost somewhere, and he should be doing much more to find her and bring her home. If only he knew where to look.

It was a cold, wet day in October, the kind where washing hung damply on the lines strung about the back streets, without any hope of drying. Irma made her way along the street to see Rose, Joe having obligingly agreed to keep an eye on the stall for the last hour of the day. Yet she heaved a great sigh, filled with sadness.

She'd lived and worked on Champion Street Market for the last twenty years, and she'd be sorry to leave it, she would really. Irma could remember when they'd all feared for their lives as bombs were dropped all over Manchester. She recalled a time when there was bunting strung everywhere and hopes were high as peace was declared. Mothers had kicked up their skirts to dance on VE Day. But what progress had they made since that glorious day?

A group of kids were crawling all over an abandoned car, some playing hopscotch on the paving stones while their mothers searched for a bargain on the open stalls, or bought a bit of bacon for their husband's tea. Nothing had changed. People were still hard pressed to make ends meet, as were the stallholders themselves. They all depended upon this market, which would soon be history.

As Irma walked into Joyce's hair salon, she felt as if she'd entered another world. A world where the chief topic of conversation was whether to go for a June Allison pageboy bob, or the Lucille Ball bubble cut, apparently all the rage.

She stood in the doorway listening, acutely aware that Joyce had seen her enter but was choosing to ignore her.

'I had a girl in here the other day who'd tried to bleach her own hair,' Joyce was telling her customer as she folded the woman's rich dark locks into a clever French pleat at the back of her head. 'She'd mixed peroxide with washing-up detergent, and I have to say it was a disaster. Young girls, or teenagers as they like to call themselves these days, where are their brains? All they think about is fashion. Crinoline-hooped petticoats that bounce and show their knickers as they walk. Tight pencil skirts under which they can barely wear any underwear at all. Then there's popper beads, baby pink lipstick and ponytails, poodle skirts and plastic hoop bracelets all up their arms. I suppose they are at least trying to look smart for their boyfriends, which is more than some women do for their own husbands. That dowdy, some of them, they're invisible. Oh, I didn't notice you standing there, Irma, were you wanting to go up?'

'If you don't mind.'

'Why would I mind? It's me mother you're attending to, not me.' And turning back to her customer Joyce went on with her conversation as if Irma were nothing more than the washer woman come to collect the dirty laundry.

Irma made no comment but quietly squeezed past two women seated under hair dryers, and others studying the latest fashion magazines as they waited their turn. Joyce seemed to be busy, not coping quite so well without Harriet to assist, and young

Grant had evidently been coerced into making coffee. Yet it was all very calm, quietly civilised and professional, so long as no one was in too much of a hurry.

'Thinking of taking up hairdressing then?' Irma joked as she reached the foot of the stairs and saw Grant heading back towards the kitchen.

'No chance. That dozy mare Harriet should be doing this, not me.'

Upstairs was a different story. Rose was in great distress. The old woman had clearly been left unattended for some hours and she was in floods of tears over having wet her bed.

'I'm worse than a babby,' she cried, wretched in her shame and despair. Irma put her arms round her old friend and gathered her close against her plump warm bosom.

'Nay, don't take on. It's not your fault. When's the last time your Joyce came up to see how you were, or if you wanted anything?'

'Dinner time.'

Irma looked shocked. 'But that's more than five hours ago. Six, if she came up around twelve.'

Rose nodded. 'She left – water.' Then shook her head as she indicated the still full glass, showing how she'd been too afraid to drink it in case she needed to relieve herself.

Irma helped the old lady out of bed and to the bathroom where she cleaned her up then sat her in a chair while she stripped and remade the bed. She could feel fury boiling up inside her. How could a woman treat her own mother in such a fashion? It was dreadful.

'I blame meself,' Irma said. 'I should have popped in for a few minutes in the middle of the afternoon. I will in future. I'll make sure our Joe is available to take over for half an hour or so every now and then, while I see to you.'

'I – I d-don't want to be no . . .' Rose struggled over the next word.

'Eeh, you're no bother, chuck, so you can put that idea right out of yer head.'

'Harriet. Want – Harriet. She'd help.' And then summoning all her failing energy Rose asked, 'Where is she, Irma? Where's my lass gone?'

'I don't know,' Irma grimly replied. 'But I mean to find out. In the meantime, I'll move into her room so's I can look after you properly till we get you on your feet again. Though mebbe I'd best ask your Joyce if it's all right, since it's her house.'

'Nay – it's not. Mine,' Rose told her, surprising her friend.

'Really? It's your house, is it? Well, strike me down with a wet feather, and there's me thinking Madam Joyce was the one with the brass. In that case, I'll go and fetch me box right now, shall I?'

Rose beamed her pleasure.

Which was how it came about that it was Irma who moved in with Joyce, and not Joe after all.

19

Harriet

Harriet wasn't coping terribly well. There were times when she cried with quiet despair into the musty old cushion that she'd found in a rubbish skip and used as a pillow; times when she ached to run back home to Nan, to a hot bath and a warm bed.

Then the sun would come up, lighting the Ship Canal, glinting on the metal struts of giant cranes, polishing the railway sleepers to a glowing silver, and she'd sneak out to buy breakfast for the lads and think: 'Where would I rather be? Here, with Vinny, having fun, or back home being harangued by Joyce, stood up by Steve, and with nothing more to look forward to than another day of constant criticism?

She missed her nan, of course. Harriet had tried ringing home a couple more times but had received the same abrupt response, so gave up. Instead, she wrote a long letter to her grandmother every week. Not that she could ever give any address for a reply, but at least it would put the old woman's mind at rest.

She still felt angry over what had happened to her, over the way Joyce had treated her since Nan had announced the truth about her mother. It was absolutely unforgivable. Harriet felt she had only one real friend, and that was Shelley, the girl who sang in the band. They would sneak off together for a frothy coffee and a giggle and gossip whenever they got the chance, swap clothes and advise each other on the right shade of lipstick. It felt good to have a friend. But Shelley kept urging Harriet to go home, to get out while she still could.

Harriet laughed at the very idea. 'Joyce would never have me back. She chucked me out, remember?'

'You're lucky you have a home to go to. I don't. My parents are both dead. Vinny's in the same boat. You could at least ask. What have you got to lose?'

'Everything. My freedom. My pride, I suppose. Vinny?'

Shelley looked at her askance. 'You aren't in love with him, are you?'

'Of course not.'

'Good, keep it that way. He'll bring you nothing but unhappiness.'

'I think you're being a bit hard on him, actually. He's had an unhappy life too. He needs friends just as much as we do.'

Shelley raised her brow and said no more.

Harriet was suffering so badly from homesickness that she decided to pay a visit to her nan. Letters were all very well but Rose was the only one who had ever cared for her, and the old lady would probably still be worrying over how her favourite grandchild was coping. Besides, Harriet missed her, and felt in desperate need of a warm hug.

She chose a Saturday evening when Harriet knew Joyce would be out at the Dog and Duck with Joe. The market too would be closed, so there'd be less danger of her running into someone she knew who would ask awkward questions. Much as she ached to see her friends she had no wish to own up to them what a mess her life was in right now.

She rang the doorbell, a slight sense of nervous excitement making her anxious even as she was eager to see her grandmother. She could hear the bell echoing through the shop, could imagine the sound of it in the flat above, but no one came, no one answered. Harriet was deeply disappointed.

Finally, she was forced to admit defeat and walked disconsolately away, tears rolling down her cheeks. Harriet told herself off for being so foolish as not to warn Nan that she was coming. Why hadn't she at least sent a postcard? Perhaps because she'd been afraid of Joyce finding out and attempting to block her, or creating some sort of scene. Harriet had been so obsessed with avoiding her stepmother that she'd messed up an opportunity to see her lovely grandmother.

A little sob caught in her throat and she briskly rubbed her tears away with the flat of her hands. Next time she'd do it properly.

Upstairs, stuck in her bed unable to move, Rose had heard the doorbell ring and wondered who could be calling. Everyone knew the market would be closed by now so it couldn't be a customer, or a commercial traveller trying to sell them shampoo. Oh, well, if it was important they'd call again, she thought.

Harriet strolled along the empty street, imagining the stacked stalls as they usually were, all decked out in their pink and white striped awnings and open for business, packed with produce, the entire market humming with people as they haggled over the price of a hand-knitted sweater or length of curtaining, bought their Fisherman's Friend or coltsfoot rock, a meat pie or chunk of cheese from Poulson's, mint chocs from Pringle's Chocolate Cabin. She thought of the times she used to sit in Bertalones' ice cream parlour enjoying a peach gelato, or chatted over a hot Vimto with her friends in Belle's café. How she missed it, all the fun and laughter, and most of all, the people.

She felt a warm acknowledgement that this was the place she belonged, almost as if she were an exile being granted a glimpse of her homeland.

Finding the big doors unlocked, Harriet couldn't resist walking through the market hall. One or two of the traders were still in the process of closing for the day, cashing up or perhaps taking the opportunity to carry out a few maintenance jobs now all the customers had gone home.

To her great relief, Winnie Holmes was not among them. The nosy old woman would only need to catch a glimpse of her for Harriet's presence to be broadcast to one and all. Joyce would be sure to hear then that she'd been back on a visit. Harriet tiptoed past Winnie's stall, almost as if she half expected the old woman to leap out from behind the locked-down grille that protected the goods on display.

Even as she laughed at her own fears, she heard her name being called and almost jumped out of her skin. Turning, she saw with relief that it wasn't Winnie, and the next instant found herself caught up in a warm hug from her friend Patsy.

'Harriet, it's so good to see you! I was just reorganising the display on the hat stall. Best chance I get to have a good clean and tidy up when we're closed, and I couldn't quite believe my eyes. How are you doing? Where are you living now?'

All the questions Harriet had dreaded. She put on a brave face. 'I'm fine, thanks. I'm with Vinny's band, as I expect you've heard.'

'Yes, I did hear something of the sort,' Patsy admitted. 'And you're happy?'

'Oh, yes,' Harriet fibbed. 'It's great fun. And they're doing really well with lots of bookings lined up.' There were only three so far, but she didn't tell Patsy that.

'We must get up a group together from Champion Street, and come and listen to it some time.'

Harriet felt the smile freeze on her face. 'That would be good.'

'What do they call themselves?'

'The Scrapyard Kids.'

'And where will they be playing next? At the Ritz or Mecca? I'd love to hear them. What sort of stuff do they play?' The conversation turned to music which was far easier than discussing possible venues. Harriet had no wish to admit that the band would be more likely to be found playing in some back-street pub rather than a high profile spot like the Ritz or Mecca ballroom. But then some instinct made her turn round and she found herself face to face with Steve.

'Harriet!

He was staring at her in shock and delight, as if he couldn't quite believe his eyes, his face wreathed in a grin as wide as that of the proverbial Cheshire cat.

'I thought I heard your voice. You're home, that's wonderful!'

'Not really, just on a visit.'

An awkward silence fell between them, in which Patsy crept away and left them to it.

Steve said, 'Fancy a coffee?'

'Er . . .' Harriet half glanced about her, as if seeking rescue. The last thing she wanted was to be interrogated by Steve over where she was living or what she was doing. Why would he care anyway? He hadn't been interested in her the last time she saw him, so why now?

When she didn't immediately answer, he hurried on, 'Come to think of it, I'm not sure Belle's café is still open.'

'It doesn't matter, it's just a flying visit . . . I have to get back. I really don't have time . . .'

'There's a new hamburger joint opened on Bridge Street, we could go there for a bite, if you like.' Steve smiled hopefully, knowing he'd give his right arm for her to say yes.

'I'm sorry, but . . .'

'There's something I need to say to you, a sort of apology.'

She looked at him more closely then and almost burst out laughing at the sheepish expression on his boyish face. At one time she would have done exactly that, and they would have hugged and both had a good laugh over their foolish quarrel and the attempt each made to make the other jealous. There wouldn't have been any need for apologies, they would both have instinctively understood and forgiven each other.

But then she thought of Vinny and of what had happened between them the other night, and knew it was too late for apologies now.

Even so she couldn't drag her gaze from his. Harriet looked into a pair of dark brown eyes which seemed to be pleading with her to agree, and felt that familiar weakness deep inside, that softening and melting which always came over her when she was close to Steve. She could sense his eagerness, smell the familiar tang of his skin, knew if she reached out her hand he would grasp her fingers and kiss them as he had used to do.

In that moment Harriet realised she still adored the way his heavy straight brows almost met when he was puzzling over something, as he was now. She loved the way his nostrils flared as his breathing grew more rapid, and how his wide mouth set above a firm square chin was always smiling. His dark hair had grown, reaching almost to his collar instead of being cut to less than half an inch all over his head. And he'd started wearing glasses, black and rather square. He looked very much the student in his corduroy jacket and slacks, and he still carried about him that air of reliability and strength.

And she still loved him. In that moment her heart ached with longing for things to be as they once were between them. Why couldn't it have worked out better for them? Why hadn't he stuck up for her against his snobby mother?

But the damage was done. It was too late now. Harriet was no longer the innocent young girl Steve had fallen in love with. She was no longer a virgin, nor the same person in any way. She rather thought that she'd fulfilled his mother's doom-laden prediction for her, and justified her fears for her son.

Harriet's stock was surely about as low as it could get. Dossing down on cardboard, smoking pot, hanging out with a bunch of losers who lived on dreams and other people's leftovers. Mrs Blackstock would indeed have fifty fits if she knew where Harriet was living now. And what Steve would think of her, she didn't bear to think.

'I have to go,' she said, spinning on her heel as if about to break into a run.

Steve grabbed her hand. 'Just five minutes, please. It wasn't how you think. I didn't really stand you up.'

The feel of his fingers curling around her arm was having a strange effect upon her, making her go all light headed. If she didn't make her escape soon, then she'd be falling into his arms and begging him to kiss her. 'Look, I really do have to go. Some other time, right?'

Harriet fled, breaking into a sweat as she pushed her way through the big doors, took to her heels and ran, not pausing even for a second as she heard his footsteps clattering behind her, nor did she respond as Steve called after her, 'Where's the band playing? I'll come over some time and we can talk properly.'

She didn't bother to reply and he stood forlorn in the empty street and watched her race away from him, her strawberry-blonde curls bobbing all about her head.

'Damn! You rushed her, you damn fool. You scared her,' he berated himself.

Patsy was at his side in a second, a comforting hand on his arm. 'It wasn't anything you did. The problem lies with Harriet, I think. Something isn't quite right. I sensed it too.'

'I didn't even tell her how sorry I was about Rose being ill.'

'Me neither. I didn't get the chance, but I assume she knows.'

Steve's gaze remained fixed on the spot where he'd last had sight of her. What a clod he was! 'Why didn't I just ask her how *she* was, if she was enjoying life? Why did I have to go charging in like a bull in a bloody china shop with a bungling attempt at an apology?'

Patsy gave his arm a little squeeze. 'It wouldn't be difficult to find out where the band is playing. Scour the local papers, read the boards outside pubs and clubs, they'll be bound to turn up sooner or later.'

He looked at her, a pained bleakness in his expressive face. 'I didn't ask their name. I've no idea what they're even called.'

'Oh, she did tell me that much at least. What was it? Yes, The Scrapyard Kids, that's it. You'll just have to keep a look-out and not give up.'

'Oh, I won't give up, Patsy. I may be fooling myself, but there was something in her expression just now which tells me it might not be such a lost cause between us after all.'

Grant came across the band quite by chance. Bored with having no success in searching for Harriet he'd hooked up with a girl he quite fancied and it was she who suggested they go to a jazz club one night. It was a bit seedy, short on electricity and smelling of drains, tucked down in a basement near Cross Lane in Salford.

Several jazz bands were playing that night, both modern and trad, and then for a change they introduced a rock group. Grant wasn't paying too much attention, being more into cool modern jazz than this sort of playground stuff, but then he saw her.

She was sitting in a corner, deep in shadow, since the club was in near-darkness, but he would have recognised her anywhere. She was his half-sister, after all, or maybe not any more, but there Harriet sat and his mouth went dry. His appetite for the lusciously plump little bird he'd brought with him vanished upon the instant.

For all Harriet's coldness towards him, or perhaps because of it, the thought of her still tormented him. In his view she'd lorded it over him all his life, stealing the attention Stan should have paid to him. Of course, as things had turned out, Stan wasn't his real father after all, but that wouldn't have mattered if Harriet had never come on the scene. No wonder his mother hated her with a vengeance, exactly as she had hated Stan. So did Grant.

And he still nursed resentment over the beating up Vinny's old gang had given him the night Joyce had thrown the stupid girl out. He'd enjoyed watching *her* suffer the beating, but hadn't expected them to turn on *him* just moments later. That was all her fault too.

She got up to jive with the singer at one point, and Grant couldn't take his eyes off her.

He'd always been fascinated by the languid way she moved, her slow smile, and the innocence in those big grey eyes which could be all soft and velvety one minute and like a storm over the sea the next.

He loved the way she would suddenly flare up into an absolute paddy because she couldn't find her lipstick, or some favourite record or other she wanted to play on her record player. She'd rail at him, accusing him of borrowing it without asking and not giving it back. Which of course was true, certainly so far as the record was concerned, although he had once or twice stolen her lipsticks too and dropped them in the canal, simply for the joy of seeing that temper in action. There was nothing he liked better than to irritate and annoy her, to see how much he got on her nerves. It all seemed to add to the fun.

The band was playing 'Love Potion No.9', then even managing a pretty fair rendition of 'Mack the Knife', considering they were amateurs. Grant noticed how she kept her eyes fixed on the band, was jiving quite close to them, talking to one guy who looked vaguely familiar.

Then Grant recognised him. Vinny Turner, no less. Of course, he was the main attraction. No doubt she was sleeping with him. Well, let her get in a bit of practice, then he'd show her what a real man could do.

He warned himself not to rush into anything. He'd get rid of the bird, Sandra or Sharon or whatever her name was, then he'd follow this so-called sister of his and see where she went. Once he knew where she was living, he could make plans at his leisure. Not taking too long about it, of course, in case they decided to move on. Bands were notorious for not staying in one place for long, but, now that he'd found her, he had every intention of keeping her in his sights. And then of enjoying her and taking his revenge for the mess she'd made of his life.

20

Joyce

Joyce and Stan had just two nights together after the hasty Register Office wedding, two passionate nights, and two long days of loving before Stan had to leave. His ship was sailing for some unknown destination overseas the very next day. Joyce was already three months pregnant, which she somehow managed to avoid mentioning. Within weeks though, she was writing to announce her pregnancy, and he wrote back with joy, saying how he'd always wanted to be a family man, and he really didn't mind whether it was a boy or a girl.

Fortunately his parents were still disapproving of their marriage and never came near. When the baby was born Stan was still overseas, and Joyce left it for several more weeks before writing to tell him he'd become a father.

In her heart she knew she couldn't get away with this subterfuge for long, and she was proved absolutely right. By the time Stan came home, instead of a small seven-month baby lying in his cot, he found a ten-month-old infant crawling around and getting into mischief. Something didn't add up, but Stan could. He knew at once that he'd been duped.

Stan looked at the child and then at Joyce. 'You saw me coming a mile off, didn't you? What a fool I was. No wonder you didn't put up much of a fight when I suggested we get married in a hurry. My parents' suspicions were correct.'

'I was in love with you,' Joyce told him, trembling with fear that he might actually walk away and she'd lose him. 'I still am, and I can explain.'

'I'm sure you can.' The sarcastic tone of his voice cut right to the heart of her. 'It's my own fault, I suppose, I should've paid more attention to that Dear John letter, shouldn't I?'

'Don't say that. Just listen to what I have to say. Please!' But he wasn't interested in listening. He was indeed walking away. Joyce felt desperate. She must stop him from leaving, she really must. 'I was raped!'

He stopped dead, whirled about to face her, eyes stretched wide in disbelief. 'Raped! Now I've heard everything. *How dare you!* How dare you try to excuse your lies and trickery by making up such a sorry excuse?'

'It's not an excuse, it's true, I swear it.'

'And you forgot to mention it until now, is that it?'

'I should have told you, I realise that now. But I didn't tell anyone, not even my own mother.'

'And why was that, I wonder? Because it never happened?'

'It did happen, at a party Eileen held. He was a sailor too, but he was a stranger to me. I'd no idea who he was. He was drunk and I—'

'Drunken sailors? That's enough, Joyce. *Enough* I say!' Stan was furious, stabbing a finger in her face. 'Do you realise my comrades, little more than boys some of them, are dying out there. And what thanks do they get for offering that ultimate sacrifice? Their girlfriends sleep around with other men, that's what happens, time after time after time. I've seen my best friends face danger every day, and all their girls can think about is the next bit of fun they can have at some dance or other. You make me sick with your excuses. You've made a fool of me once, Joyce, but don't think you can make a habit of it. We may be stuck with each other, for the moment at least, but I don't have to like it.'

Joyce was certain that was when he started seeing other women, or at least one in particular.

Now, of course, she was the one having the affair, stealing, or at least attempting to steal, someone else's husband. Joyce deeply resented Irma Southworth's presence in her house. There she would be in the kitchen every morning, coddling eggs for Rose and frying bacon for herself. She left Joyce, of course, to make her own breakfast, and the kitchen in the flat was really far too small for two women who disliked each other as intensely as these two did, to share, particularly when one of them was Irma's size.

'How long are you going to take in there?' Joyce would demand. 'I've the salon to open. I take exception to being shut out of me own kitchen.'

Irma would cast her barely more than a scathing glance. 'And I take exception to you leaving your own mother to pee in her bed because you can't be bothered to nip upstairs and look after her. Anyroad, I'm not standing in your way. I'm done, it's all yours.'

And the two women would do a little two-step as Irma attempted to exit, tray balanced precariously, while Joyce barged in.

But having taken Rose's breakfast upstairs, Irma would then return and have the effrontery to eat her own breakfast at the living-room table – more often than not without even Grant to leaven the silence between them as he was usually still in bed, snoring his head off.

Irma was a very determined lady. She wasn't going to be hindered in her self-appointed task to make Rose better just because of any bad feeling there might be between herself and her husband's mistress. How many times in the past had she been in similar tricky situations, being obliged to behave normally with a woman who was sleeping with her man? She'd learned long since that whatever Joe got up to was his business. On this occasion, Irma had a job to do, and if that caused Joyce Ashton some discomfort and embarrassment, so be it.

Half an hour later Irma was serving Winnie with half a pound of mixed biscuits, paying particular attention to fig rolls, for which her friend had a weakness. She cast a glance over her shoulder to where Joe was packing a birthday cake ready for delivery. She'd seriously considered giving him the order of the boot because of this latest infidelity, but had decided, after careful deliberation, that he might be worth hanging on to.

Even if he did spend too much time on his beloved committees and with other women, Joe was still handy to have around. She was able to leave him in charge of the stall while she took a break, without the need to employ anyone. He drove the van when she had a cake delivery to make, as Irma didn't even drive. He could fix the guttering on the house when it fell down, and dig their vegetable patch on the allotment. And he was really no bother.

Winnie interrupted, instinctively reading her thoughts. 'He's working hard on this new campaign committee is your Joe. I've not seen him in the Dog and Duck nearly so often lately.'

Irma met her friend's bland gaze, interpreting this apparently innocent remark as an indication that he hadn't been seeing as much of Joyce Ashton either.

'Aye, that's happen true,' Irma agreed. 'There's nothing Joe loves more than a bit of committee business to get his teeth into. And he's been doing a few jobs for me around the house.'

On balance, Irma had decided Joe was worth keeping, although last night they'd had a real set-to when he'd actually threatened to move out. Well, more a tentative offer rather than a threat. Irma had laughed at him.

'Move out, and where would you move to?'

'I'd find somewhere.'

'You'd never manage on yer own. Who'd wash yer mucky socks or pick your clothes up off the floor? Who'd cook yer dinner or wipe round the bath after you climbed out of it? If you lived on yer own, the place would be like a pigsty in no time.'

'Aye, but I might not be on me own, I might lodge with someone.'

'Nay, who'd have you?'

'Someone might.'

'Well, if you were thinking of shacking up with that Joyce Ashton I wouldn't recommend it, not if you value your livelihood, not to mention your manhood.'

Joe had looked devastated, blithely unaware his wife even knew about that particular friendship, let alone the fact that Joyce had suggested he move in with her. 'What are you suggesting?'

'That if you want to continue earning your living working on this biscuit stall, and expect to share in the profits from my little cake business, then you aren't going anywhere. You don't start getting itchy feet, or any romantic notions in your daft noddle, if you catch my drift. Anyroad, you'd miss my steak and kidney puddings. See, I've made you a gradely one tonight, so stop dreaming and get that down your neck.'

Joe's eyes lit up as she placed the feast before him. 'Eeh, Irma, yer a good wife to me. What would I do without you?'

'Aye, what indeed? We're all right, you and me. We've been together too long to suffer any nasty surprises, so eat up and be grateful for what you've got, lad.'

'Oh, I am, Irma, I am,' Joe said, tucking in, all thoughts of leaving quite gone from his mind.

Now, the morning after his pathetic bid for freedom, as if suddenly aware of her eyes upon him, Joe managed a timid smile which he intended to be reassuring. 'I've done all the packing. Is it all right if I slip over to Belle's café for a frothy café?' he politely asked of his wife. 'I'll not be more'n ten minutes.'

'Ah, chuck, you go. I'll mind the family jewels,' indicating the cash box behind the stall. 'But don't spoil your appetite. I've got a lamb hotpot in the oven for us tea tonight.'

He beamed at her in delight. 'Eeh, right y'are, Irma, love. I won't.'

Irma rolled her eyes as she watched him stride away, and smiled at Winnie. 'The only certainty in life is my husband. I'll say one thing for Joe, he's predictable. Like all men, you know exactly where you are with him. Wherever other parts of his anatomy might lead him, he'll allus come home to be fed.'

Winnie went away chortling.

After another week of Irma's large presence in her kitchen, Joyce had had enough and went to see Joe. 'You've got to get that woman out of my house.'

'What can *I* do?'

Joe was not unaware of the difficulties his wife was causing by this unexpected decision to involve herself in Rose's troubles, but was loath to interfere. His mouth watered as he recalled the custard tart she'd served him last night for his tea, following a delicious dish of macaroni cheese. He really didn't know how she coped, how she managed to fit so much into her day. She was a miracle worker, that woman. But however busy she was, she never neglected him, never failed to provide him with a good dinner and a clean shirt. What more could a man ask?

Joyce's voice had become shrill with temper. 'Tell her it's not appropriate for her to be living with me, that she's creating gossip, that I don't need her, thank you very much.'

'*You* tell her. It's nowt to do wi' me what Irma does.'

'She's your wife, for goodness' sake!'

'Nay, I can't control her, never could. She's her own woman, is Irma.'

Joyce clenched her fists and stamped her foot, unable to control her rage. 'Damn you, Joe, this isn't fair. You swore that once Stan was gone we'd be together. Instead I'm lumbered with your flamin' *wife*.'

'That's not my fault. I wasn't to know your mother would have a stroke, was I? And I wish Rose a speedy recovery, I do really.'

Joyce came close to hitting him then, but knew it would be like batting a pillow. What was wrong with the man? He seemed to be completely oblivious to her problem.

Joe was thinking that perhaps Joyce Ashton was becoming a bit of a problem herself. He'd had some ding-dong battles with Belle Garside over the years when they were enjoying a bit of a fling, but at least Belle had fire in her soul, and she'd often provided him with a good breakfast at her café, if Irma hadn't time because of a rush order for her cake making.

'I don't see how I can help,' Joe admitted. 'Sorry, but I'd better be getting back to work. I'm minding the stall for the next couple of hours while Irma does exercises with your mam.'

How could she argue with that?

In despair Joyce turned to her son. 'Find our Harriet,' she instructed Grant, through gritted teeth. 'Fast. I've had enough of this. It's time to fetch the girl home where she belongs.'

Grant smiled, choosing not to mention that he'd found her already. 'And how do I persuade her? How do I get her to come back after the way you chucked her out?'

'Tell her Steve is pining for her, tell her anything you like, but get her back here where she can be of some use.'

Just as Joyce was about to close the salon after a long tiring day constantly interrupted by a stream of visitors, Belle Garside popped across to make an appointment. The other woman stood impatiently tapping her long scarlet fingernails on the counter top as she waited for Joyce to write out a card. 'I see Irma has moved in to help with your poor mother. That must be convenient for you? Though perhaps not in every respect.'

Joyce cast the other woman a questioning glance. Belle no doubt found it highly amusing that her little affair with Joe had been stifled by the omnipresence of his own wife on the premises. Determined not to rise to the bait, she agreed that Irma had been most attentive. 'I'm pleased to report that my mother is making good progress.'

'Excellent. No sign of your Harriet yet then?'

Joyce took a breath, reminding herself that this was a valued client she was speaking to and she couldn't simply snap her head off saying, *she's not my Harriet*. She managed a chilling smile instead. 'Not yet.'

'How dreadful, and with her grandmother seriously ill. You never got your party then?' Belle continued, enjoying finding new ways to make her rival squirm.

'Party, what party?'

'Ooh, have I let the cat out of the bag?' she asked, in all innocence. 'I thought that was why Grant was asking all those questions about your old flames, about what went on during the war. He said he was planning a surprise party, so I assumed he wanted to invite them all. We talked a bit about it the last time I was in, if you remember?'

Joyce found it a struggle to recall a conversation she'd had yesterday, let alone weeks ago, but that bit of gossip did come back to her with surprising clarity, now that Belle mentioned it. Grant had been going on a bit about her old friends. Joyce frowned. 'Yes, I do remember something about that, now I come to think of it, but I don't recall any mention of a party.'

'No? Well, I obviously had more discretion then than I'm showing now. Forget I ever mentioned it. I've no wish to spoil the lad's surprise. Anyroad, I was no help to him, you'll be glad to hear, so I suggested he talk to Frankie Morris. You used to be quite pally with him once-over, I seem to remember.'

After she'd gone, Joyce quietly closed the door and carefully locked it. She made no move to go upstairs, simply stood in the empty salon, silently contemplating what Belle had just told her. Frankie Morris? If Grant ever started asking Frankie the same questions he'd asked Belle, she would really have a problem on her hands. The last thing she wanted was for her precious son to hear the whole terrible story of how he was conceived, let alone the rest of it.

Without pausing to give the matter any further thought, she pulled on her coat, let herself out of the salon, and hurried across the road to the fish and chip shop opposite. She didn't have the energy to cook tonight anyway.

'Hello, chuck, what'll it be?' Frankie asked, his round shiny face beaming a wide smile. 'Haddock or cod?'

She chose cod. As Frankie wrapped the fish and chips, first in greaseproof paper, and then in yesterday's newspaper with a picture of a smiling John Kennedy who was running for president in America, Joyce chewed on her lip, worrying over what she should say.

As he handed over the hot parcel, aromatic with the scent of freshly cooked fish and chips, it all came out in a rush. 'Our Grant has taken it into his head to do a bit of probing. He's asking questions about my past, my old friends and such, so I'd appreciate it if you'd keep your trap shut.'

Frankie looked at her with brows raised, sympathy wiping the smile from his fat face. 'Really, and why would he be interested?'

'Summat to do with a surprise party he's planning. And you know how I feel about parties, Frankie. Say nowt, right?'

'You know you can rely on me,' Frankie smoothly promised, but as Joyce dashed away with her supper tucked under her arm, he muttered to himself. 'Not that I care what happens to you, madam. But then it's not you I've been protecting all these years, is it?'

21

Harriet

They called themselves The Scrapyard Kids and played not only rock 'n' roll but the blues, which they'd jazz up, reworking songs and practising for hour after hour, sometimes with barely a break.

Vinny had a go at composing his own songs, although not terribly successfully. On one occasion he sat up all night frantically scribbling notes on paper, so certain he was producing something brilliant he refused all suggestion that he should at least get some sleep. But the next morning, as he started to strum the tune on his guitar, he suddenly decided it was no good, flew into a temper and ripped the paper to shreds.

Harriet rushed to console him but he pushed her away and remained in a glum mood all day, only livening up when the beer and cigarettes came out in the evening.

They'd had one or two small gigs in pubs and clubs and the like, at first earning nothing beyond their supper, but their biggest booking so far was at a dance at the Cooperative Rooms in Salford on a Saturday night in early November. Their hard work seemed at last to be paying off, as they were well received and came away with real money in their pocket, a fiver each no less. The lads thought this much more fun than working in a boring factory, and far more profitable.

This success was followed by another and another, till soon they had a rush of bookings which meant the band was working most weekends, sometimes with the odd gig during the week too. Harriet didn't mind the fact there was no routine, no pattern to their days except sleep, eat, practise and play in the gigs. It thrilled her to think she was part of something momentous.

Not that this was exactly the big time they'd expected or at least hoped for, and there was no sign of any talent scout so there seemed little chance yet of the band actually cutting a record deal. When Harriet had asked Vinny why this was, he was irritated by her question, pointing out there were any number of skiffle groups and rock bands in Manchester alone, not counting the rest of the country.

'You think it's easy?' he snapped. 'You do it then,' and he flung his guitar at her and stalked off in a rage. She never asked him again.

But the pay was good, coming in regularly, and they began to get themselves a name, even a fan club of sorts. Kids had money to spend. Dancing and going to gigs was the way they liked to spend it.

Girls would scream at the boys as they played, just as if they were Elvis or Tommy Steele or someone really famous. There was always a gang of avid fans following them around, asking where the next gig was going to be. Neither Bruno nor Duffy ever missed out on a chance to mingle with the girls, dancing and smooching, drinking and smoking with them just the moment they finished playing.

Harriet kept a close eye on Vinny, but so far he'd shown no inclination to do the same. He seemed to have eyes only for her, which was deeply flattering, although admittedly he was often so stoned he could hardly see straight, let alone show any interest in other girls.

However much Harriet might deny she was in love with him, she was, in fact, completely and utterly besotted. She found him fascinating, very different from any other boy she'd ever met. There was an edge to Vinny Turner, which, in her present mood, she found compelling and exhilarating. She relished the aura of danger which emanated from him, and if that led her to taking risks, so be it.

Harriet was only too aware that her sense of self-worth was

low, that she put herself down. Shelley was constantly telling her as much, nagging her about not allowing herself to turn into a doormat for Vinny to wipe his feet on.

But she didn't care. She wanted to hurt herself, to do something, *anything*, which caused more pain than discovering she no longer had a mother. She needed to shut out the memory that she'd been thrown out and rejected, even by the boy who claimed to adore her.

Fortunately they now made enough money to stop sleeping on cardboard in the old warehouse, and could afford to book themselves into small hotels and B&Bs. Harriet found them places to stay and made sure their landladies got paid, usually up front, to keep them sweet. It made more sense for Vinny and Harriet to share a room, as it was cheaper, Harriet decided, ever practical.

'You're a fool,' Shelley told her.

'So what? I like him, he's fun.'

'Vinny Turner is totally wrapped up in himself. He's a taker, not a giver.'

'Now that's where you're wrong. He's very giving, and loving. Anyway, it's my life, what business is it of yours?'

Shelley shrugged. 'Suit yourself.'

Harriet enjoyed the feeling of being safely cuddled up to Vinny in a warm bed. She liked the sensation of waking up with him sprawled beside her, always ready to make love to her the minute he woke whether it was breakfast time or late afternoon.

Shelley was wrong. He wasn't selfish at all, but really good to her.

One day he took her out shopping to some of the best shops in Manchester: Kendals and Lewis's, and some smart little boutiques in St Anne's Square. Vinny generously treated her to a couple of sleek sheath dresses, quite short as they came to just above her knees, plus an A-line blue taffeta dress with an empire waist for evenings. Harriet bought herself a new pair of blue jeans, some stretch pants with stirrups that went under her feet to pull them tight, bags, shoes, and a couple of cool new blouses in a flimsy see-through fabric. She felt so chic and stylish.

Vinny bought himself an Italian-style suit and several silk shirts and ties, really cool and trendy so that he looked like a mod, putting an end to the Teddy boy image for good. He might only play in a cheap little band, but he looked a million dollars, so sexy!

When they'd finished shopping he took her to lunch in a trendy little pub where a jukebox played loud music and they were served chicken and chips in a basket.

He said they deserved to celebrate the band's success, and the fact that national service had been abolished so he wouldn't have to risk losing his freedom, or her, for two years.

Freedom, Harriet thought, was what this was all about. Oh, and didn't she just love it?

The band were performing one evening at The Hare & Hounds on Broad Street. It was not exactly the Ritz and was due to be closed soon as it awaited demolition. Harriet had accepted the booking because they were skint. Money seemed to be going out faster than it was coming in, and she really felt they needed to take everything on offer until they had some savings behind them. Vinny did not agree, and he grumbled and muttered and bitterly complained as the lads tuned up and prepared to go on.

'We should be appearing at the Plaza, or Belle Vue, not some tuppenny-ha'penny flea pit.'

'Smile,' Shelley said. 'Or you'll frighten away the punters.'

As usual, Harriet found herself a spot right at the back where she could watch in peace without disturbing the audience. She crossed her fingers, praying Vinny would behave himself tonight and not go stalking off in a temper as he was wont to do when in a mood.

She glanced around, trying to assess how many people were present – little more than twenty or thirty she thought, and most of them were busy talking and paying little attention to the lads playing their hearts out on the small stage. She felt sorry for them, knowing how much effort they put into their perform-ances. There was perfunctory applause at the end of the first number and then Shelley came on to sing, which perked up the men's attention no end.

Shelley was wearing the shortest skirt Harriet had ever seen, scarcely skimming her bottom, and the neckline was so low the two nearly met. No wonder a reverent silence had fallen over the assembled drinkers, although it had little to do with the quality of her singing despite it being excellent, as always.

Harriet shook her head in despair. This wouldn't please Vinny either, if Shelley got all the adulation and attention, and, judging by the applause which followed, that's exactly what was happening. She couldn't help but smile though as she watched the intent expressions on the faces of the audience, all whistling and cheering, begging Shelley for an encore.

It was then that Harriet noticed one man who wasn't even looking at the stage, let alone joining in the applause. He too was scanning the crowd, looking all round him as if searching for someone. Her heart gave a loud thump as she realised it was Steve, his gaze fixing on hers at exactly the same moment.

Oh, lord, he was coming over. He began to weave his way towards her between the tables.

Harriet often thought about Steve, particularly at night when she lay curled up alone in some anonymous hotel room, wondering where Vinny was, what he was doing, or with whom. She would dream up scenarios of what might have happened if Nan hadn't given her that devastating news, if Joyce hadn't kicked her out, or if she hadn't been attacked by that gang or Vinny hadn't come to her rescue. Steve had always been her friend. They'd been together since their school days, and she missed him.

The next instant he was standing before her, a great big grin on his face, and Harriet couldn't help but smile back.

'What are you doing here?' she asked, not knowing what else to say.

'I said I'd come and see the band, didn't I? I've been keeping a look-out for one of their gigs, is that the right word?'

Harriet agreed that it was. She cast a quick glance in the direction of the stage, hoping Vinny wouldn't notice her talking to

Steve; then again, seeing her with another bloke might make him jealous and appreciate her all the more.

'It's good of you to come, but you must think this a bit third rate, after the kind of shows you see with your college friends.'

Steve frowned. 'Don't be daft. You know I'm not the sort to go to the Philharmonic or watch Shakespeare. I'm going to teach maths and geography, not be a professor. I think they're great.' He turned to listen for a moment, then asked, 'Which one's Vinny?'

Harriet casually pointed him out, not wanting to make too much of it.

'I liked the way they played "Red River Rock," it had a real beat to it.'

'Thanks, I'll tell Vinny you said that. He'll be pleased.'

'So, what are you doing with yourself these days? Where are you working now?'

Harriet didn't quite know how to answer this, except with the truth. 'I work for Vinny. I – I help with the band.' It sounded so inadequate, put like that.

His eyebrows climbed in surprise. 'You mean you manage them, do all the bookings, and promotions and stuff? Are they so successful?'

Harriet shook her head, her cheeks flushed, although there was a defiance in her tone. 'Not exactly, and Vinny does all of that, but I look after the money side of things. And I look after him, of course.'

There was a small silence while Steve absorbed this. 'Right,' he said, sounding thoughtful. 'I see.'

Would she have found the courage to do something more worthwhile with her life if she'd stayed in Champion Street? Harriet wondered. She might have gone to college too, if she'd been clever enough, or at least stuck at her secretarial course. Maybe then Steve wouldn't have dumped her, illegitimate or not.

Was she happy trailing after the band and sticking by Vinny? Where *was* she going? What was she doing with her life?

Harriet swallowed, staring unseeing at The Scrapyard Kids as they tuned up for their next number. And would she have been any happier if she was still waiting for Steve back home in Champion Street? She might have felt safer, but that wasn't quite the same thing, was it? In any case, he'd changed, and not simply in appearance. He seemed more assured, more mature somehow. No doubt he'd found himself a 'nice' girl by this time, at that fancy college he attended, someone classy to spend his life with, if only to please his flipping mother. She could see that he was used to hanging around with a different crowd these days. He proved it with his next words.

'He looks a bit wild.'

'What?'

'The way he strums that guitar, as if he's beating the hell out of it. I hope he doesn't treat you like that.'

Harriet was incensed. 'Why would you imagine that he would? Anyway, what's it got to do with you how he treats me?'

'Because I believe you'll regret ever getting involved with him, if I know you as well as I think I do. You're wasting your life hanging around with the likes of Vinny Turner, Harriet.'

'Why are people always so anxious to tell me what to do with my life, always so bloody condemning and critical of everything I do? You sound just like Joyce.'

'No I don't, but I can see that he's trouble, with a capital T.'

'Well, that's where you're wrong,' Harriet fumed. 'He's lovely, is Vinny, if you want to know. Really kind and generous, buys me clothes and everything.'

Steve gave her a look of utter disdain. 'I don't believe you said that. I can't believe you'd settle for being some guy's plaything, being bought presents and such. Why would you do such a thing?'

Harriet could feel herself growing all hot and bothered. 'If you're implying they were gifts for services rendered, you can just take that back.'

'I never said that!' Now it was Steve's turn to blush as a stain of colour flooded right up to his hair line. 'I just think you're perfectly capable of getting a good job of your own, of building a life for yourself. The independent-minded Harriet I once knew would never have agreed to being some chap's pampered pet.'

'I'm not a pampered pet!' Harriet raged, 'and you can keep your comments to yourself, if you don't mind.' She knew she was making too much of this, could feel herself coming dangerously close to tears, but couldn't help herself. Inside her head a small voice was screaming, *It's too late to defend yourself. It's too late!*

Too much had happened since Steve Blackstock had been the love of her life. He'd made it very clear that he was no longer interested in her as a girlfriend, so why even bother to concern herself about what he thought of her? It was too late to turn back the clock. What was the point in remembering how much she'd adored him? His parents hated her. *He* hated her. For heavens' sake, she even hated herself. She was no longer the innocent young virgin Steve fondly remembered. She'd given herself to Vinny now.

'Just leave me alone.'

Steve was trying to placate her, as always, flapping his hands as he used to do when she'd accused him of ruining her skipping game in the playground. 'OK, OK, keep your hair on. I just wanted to ask when you'd be coming home, that's all. But obviously you aren't by the sound of it.'

'No, actually, I'm not. I'm staying with Vinny, thanks. And it would be best if you just forgot all about me.'

He was looking at her now with a sadness in his gaze. 'I see. That's what you want, is it, to be with Vinny?'

Harriet looked away. 'Yes, it is.'

'I'll leave you to it then,' and with a curt nod he walked away, out of the pub, out of her life.

Harriet slapped the tears from her cheeks and stared at Vinny, her new love, leaping about like a mad thing. She could never go back, not with the way things stood, so why fret about it?

She'd made her choices, and she would stand by them.

22

Rose

Little by little, and by dint of sheer willpower and bloody-mindedness, Irma forced Rose to get going again. She made the old woman do regular exercises, first with her hands and arms, which she would massage and manipulate, and then her legs. Irma would make her lie on her back while she rubbed and bent them up and down, up and down. Then she'd make her sit on a chair while she did the same there. After a few weeks of this, she started hoisting her to her feet, holding the fragile old woman safe in her big arms while Rose got the feel of the weight of her own body again.

Oh, it sometimes went all wrong. Rose would lose her balance, or she'd use the wrong word, and they'd fall about laughing like a pair of silly teenagers. But that was no bad thing.

Irma absolutely refused to allow her friend to sink into depression. She kept Rose alert by reading to her, by persuading her to listen to her favourite programmes on the wireless: *Woman's Hour*, *Paul Temple* and Valentine Dyal as *The Man In Black*, whom she loved. And Irma talked and talked and talked, mostly nonsense but it didn't matter. Anything she could think of to stimulate her friend's mind and prevent her from just lying there doing nothing.

Joyce frequently objected to the noise they made, claiming that the loud music disturbed her customers, that their shrieks of laughter were doing her head in. She objected even more when a constant stream of visitors began to trickle through the hair salon, all asking if they could just pop upstairs and have a bit of a crack with Rose.

'We miss seeing her out and about on the market,' Winnie

explained. 'Anyroad, she'll want to know all about this campaign that she's started.'

'What campaign?'

'To save the market. It were Rose's idea that we investigate thoroughly what's happening and then set up a special committee to fight the closure. We're not going to let them get away with it. She's very determined, your mother, when she sets her mind to summat. Anyroad, you'll be glad of the help to get her back on her feet, I reckon, even if it's not coming from the direction you would have sought.'

'I'm afraid I don't understand what you're implying, Winnie.'

'No, course you don't. Why would you? I'll just go up, shall I?'

The whole of Champion Street Market seemed to be trailing through her salon and up Joyce's stairs at one time or another. It was infuriating.

Joyce hated to feel beholden to anyone, and loathed having Irma in the house. Apart from the fact that it put paid to any hope of secret trysts with the silly woman's husband, Joyce deeply resented the intrusion into her own private domain. And she hated to be at the mercy of the market gossips.

Steve could have kicked himself. He'd messed it up yet again. He seemed to make a habit of saying the wrong thing. Not only had he upset Harriet by implying she was letting herself down, but he'd criticised her precious new boyfriend too, which apparently was unforgivable. Why was she behaving so stupidly? He couldn't understand it. Yes, he could.

After all she'd been through he could understand perfectly. It was difficult to imagine how anyone would react to suddenly discovering that your mother wasn't your mother, after all. Even if Joyce Ashton hadn't been the easiest woman in the world to live with, she was the only mother Harriet had ever known. Steve's own mother could be a pain at times, but he still loved her.

Worse, because of their quarrel, he'd again forgotten to tell her that Rose was ill. Harriet would be furious with him if she ever found out that he'd known about her nan's stroke yet had failed to mention the fact. And Joyce clearly didn't intend making any effort to trace Harriet and inform her of the state of her grandmother's health.

There was no help for it, he'd have to pay another visit to a gig by The Scrapyard Kids, and tell her. Apologise to her yet again, this time for failing to tell her that her grandmother was ill.

Steve felt a spark of hope. At least it would give him a perfect excuse for seeing her again. He certainly wasn't going to give up on her, or forget her, despite Harriet having told him to do so, even if she was behaving stupidly.

The problem was that his time was limited since he was at college during the week, which meant he only had the weekends, and, once his workload increased as the course progressed, even those would be in jeopardy. He spent the very next weekend trailing around from pub to pub, like some sort of desperate inebriate, looking for any sign that The Scrapyard Kids were due to perform. He spotted Grant in one pub, and then in another, and turned the other way, wanting to avoid him.

The next weekend, Steve followed the same routine, with little better luck, and yet again he spotted Grant. What was the lad up to?

Grant had followed Harriet back to her digs, and, now that he knew exactly where she was staying, kept a close eye on her movements, covertly following her wherever she went.

He would see her call in at a baker's shop to buy them sandwiches or pastries, or go to a take-away for burgers or fish and chips. At other times she'd visit some pub or other, presumably to talk with the landlord about a possible booking. Grant thought he was being really rather clever trailing her as she went back and forth on what seemed to be a constant stream of errands for the band while they rehearsed in that decrepit old warehouse. It amused him to think of her as being little more than an errand girl.

One evening she called at several public houses, then recklessly chose to take a short cut down a side street, clearly anxious to get back to lover-boy as quickly as possible. Grant followed her. Dusk was falling and he thought that maybe this could be the very opportunity he'd been waiting for. He pictured in his head what he would do to her.

He would shove her down into the gutter where she belonged, strip her of her dignity, pummel her soft white flesh with bruises and reduce her to tears. He'd make her beg for mercy, plead with him with tears in her lovely grey eyes for him not to hurt her. Oh, but he would hurt her. If she could open her legs for all and sundry in that band, she could open them for him too. She deserved to be humiliated. She needed to be made to understand the injury she'd done to him over the years, the neglect she'd caused him, just by being Stan's favourite.

Grant slipped from one doorway to another as he made his way along the street, making sure that he kept a safe distance between them. As she reached the bottom and swiftly turned the corner, he put on a little spurt so that he didn't lose her. Then, edging slowly round the corner, he found to his utter shock and horror that he'd walked right into her. She was standing waiting for him, hands on her hips and an expression of cold fury on her face.

'So what is this all about, Grant, this creeping about behind me like some tin-pot detective?'

He valiantly attempted to recover his equilibrium, though he was sweating furiously. 'Good evening, sister dear, I wondered if it might be you. What a coincidence!'

'Coincidence my foot, you've been following me for days. Did Joyce put you up to this, or is this all your own idea?'

'I can't think what you mean?'

There was something about her demeanour which unnerved him. She'd never been the meek and mild sort, always considering herself to be a cut above him, and completely unmoved when he, as her older brother, after all, exercised his right to discipline her. She'd always been a cocky little madam who refused to do as she was told. Grant hated her for that attitude alone.

She might think she was somebody because she was involved with this cheap little band, living in cheap little boarding houses, but she wasn't at all. Harriet was nothing but a bastard, the scum of the earth. So what right did she have to lord it over him?

Grant curled his upper lip in a sour smile. 'If you want to know, I came out for a bevy and I spotted you in that pub. It's really not the sort of place a young girl like yourself should visit on your own. I won't allow any sister of mine to make herself look cheap in that way, so I followed you to check that you were OK.'

'Don't lie to me, Grant. And don't creep about. I'm not stupid and I won't be spied on. You go back home and tell Joyce that I'm fine, thank you very much. I might be homeless but I'm not starving, and I'm not without friends, so don't for a moment think of trying anything.'

Grant adopted an injured expression of outraged innocence. 'What are you suggesting, sister dear?'

'You're a nasty little sneak, Grant, but you don't frighten me. You forget that I'm used to your grubby little ways. They don't intimidate me in the slightest. And call me by my proper name, if you please. Show some proper respect.'

Grant took a step towards her, a threatening note coming into his voice. 'Or else what, *sister* dear?'

'Or you'll have me to deal with.' The voice came from quite a different direction, and Grant spun about to find himself face to face with Steve Blackstock. By heck, did she have two lovers on the go? But then he noticed that Harriet was equally surprised by his appearance.

'Steve, what in heaven's name are you . . . ?' she began as if she'd had no idea he was there.

'I rather suspected this creepy little toad was up to something, and decided to keep an eye on him. I've been proved correct. Do you realise he's been following you for days?'

'Yes,' Harriet snapped. 'I'm fully aware of that fact, and I really don't need you hanging around as well, appointing yourself as some sort of glorified protector. In fact, I'm pretty fed up with the pair of you. I don't need anyone to look after me. I can look after myself, thank you very much, so will you both get off my back and leave me alone!' Upon which note she walked away, leaving both young men feeling decidedly foolish.

The day came when Irma decided it was time Rose ventured downstairs. She refused, point blank.

'Nay, I'll fall.'

'Not if I'm holding on to you.'

'Can't walk – far. Couldn't get down them – blame stairs.'

Not to be thwarted in her plan, Irma assured Rose she'd soon fix that. She took the problem straight to Joyce. 'I don't understand why you're keeping your mother trapped upstairs when there's a perfectly good room at the back here which your Stan used.'

Joyce regarded the other woman with a chilling glare. 'You surely don't expect me to give up my office?' She'd taken the room over within days of Stan's death, clearing out all his belongings, packing them into bags, ordering Grant to dump them at the tip. Good riddance to bad rubbish, had been Joyce's view on the clothes, medals, books and personal mementoes that her husband had collected over the years. Then she'd set out the room as an office to her own impeccable taste. She rarely used the room, truth be told, but it looked rather smart, and she certainly had no intention of being evicted from her own personal, private space.

Irma said, 'I'm fetching her downstairs tomorrow, like it or lump it, so we'll set up her bed in here, shall we? Just till she's stronger and can get up and down them stairs under her own steam.' Irma caught sight of Stan's wheelchair tucked in a corner. Joyce was still waiting for Grant to dispose of this bulky item. 'Eeh, and we could make use of that an' all.'

Joyce was outraged. She couldn't believe this was happening to her all over again. 'I'll never agree to that!' The thought of her mother within feet of her precious clients in the salon, and trundling about in that wheelchair, sent shudders down her spine. Hadn't she suffered the indignity of enduring an invalid in this room for more years than she cared to count? When would she ever be free? 'Never in a million years,' Joyce announced, lips thinning to their trademark line.

'Oh, I reckon you will. I've kept quiet about what I found here, but if I ever started talking about the way you were treating your old mother before I arrived on the scene, I doubt I'd be able to stop. No food for hours, only a glass of water to drink all day, and no help to get to the bathroom. I can be a right jabber-mouth, me, when I want to be.'

'Is that some sort of threat?'

Irma smiled. 'Joe would back me up. Shall I ask him? Anyroad, I'm sure he'd come over and give us a hand to move her bed and stuff, if *I* asked him.'

Joyce discovered, to her dismay, that Irma was not, in fact, asking her permission. She was simply informing Joyce of her intention. In no time at all, Joyce's desk, chair, lamp, and even the old typewriter she'd purloined from Harriet's room, which had looked so important set out on the desk even if it was never used, were all stacked up against the wall, or shut away in cupboards.

And in their place stood her mother's narrow divan bed, small wardrobe and chest of drawers, all brought downstairs with Joe's help. It seemed almost bizarre that her lover, together with his wife, should be moving her invalid mother and all her posses-sions without even a by-your-leave. But then wasn't that the story of Joyce's life? When did she ever have control over anything? At least she'd put her foot down over that irritating child and banished her from the house. Long may she stay away.

Irma and Rose were celebrating a good progress report from the doctor by happily eating a Knickerbocker Glory in Bertalones' ice cream parlour. Papa Bertalone had put extra strawberry syrup over the peaches, strawberries, grapes and melon pieces and two scoops of ice cream, topped off with a swirl of cream, flaked almonds and a fan wafer. Irma licked her spoon in delight, savouring every delicious mouthful.

'A little of what you fancy does you good, eh?'

Rose chuckled. She was feeling particularly buoyant as the morning outing had done her a world of good. Frustrated though she might be with her own progress, the doctor seemed pleased enough with her. 'It's thanks to you . . . Irma . . . I can sit here . . . and eat this . . . wicked stuff.' Her words were still slow in coming, but made better sense these days.

Papa Bertalone was patiently listening to what she had to say too and scolded her gently, taking issue with her choice of words. 'My Italian ice-a creama not wicked. It good for you, Rose. It full of the best ingredients, eggs, cream, and the finest fruit.'

'I know, Marco, I wasn't . . . complaining. Enjoy . . . every . . . mouthful. Happy! Out and about . . . even though,' and she slapped the wheelchair with one hand as if to indicate she resented it.

'We are happy to see you,' he agreed, clapping his hands with pleasure. 'But do not worry about the chair. My Gina spend many months in one after she have the polio, but look at her now, walking, working for Dena, and living life to the full.'

'How is Gina?'

Papa Bertalone beamed. 'She very happy. She is to be married soon, to Luc, the love of her life.'

'A fine young man,' Irma said. 'I hope they'll both be very happy.'

'Then she will give me many grandchildren, many bambinos.'

'Grand,' Rose agreed. 'Grandchildren can bring problems, Marco.'

Rose's expression grew serious as she thought of her own. She was quite certain young Grant was up to no good. Rose could see it in the sly way he watched her sometimes, but she couldn't quite put her finger on what the problem was. As for Harriet . . . The old woman sighed, and shook her head. 'Wish my lass were here. I . . . miss her.'

Seeing that he had upset his customer, Papa Bertalone dashed off to bring them both an extra cherry to pop on the top of their ice creams, which made Rose smile through her tears. Irma put her plump arms about her friend and hugged her. 'She'll be home soon, I'm sure of it.'

23

Harriet

Was Steve's assessment of Vinny right? This thought tormented Harriet in the days following their encounter. Surely not. It might be true that he was a little on the wild side, but wrong to imply he treated her badly or had no heart. He cared about his family, for one thing. Harriet knew he sent money home most weeks to his younger brothers and sister because she posted the postal orders for him.

Even so, Harriet was aware that she really shouldn't be getting involved with the likes of Vinny Turner yet couldn't seem able to resist him. He was lovely, utterly gorgeous, the best looking of the group. And he made her feel special. It was so good to know that somebody, at least, cared for her, after all she'd been through.

And the way he made love to her was exciting and thrilling.

There was something in the way he touched her that was forever her undoing. He only had to look at her and she would melt inside. Then, everything Nan had ever told her about keeping herself decent and respectable would crumble to dust in her head.

Harriet was running herself a bath, crumbling in a sweetly scented bath cube so that she'd smell nice for him. It was past eleven and he still hadn't returned from tonight's gig. No doubt he'd be out with the lads celebrating, knocking back a few beers. Harriet had chosen to return to the hotel because of a headache but he'd promised her faithfully that he wouldn't be long.

'You can keep the bed warm for me, babe,' he smirked with a suggestive little wink.

'Don't I always?'

Harriet smiled as she recalled the evidence of jealousy when he'd spotted her engrossed in deep conversation with Steve.

'You don't still fancy Stevey boy, do you?' he'd asked, making a beeline for her the minute Steve had left.

'Don't be daft. I'm with you now, only I had to be polite and talk to him, didn't I, since he'd come all this way to see the band?'

'Can't think why he would. I expect it was you he was really wanting to see.'

'Not jealous, are you?' Harriet had teased, widening her eyes appealingly.

'You're a free spirit, girl. I put no chains on you,' he casually responded, and with a shrug of his shoulders he had leapt back on stage for the next number. It wasn't quite the answer she'd hoped for but Harriet knew it was only bluff. Vinny liked to pretend he didn't care about anything or anyone, which was how he coped with the problems in his life.

Yet when they were alone he would tell her she provided the oil which kept his motor running, or she was the butter on his bread, and they'd fall about laughing. He had such a funny way with words, all a cover to pretend he didn't care.

No, Steve was entirely wrong about him. Vinny might have problems but he was decent and kind inside, warm and loving. This was her life now, with Vinny.

Of course there were aspects to his character she really didn't care for, Harriet thought as she lay back with a sigh in the lemon-scented water. Privately, she considered that he drank far too much. He often came back the worse for drink after a night out with the lads, and he really shouldn't smoke those weeds. She absolutely refused to share one of the smelly cigarettes with him now. The woozy feeling no longer appealed as they made her feel slightly sick and out of control. Harriet would watch with some concern as he smoked one after the other and then be comatose for hours, sometimes days, often missing any number of rehearsals.

On one occasion he actually missed a gig, and was furious with her, blaming her for not waking him up in time.

'I tried,' Harriet told him, mortified that he should consider it was her fault.

Perverse as ever, he'd laughed at her, pretending he was only worn out because her demands upon him were so insatiable, and Harriet had fallen into a fit of giggles, blushing with embarrassment.

He was such fun to be with. What did it matter if he missed the odd show? Vinny didn't have anyone to answer to but himself. Neither did she. She no longer had Joyce nagging her, manufacturing an interest in her education or pretending to care about her career prospects which was all put on simply for the sake of appearances.

Not for the world would Harriet attempt to lecture Vinny on how to behave. They'd both opted for freedom, and she respected his right to it. It wasn't as if she was in love with him, or anything silly and sentimental like that, so why should it matter to her what he got up to? She was simply grateful that he had at least included her in this adventure.

'We're just having a bit of fun,' she told herself firmly. 'It's not in the least bit important. I don't care what he does.'

Yet when he was late back, like tonight, she couldn't keep her eyes off the clock.

Harriet carefully shaved her legs as she lay soaking herself in the foaming hot water. Vinny hated girls with hairy legs, preferring them to be smooth and silky. He was always complimenting her on the softness of her skin, and the sweet scent of her. She felt a warm glow of anticipation inside as she patted herself dry and pulled on a pair of baby-doll pyjamas, an outfit he adored. He'd be back soon, and she meant to be wide awake, waiting for him.

Even if there were times, like now, when he would sometimes neglect her, leaving her kicking her heels with nothing to do while he and the lads beat out music all day, or sat up half the night drinking and smoking, Harriet judged it wise to make no comment. Maybe she was afraid of being told to pack her bags and leave, as her own mother – Joyce – had done. Much as she might want him to be with her, Harriet accepted this behaviour as an essential part of his nature, and of the world he was involved with.

She lay in bed in the shabby hotel room trying to concentrate on a romantic serial in *Woman's Own*, fighting tiredness to keep her eyes open so that she'd be alert and ready for love when he finally appeared. But sleep overcame her in the end, and when she woke it was to find sun streaming through the window, and he still wasn't back.

Harriet felt a keen disappointment but not for the world would she complain when he finally did show. No doubt he'd got caught up in a jam session, or the lads were involved in composing a new number and he'd quite forgotten the time. Why would she expect him to give up any of that just for her? Harriet was determined to go along with whatever Vinny wanted. Wasn't she content simply to be a part of his life?

At the very next gig there he was again, waiting for her, just as if she'd never ordered him to forget her, or told him off for following her and playing guardian over her well-being. If Steve had come to lecture her yet again she'd give him what for. Harriet marched right over and demanded to know what the hell he was playing at. 'Are you following me, Steve Blackstock?'

'Hello, Harriet, you're looking well.'

'Don't try your soft soap on me. Why are you here? Don't tell me you've just developed a passion for rock 'n' roll. Or is this yet another apology, because if so . . .'

'Actually no, it isn't.' Steve took his hands out of his pockets to hold her gently by the shoulders as he faced her with an uncharacteristically serious expression on his face. 'There's something I meant to tell you last time, and because we had words . . .'

'A flaming quarrel, you mean – yet again.' She wanted to shake his hands away but that would seem petty, and Harriet suddenly felt very safe and warm being held by Steve again.

Steve ignored the remark, and his face now held a sadness that filled her with sudden fear. His next words confirmed it. 'I meant to tell you about Rose. Your nan's not well. I thought you'd want to know.'

Harriet looked at him in dismay, all anger draining from her. 'Nan's ill?'

'She's had a stroke. It's OK, don't panic. She's being well looked after by Irma Southworth.'

'Where?'

'At yours, where else? Irma calls in countless times during the day to see to her, and she's sleeping there too, I believe, so she can be on hand to look after her during the night.'

Had this news not been so very serious Harriet would have burst out laughing at the thought of Irma and Joyce sharing a house. It seemed ironic, in the circumstances. But she was already searching for her coat. 'I must see her. Will you come with me?'

'I've got my car outside, I'll give you a lift.'

Harriet glanced across at Vinny and the lads, strumming away, Shelley singing for all she was worth. She could hardly interrupt them in mid-flow, so she left a message for them with the barman and gladly accepted Steve's offer.

Joyce was as unwelcoming as ever. 'And what ill wind has blown you in?' was her opening remark as she opened the door to find Harriet and Steve Blackstock standing on her doorstep.

'I've just heard that Nan is ill. Why was it left to Steve to let me know?'

Joyce looked down her nose at her stepdaughter. 'How did we know where you were? You could be anywhere. Might not even have been in Manchester.'

'Of course I was still in Manchester, and it wouldn't have been difficult to find me, if you really wanted to. An announcement in the paper might have done the trick, for a start.'

Harriet turned to Steve and thanked him for the lift. They'd said little to each other in the car as he'd driven her home, beyond expressing their mutual concern over Rose. But there'd been an awkwardness between them, one which seemed impossible to bridge. Too many wrong words, too much bad feeling, and Harriet could still sense the disapproval emanating from him which was almost unbearable. They'd given up on the stilted conversation and her thoughts had turned inward as she became pre-occupied with her own worries over her grandmother. Steve had kept his eyes on the road. Now, she tried to smile, put a hand on his arm to show her appreciation.

'Will you be wanting a lift back later?' he asked. 'Or will you be staying overnight?'

'She's not staying here,' Joyce said, her tone as sharp as ever. 'We've no spare bed now Irma is resident.'

'I wouldn't dream of putting you out,' Harriet coolly remarked. 'Thanks, Steve, I'd appreciate a lift back, if you don't mind.'

He was secretly delighted. 'No trouble. I'll pick you up in about an hour, will that be enough time, or do you need longer?'

'That'll be fine.'

As he strode away, Joyce reluctantly opened the door wider and allowed Harriet inside. 'There's no need for you to be here at all. We're managing fine without you.'

'I'm sure you are, but I want to see Nan. Where is she?'

Joyce nodded in the direction of Stan's old room and without another word, Harriet knocked softly on the door, then went in to see her grandmother.

Rose was beside herself with joy at the sight of her beloved granddaughter. 'Eeh, chuck, I've been that worried. Are you all right? Are you eating proper?'

Harriet laughed and wrapped her arms about the fragile old woman. 'You're the one I'm concerned about, not me.'

'I'm doing champion, thanks to Irma here.'

Irma was seated by the bed and smiled at Harriet as she got quietly to her feet. 'I'll fetch us all a cuppa, give you two a bit of privacy,' and she slipped quietly out of the room.

'She's lovely, is Irma,' Rose said. 'Can't think how I'd've managed without her.' And she told Harriet all about the exercises she was putting her through, the constant stream of music and chatter. 'I couldn't even talk at first,' Rose explained.

Harriet squeezed her hand. 'You sound like you've got your voice back now all right.'

'Tell me all about yourself, lass. Where are you living, what are you doing? How are you surviving?'

'Don't worry about me, I'm doing fine.' Harriet gave her nan a carefully sanitised version of her life with the band, giving the impression it was very much a temporary situation until she got herself sorted out and made some long-reaching decisions about her life. She told her how good Vinny was to her, and showed off her new clothes. Rose said nothing.

Irma came back with the tea and as they drank it, enjoying a slice of Irma's best sultana and walnut cake, they talked about the campaign to save the market. Rose was full of it, and it was clearly giving her a focus and helping her to get over the stroke. Then quite out of the blue Irma took Harriet's hand, and turning it palm up began to trace the lines with one finger, examining them closely.

'You're not strong on ambition, love, but you have a great deal of heart and deep compassion,' Irma told her.

Harriet was startled, pulling her hand away. 'I'm not sure I believe in all of that stuff.'

Rose said, 'Listen to her. She's a dab hand at fortune telling is this mate o' mine.'

Again Irma examined Harriet's palm. 'There's some indication of emotional turmoil here which has been making you very unhappy.' She looked keenly at Harriet, who sat mute, intrigued now despite her instinctive dismissal that it was all superstitious nonsense. 'I'd say you are too intense, too sensitive, too giving. You allow people to use you, and that's not a good trait.'

'Will I have a long life?' Harriet teased, as jauntily as she could manage, not wishing to reveal how Irma's words had touched a raw nerve and inflamed her deep sense of insecurity. Nevertheless, Irma seemed to sense it and her voice softened.

'You've suffered a serious change in your life, some cataclysmic event.'

'I think we all know this,' Harriet said.

'But there's more to come, I'm afraid,' Irma continued, as if she hadn't been interrupted. 'Your general health seems uncertain, lacking vigour and strength, and I'd say the cause of that is largely because you allow your heart to rule your head.'

'Our Harriet allus was soft as butter,' Rose put in.

'Looking at your fate line I'd say you still have many obstacles to overcome.' Irma turned the hand a little, examining the edge of it, the fingers, pressing the pads of it here and there. 'I see problems with a man. You'd do well to be wary of this person as he is the one draining away your ability to make decisions. Perhaps because he is too demanding or self-serving. You need to break free and go your own way, not pander to the needs of others all the time.' She lifted Harriet's other hand and compared the two. 'There is every sign of happiness for you in the long-term. You will find a man to love. You'll marry and have three children.'

'And does it tell you his name?'

'Don't be flippant, Harriet,' Rose scolded. 'Irma is only trying to be helpful.'

Irma let go of Harriet's hands with a smile. 'When you have had time to think on what I've said, then you should act upon it. Remember, your hands only tell so much, the rest is up to you.'

Harriet swallowed. There was something knowing in the older woman's steady gaze, as if she could read Harriet's soul, see all her miseries and problems, her insecurities and needs. She got up. 'I have to go.'

She kissed her grandmother goodbye, promising to call again soon. The next moment she was climbing into Steve's beat-up old Ford car and driving away, Joyce not even troubling to come downstairs to see her off. Not that Harriet cared, she was only too relieved to be returning to Vinny and the band, and her new friend Shelley. They were the ones who mattered now, and no superstitious nonsense spouted by two credulous old women was going to unnerve her.

There was even less conversation between herself and Steve on the way back, and Harriet got him to drop her at the corner of Cross Street, rather than directly outside the hotel. She really didn't want him to know where she was staying. Before getting out, she thanked him for taking so much trouble to inform her of Nan's illness.

'I appreciate your kindness, but don't take this as any indication that you and I could get back together. I meant what I said, Steve. Best you forget all about me. I'm not worthy of your love, not any more,' then she climbed out of the car, closed the door and walked away. But not before she'd heard Steve say that he never could forget her, not as long as he lived.

24

As the weeks passed and autumn slid into winter, the band became busier than ever, particularly over Christmas, with gigs night after night. Harriet was pleased to be busy as it stopped her from thinking too deeply about where she was going and what she was doing with her life.

Even so, she'd been haunted by what Irma had apparently read in her palm. Despite her scepticism it had touched a chord. Harriet had been unnerved by the woman's accurate assessment of her character as well as what was going on in her life. It seemed to tally so exactly with Steve's attitude, and even the warnings Shelley had made that she shouldn't rely too much on Vinny but depend only upon herself.

A part of her wondered if perhaps she should start listening to these people. Why was she sticking by Vinny Turner? Was this love she felt for him the kind which would last, upon which she could base the sort of happiness which Irma had predicted, with marriage and three children? Harriet very much doubted it, but was that even what she wanted?

Every week, without fail, she would ring the salon and leave a message for Nan, even if Joyce was always frosty with her on the phone.

'I'm not your message boy, why don't you just write to her?'

'I do write to her, as often as I can, but since you've got a telephone why shouldn't I ring and ask how Nan is? Just give her my love, that's all.'

'Fine,' Joyce would snap, followed by a sharp click as the receiver clattered down. Not once did she ever ask Harriet how *she* was, if she was well, or if she was thinking of coming over.

It was as if those years of bringing her up had never existed, as if her own mother – *stepmother* – didn't care if she lived or died.

As they entered a new decade January too was busy with the band playing at many parties left over from the New Year. Now it was February and they were enjoying a well-earned break, sitting on their bed while Vinny sang to her.

> *Never knew what I missed till I kissed ya', uh huh.*
> *I kissed ya', oh yeah . . .*

Harriet let him sing the Everly Brothers number all the way through to the end before rewarding him with the kiss he clearly wanted. He was in one of his soft, caring, benevolent moods this evening, and she meant to take advantage of it to try to get to know a bit more about him. Maybe then she'd be better able to judge whether these well-wishers were right and her future with Vinny was doomed from the start.

'When did you first start playing the guitar?' Harriet asked as she sat beside him, arms wrapped about her knees, content to watch as he strummed on his precious instrument.

'You don't want to hear all of that rubbish.'

'I do. I want to know all about you. You've told me about your parents, your background, so tell me about your music.'

He smiled at her, that enigmatic, sensual smile that set her heart racing. 'You ask too many questions, Harriet.'

'Only when I like someone.'

He considered her, eyebrows raised in mock disbelief, a cynical twist to his mouth which sent a shiver right down to her toes. 'Don't get to like me, babe, I'm not the likeable sort.'

'I beg to disagree.'

He rolled his eyes. 'God, don't go all needy on me. The last thing I want is a needy woman, or commitment or responsibility of any sort.'

Harriet looked down, avoiding his gaze for a moment as she strove not to show any reaction to this stark comment. A nagging worry had recently crept into the back of her mind, which, if it turned out to be true, would mean responsibility of the kind even she hadn't bargained for, although perhaps she should have. Maybe it was one of the obstacles Irma had warned her of.

Usually she was so regular, and marking the dates off in her pocket diary was merely a matter of form. Now she was late, by only three days, admittedly, but it had never happened before. Harriet couldn't believe it had happened now, not to her. They'd been careful to use johnnies, so what had gone wrong? Had Vinny slipped up one night when he was far gone on the drink or the pot he smoked? Maybe she should have gone for some of those new birth-control pills Shelley kept mentioning to her.

If it was true and she was indeed pregnant, then she didn't know what she'd do. Joyce would call her a slut, saying it proved she had bad blood in her veins, and Winnie Holmes would spread the gossip all round the market. She'd really be a pariah then. Harriet tried to pretend that she didn't care if people talked about her, but deep down her sensitive soul cared very much.

He'd have to marry her; she couldn't manage on her own. A baby might curtail this great desire they both had for freedom, but that's life, Harriet thought. They'd be a family then, able to take care of each other. She felt a warm glow inside at the prospect.

But she was getting a bit ahead of herself here. Three days overdue didn't mean a thing. It could simply be a false alarm, so no need to mention it just yet. Harriet smiled brightly at Vinny, giving no indication of her innermost thoughts. What was it they'd been talking about? Oh, yes, she'd been asking him about his guitar. She did so love to have him all to herself, talking to her as an intelligent person.

'Did your mother teach you to play?'

He laughed. 'She taught me to love music. I'll say one good thing for my ma, she could sing like a canary as well as look like one. She'd come home from that munitions factory exhausted, rush into the house, change and dash straight out again, off to some pub or other to sing her heart out for a few more bob. Course, the silly mare never got home till the early hours so I'm sure there was a great deal more involved than singing.'

'What a thing to say about your own mother!' Harriet said, shocked.

'If you're looking for a perfect world, don't hang around with me. Don't know why you *are* hanging around, anyway, good-looking chick like you from a decent home.'

'Decent home? You have to be joking. Go on, you were telling me about your music.'

Vinny carried on strumming his guitar for a while, saying nothing. Harriet was the only one who ever asked him to talk about himself. He liked that in her. 'It all started one night when I went looking for her. Probably because she'd forgotten to leave us anything to eat, yet again.'

After another silence, Harriet prompted him to continue. 'Did you find her?'

'Sure, in some pub or other, and she was all contrite, morti-fied to think she'd left us penniless with not so much as a crust of bread in the place. Our Sal was little more than a toddler at the time. Mam dashes off to find us some money, and is gone ages. When she comes back I'm tinkling on the piano keys and not making too bad a job of it. The customers are egging me on, paying me with lemonade and crisps, and I'm lapping it up. After that she did find time to give me a few lessons. The pub land-lord let her borrow the piano occasionally when the pub was closed.'

'And then she bought you a guitar?'

Vinny shook his head. 'Naw, but it was Mam what taught me my scales, and, as I say, to love music. I didn't actually get me hands on a guitar till after she was dead and we were in the orphanage. There was this teacher, a po-faced, hard-hearted old git with glasses and a beard. He found me playing "How Much Is That Doggy in the Window" on the school piano one day, so he began to take an interest. He had other interests in me too, but we won't go into those, eh? Whatever I had to put up with was worth it.'

'I'm not sure what you mean . . .' Harriet interrupted.

'Let's just say his wasn't the first pink appendage I'd seen waved about, or been obliged to avoid. I managed to confine him to the odd feel.'

Harriet's eyes widened with shock. 'You can't be serious. Oh, that's dreadful.'

'No, lovey, that's real life. Where've you been living all these years, under a cabbage leaf? Anyway, in return I persuaded him to buy me my first guitar and he taught me the chords. D-seven was the first one I learned, I seem to remember, then the rest, one by one. It was slow going, hard on the fingers.' He held out his hands to show her. 'They've never been without calluses since. But I stuck with it and learnt to play the damn thing in the end. It made me feel good to be able to play the piano, and the guitar. I was no longer a dead-leg, I had a skill at my fingertips, literally. One that might make my fortune one day, eh, you never know.' He grinned at her, then leaned over to kiss her full on the mouth.

'You deserve to do well. I think you're wonderful!' she murmured, moving into his arms.

'You're not too bad yerself.'

Pushing her down on the bed he stroked and caressed her, touched and explored her body which he'd come to know almost as well as his own. He teased her with his fingers, with his tongue, till she was gasping and begging him to love her, and finally, exhausted from their love making, they fell asleep in each other's arms.

When morning came the first thing he did was reach for her again. She was all sleepy and warm and instantly wound her arms about his neck, eager for more loving. Vinny liked that in her too, that eagerness to please.

Harriet simply loved him all the more, no thought now in her head of leaving him.

★

The Scrapyard Kids were beginning to do really well. They played at hotels and clubs, church halls and ballrooms all over Manchester, including Belle Vue and the Locarno. They played in the interval at the Classic Cinema on Oxford Road, and even at the Ritz on pancake night, which was hilarious with the girls tossing pancakes then feeding them as fast as possible to their man. They were making more money than some professional bands.

Unfortunately, despite Harriet striving to encourage restraint, the lads were spending the money as fast as it came in. Several of them bought cars, and smart new suits. It never occurred to them to save, or rent a place of their own, or cook a meal. They simply stayed at better hotels, ate out every night, and spent the remainder on drinking in bars and idling away hours on end in snooker clubs and taking girls out. It was a hedonistic sort of lifestyle, with no thought of tomorrow, which was worrying.

Nevertheless, she was content to be here with Vinny and the others. It was fun, exciting, and every day was different. Life was never dull. Even if they hadn't hit the big time, they were a success in their own way, and Vinny remained convinced that one day some record producer would walk in and catch their act. Then their fortunes would truly be made. The other lads would laugh at his dreams, content simply to have a bit of money in their pockets.

Most of the time they all got on well and everything went smoothly, although there was occasional friction between Vinny and Al, the drummer. Vinny seemed to hate it if anyone got more attention than he, or if Al's drum solo went on for longer than he liked. He'd suddenly leap in front of him and start banging on his guitar, stopping the solo in mid-flow.

Mostly Al would be fairly philosophical about this attitude, but one night Vinny allowed him even less time than usual. Al had scarcely got started before Vinny stepped forward and brought the guitars back in far too soon. It was evident Al was annoyed. Later, after a drink or two, the pair of them had a real set-to, in which Vinny got so furious he accused Al of deliberately trying to undermine his authority. Al argued vehemently that he was doing nothing of the kind, that Vinny wasn't some star who could hog all the limelight.

At this Vinny flew into a rage and smashed his guitar on a bar stool, swearing never to play the damn thing again.

He sulked for days after that. Eventually though, he went out and bought himself another guitar, but he wasn't happy. Vinny had loved that old instrument, had had it for years, and blamed Al entirely for the loss of it. At the very next gig he made it clear before they even went on that he was the one in charge of the band and the drum solo would end when he said so.

But Al still wasn't having it. 'You don't interrupt till I'm good and ready, that was our deal, if you remember. I get one full minute, nothing less.'

'You'll get thirty seconds, if you're lucky.'

'Perhaps you'd prefer to find yourself another drummer then?' Al taunted him.

'Good idea. You're sacked.'

Harriet instantly stepped in to calm frayed tempers. 'Vinny, you can't do this, not right now. This isn't the moment to settle this quarrel, not with an audience waiting. Listen to them, they're getting impatient, doing the slow hand clap. Sort this out later, for goodness' sake, and get on that stage. *Now!*'

'Why does everyone think they can tell me what to do?' Vinny yelled, and stormed out of the hall. The band did not go on that night, and the following morning Al packed his bags and left.

'You'd be wise to leave too,' he warned Harriet. 'He's falling apart. I know the band is doing well and Vinny is on a high, but it won't last. He'll go all the way down, right to the bottom.'

'Not if his friends stand by him, he won't,' Harriet stubbornly retorted.

25

It took them over a month to find another drummer, missing several gigs in the meantime, and even when they found one he wasn't half as good as Al. The row between the two friends, united in their passion for music, had distressed Harriet as it was so unnecessary.

It had been Al who'd encouraged the band to widen their repertoire and try a few different numbers such as 'La Bamba', a Ritchie Valens number, 'Bongo Rock', and 'Everybody Likes to Cha Cha Cha', a dance craze that was doing the rounds. It boosted their popularity ratings enormously.

In her heart of hearts, Harriet realised that she was in more trouble than she cared to admit. Even if the band was no longer sleeping rough, or living in poverty, she was on the fringes of a world she neither understood nor fitted into. She'd lost her innocence, her naivety. She recognised the funny cigarettes for marijuana now, and it was clear that Vinny was becoming increasingly unpredictable, and so volatile she worried for his health.

He seemed to have boundless enthusiasm and energy, high on something or other. Sometimes he would be completely out of control, leaping about and pounding on the strings of his guitar, screaming instructions to everyone, urging them to greater heights of creativity, refusing to stop practising even when everyone else was exhausted. On other occasions he'd have no energy at all. He'd retreat to his bed and refuse to speak to anyone for days, apparently swamped in deep depression. At those times it was impossible to please him or do anything right.

Harriet was growing more and more certain that he had a serious problem, that the pot he smoked was doing him no good at all, and that maybe he was involved with other drugs too.

Harriet put the question to him one evening and could see at once that she'd made a bad mistake. They'd been sitting in bed together, in some overpriced hotel near Piccadilly Gardens having just made love, and she'd thought this a good moment to make her plea. Instead, he glared coldly at her.

'You stupid bitch! You think that's what this is all about, drugs? In any case, what business is it of yours what I do?'

Harriet was appalled by his reaction, seeing it as interference. 'I – I'm just concerned for you.'

He seemed to speak through gritted teeth as his jaw tightened, green-gold eyes flashing fire. 'That's all you imagine trash like me is fit for, is it? I'm just some no-good Irish lad who spent his youth in institutions, so I must be a drug addict, or evil in some way? You don't think that maybe I'm in the music business simply because I enjoy it, might even have a modicum of talent?'

Harriet was mortified, never having realised he could be so touchy. Vinny clearly carried a great big chip on his shoulders over his difficult background, and she'd just made matters worse. She stroked his arm, trying to pacify him. 'Look, I apologise. I shouldn't have said anything. I'm sorry, I really am. Forget I asked.'

Pushing her roughly away, he taunted her. 'Naw, come on, get it off your chest, why don't you? There must be a reason why you asked. Is it because I'm not good enough for you, Miss Goody-Two-Shoes?'

Something inside Harriet snapped at his sarcasm, reminding her as it did of Joyce. 'Don't be ridiculous, but OK, I'll be honest. I hate you smoking that weed. I don't think it's doing you any good at all and I want you to stop.'

He looked at her askance. '*You* want *me* to stop?'

'Yes!'

'And why in hell should *I* do what *you* say?'

'Because I ask you to.'

He put back his head and roared with laughter. 'You're a real treasure, you know that, babe? You ought to put yourself up for sainthood.'

Harriet said no more, simply flounced away from him and curled up at the far side of the bed, swamped in misery.

Before morning he'd apologised for 'his callousness', pulled her to him and made love to her so passionately, so sweetly, that for the first time Harriet admitted to herself the dangerous path she trod. She realised it was far too late now to deny she had feelings for him, or pretend their relationship was simply physical. She was mesmerised by him, addicted to Vinny as much as he was to that weed. And she still hadn't told him about her condition.

'Don't I just love it when you heckle and fuss over me,' he said, purring softly into her neck, licking her throat with his tongue, nibbling her ear, pretending she was his pet kitten and he wanted to stroke her.

'So will you do as I ask?' Harriet risked repeating the question, certain he must love her a little, deep down, or he wouldn't have apologised for his bad behaviour, would he?

Vinny looked at her blank eyed, shaking his head in a bemused fashion as he adopted his most Irish accent with not a trace of Manchester in it. 'Sure and I haven't the first idea what it is yer wanting me to do? Aren't I the picture of innocence already?'

He indeed looked so innocent in that moment, Harriet couldn't help but giggle. 'All right, I give up, but please try to cut down. Will you do that for me, at least?'

By way of an answer he sat up in bed and lit up another spliff, grinning cheekily at her as he did so.

Harriet took this as a warning to keep her nose out of his private life.

There were times when Vinny wondered why he bothered with her when there were any number of adoring fans around eager to enjoy his attention. Harriet was pretty enough with that heart-shaped face and bouncy bob of blond hair which curled under her pointed chin, and those solemn, slate-grey eyes looking so adoringly up at him. But she came from a different world.

For all her parents might not have been happily married, her father had clearly adored her, as had her grandmother. And although Champion Street might not be a well-off neighbour-hood, some of the houses falling apart at the seams, and the bit where Vinny lived behind the new fish market should have been condemned back in the dark ages, nevertheless, nobody could deny its innate decency. It was a tight-knit community in which people cared about each other. Harriet might tactfully never say as much, but Vinny was all too aware that she had a completely different set of morals from his own.

Yet perhaps it was because of these differences that he found her so enchanting. He liked having her around. She was brave and intelligent, determined and strong, hard working and uncom-plaining, although he didn't find her easy to understand. Harriet Ashton was different from all the other girls who fawned upon him, always managing to keep a part of herself private. She repre-sented a challenge, one he couldn't resist.

Most of all she was warm and loving, always willing to listen to him talk and sympathise with his problems. He needed her, liked her fussing and caring for him like some sort of mother hen, and in one respect at least he knew her intimately. He knew how she liked to be touched, how to tease and provoke her till she was begging for him to take her. She was so giving, so loving, that sex with Harriet was never dull.

They couldn't get enough of each other. He only had to touch her, to kiss her, as he was doing now, pulling open her blouse and suckling each nipple of her pert, firm breasts before she moaned in ecstasy, unable to resist, desperate for more. He was always on a high after a successful gig, he thought, as he pushed her, unprotesting, down on the grubby floor of the pub's back office which was serving as a dressing room.

'Someone might walk in,' Harriet gasped, in a futile attempt to be sensible.

'Let them,' he cried, reaching under her skirt to remove her panties. Then he was rubbing himself against her, pushing himself inside, filling her with his love as they both moved instinctively together, savouring their pleasure in each other.

The door opened and Duffy and the rest walked in. Harriet leapt to her feet, embarrassed, tucking her blouse into her skirt, snatching up discarded clothing, feeling a burning shame in her cheeks as she searched for her shoes.

Vinny just put back his head and roared with laughter. 'Right on cue, lads, as always,' he said. Turning to Harriet, he kissed her on the nose. 'Go back to the hotel, there's a good girl.'

She was disappointed. 'Aren't you coming?'

'I'll see you later, right?'

For all he enjoyed that vulnerability and need in her, perversely there were times when it cramped his style somewhat to know that wherever he went, whatever he did, she would be waiting for him back at the hotel. She wasn't, after all, the only girl in the world. And once he hit the big time, when he got the call from London, he'd move on, and this little dalliance with Harriet Ashton would simply be a fond memory. Freedom, that was the name of the game.

The next morning, feeling guilty over his apparent neglect, since he hadn't climbed into her bed until past five in the morning, Vinny suggested they take a day off and have some fun. 'Why don't we go to the Speedway at Belle Vue? Or would you prefer the Water Chute? How about that? We're getting far too wrapped up in problems.'

Harriet smiled at him, as if he were a small boy she had to humour. Vinny might be a rogue, but he was fun. 'Can we go out to play tomorrow instead? Today, there's something far more important we need to talk about.'

He pretended to sulk. 'What? What can be more important than a day out with me?'

'I'm pregnant.'

He stared at her for a long moment as if he hadn't quite understood, and then his face lit up. 'You're having a baby? Are you serious?'

She nodded. 'I'm afraid so.'

To Harriet's utter astonishment he wrapped his arms about her and hugged her tight, raining kisses all over her face. 'Aw, now isn't that lovely? Don't I just love kids? The more the merrier my ma used to say. And I could teach him to play the guitar, assuming he's a boy of course.'

Harriet laughed with relief. She couldn't believe how well he was taking it. It was astonishing. She'd expected shock, denial, even anger or resentment. Never for a moment had she anticipated this open-hearted joy. She could have cried with happiness, realising how tense she'd become over the last few weeks. 'So today we need to start making plans.'

He kissed her delightful snub nose. 'What sort of plans?'

'For the baby. For us.'

'We'll call him Dylan. Didn't I always want a son called Dylan? That's a good Irish name, to be sure.'

'You can call him whatever you like,' Harriet told him fondly, quite light headed with relief. 'The point is, I'm still under age, so we'll have to get Joyce's permission before we can marry. Even though she's no longer my real mother, I suppose she's still my legal guardian, or whatever they call it. I don't expect her to object. She'll be only too pleased to be rid of the responsibility.'

'Responsibility? Hey, I don't do all that stuff. I put you in charge of responsibility.'

Harriet tweaked his nose. 'Of course I am. Don't worry, you can leave everything safely in my hands. She's *my* mother – er, stepmother, after all, so I'll go and talk to her, shall I? Get her to sign the forms.'

'Forms?'

Harriet felt her cheeks grow warm before his enquiring gaze. 'Well . . . I picked them up from the Register Office the other day. It's OK, I'm not expecting you to go down on bended knee and propose, or anything vaguely romantic like that, but I thought I'd save you the trouble since you're so busy with the band. I just need to get Joyce to sign them, then we can have a quick and easy little ceremony. No fuss, no bother.'

'What I want is a quick and easy bit of the other,' he said, pulling her into his arms, kissing her with a thoroughness that excited her as it seemed to be proof of his love. 'That's enough talk about responsibility, let's celebrate our baby.'

Vinny wanted her, and her child, so what else mattered?

He'd surprised her by his warm response, but then he was ever unpredictable. He always seemed so different when they were making love, as if his thoughts were only for her, his edginess quite dissolved. He stopped being cynical and sarcastic and became sweetly loving. Just the sensual way he kissed her caused Harriet to believe that, deep down, he cared for her very much indeed, for all he might pretend otherwise.

She loved the hard pressure of his mouth, the curl of his tongue against hers and the feather-light touch of his fingers as they slid over her upper thighs to that secret part of her.

'Let's make music,' he murmured, in that teasing way of his.

'Oh, yes please, don't ever stop,' she begged, groaning with delight as shafts of pleasure rippled through her.

'I wouldn't dream of it,' he murmured, drawing off the sexy black lace nightdress he'd bought for her so he could kiss and suckle her nipples. 'I'm going all the way, sweetie, right to the top.'

Harriet giggled, knowing he was referring to his career, but also hoping that he was secretly telling her that he'd take her with him all the way too.

She climbed astride him, pushing herself on to him, moving slowly at first, revelling in her power. Then he rolled her over, pulled her beneath him and brought her to such a height of passion, Harriet didn't care what happened to her, as she fell once more under his spell.

Moments later, instead of falling asleep as he was inclined to do after one of their love-making sessions, he leapt from the bed and began pulling on jeans and a sweater. His back was turned towards her as Harriet chattered on about the sort of dress she might wear for the wedding, too busy making plans to notice his slight withdrawal.

'We might have a bit of a bash afterwards, what do you think? Nothing too expensive, and we can think about serious stuff like babies and houses later.'

Vinny picked up his guitar as he glanced at her, his expression quite blank. 'You know I don't care for serious, babe. Why do we have to be *serious?*'

'It's what grown-ups do, Vinny.'

'That's OK then. You be the grown-up. I'm not, nor ever intend to be. You do what you like, babe. I'm off to the Belle Vue Speedway with the lads.'

'Vinny . . .' but he'd gone, guitar in hand.

Harriet shook her head in fond despair. What a child he was, but at least he'd taken the news so much better than she'd expected. All she had to do now was speak to Joyce.

26

Joyce

'By heck, it must be a day for bad pennies turning up.'

Harriet had chosen lunch-time to call, knowing the salon would be closed for an hour, thereby avoiding an audience to their conversation.

She'd wasted no time strolling round the market, much as she might have wished to catch up with old friends. Champion Street looked much the same as ever on this cold March day, grubby awnings flapping in a chill wind; pinched-faced customers arguing over the price of fish. The steaming, appetising aroma of Benny's hot potato cart wafted tantalising across to her. She'd maybe buy one later, when she was done.

A small child was having a tantrum because his mother refused to buy him a plastic windmill that whizzed round when you blew on it. Harriet felt a warm glow inside to think she'd soon be a mum too, with a small child of her own. Oh, and wouldn't she give it all the love her own so-called mother had always denied her?

She arrived at the salon just as Joyce was dropping the latch on the front door, judging her moment perfectly in case she should decide to go off and have dinner with Joe in Belle's café. Her greeting, if that's what you could call it, was as cold and unwelcoming as ever.

'Is that what I am then, a bad penny? Well, it's good to see you too, Joyce. You don't mind if I call you that, so that we're both clear where we stand. And don't fret, I haven't come home for good. I won't take up more than a moment of your time.'

'You'd best come in then afore Winnie sees you and comes dashing over, ear-lugs flapping.'

Joyce didn't take her upstairs, or offer any sort of refreshment. She swivelled a hair dryer out of the way and indicated Harriet should sit on one of the salon chairs.

Harriet looked round. 'Where's Nan? I'd like to see her while I'm here.'

'She's off out gallivanting with Irma Southworth. She might not be back till this evening.'

Harriet felt a burst of disappointment. What bad luck! She'd been so looking forward to seeing her grandmother. But this had been a rather spur-of-the-moment decision, not quite knowing when she'd find the courage to tell Vinny about the baby, so she hadn't mentioned in her latest letter that she might pop over.

'Not having her cards read again, is she? Are you sure she won't be back before this evening, or I could go over to Irma's and . . .'

'I've told you, they're both out for the day, so it's not worth your while waiting.'

Irma had taken Rose to the doctor, but not for the world did Joyce intend to tell Harriet that. Like it or not Irma was having some success with her regime of exercises, which meant that Rose was on the mend. She might soon be free of that blasted wheelchair and the last thing Joyce wanted was to have Stan's daughter back home, fussing over her precious nan and reminding her of how she'd messed up her life. She'd quite changed her mind on that score.

'I haven't got all day so say whatever you've come to say, and get it over with. If it's money you're wanting . . .'

'No, I don't want your money. Have you seen Steve recently?' Harriet asked, again putting off the evil moment. She hadn't seen Steve in weeks, not since the night he'd brought her to visit Nan, and that was before Christmas. Maybe he'd got the message at last to leave her alone. Even so, she thought about him a great deal and wanted to know that he was well.

'He's doing well at that college I believe, according to the weekly bulletins issued by that snobby mother of his.'

'Does he ever ask about me?'

Joyce was thinking of her dinner going cold upstairs and impatiently shook her head. She stood ramrod-straight, arms folded, making it all too clear she was not in the mood for casual conversation.

She looked thinner than ever, Harriet thought. Her hair seemed darker, almost black, and the plucked eyebrows more finely drawn, the mouth tighter and deeply puckered.

'Well, the fact is . . .' Harriet took a breath '. . . I'm getting married.'

Joyce stared at her without comprehension for a moment. 'Married? But you're only . . . oh, my God! You're pregnant!' Anger flooded through her, clouding her vision, and her heart started to thump. Joyce could see Harreit's mouth moving, knew she was still talking but the sound of the girl's voice became a roaring in her ears.

All these years of carefully nurturing an aura of respectability seemed to come crashing down around her. She'd dragged herself up from the pits of Ancoats despite the shame of a dustman for a father, overcome a rape with no help from anyone, a straying husband and having this cuckoo child foisted upon her, to building herself a fine, respectable business. She was respected on this market, everyone came to Joyce's to have their hair done. And not a word of scandal had ever crept out in all the years she'd been here. Now this little madam, this trollop, had brought shame upon them all.

Joyce could feel herself trembling with rage, was having difficulty keeping her hand from slapping the little slattern, and her voice shook as she finally found her voice. 'Why am I not surprised? I allus said there was bad blood in you, girl. Like mother, like daughter.'

'Are you going to tell me who she is – or rather was – this mother of mine?'

'What the hangment does it matter now, after all this time?

She was a nobody, a bit of skirt or fluff Stan picked up. A slut, exactly like you.'

Harriet bristled, inwardly chiding herself to remain calm. 'I'm not going to enter into a slanging match with you, Joyce. I just brought these.' Handing over the forms she briefly explained how, as her guardian, her stepmother's signature was necessary since she was still under age. Joyce snatched up the pen and signed in a fury, without blinking, without even asking his name.

'Thank God he's prepared to marry you. Make sure it's quick. How far gone are you?'

'Not even three months yet. Don't you want to know who I'm marrying?'

Joyce's upper lip curled. 'If it's that Vinny Turner, you'll rue the day. He'll bring you nowt but misery, which pleases me greatly. Why should *you* be happy? I never was, with your flamin' father.'

Harriet got up, anxious now to be gone. She'd considered calling on a few friends, once this difficult interview was over, but now she just longed to dash back to Vinny.

'Tell Nan I'm sorry to have missed her this time, but I'll call again soon. And I'll bring my husband with me.' Then she walked out without a backward glance.

Joyce slammed the door after her, marched upstairs and picked up her mug of cold tea, then flung it in the sink where it smashed into a dozen pieces.

Harriet had hardly turned the corner of Champion Street when there was another knock on the salon door. Joyce, in no mood to be interrupted yet again, stamped down the stairs and flung it open.

'Yes?' she snapped, to her surprise finding Steve Blackstock kicking his heels on the doorstep, looking all hangdog with his hands in his pockets. 'Flaming 'arry, what a morning I'm having. I thought you were away at college?'

'I'm home for the weekend, so I thought I'd just pop over.'

'What for this time?' Joyce groaned. 'You're never away.'

'I was wondering if you'd heard anything of Harriet lately?'

Steve asked, as politely as he could manage. He didn't much care for Joyce, but despite Harriet's earnest pleadings that he forget about her, he simply wasn't capable of doing so. He'd kept away for as long as he could, but some instinct, some need in him, always brought him back here in the end.

'If you've got an address I'd like to know what it is, so's I can write to her. Just to keep in touch, since we're such old friends.'

'I haven't the first idea where she lives. I should think, since she's with that Vinny Turner, she's barely in one place long enough to wash her socks,' Joyce snapped. 'Anyroad, you've just missed her.'

Steve looked aghast. 'Missed her, why, has she been here?'

Joyce glanced up the street, as if she half expected to see Harriet still walking along it. Steve did the same. 'She was here just now . . . only just this minute gone.'

'Did she ask after me?'

Joyce frowned. 'I'm not sure, er, yes, I think she did enquire as to how you were. I told her you were doing well at that college, or at least so your mam says whenever she comes in to have her hair done.'

Steve was edging away from the door, lifting himself on to the balls of his feet, as if about to run. 'How long has she been gone? Do you reckon I might catch up with her if I hurry? Which way did she go?'

'I've no idea. Anyroad, don't waste your time, lad, she isn't interested in you any more. You're history. She brought some forms for me to sign, to give her permission to marry her lover-boy.' Joyce was itching to shut the door, to go back upstairs and pour herself a rum and coke. She needed one to help her cope with the shame Harriet was about to inflict upon her.

'Marry?' Steve froze, his face going rigid with shock.

'Aye, that Vinny Turner is her intended now, so go back to your nice college, lad, and find yourself another girl.'

The leftover stew was tasteless and almost cold by the time Joyce finally got round to eating it. She could strangle the girl, she could really. Why did she always have to ruin things? Why was her life so blighted by the faults of others? Joyce attached no blame to herself. Why should she? Hadn't she taken the lass in as her own when most betrayed wives would have flung both husband and by-blow on to the muck heap? But what good had it done? She was a fool to herself, that was her trouble.

And she'd been so looking forward to this day on her own, without Irma constantly under her feet, or her mother demanding this, that or the other. Or ringing that flaming bell Irma had provided her with, for the times when she herself wasn't at her patient's side ready and willing to do her every bidding.

Joyce was heartily sick of the pair of them.

Following her appointment with the doctor, Irma was taking Rose out to lunch at the Midland Hotel for a treat. As if she deserved one, Joyce thought in disgust. Her mother hadn't done a lick of work in weeks, just lay in bed all day being waited on. What right had she to a lunch out while Joyce was still slaving away with no thanks from anyone?

She didn't even have time for five minutes with the *Daily Express* as she usually did. There wasn't a moment in this awful day to relax before she was back downstairs in the salon, shampooing Helen Catlow's hair.

'Just a little trim, is it?' Joyce asked her customer in the practised, professional tones which skilfully disguised her ill temper. She found that she needed to breathe slowly and deeply, to calm herself. 'Going somewhere nice this evening, are we?'

'I'm having dinner at the Shackletons', such lovely people. John is hoping to be our next MP,' the other woman bragged.

Joyce mentally switched off as the boring catalogue of engagements continued, as if life was most wearisome for someone such as herself with a busy social life. As she shampooed and rinsed, slapped on conditioner and rubbed Helen Catlow's scalp with more vigour than was quite necessary, Joyce furiously mulled over her own problems in a welter of self-pity.

She'd believed herself to be free at last, having kicked the hussy out. Now the stupid girl had robbed her of what little peace and respectability she had left in her life. Nothing seemed to go right for her these days.

By the time Joyce was combing out the tangles of wet hair, Helen Catlow had changed tack and was now into a litany of complaints about her husband, who was apparently seeing rather a lot of Judy Beckett.

'Not content with stealing my husband, that Beckett woman has the bare-faced cheek to return to the market and open up her cheap-jack little art stall again. She's selling her silly little paintings as if she's some sort of renowned artist.'

'I heard she was doing rather well, actually,' Joyce said. 'Anyway, I thought you and Leo were getting divorced?'

'We are, but that's no excuse, is it?'

Joyce mumbled some non-committal response to this, since everyone knew that Leo Catlow had stuck faithfully to his wife despite her own rampant infidelity, long after any other man would have strangled the woman. Besides, as Joyce herself was likewise embroiled in an extra-marital affair with the ever-indolent Joe, what right did she have to criticise?

Why was Joe obstinately resisting any attempt to move in with her, even though Irma was back in her own bed? He still seemed keen enough on the bedroom front, so what was the attraction in staying with his wife? Irma wasn't exactly a pin-up. No Marilyn Monroe, that was for sure.

Joyce had rather hoped to persuade him to pop over at some point today, as she'd seen very little of him lately. But of course with Irma out with Rose, Joe was tied to the biscuit stall. It was all most frustrating.

As she towel-dried her client's hair, Joyce couldn't resist one cheeky question. 'And what's Sam Beckett doing these days? I used to see him regular in the Dog and Duck, but haven't clapped eyes on him for weeks.'

Helen's coral lips tightened slightly, her porcelain complexion taking on the faintest flush of pink. 'He's left the market, I believe. There was a time when I used to see quite a lot of him myself.'

I know you did, Joyce thought, generally in his back office with the closed notice on the door. It had been the talk of the market for months that Sam had been Helen's lover, and an absolute brute to Judy, his lovely wife. 'So that's why his little ironmonger's shop is all boarded up and empty?' she innocently enquired.

'Apparently so. He accepted an offer from the developers he couldn't afford to turn down, and he's gone. Planning to emigrate to Canada, or so I'm told.'

'Dear me, that won't go down well with the other stallholders. My mother, for one, will go light. Just as well he's leaving the country before she gets hold of him. They still hang traitors from trees round here. Good riddance though, is what I say.'

'Yes, indeed,' Helen agreed, with characteristic coldness in her tone. 'My sentiment entirely.'

But as Joyce applied the razor to Helen's fine blond hair, cropping it fashionably short with a feathery fringe over her forehead, her mind returned to her own recent visitors, to Harriet and to young Steve.

She could see the lad had been pole-axed by the news, though at least she'd spared him the reason for the hasty nuptials.

Joyce had never believed that particular relationship would amount to anything, not with that snobby mother of his. Nevertheless, she felt some sympathy for the lad as she could still remember what it felt like to be in love, and to feel hurt by a loved one's betrayal. Shame and humiliation were only a part of it.

Back in 1940 at the start of what appeared to be the shortest marriage in the history of the universe, Joyce had been riddled with guilt. She knew in her heart that she should have told Stan the truth from the start. And she should never have let him talk her into going out with him again after she'd sent him that Dear John letter calling it all off. How stupid she'd been! It was true what he'd said, she had tricked him. But the prospect of a respectable marriage, particularly to Stan Ashton with whom she was already madly in love, had been too tempting to resist.

It was as if her entire life had fallen apart, as if she'd failed in some way, that it was all her own fault. Joyce hated that feeling more than anything.

In the end she'd convinced herself that Stan was the one really to blame. From the day he'd realised Grant wasn't his child, their relationship had gone from bad to worse. He could have accepted the boy as his son, if he'd loved her enough. Just because she hadn't told him the truth at the time of their marriage was no fault of the child's. But Stan was far too selfish to overlook her lies, seeking any excuse to play the field. That much was obvious, Joyce thought, appeasing her conscience.

He'd hurt her precious son badly, so was it any wonder if now she hurt his child?

27

Harriet

They were in Seedley Park Science Museum of all places, looking at the stuffed animals and birds in cases, at the birds' eggs, rocks and minerals, and other exhibits. There was even an elephant, a small one admittedly, and close by it a tiny mouse in a glass case. Harriet felt like that mouse, stuffed and stiff, trapped behind a glass wall she couldn't penetrate, and Vinny was the huge elephant, blundering through life doing exactly as he pleased, irrespective of all those around him.

He pulled one of his vile cigarettes from his pocket and lit up. Harriet was instantly filled with shame, glancing about her to meet several disapproving glares.

'You can't smoke in here, Vinny. Put it out,' she hissed, fearing the museum curator might appear at any minute and catch him smoking.

'Why?'

'Because you can't!' As so often these days, she felt as if she were speaking to a petulant child. 'Come on, let's go outside. I don't know why you wanted to come here in the first place.'

He would often insist on doing strange things, such as spending the day riding on buses and trams, back and forth through the city, going nowhere in particular. Or he'd count every step, sometimes backwards, as they walked along the towpath. He'd get up in the middle of the night and start scattering sheets of music all over the place, frantically searching for one he couldn't seem to find. He'd lose patience with the lads when they were practising a number and change to another one half way through. He would do this over and over, so that they never reached the end of a song. Then there'd be an almighty row and Vinny would stalk off, refusing to speak to anyone for hours.

Harriet was growing concerned. At first she'd put his odd behaviour down to overwork and insufficient sleep. For weeks now she'd been begging him to see a doctor, insisting he was overdoing it but he point-blank refused. He had, however, agreed to this day out in the park in order to allow himself time to relax, to breathe in some fresh air, and to stop smoking cannabis for a whole day. Now he'd broken this promise and she was in despair.

Vinny, however, thought it all a huge joke, and was chuckling over her fussing and her frown of disapproval.

Afraid to take him to task over the issue in public, as this could provoke him into doing something really wild, like when he climbed on top of the bus shelter the other day, yelling at everyone, Harriet made him sit by the fountain while she went to buy a pot of tea and sandwiches. He hadn't eaten a thing so far today, for all it was Sunday and supposedly a free day in which to enjoy themselves.

Later, after they'd enjoyed their snack, they lay on the grass while he kissed her, long and hard, and she melted inside as he held her close. He could be so gentle, so loving, she really didn't understand why he would sometimes be unpredictable, so difficult at times.

Was it because of his terrible childhood, having been brought up largely in an institution, some dreadful orphanage or other, and then having been abused by one of the teachers? It was not surprising if it had made him deeply insecure and distrustful of everyone. She might complain about her own situation, but surely Vinny's had been worse. Unimaginable. Obviously that sort of thing left its mark.

Deep down the fear was growing that his problem was much more serious. If only she could stop him smoking, just for a week or two, then she could see if his health improved. She needed him to start sleeping and eating better, be less irascible.

'I want to get some practice in later,' he was telling her, as if she was preventing him from working. 'I'm working on a new number, new to me that is: "Stagger Lee", and I must get it right.'

'Of course you do, you've got a gig tonight, remember? I might pop over and see Nan, if you can spare me for an hour or two. I missed her last time.' It didn't surprise Harriet when he shook his head, saying he needed her by his side, as always. He never seemed to let her out of his sight for a minute these days.

Vinny was frowning at her through the hazy smoke of his cigarette, eyes half closed. 'You aren't thinking of leaving me, are you? I missed you when you were away the other day, babe. I kept thinking you might decide not to come back.'

Harriet laughed, instantly warming to his childish anxiety. 'I'm glad you missed me but you've really no need to worry. I couldn't wait to get back to you.'

'You're the only one who understands me, do you see, babe?' he told her, his voice tender. 'And I'm the only one who understands the band, and the music. We make a good team.'

'Of course we do.'

She'd already shown him the forms: the one which Joyce had readily signed, and the licence she'd got from the Register Office, all duly filled in and waiting only for his signature. But it hadn't seemed to penetrate his mind that this meant they could now go ahead with the wedding. Harriet didn't want to be the one to make the arrangements, that should be Vinny's task, surely. So she was patiently waiting for him to offer.

'Why would I want to stay in Champion Street when I have you?'

He tucked a blond curl behind her ear, punctuating his next words by raining little kisses all over her face and throat. 'You might want to go back to that secretarial course, to your precious market, to the hair salon and your nan, even if Joyce isn't your real mother.'

Embarrassed someone might see them kissing, she moved a little away from him. 'Why would I? And aren't we about to be married, so we'll be together always then? It's just that I didn't get to see Nan.' She was kicking herself for not having gone over to Irma's, if only to make sure Joyce was telling the truth. What if Nan had suffered another stroke, or a bad turn, would Joyce even tell her? 'That's why I thought I'd take the bus over there this evening, just for an hour, but I won't if you don't want me to. Or we could go over together, tomorrow if you like? You could visit Hall's Music shop, have a lovely rummage through their huge selection of sheet music.'

Vinny seemed to perk up at this. 'Aw, and isn't that a grand idea? And I could call in and see me little sister, Sal. I'd like that.'

'That's a lovely idea, then you could properly meet Nan, at last.'

The smile instantly faded. 'Aw no, if you get involved with family again, you might change your mind, and decide to stay with them. And what would your lovely nan say about this?' Vinny queried, lightly patting her rounded belly, clearly indicating her pregnancy.

Harriet paled. She'd forgotten for a moment that although Joyce was aware of her condition, it was by no means certain she'd told Nan. The shame of her stepdaughter's condition would have hit Joyce hard, and Harriet was still unmarried.

Vinny lay back on the grass, chuckling to himself, but at least he hadn't lit up another spliff.

Harriet smiled shyly at him, tickling his nose with a daisy. 'Perhaps we'll wait a little longer then, so that the next time I visit my family you can come with me as my husband. Would that be better? More appropriate, don't you think? And you might feel more secure too. Anyway, what are we waiting for? Let's get on with it, shall we? I think you just have to sign this form some-where,' and she handed him a pen.

Ever perverse, Vinny didn't take it from her but abruptly sat up, brushing her aside. 'Are you sure trailing around with the band is a good idea? Particularly now, with a baby coming.'

'Don't be silly, of course it is. I want to be with *you*. What's all this? You've just said you can't bear to be parted from me, now you question why I'm even here? You aren't having doubts, are you?' Oh, she did hope not.

A few seconds passed before Vinny answered, and even then his tone was no longer soft and sexy, but hard and mocking. 'Maybe you already care about this baby more than me.'

'Now you're being silly, it isn't even born yet. Goodness, look at the time. You should be getting ready for the next gig. Where is it tonight? The St Philips Hotel on Oldfield Road, isn't it? We'd best get going.'

Vinny pulled out another cigarette, half talking to himself. 'I don't feel in the mood for making music tonight. I need to be quiet, and alone. I've got things to work out in my head, matters I need to plan.' A note of caution had crept into his voice and Harriet frowned.

'What things? What plans?'

'I've just told you. I've explained. Weren't you listening to anything I said? Why don't you listen?' He was shouting now, causing heads to turn and people to look at him, puzzled.

'You aren't making any sense, Vinny. Come on, love, let's get back. You're going to be late.'

He became angry. 'I've told you, I'm not going to any damn gig. You'll have to ring and cancel.'

Harriet was aghast. 'Oh, no, not again! We've cancelled so many lately. This will ruin us. There are cinemas and pubs closing every week in Salford, any amount of demolition going on with all these new flats and houses being built. We're lucky to get the booking at all. We certainly can't afford to lose it.'

'You'll do as I tell you,' he roared. 'I'm in charge, not you, and I say cancel!' Then he marched back to the hotel in a silent fury, flung himself on to the bed and refused to leave it, or speak another word for the next twenty-four hours.

Harriet was seriously alarmed. Vinny's moods were growing ever more erratic, changing as swiftly as if someone had flicked a switch. It certainly didn't improve in the days and weeks following, even after he'd recovered from his latest sulk and was thumping out tunes with a skill and dexterity that was astonishing, almost as if nothing untoward had occurred. Harriet didn't dare mention how furious the manager of the pub had been when she'd gone round personally to apologise, making the excuse Vinny was ill.

'That's the last booking he gets off me.'

Sadly, this was by no means the last cancellation either in the coming weeks. Even the other band members began to grow concerned, and urged Harriet to do something about it.

'I'm trying, but you know how difficult he can be at times.'

Vinny was in such a strange mood she didn't even try to raise the subject of the marriage licence again, nor suggest going to see her nan. Everything she said was wrong. And she didn't feel well in herself, nauseous for most of the day, not just in the mornings, and lethargic and strangely tearful at the same time. She needed Vinny to take better control of things, to comfort her for a change, but he seemed oblivious to everyone else's troubles. Whenever she attempted to discuss the number of people they'd let down he'd sink into deeper depression, refuse to discuss it, or just shout at her.

His behaviour tonight was typical. When she'd gently pointed out that they were running short of money, he studiously refused to discuss the problem. He just snorted with laughter as if at some private joke, and, as always, lit up another stinking weed.

'You're never satisfied, you. I wonder sometimes why you bother to stick around. A bird like you, all decent and proper and well brought up, a *good* girl, slumming it with a rough sort of guy like me, you must be bored out of your mind. Why not go back to good ole Stevey boy?'

Harriet fleetingly wondered why she didn't. It would be so much less complicated. Vinny was becoming impossible. It was a constant battle to get him to concentrate on anything. He might talk wildly about success, of plans and dreams and things he needed to sort out, but trying to pin down exactly what he was thinking or feeling about anything was quite beyond her. Harriet never quite knew where she was with him.

And he still hadn't got round to signing those blasted forms.

But did she really want him to? Did she want to spend her life trailing after the band with a baby in tow, worrying about what Vinny was up to half the time? Was Irma right when she suggested some man, Vinny himself perhaps, was blocking her happiness? Harriet felt a knot of anxiety rise up from the pit of her stomach, threatening to choke her.

She couldn't think clearly, and was experiencing serious doubts over marrying him. Yet what choice did she have? Joyce had made her opinion on Harriet's situation very clear on her last visit to the salon. She'd felt like a pariah in her own home.

And the very idea of coping alone, of bearing a child who would be forced to go through life with the shameful stigma of illegitimacy attached, exactly as she herself was suffering, was unthinkable. And despite Steve's protestations of loyalty he would never have her back, not with another man's child in her belly. Nobody wanted her. Nobody liked her. She didn't even like herself very much.

Vinny suddenly got to his feet. 'I'm off out.'

'But it's past midnight.'

'So? I like going out at night. I like walking for mile after mile, just looking at the stars, or sitting by the canal playing my guitar. Don't you ever want to do something wild and exciting, something dangerous and thrilling? An adventure.'

Harriet went to him and put her arms about his neck. 'Of course I do. Didn't I choose to do exactly that when I agreed to join you in *this* adventure?' Wanting to please him, she gave him a long, sensual kiss, curling her tongue round his, losing herself in the ecstasy of the moment. As they broke apart she smiled at the wicked twinkle that came into those green-gold eyes. 'Happier now?'

'Oh yes,' he murmured.

'Good.' She drew him back to bed, making him lie down and covering him with the sheet, snuggling in beside him to wrap her arms about him as if he were a child. 'Maybe I too needed a bit of fizz putting into my life, but we've done that, haven't we?' She wanted to go on to say it was time now for them to settle down and be more grown up and sensible, but couldn't quite get the words out.

He was chuckling to himself, as if at some private joke in his head. 'A bit of fizz, that's it exactly. Maybe we should be even more adventurous, what do you think? I'll maybe ask Shelley if she has any suggestions.'

Harriet frowned. 'Why involve Shelley? What's it got to do with her what we do?'

'Shelley can be very inventive. Haven't you noticed?'

Curled in the crook of his arm, intent only on having him make love to her, Harriet wasn't sure where this conversation was leading, but she was mildly concerned. She rolled over on to her back to gaze up at him so that she could more carefully study his expression. Unfortunately, it was perfectly bland, as unreadable as ever, and then his eyelids drooped closed and the next instant he was fast asleep, snoring gently.

Harriet's heart had begun a slow pounding as she thought of all the nights when Vinny wasn't beside her in whatever hotel room they were occupying at the time. She'd always assumed he was with the lads, but what if he wasn't? What if he was with Shelley on all those nights she'd believed him to be innocently strumming his guitar? Oh, lord, she did hope not.

A night or two later, as she helped her friend to get ready for the next gig in the cramped washrooms of some seedy pub, Harriet resolved to ask her straight out. The thought of Shelley and Vinny together had become a nagging worry at the back of her mind.

'Can I ask you a question?'

'Sure, fire away.'

'Are you and Vinny lovers?

Shelley looked startled, and then burst out laughing, as if Harriet had cracked some sort of joke. 'Would it matter if we were?'

Harriet stiffened, could sense herself sounding all disapproving like some sort of maiden aunt. 'It might.'

'I thought you and me were best friends,' Shelley said, briskly brushing out her dark cropped curls till they seemed to stand on end. 'And friends share everything, don't they?'

'Not their men, they don't.'

Shelley stabbed at her lips with a pale pink lipstick. With those huge Bambi eyes, and elfin hair cut, she looked positively frail, more like a child. Yet she was anything but. She only had to start singing, with that throbbing husky voice of hers, and men fell at her feet, shivering with desire. 'Anyway, I thought you weren't in love with Vinny.'

'I'm not!' Even as Harriet issued the hot denial it sounded strangely hollow and unconvincing. Who was she kidding? If she didn't love him, why did she stay? Because he made her feel wanted maybe? Yet it seemed nothing like the love she'd felt for Steve.

Shelley shrugged her shoulders as she began to apply violet-blue eye shadow. 'Well then, if you don't love him, what does it matter who else he might be sleeping with?'

This wasn't at all the response Harriet had hoped for, or expected, and her voice trembled with anger as she answered. 'Maybe because I believe a bloke should be faithful to the girl he's dating, that he should only go out with one person at a time.'

Shelley applied a line of kohl above and below her black spiky lashes, and giggled. 'What a funny, old-fashioned girl you are. You can't have it both ways. You can't claim not to be in love a guy and yet want him all to yourself.'

'Why can't I? That's the decent way of going about things, certainly in my book.'

'Oh, well then, if you say it's the decent thing to do, it must be, mustn't it? You're the one who's an expert on morals.'

Grabbing hold of Shelley's arm Harriet gave the other girl a furious shake. 'This isn't some silly joke that we can all have a good laugh about. This is my life, my *future!*' It crossed her mind to confess about her pregnancy, but at the last moment something held her back, a need for privacy perhaps. 'You leave Vinny alone, right? He's mine.'

Shelley shook her off, instinctively tweaking her fly-away curls and checking her lipstick, as she'd be out there singing before a drunken audience in less than five minutes. 'Making claims on him now, are you? You really are a glutton for punishment. Living on dreams, more like. Trying to turn Vinny Turner into something he isn't and never could be.'

'And what exactly do you mean by that?'

'Nothing, nothing at all.'

'Well, just you remember, Vinny and me are planning a future *together*, so you keep your grasping little mitts off my man. Right?'

'Ooer! I'm shaking in my shoes.'

'Go and chase Duffy instead. He's not choosy about which girls he sleeps with, and leave Vinny alone or you'll have me to deal with.'

Shelley moved away from the mirror, dusting a few traces of powder from the tight shirtwaister dress she was wearing. At the door of the washroom she paused, smiling as she issued her parting words. 'Vinny Turner is great fun, but as for planning a future with him, I'd think again if I were you. However, if you're determined you want him, love, you can have him and welcome. He's all yours, and good luck to you.'

So why, when her erstwhile friend sashayed into the bar lounge to a huge round of cheering and applause, didn't Harriet feel more elated by her victory?

28

Joyce

Having discovered the full facts, Stan obstinately refused to believe Joyce's version of events and deliberately set out to provoke her by flirting with her best friend.

Eileen seemed to think the whole thing hilarious. She took the view that this fledgling marriage was already on the rocks and had no compunction in enjoying Stan's company. He was a good-looking chap, after all, and hugely entertaining. They went everywhere together, to dances, to the cinema, and on long romantic walks by the canal. He even took her to Liverpool to see his ship. Whenever he was home on leave, however little time he might have, he would spend most of it with Eileen rather than with his own wife. Yet she swore to Joyce that's all it was, a close friendship, a flirtation, and not a full-blown affair.

Joyce didn't believe her, of course. She was deeply hurt and very angry over this betrayal by her best friend. It made her feel sick inside just to picture them together. Images of them making love haunted her dreams and stopped her thinking straight during the day. She couldn't concentrate on her work, couldn't bear for her husband to be out of her sight for a moment, the jealousy eating away at her like a canker. Joyce hated herself for being so needy, constantly threatened to leave him, but could never quite bring herself to do so.

'How dare you go off with her! How dare you cheat on me!' she would scream at him, picking up a vase that was handy and throwing it at his head.

Stan became adept at ducking, his burst of laughter failing to brighten the grim set of his face. '*You've* no right to complain. You only married me in order to provide a father for your son, so you've only yourself to blame if it's all gone wrong. What did you imagine? That I'd be so stupid I'd never have the wit to notice, or add up the discrepancy in his age? Eileen and me are having a good time, that's all there is to it, and I reckon I deserve a bit of fun.'

'Bit of fun? You're sleeping with her!'

'I'm not, actually, but what business would it be of yours even if I were? You can hardly claim our marriage to have been made in heaven, can you? You were the one who cheated first, not me.'

'I've told you a thousand times, I was *raped*!'

'So you say, a fact you quite forgot to mention until you discovered the consequences of your betrayal.'

'Once this war is over, you can go hang yourself off the yard-arm,' Joyce yelled, flinging her favourite vase after the first and then bursting into tears when it smashed to smithereens against the wall.

Yet she loved him so much that even as tempers flared and passions grew heated, even in the throes of her rage she would fling herself into his arms, profusely apologising for her lack of honesty and begging for his forgiveness. 'Love me, give *me* a child!'

And perhaps intrigued by her neediness, captivated still by his sexy wife, Stan would laughingly take her to bed and make love to her till she cried out in ecstasy. This sort of behaviour was typical of the blow hot, blow cold nature of their relationship. Joyce loved Stan and hated him in equal proportions, and he felt the same way about her.

To her utter delight Joyce did indeed fall pregnant again, and joyously celebrated, writing to Stan at once to tell him the good news. But no sooner had she posted the letter than she started bleeding and lost the baby. She was devastated.

His reply, when she wrote a second time to tell him what had happened, was to accuse her of lying to him yet again. 'How do I know you weren't just claiming to be pregnant in order to keep me? You probably weren't pregnant at all,' he wrote. 'Or maybe your lover put you in the family way again, and that's why you threw yourself at me.'

'If that's what you think then don't bother coming home again,' she wrote back, in a frenzy of rage.

But of course he always did come home, and they'd row and make love with equal intensity all over again, jealously accusing each other of rampant infidelity. Long before one war ended, another had already begun.

But Joyce had no intention of allowing Stan to win it. She'd force him to love her, make him give her another child, insist that he be a good husband to her, no matter what the cost. Failure didn't bear thinking of, and divorce was quite out of the question. Far too shaming for words.

Fortunately, with Stan being a Catholic, his religion didn't approve of divorce, which was some consolation. If nothing else, Joyce intended to protect her reputation.

Even now, years later, Joyce was still on the same mission, obsessed by her desire to keep her good name unsullied. Keeping her son on the straight and narrow had been difficult enough, and now Harriet had let her down badly. Was any woman more beset with problems than she?

She was backcombing Patsy Bertalone's hair when her son came in, giving Patsy's usually sleek, silver-blond hair some lift on the crown to make it more stylish. Grant was doing a bit of portering for Leo Catlow so at last had a regular income coming in. Since it was Friday, his mother told him to leave his contribution towards the housekeeping on the kitchen table.

Grant mumbled a protest, though not very loud. His mother could be soft as butter with him at times, but never when it came to money. He had to pay his whack; his board, as she called it. Which was a nuisance considering how much it cost him to take part in the nightly card games he and his mates enjoyed playing.

'Have you seen your grandmother by any chance, son?' Joyce

asked, in that mincing way she had of speaking in front of her clients.

Grant shook his head. 'There's a meeting going on at the market hall, so I expect that's where she is. Putting in her four pennyworth.'

Joyce twittered with polite laughter. 'I dare say you're right. What a character she is, my dear mother. Put the kettle on,' she instructed him. Halfway to the stairs Grant pulled a face, which fortunately Joyce didn't see. 'I'm fair gasping. Coffee for you, dear?' she asked of her customer.

Patsy shook her head. 'No thanks, I have to get back to the stall.'

'And will you be accepting the developers' offer, I wonder. Or rather, will Clara Higginson be accepting?'

'I really wouldn't know. You'd have to ask Clara,' Patsy said, carefully guarded. 'Don't overdo the backcombing, Joyce. I often have to model a hat, don't forget, so it's hardly worth it.'

'Yes, but we must keep you in the forefront of fashion, so you can show the hats off at their best,' Joyce demurred, teasing and smoothing and patting till finally even Patsy ran out of patience.

'That's fine, Joyce. And I like the way you've got it to flip up at the ends. It looks lovely, for as long as it lasts.'

'Oh, it'll last,' Joyce assured her, waving a can of hair lacquer about and spraying the new hair style so thoroughly even a force nine gale wouldn't shift it. Patsy paid up and fled, wishing she'd just trimmed it herself, as she usually did.

Grant produced the tea, weak and milky with two sugars, just as his mother liked it. As he made to escape, Joyce said, 'I hope you're not still wasting your time looking for our Harriet?'

He paused, puzzled by this remark. Hadn't Harriet called at the salon a couple of times, and once to see Nan? 'I did catch sight of her one night with that band, if you recall, but that was months ago. Then I lost her again. If you'd wanted to know where she was living, you should've said. I could've followed her after her last visit.'

'No, I don't particularly want you to find her. That's why I'm mentioning it. It's not important now that Mother is on the mend. And I don't want her upset.'

Joyce had said nothing to Rose about Harriet's most recent visit, although Grant was aware that his sister was about to embark upon a shotgun marriage, which hopefully would have taken place by now. Joyce sincerely hoped so, in view of the circumstances. It still filled her with rage to think of the shame that harlot had brought upon them all. Keeping quiet seemed the only solution. She certainly had no intention of spreading the scandal. Joyce had little sympathy for the girl, none whatsoever, in fact. This was nothing like the situation Joyce had found herself in. Harriet hadn't been raped, she'd brought this disgrace upon herself.

'Don't you even want to know what's happened to her?' Grant was asking. 'She's still your stepdaughter, after all. Maybe she's had a hard winter. She could be holed up in some rat-hole somewhere, half starved.'

'Good heavens, what's this? Don't tell me you've developed a conscience all of a sudden. That'd be a first.'

Grant shrugged his broad shoulders. 'Why would I care? You're the one who seems troubled by a conscience, not me.'

Joyce frowned at this enigmatic remark, wondering what exactly he meant by it. 'You've not been pestering folk with more questions, have you?' she snapped.

'No!' Grant shook his head, a picture of innocence. 'Why would I?'

'Why indeed?' Joyce watched her lazy son slouch away, chin thrust forward, shoulders hunched about his thick neck. Was he a blessing or a curse? Much as she loved and adored him, she'd never quite made up her mind.

Alone in his grandmother's room, Grant glanced through the pile of letters from Harriet, as he often did when Nan was out and about around the market, or at one of her committee meetings. He was seeking an address. Harriet wrote regularly every week to her grandmother, even though she hadn't visited the old lady for some time.

Rose kept making excuses for her, saying the poor girl was probably busy helping to organise the band, that her lovely granddaughter would come home just as soon as she could. It was annoying that Joyce still hadn't told Rose that Harriet was pregnant, and had threatened Grant with blue murder if he let that particular cat out of the bag.

'The last thing I need to cope with right now, is for your grandmother to suffer another stroke, so keep them lips buttoned, right?'

'She'll have to know some time,' Grant had objected. He'd rather relished the job of whistle-blower, and he'd love nothing more than to see his prissy half-sister brought down in his grandmother's eyes. It would be justified punishment for always being his nan's favourite.

'You'll say nowt,' Joyce insisted. 'At least, not until Rose is fully recovered. So think on. Keep your gob shut!' His mother could sound so vulgar at times.

Grant picked up the latest envelope, noticing that it was dated nearly three months ago. Frowning, he realised this was strange. The last time she'd written, back in March, shortly after asking Mam to sign some permission forms so she could get wed to that Vinny Turner, Harriet had been adamant that she'd be coming to see Nan any day. Yet not a word since. Shrugging his shoulders, he dropped the letter back on to the pile.

Then he expertly picked the lock of the little jewellery box where Rose hid her pension, with the skill of long practice, and helped himself to a couple of five-pound notes. His need was greater than hers. The old woman had nothing to spend her money on anyway.

No matter what his faults, Joyce adored her son. Because of the way he'd been conceived she hadn't expected to care for him at all, but the moment they'd put Grant into her arms she'd fallen in love with him at first sight. Perhaps because he was hers, and hers alone.

After the miscarriage, she'd felt no real desire to go through all the pain and agony again, or bear the responsibility of another child, but nor did she wish to risk losing her husband.

If a child was what it took to keep him, then that's what she'd have.

Until that happy day dawned, the pair of them seemed hell-bent on destroying each other, both bitter over the way things had turned out. And whenever she complained about his attitude towards Grant, Stan would insist this dreadful situation was all of her own making, her own fault for tricking him into marriage in the first place. She'd lied to him so must now suffer the consequences.

Yet he made no bones about the fact that he wanted a child of his own, and that he was disappointed over Joyce losing the baby, if that were indeed the truth. Sadly, she very much doubted she'd be able to provide him with another. Joyce had endured a difficult birth with Grant, a tragic miscarriage, and now she didn't seem able to even conceive. She was willing to keep trying, if only because it kept Stan in her bed, but his home leaves were becoming less frequent, and hope was fading.

'I'll stick by you for the duration,' he promised. 'But once peace is declared, if you haven't managed to give me a child by then, you're on your own.'

'I can never resist a challenge,' Joyce bit back.

It was then that she'd enrolled on a course in hairdressing, realising she'd need a decent income to support herself and her son when peace finally came. To her surprise, she found she enjoyed the course and had a natural flair for styling hair, but the prospect of life alone without Stan brought little comfort.

She still loved him, that was the trouble.

29

Harriet

The two girls hardly spoke to each other for days, their friendship severely dented by the quarrel. Instead of sitting
gossiping together in the breaks between rehearsals, or sharing a
sandwich and a giggle, there was an awkwardness between them,
and a distinct coolness.

Harriet wanted to feel pleased by the fact she'd won the battle
but it somehow seemed so tawdry to be fighting over a man. So
clichéd and silly. The only emotion she felt was one of foolish-
ness over the pointlessness of it all. What was it she expected
from Vinny? Security? Love? Some sort of emotional commitment? And could he possibly provide it? Oh, she did hope so,
otherwise, what else did she have?

But Shelley's words still rang in her head. *Making claims on
him now, are you? You really are a glutton for punishment.* What had
she meant by that?

She seemed to be implying that what Harriet felt for Vinny
was not really love at all, but simply a physical attraction born
out of a desire for revenge against Joyce, or as a means to hurt
herself.

Was that true? Was that what this was all about? Self-punishment?
But why would she do such a thing after all that had happened
to her? Hadn't she a right to a decent, happy life like everyone
else, Harriet thought, in a welter of uncharacteristic self-pity.
Shelley wasn't the easiest person to understand. Her parents had
both died in an horrific car crash and she was almost as confused
and bitter about life as Vinny himself. But never one to bear a

grudge, after nearly a week had gone by Harriet could take no more of the other girl's huffy silence.

'Are we still friends?'

Shelley instantly gathered Harriet into her arms for a big warm hug. 'Course we are. Why would we not be? I've been every bit as miserable as you. We certainly aren't going to fall out over Vinny Turner. I know about the baby so I can see now why you were so upset, and I just want you to know that you can rely on me, no matter what.'

Harriet instinctively smoothed the flat of one hand over her emerging bump. 'Thanks, that means a lot. Everything's going to be fine, I know it is. It's just that Vinny's so booked up with gigs at the moment we haven't had time to fix a day to pop down to the Register Office.'

Shelley didn't look at her as she turned her back to Harriet so she could pull down the zip of the new mini dress she'd worn for the gig that night. 'Maybe he will do soon. But if there's any problem, I'm here, don't forget.'

Harriet helped her out of the dress and placed it on its hanger, smoothing the soft blue fabric. She suddenly envied her friend's beauty and her free and easy style. Harriet would never summon up the nerve to wear a dress so short even if she'd still been slim, and certainly not now with her swollen tummy and breasts bursting out of her bra. Was it any wonder if Vinny wasn't quite as enamoured of her as he used to be? Still, he was pleased about the baby, she must remember that, which surely proved that he meant to stand by her. 'Why would there be a problem?'

'Exactly!' Shelley agreed, pulling a Sloppy Joe sweater on over her stretch pants. 'I'm just saying, all for one, and one for all, isn't that what the band stands for?'

Despite herself, Harriet found herself giggling, remembering how Vinny used to say the same thing. 'Only when I'm paying for the fish and chips,' she reminded Shelley.

'Right, then let's go and buy some. And you're paying.'

★

The silly squabble was forgotten and everything was back to normal. The band was booked for so many gigs they rarely had a free night. Not one was cancelled as Vinny too seemed to be on a more even keel, working hard but seemingly relaxed and enjoying life. Harriet took great care not to upset him, or to mention how anxious she was for them to be married. She still had the forms, safely stowed away in her bag, waiting for the right moment.

But as May slipped by and June arrived with the promise of summer in the air, Harriet was forced to admit it was harder to disguise her condition. And she'd quite lost her nerve to call on Nan again. What would the old lady say if she saw the state of her now, nearly five months gone and still unwed? Being a strong chapel-going Methodist with high moral standards, the old lady would be appalled to find her granddaughter in such a condition. Much as Harriet longed to visit her, she no longer dared do so.

She was growing bigger by the day and it was far too warm now to hide her bump under a baggy sweater. Harriet bought herself an A-line dress, one size too large, hoping that would hide her condition a bit longer, but really she was growing frantic over Vinny's continued silence on the subject of their planned Register Office wedding.

'Will we find time soon, or shall we wait till we can wheel the baby there in the pram?' she joked one day, struggling not to show her desperation.

'That's an idea. Do they do christenings as well? Two for the price of one, eh?' he laughed, without lifting his head from his guitar. He'd been practising all morning, trying to learn 'The Twist', a Chubby Checker number which was turning into a real dance craze. Everyone was asking for it. Music styles were changing and Harriet sensed Vinny was finding it harder to keep pace with the change.

This wasn't how she'd expected things to turn out, not at all how it was meant to be. They'd marry soon, she told herself, and he'd give up the band and settle down, then everything would be fine. It was just that he was particularly busy right now, that was all. Harriet knew she was making excuses for him, but didn't care to consider any other reason why he would drag his heels.

Love-making wasn't quite what it used to be either, as she was feeling increasingly bulky and awkward, or had to keep running to the lavatory, but Vinny was surprisingly patient with her. One night she simply didn't feel in the mood at all, yet he didn't blame her. He simply held her close as she dozed off, lying contentedly in his arms. She was almost asleep when she became vaguely aware that he'd left her side, but when she woke again, moments later perhaps, he was back beside her, so didn't trouble to ask where he'd been.

The same thing happened the next night, and the one after that, until at last she dared to ask, 'Where've you been? Do you have a problem?'

'No, not at all,' he murmured, smoothing her hair back from her face, all warm and sleepy as he kissed it. 'Go back to sleep, babe.'

'Don't keep leaving me on my own then.'

'I won't, I'll stay right here.'

The following night Harriet wasn't sure how long she'd been asleep when some sound woke her. It was a door opening. Shelley slipped into the bedroom on silent feet, and the next instant was lying beside Vinny in the big bed on the opposite side to Harriet.

Harriet clearly heard her loud whisper. 'Since you didn't come to me tonight, I thought I'd join you both here instead,' and smiling impishly she wrapped her arms about his waist. 'You don't mind, do you?' she said to Harriet.

Harriet was stunned, not having the first idea what to say, or how to deal with this. She'd believed that she'd made her feelings on the subject of sharing very clear, yet her comments had apparently fallen on deaf ears. Fighting through a fog of sleep she struggled to focus on exactly what Shelley had said: *Since you didn't come to me* . . . What on earth was going on?

'Shelley, what are you doing? Why are you here?'

Her friend giggled. 'Vinny told me ages ago you wanted to spice things up a bit, and since we've patched up our differences,

I assumed you were perfectly willing for me to share in the fun now.'

'But, I explained to you . . .' Harriet stopped and looked at Vinny, at the way he slid his arm casually around Shelley's shoulder, how his fingers instinctively traced the mole at the top of her arm, and knew with a chilling certainty that this wasn't the first time her so-called friend had been in his bed, or he'd visited hers. As if to emphasis this fact, he gave the other girl a welcoming kiss full on her lips. Harriet turned abruptly away, the blood pounding in her head, unable to bear the sight of their intimacy. She felt as if she'd been punched in the face. Her heart was pounding and she felt dangerously close to tears. She made to leave but Vinny grasped her wrist to prevent her from moving.

'Don't go, Harriet. Remember, love is an adventure to share between friends.'

'Are you serious?' She felt overcome by confusion, trying to decide if this was normal behaviour. It didn't sound normal, and Harriet certainly had no wish to share Vinny with anyone, least of all with Shelley.

'Why not?' he was saying. 'Could be fun, don't you reckon?'

'Is this because I'm pregnant, and not quite up to love-making any more?'

'No, of course not. Anyway, it's nothing to do with the pregnancy. Our love-making has just got a bit staid and boring, that's all.'

'Staid and boring?'

Vinny looked away, refusing to meet her shocked gaze. 'You know how it is, babe, how I *hate* to be predictable. You agreed we needed to put a bit more fizz into things, so don't go all uppity on me. We can all have a good time together. Just because I like Shelley doesn't mean I don't want you too. I can have you both, can't I?'

'No,' Harriet said. 'Actually, you can't.'

Vinny chuckled, nuzzling into her neck, nibbling her ear. 'Sweetheart. Stop being so prissy. You should learn to relax and enjoy yourself a bit more, otherwise why are you even here with my rackety band?'

It was a good question. One to which she couldn't easily find an answer.

Harriet gazed into those dazzling green-gold eyes and for a second found herself hesitating, baffled and bewildered by what he was saying to her. In that moment she almost longed to be the kind of girl who could happily agree to such an adventure. Yet in reality she wanted only to run as fast and as far away as possible from these two people who held such a different moral outlook to her own on what was right and wrong.

But where would she run to? To Joyce, who was even more of a straight-laced, moralising puritan? To Nan, who still didn't know anything about her condition? And did Harriet really want to risk losing him? Hadn't she finally admitted that she loved Vinny, or was Steve the man she truly loved and still pined for? One thing was certain, Harriet would never want Steve in bed with her at the same time as Vinny. Was that because she loved her ex-boy friend more, or because she was indeed provincial and old fash-ioned, as Shelley had suggested?

Vinny wasn't even bothering to wait for her answer. He was again kissing Shelley, with more fervour this time, her slender legs and arms curled enticingly around him. He grinned over his shoulder at Harriet. 'Just relax, babe. Your turn next.'

'Or join in, if you feel like it,' Shelley murmured, arms wrapped possessively about Vinny's waist as she slid the flat of her hands up and down his bare back. 'What does a little three-in-a-bed romp matter between friends?'

Apparently Harriet was expected to remain by his side while he made love to her best friend. She lay for a whole five seconds as if turned to stone while the couple writhed and moaned, kissed and petted in the bed beside her. It felt like five minutes, *five hours*! Never, in all her life, had Harriet experienced such shame. She longed to vanish in a puff of smoke, to crawl into some black hole and disappear so that her misery would no longer be visible, even to herself. Why didn't she shout at him? Why couldn't she move? Why didn't she simply run away? Because she loved him? Because she was weak?

Maybe what Shelley suggested was true. She no longer cared what happened to her, but was simply desperate to hurt herself in order to spare everyone else the trouble.

Had she lost everything, even her own self-respect the moment she climbed into bed with this exciting, dangerous man?

At this thought a small curl of anger was ignited deep in the pit of her stomach. It began to grow and spread, burning and scalding, till her breath became shallow and rapid, her heart pounded and a rosy mist of fury swam before her eyes. How dare this girl pretend to be her friend, and then attempt to steal her man right before her eyes?

How dare this man use her so badly? People just seemed to walk all over her. Joyce, Steve, Grant, and now Shelley and Vinny. She really wasn't putting up with it any more.

With every scrap of energy she possessed, Harriet flung herself off the bed. 'Stop this at once!' she screamed. 'It *matters* what we do because I'm a real person, not some bit of scum brought in on the heel of your shoe. What's more, we're about to get married because I'm carrying his child!'

Vinny calmly looked up at her, eyes hooded, and said, 'I'm pleased about the baby, you know I am. But I never said anything about getting married. That was all your idea, not mine. I'm a free spirit, babe, always will be.'

Shelley regretted what she'd done the moment her friend left, slamming the door behind her. 'That wasn't very nice of us, Vinny. Harriet doesn't think like you and me. She's a decent soul, innocent, with a heart of pure gold. We should have given her more time to get used to the idea. We've upset her.'

Vinny reached for another bottle of beer. 'You reckon? Well, she shouldn't make out she's right all the time. Too damned bossy. Come here, sweetheart, let's you and me have some fun on our own.'

But Shelley was concerned for her friend, no longer interested in love-making as she tried to untangle herself from the sheets. All the fun had gone out of it as she recalled the expression of hatred on Harriet's face, some of it directed at herself. 'Not now, I'd only feel responsible if anything happened to her. I think we should go and look for her. Come on, wake up, lazy-bones. We can't let any harm come to her. Harriet is in trouble.'

Vinny struggled to focus but his heavy eyelids dropped closed as he flopped back on the bed. 'She'll be fine,' he muttered. 'Stop worrying.'

'That's just it, I do worry. She expects you to play the hero and save her from herself, you idiot. Maybe the daft mare even imagines herself in love with you. Did that never occur to you? And I was horrid to her. OK, so you're out of it, stoned out of your mind as usual. Why any of us bother with you, is quite beyond me.' Leaning over, she gently kissed him. 'You get some sleep then. I'll see you later.'

Dashing back to her room Shelley hastily pulled on jeans and a sweater, then headed down the stairs and out into the empty darkness. Where had the silly cow gone?

Harriet hadn't the first idea where she was, or where she was going. She knew only that it was cold and dark, and it was raining. She also knew that she was afraid. Huge blocks of warehouses, cranes, stacks of timber and boxes waiting to be loaded on to ships and barges, loomed ominously close, but she couldn't find her way out of the docks. Maybe because as well as the darkness, she was also blinded by her own tears. How she had stumbled on to these wharves in the first place was quite beyond her.

She felt as if she'd been walking for hours but could remember very little of where, exactly, she'd been. Maybe round and round in circles.

Following the humiliation of that little scene back at the hotel, she'd flung a few things into a bag and run out into the night. Harriet could see that it had been a very foolish thing to do. She hadn't even remembered to pick up her purse. So here she was with no money, no bed for the night, and nowhere to go.

She was also pregnant with Vinny's child, and he hadn't moved a muscle to prevent her frantic departure. He'd just sat back, his arm round Shelley's shoulder, watching her frantic packing and abrupt departure. There clearly wasn't going to be any Register Office wedding, so being lost seemed of small concern by comparison.

Harriet had never felt so low in all her life. There didn't seem to be any way forward, no future she could bear to contemplate. When Nan had made that blunt announcement on the day of her lovely dad's funeral, her security had vanished forever. She'd felt then as if she were hanging over a cliff. Now she'd fallen into a raging sea that had tossed her about as if she were no more than a piece of flotsam, and Harriet knew she didn't have the energy, or the willpower, to climb out of it.

Where was the point? Her father was dead. The mother she'd accepted and loved all her life despite Joyce's inability to show any affection, was not, in fact, her mother at all. Steve, the boy she'd loved with all her heart, had turned from her when she'd needed him most. And now she'd lost Vinny.

It came to Harriet then, in a moment of unexpected clarity, that her relationship with Vinny had been pure fantasy, a bit of fun, yes, as she'd first claimed it to be, but nothing more. She'd run away with him out of desperation, fallen in love with an image that she had created, and not with the real Vinny Turner at all. Perhaps her naivety had been brought about by a desperation to prove something to herself: that she was still attractive, or that someone at least wanted her.

But it had all been a complete fallacy. Vinny didn't love her at all, except in Harriet's own imagination. All Vinny loved was himself, and the dratted grass he smoked. Nobody, in fact, loved her. Not a single soul, save for Nan, cared if she even lived or died. And she couldn't for shame face her lovely grandmother. She'd lost everything that mattered to her, even her own self-respect.

Harriet walked on, dazed with pain, found the dock gates quite by accident, but they were locked fast. How had she got in? She couldn't remember. She didn't even know if the hotel was nearby or miles away, and she hadn't the first idea how to retrace her steps. Moments later, she found herself walking over a bridge. She paused to look down into the smoothly flowing black water beneath, visible only by the light of a thin sliver of moon. She stared into its velvety blackness and longed for oblivion to put an end to this pain that was tearing the heart out of her.

What a mess she'd made of her life. When Joyce had thrown her out, she should have done something sensible with the twenty-five pounds she'd given her. She should have got herself a proper job. The money would have paid for respectable lodgings for several weeks. Instead, she'd wasted it all on fish and chips and beer for that stupid rock group who spent money without any thought for the future.

She should be thinking of her own future now. Hers and the baby's. But she didn't seem to have one. She was nearly five months pregnant yet wasn't fit to be a mother. And how could she bring it up on her own with no home, no job, no father, and no one to help her? Oblivion, that was what she craved. An end to this pain. Dry eyed, Harriet began to climb on to the parapet of the bridge.

30

Rose

Rose was well on the road to recovery, and for the first time in many weeks was walking through the market under her own steam, albeit with the aid of a walking stick. Stan's wheelchair had been abandoned, returned to the doctor who had given her a clean bill of health and told her to get out more and enjoy life to the full, which was exactly what Rose intended to do.

She'd certainly had enough of sitting in that back room hour after hour, waiting for someone to call in for a chat, or to wheel her out so she could escape for a short while from her prison. How Stan had tolerated his wife largely ignoring him for so many years she couldn't imagine. She was beginning to see her son-in-law in quite a different light these days.

She struck out with as much vigour as she could muster, revelling in the warmth of the sun on her face, smiling as friends hailed her as she passed by. Big Molly gave her a cheery wave, calling Rose over and insisting on giving her old friend a pork pie.

'On the house, I'm that glad to see you out and about again.'

Barry Holmes tossed her a rosy red apple, saying it matched her cheeks, which made Rose laugh and feel all girlish.

The June day was warm with the promise of summer, mingling with the scent from Betty Hemley's flowers, and Rose sighed with pleasure. How she loved the market. How many years had she lived here? Nearly twenty. A long time. They'd come to Champion Street following the trauma of losing their old house in Ancoats, their lives having gone up in flames. Joyce was already working on the market, helping out at various stalls. Then she'd started up the hairdressing business on her own.

'You have to hand it to that lass of mine,' Rose muttered to herself. 'She might not suffer fools gladly, but she doesn't believe in sitting on her hands and moping.'

Oh, but nothing had been the same since that day. Everything had changed, in some ways best not remembered at all.

Rose stopped for a moment to catch her breath and wipe away a stray tear. The war had been over for fifteen years. Let it go, she chided herself. It was a different world. Princess Margaret has married the son of a lawyer instead of a royal prince. A handsome young John F. Kennedy is promising a new dawn, and folk are frightening themselves to death watching that new film, *Psycho*, at the pictures.

'What is the world coming to?'

Rose rested her weary limbs on the bench by the ancient horse trough. Her left leg was still playing up, not quite behaving as it should, but good progress was most definitely being made. She massaged her knee, as her old friend had advised her to do. She was grateful to Irma for all the hard work and exercises, difficult though they'd been at times. Today she felt a new woman, not a worry in the world save for Harriet, of course, and that letter she still carried in her pocket. Unfortunately, Irma had been no real help to her there, merely saying the answer would come to her if she followed her instincts. Rose let her mind again slip back to the past, as old women tended to do.

She recalled how old Mr Lee, who'd been wounded in the first World War, used to sit here selling his matches. Gone now, poor old chap, although plenty of his colleagues in flat caps and mufflers were still gathered in a huddle, smoking their pipes and putting the world to rights, remembering the good old days.

The market was changing too. The Lascars were all gone, the Indian seamen, and Rose missed the colour and character they had brought to the street. They used to be on the flat iron market too.

The grizzled old men were entertaining themselves this morning by watching open mouthed as the youth of today sauntered past. Dressed in their Italian suits and winkle-picker shoes, Slim-Jim ties and fancy waistcoats, they looked proper dandies. And these were just the young men.

The girls all looked like Brigitte Bardot in their skinny raincoats, or tight-fitting blouses tucked into the waist of their Capri pants. One girl tottered by looking very like Minnie Mouse in her impossibly high-heeled white court shoes, outlandishly dressed in a tight black and white spangled top and the greenest, brightest, checked trousers. She reminded Rose of the clowns that used to feature in the Belle Vue Circus. Eeh, maybe she was getting old.

Rose thought of her beloved granddaughter, whom she hadn't seen in months, and wondered if Harriet had started wearing outlandish clothes in that band she'd joined. She'd used to telephone and leave messages, and had written many letters and jokey postcards, but there'd been fewer of those lately. Rose was desperate to see her, to give her a hug and a kiss. Rose would know then what she was wearing, wouldn't she? She'd know if she was well and happy, eating properly and looking after herself, instead of worrying herself sick night and day. In her heart Rose was convinced something was wrong. Harriet would never willingly stay away so long, or keep so quiet. There must be a good reason.

She dabbed away a stray tear as Dena Dobson came by in a pink slouch cap and blouse, short burgundy skirt, clanking beads and a long crocheted woollen jacket. The young girl paused to tell Rose how delighted she was to see her looking so well, which pleased the old lady.

'I'm in the pink, and so are you by the looks of it,' Rose drily remarked. 'Apart from the length of that skirt, which shows all of your knees I'll have you know, you look like my maiden aunt in that jacket.' Rose fingered the fabric with appreciative curiosity. 'Did you crochet it yourself?'

Dena laughed. 'Don't be daft, I've no skills in that direction at all, only with a sewing machine. I'll accept your remarks as a compliment though, even if you don't like my knees.'

'What happened to all them fluffy can-can petticoats? They were pretty, they were.'

'They're on the way out. Things are changing, Rose. Skirts will be going even shorter soon, mark my words. They call them minis. You'll blush when you see one of those.'

'Eeh, heck, standards are indeed slipping. Morals will soon be a thing of the past. It's all coffee bars, jazz cellars and stiletto hells that drill holes in the floor. And nobody stands up for old ladies on the bus now. Where will it all end? With women flaunting themselves and practically showing their bottoms? Shocking!'

Dena kissed the old woman fondly. 'Just make sure you save our market, Rose, and leave the fashion scene to me.' And Dena hurried off leaving Rose shaking her head in despair.

Having rested her bad leg, Rose made a beeline for Irma's biscuit stall, anxious to prove to her old friend how well she was doing. 'Look at me,' she called, as she approached. 'I'll be doing the boogie-woogie next.'

Irma shouted for her husband. 'Joe, fetch Rose a chair. She'll be wanting a rest.'

Rose protested. 'Nay, I'm fine. I put me feet up for a while on the bench, so don't fret about me.'

But Irma wouldn't take no for an answer. Joe produced the chair and Irma poured a mug of tea out of her flask, plus a few chocolate biscuits to help it down. And as folk stopped to ask how she was, Rose felt like the Queen of the market. 'Watch out, Belle Garside, they'll have me as Market Superintendent next,' she chortled. 'I feel fit for anything.'

'If that's the case,' Joe said, 'then we could do with you this afternoon at the committee meeting.'

'Right, you're on. I'll be there.'

True to her word, Rose presented herself, stick in hand, at the market committee meeting to discuss progress on the campaign. She opted to sit at the back, where she could listen to the arguments ranging back and forth.

As she made herself comfortable, Joe was on his feet talking about high-rise flats shooting up everywhere, of people complaining they were being forced out of their much-loved homes and street communities where they'd lived happily for years. 'It's cruel. Wicked!' he fumed. 'And they'll do the same to us here in Champion Street, if we let them.'

Chris George stood up to say that Champion Street was happen in need of some decent housing, then he quietly announced that his father, who owned the bakery where he and his wife Amy now lived and worked, had decided to sell. 'I'm sorry, but the decision was taken out of my hands.'

A dreadful hush fell upon the assembled company. Jimmy Ramsay was the first to recover.

'Nay, lad, that's a bit of a blow. You're the second to accept the developers' offer. Sam Beckett has already taken their money and run. He's shut up shop and done a moonlight flit. You can't do this to us.'

'Like I say, I'm sorry,' Chris said. 'We need the money. Dad could do with a bit more for his retirement on the Fylde Coast, and me and Amy, well, we've two mouths to feed now. And we're young and ambitious. This money will set us up properly in a business of our own, plus a down payment on a house. It's not to be sniffed at. Amy's all for it.'

Big Molly leaped to her feet, waving her huge fists in the air, as if ready to defend her daughter to the death. 'I can't believe our Amy wants to leave the market. She's been bullied into this by *your* over-ambitious family which *my* girl was daft enough to marry into. I knew it would all end in tears.'

'Calm down, Moll,' Betty Hemley urged, tugging her friend back down into her seat. 'The young have to live their own lives. We can't dictate to them what they should and shouldn't do.'

There was a noisy outburst following this, with everyone wanting their say, some folk shouting out that it was the young who were ruining everything, and others objecting that the old ways were not necessarily the best. Names were mentioned of other residents in the street anxious to take advantage of the huge sums being offered by the developers. Things were getting heated and it took Jimmy Ramsay to calm everyone down, his big voice booming out loud and clear, gradually bringing the meeting to order.

'Hold on, hold on, let's not get too excited. I'll admit it's a blow. If some folk have already agreed to sell, then others will surely follow. It puts the rest of us in a weaker position as we'll find it harder to hold our ground. It's a chink in our armour, that's what it is. What we have to do is to plug every hole with new faith in the future of Champion Street Market, otherwise we'll have a sinking ship on our hands.'

A small silence followed while folk digested these mixed metaphors, but then tempers flared once more, voices were raised, and matters threatened to again get out of hand. Marco Bertalone and Winnie Homes were arguing so fiercely neither could possibly hear a word the other was saying; Belle Garside was calling for order and nobody was listening; and Big Molly was threatening to lather the floor with her son-in-law's brains, if he had any.

Rose struggled awkwardly to her feet, holding up her stick to gain attention. Little by little, out of respect for this long-serving member, only shortly recovered from a serious illness, voices quietened and silence fell upon the assembled company.

'I went to the library the other day and read up all about the history of markets in Manchester,' Rose quietly began. 'All about the Acres Fair, which was held in St Ann's Square from the thirteenth century, and later moved to Shudehill before turning itself into Campfield. And, as we know, the whole area around Smithfield became the fruit and veg market. Then they started up the wholesale fish market in 1872. An old uncle of mine used to work there, years back. We'd get a box of sardines for pennies in them days. Anyroad, the market has kept on spreading, with more and more traders and barrows, just like we have here. Now there's talk that the streets are getting too crowded and it'll have to move soon, with some of it relocated.

'But it's not only markets that are suffering. There used to be a picture house in every neighbourhood, a couple of churches and half a dozen pubs. Now look what's happening. They're being knocked down like ninepins all over Manchester and Salford.

'What I'm saying is, nothing stays the same. We might object to all this demolition, and want it to stop. We might not want great blocks of flats all over the show. We might like our grand Victorian monstrosities, place more value on our industrial heritage than our leaders do, but nothing stays the same. In the end we all have to accept that fact. I'm not saying we should give up on our fight. Never! We'll take it right to the wire. I'm suggesting that mebbe we should also start looking for a new home too, instead of just complaining about losing our old one. If we lose this battle, lose our street, then we'll need somewhere to take our beloved market.'

The silence following this astonishing statement was thoughtful and prolonged. It was Belle Garside who broke it. Surprisingly, she agreed with Rose, took a vote and the motion was passed. But then Rose had a happy knack of putting her finger right on the button.

It was a day or two later and Rose was sitting in Belle's café with Irma enjoying a cup of tea. 'Will you read me palm, tell me when our Harriet is coming home for good?'

Irma looked at her friend sadly. 'It's not quite that easy.'

'What about the cards then? Is it worth trying them again? I need to know how she is, if she's well.'

Irma's big heart went out to her friend. 'Yes, I can understand you must be concerned.' They were interrupted by Belle placing the cups and saucers before them. She took the opportunity to thank Rose for her little speech in the committee meeting the other day. 'You did well, said what I'd been trying to tell them for ages.'

'The battle's not over yet though,' Rose warned.

'And it could well be a futile one, as you pointed out, so alternative solutions need to be sought. We'll speak about it some more, Rose, enjoy your tea. Can I get you anything else, a scone or a bacon sandwich?' Both women refused, and with a rare smile Belle left them to it.

Irma looked at Rose's teacup. 'Ah, I can see a few leaves floating on the surface.'

'What does that signify?'

'You're going to get a visitor.'

Rose's wrinkled old face lit with fresh hope. 'Our Harriet?'

'Tea leaves don't give names, unfortunately. It could be anyone. I could read your tea leaves, if you like.'

'Eeh, that'd be grand.'

'It's important for you to relax and enjoy the tea first, let any thoughts come and go in your head. Just let them flow. We'll enjoy our tea, quietly and comfortably, then you must leave just a small amount of liquid in the bottom.'

Rose did her best to relax, although she didn't find it easy. Finally, the tea was drunk and Irma set about her task. She held the cup in her left hand and swirled the liquid around, making sure the tea was well distributed in the bowl of the cup, then she upended it on to the saucer.

Next, she turned the cup upright to examine the tea leaves left behind. She rotated it in her hands so that the handle was directed towards Rose. 'We read the leaves in relation to the handle, which is meant to represent you,' Irma explained. 'And I can tell right away, by the fact that some of the liquid has remained in the cup, that there will be tears, I'm sorry to say.'

Rose paled. 'Not again. I can't take no more bad news.'

Irma looked concerned. 'Would you prefer me to stop?'

But Rose shook her head, took a breath and told her friend to carry on. 'No, I want to know, I need to be prepared. I've still a big worry on me mind. Worrying about where our Harriet is and what she is doing is only part of it.'

'Well, from the fact that most of the leaves are some distance to the left of the handle, I would say that your worries are still tied to the past. I believe the cards told us the same thing?' Irma glanced questioningly at her friend. Rose said nothing.

'There's a large clump of leaves here which seems to indicate trouble of some sort, and here is a short stalk which could be a woman, possibly she too is from the past. Does that makes sense?'

Still Rose said nothing.

'And here they are slanted, which could mean a person or persons who aren't entirely trustworthy. Probably, by the shape and size I'd say male this time.'

'Anything else?'

'Only something which might represent a kite, in which case prepare yourself for a scandal.'

'Oh, hecky thump, we've had enough of them already.'

Irma set the cup back on the saucer. 'That's all, I'm afraid. Nothing particularly helpful then? I'm so sorry.'

'Was there nowt about a letter? The cards mentioned a letter last time.'

Irma shook her head.

'I have a problem over a letter, d'you see. And I can't make up me mind what's best to do about it.'

Irma looked sympathetic. 'Then maybe I could help you with that simply as a friend.'

'Aye,' Rose agreed, 'maybe you can, when I'm ready to talk about it.'

'When you are,' Irma gently told her. 'I'll listen.'

3 1

Joyce

Joyce deeply regretted her marriage. It had been a bad mistake to marry Stan Ashton. If it hadn't all happened in such a rush she might well have stopped to consider more carefully the risk she was taking by not telling him the truth. But she'd been at a loss to know how to deal with that rape and the resulting pregnancy, and she'd been desperately in love. No matter how much her mother might criticise, it had seemed the best solution at the time.

Rose, naturally, took a close interest in her daughter's welfare, and was not blind to the fact that her marriage seemed to be falling apart. When, on occasions, Stan spent barely more than the odd night at home in the entire length of his leave, she challenged Joyce on the subject.

'Is that Yorkshireman knocking you about?' she asked, certain this could be the only reason any marriage wouldn't work.

'Of course he isn't, Mother, don't talk daft. We've got a bit of a problem, that's all.'

'What sort of a problem? Another woman, is that it?'

And for the first time in her life Joyce burst into tears, blurting out how she believed her husband was having an affair with her best friend.

Rose was incensed. 'I allus knew he were a wrong un. I'll give him what for when I catch him.'

'No, don't. Don't say anything! It's nothing to do with you. Anyway, you don't know the whole story,' Joyce protested, as her mother ranted on, seemingly prepared to lie in wait for him

behind the front door next time he came home on leave, rolling-
pin in hand.

'What story, don't tell me you've been at it an' all?'

'No, of course I haven't, nothing like that. Not willingly anyway.'

'And what's that supposed to mean? You either have or you
haven't.'

'I'm afraid I haven't been entirely honest and open with you
either, Mother.'

'If you mean did I realise that young Grant was conceived
quite a few months before you wed his father, then spare yourself the trouble. I wasn't brought in with the morning fish.'

'I'm afraid it's a bit more complicated than that. Stan isn't his
father.'

And so, at last, driven by despair, Joyce confessed to her mother
the whole truth, the entire tale from start to finish. How Grant
was the result of 'an unpleasant encounter', a careful choice of
words, at a friend's party, and how she'd been three months pregnant when she and Stan had married, of which he'd been entirely
ignorant. Joyce found it distasteful to use the word rape, but her
mother used it for her.

'When you say that you weren't willing, do you mean that this
bloke, whoever he was, raped you?'

'Don't be coarse, Mother, but yes, I am. It all happened so
quickly. One minute I was having a laugh with this silly young
drunken sailor, the next . . . Oh, it really doesn't bear thinking
about. And the trouble is, Stan doesn't believe a word I say on
the subject. He doesn't believe I *was* raped!'

'Not surprising, if you failed to mention it till months after
your marriage that there were actually three of you present at
that little wedding ceremony.'

Rose then proceeded to give Joyce a long lecture on the question of trust in marriage, on how, even though Stan was not
without fault in this, Joyce had only herself to blame. 'I told you
not to marry him.'

'No, you didn't,' Joyce wearily protested. 'You said something
rude like, "Well, if that's the best you can do, I suppose I'll have

to accept him." You'd decided you didn't like Stan long before you even met him.'

'Aye, well, he's the wrong religion, and from the wrong side of the Pennines. Now he's playing away from home an' all, so me first instincts were right, weren't they? Why would I like him?'

'Oh, Mother!' Joyce endured the prolonged lecture with all the fortitude she could muster, thankful when Rose finally ran out of breath. She gave her mother a long suffering look. 'Please don't go on about it any more. I feel bad enough as it is. Don't make it any worse.'

'I'm not sure it could be any worse.'

But in this, she was wrong. When Stan arrived home later that same evening, it was to announce that Eileen was pregnant.

Joyce's first reaction was blind fury. How dare this woman, this so-called friend, be pregnant with her own husband's child when she had utterly failed him in that respect? How would she endure it? She wanted to scream and claw out his eyes, beat him about the head for what he'd done to her. Was this Stan Ashton's idea of revenge because of one small lie she'd told him? 'You assured me you weren't sleeping with her. You *swore* you were just good friends.'

Stan gave her a pitying look. 'That was months ago. In any case, since you clearly believed I was having it off with her, there didn't seem any reason not to. Eileen's keen for us to wed, so obviously you'll have to give me a divorce. My family will never speak to me again, of course, although they already seem to have cut me off without a penny, thanks to your lies. Father Dimmock will no doubt excommunicate me or something, but I can't see any other solution. In the meantime, I'm moving Eileen in here.'

'You're *what*?'

'She can't live on her own, not in her condition, and with a war on. Besides, her parents have thrown her out. I'll fetch her in, shall I? She's waiting outside.'

And both Joyce and Rose watched in open-mouthed disbelief

as Stan moved his mistress into the spare room, and then went to join her in it.

'By heck,' Rose said. 'This beats the filums any day.'

No one could say she hadn't tried her best to make her marriage work, for all events had conspired against her. Now Joyce had quite lost patience and had no intention of trying to please him any further.

In a fit of jealous rage, she embarked upon a fling of her own, with an old friend of hers, Frankie Morris, if only to prove she didn't give a damn what Stan did. A bit of tit for tat, and why not? Foolishly, in the throes of passion and wanting to put Stan in as bad a light as possible, Joyce told Frankie the whole sorry tale from start to finish, and was astonished when he claimed to know the drunken sailor responsible for ravishing her.

'I reckon it were our Pat. He's a right boyo is my young brother. Can't hold his whisky, and I know he were at that party of Eileen's.'

Joyce was annoyed, telling him she really didn't want to know who the man was. She much preferred him to remain anonymous. Furious with herself and deeply embarrassed, she dumped Frankie, wishing she'd kept her silly mouth shut. He wasn't pleased and turned nasty as a result, threatening to reveal Pat's name and the circumstances of their encounter to all and sundry if she didn't agree to go on sleeping with him.

Joyce was having none of that. She hadn't successfully protected her reputation to have it blown apart by Frankie flipping Morris.

'I don't think so, Frankie. If you do that, I'll have to tell everyone about that little encounter you had with Billy Carlton behind the bike sheds.'

He blushed scarlet with fury. 'What encounter? I never did any such thing. That's a bare-faced lie!'

'But could you prove it?'

Smiling to herself, Joyce knew she'd silenced him for good. Her reputation was safe and she'd not make such a silly mistake again.

★

Remembering those dark days, Joyce marvelled that they'd ever got through them. Although they hadn't, in a way. Relations between herself and Eileen had gone from bad to worse, soured to a wretched bitterness and near-hatred between the two women, culminating in a battle in which someone had to lose, so was it any wonder if things had turned out as they did?

A shiver ran down her spine at the memory. If she'd thrown her erstwhile friend out, instead of attempting to go along with Stan's wishes, then maybe everything would have been different. But then if Eileen had never invited Joyce to that party in the first place, she would not have suffered that assault. Which of them should bear the blame for the disaster that had overtaken them, or were they both equally responsible?

Joyce looked about her small salon, at its pink and grey décor, the row of sinks and the pretty net curtains protecting her clients from the curious gaze of onlookers as they sat under the dryer. If this was evidence of her victory, it had been hard won. As she pulled on her coat, preparatory to meeting Joe in the Dog and Duck, she thought of all the money and effort, all the hard work she'd put into this little business over the years.

Surprisingly, her mother had been most supportive in the years immediately after the war, during what became one of the most difficult periods of her life. Dealing with a crippled, mentally scarred, war-damaged husband had been bad enough, let alone the aftermath of the other more personal and emotional war between one-time friends. It had all taken a terrible toll upon her.

And when, on top of everything else, Joyce had been threatened with eviction because the landlord decided he wished to sell the place, Rose had gone so far as to step in and buy the property herself. Joyce had been astonished, not even aware her mother possessed the kind of money to be able to afford to make such an offer. But the generous gesture had meant they were all safe, even though her useless husband hadn't brought a penny into the marriage himself.

Joyce recalled how Rose had helped to mind Grant in those early years of peace. How she'd been the one to take Harriet under her wing when Joyce had been quite unable to bear even to look at the child.

Where was the girl now, Joyce wondered, and did she care? It was to be hoped they were married by now, at least. Joyce felt nothing but shame over the girl's condition, and not a scrap of pity. She was the author of her own misfortune, and the last thing Joyce wanted was to have her own respectability tarnished; her own efforts to be accepted as a worthwhile member of the community ruined by the stupidity of that cheap little tart.

She certainly hadn't endured a loveless marriage in order to protect her precious son, only to have the entire edifice of her carefully constructed high moral standing brought tumbling down by the actions of one silly girl. Not after the lengths she'd gone to to guard it.

Life had been an endless struggle, no doubt about that. A struggle which had taken its toll over the years, and Joyce never could quite rid herself of that sense of guilt which still hung over her like a black cloud. She was only too aware that it had turned her into a bitter woman, and was it any wonder? she thought, wallowing in self pity.

She called up the stairs to Rose. 'I'm off down the pub. Do you need owt?'

'Aye, a new left leg. But if you don't find one hanging around, I'll have to carry on hobbling around on this one.'

Joyce didn't even smile at her mother's droll wit as she let herself out of the salon, carefully locking the door behind her. Her mind was busily engaged elsewhere. She'd had enough, of that she was quite certain.

She felt the need for some peace in her life. Joyce wanted someone else to lift these cares from her shoulders, to carry the burden of responsibility for earning a good living, and giving her a little fun for a change. She needed Joe to leave Irma.

'Nay, Joyce love, it's not that easy,' Joe informed her with a sad shake of his head as, moments later, she put this point to him over her usual rum and coke. 'I can't just abandon the biscuit business we've built up together over the years. It would be difficult to separate which bit was hers, and which mine, if you catch my drift?'

'It seems perfectly obvious to me. You keep the biscuit stall and leave Irma her cake-making business.'

'Nay, it's not that simple. She needs me to drive the van, for deliveries. And I need her to do the accounts.'

Joyce silently ground her teeth then tucked her arm into his, smiling winningly up at him. 'You could always sell the lot to those developers. I could sell them my property too. Then you and I could take off into the wide blue yonder, go somewhere new, do something entirely different. We could start afresh, just the two of us. Maybe Australia, or Canada. Plenty of people are emigrating in search of a better life. Why don't we join them?'

Joe felt a wave of panic. This was the craziest idea she'd come up with yet, and some of them had been pretty daft, like him moving in above the hair salon with Rose and Grant. But what on earth had made her dream up this daft notion? It was totally unexpected and scared the pants off him. He could see the light of excitement in her face, and did his best to calm her down before it all got quite out of hand.

'Eeh, Joyce love, I don't know about that. It's a long way from Champion Street is Australia. Anyroad, selling would be letting everyone down. And what about Rose, your mam? I thought she owned the shop. If so, she'd never agree.'

'Her health is pretty shaky, and those stairs are hard on her bad leg. I could persuade her.'

'I very much doubt it. Rose is fighting as hard as anyone to save this market, mounting a substantial battle against them developers. Even now she's in the process of organising a special meeting between the market committee and the city council members, politicians and the like. She's insisting if they make us close down and move out, it's their responsibility to find us an alternative location. She's a little demon, your mam, when she gets going. I've seen her make them councillors tremble. How could we fly in the face of all her efforts and just sell up, take the money and run? It would be criminal. Wicked!'

'It would be plain common sense.'

'And how would Irma manage? Our pension is tied up in that biscuit business. I couldn't just abandon her. She is still me wife, after all.'

This wasn't at all the answer Joyce had hoped for. 'So what you're saying is that, given the choice between the two of us, you choose Irma. Is that the way of it?'

'There's no need to put it quite so bluntly,' Joe demurred, fidgeting with discomfort. 'You and me can still – you know – be friends, like.'

'You mean you can still come and visit my bed whenever the fancy takes you to enjoy my "favours", without taking any responsibility for my respectability, my good name. Or even my happiness?'

'I wouldn't put it quite like that.'

'I'm sure you wouldn't.' Joyce had had enough. She got unsteadily to her feet, drunk on the pain of broken dreams rather than the single rum and coke she'd enjoyed. She looked at the second one which Joe had placed before her, and she smiled at him, a bitter, hard mockery of a smile, one that had frequently brought a chill to her husband's heart. 'It's your decision, Joe, one you might well live to regret,' then she picked up the glass and upended the contents over his head. She didn't even glance back to enjoy the uproar she created in the pub as she walked away.

32

Harriet

The day that Shelley brought Harriet home to Champion Street, pregnant and still unmarried, was a day which would live forever in her mind. Harriet needed only to glance into her stepmother's dark, forbidding gaze to appreciate how badly she'd transgressed. Joyce would never forgive her for bringing such shame upon the family. Harriet knew she should be filled with guilt, but she felt nothing.

Since her friend had found her climbing on to the parapet of that bridge, and had come screaming towards her in a welter of panic and self-recrimination, she'd felt numb inside. Nothing seemed quite real.

In a strange way, despite it being Shelley's own actions which had led to that reckless act, Harriet had welcomed her intervention, experienced a strange feeling of relief as she'd gently been urged back on to solid ground. Harriet had offered no resistance, allowing her friend to quietly lead her from the bridge, answering her questions about her home address in a monotone, without thought or question.

It hadn't seemed the moment for blame, to point out that had Shelley not attempted to intervene, trying to muscle in upon her relationship with Vinny, then she might never have run or threatened to seek oblivion in the murky waters of the Ship Canal.

Now Harriet couldn't believe she was back home in the salon. But neither did she feel in any position to judge whether it was the right thing for Shelley to have brought her here. She simply felt grateful she was still alive, and deeply ashamed of her own momentary weakness which had led her to do such a stupid thing. What on earth had come over her? How dare she dissolve into self-pity when she was carrying this precious child?

Now Harriet looked at her stepmother and wondered what would happen next.

Fortunately, she'd insisted they hang back till she was quite certain all the customers had left and the salon was empty before allowing Shelley to take her inside. Merely the way Joyce flew to bolt the door behind her and ordered her straight upstairs said everything. The disgrace of her condition must be hushed up, hidden away from prying eyes and market gossip. Her first words made that very clear.

'Upstairs, and don't go anywhere near the window, miss. I'll speak to your friend down here, then I'll be right up.' It sounded more like a threat than a welcome.

Harriet knew it was a mistake to argue yet she did so. 'Not until I've seen Nan.'

Instinct led her straight to her grandmother. As she entered the old woman's bedroom at the back of the shop, Harriet was shocked and alarmed by the sight of her grandmother, looking even more frail than the last time she'd seen her. Despite her indomitable spirit, she seemed to have grown old suddenly. She felt shame and anguish for having neglected her for so long. And why? For what reason? Was it as a result of genuine shame, or misplaced pride? She could see that Rose was equally shocked by her own appearance, clearly having been completely unaware of her condition. Even so, Harriet ran straight into her arms.

'There, there, lass, don't fret. You're safe and sound now. Nan won't let owt bad happen to you,' and as her grandmother pressed her close against the cushion of her uncorseted breast, Harriet felt she was home at last, and let the tears come.

'Did anyone we know see you arrive?' Joyce fired the question at Harriet the moment she entered the room. Harriet shook her head.

'Not that I'm aware of. I made sure all the customers had left the salon before we came in.'

'Well, you showed some common sense there, at least. But if you think I'm going to allow you to set foot outside this house looking like that, you've got another think coming.'

Arms folded, pencilled brows almost meeting in a deep, censorious frown, small mouth drawn into a thin tight line, Joyce glared at her stepdaughter. She felt deeply disappointed and let down, furious that the girl should be so stupid as to get herself into this condition. Her wanton behaviour was quite beyond belief. Joyce refused to see the situation as a youthful act of rebellion, a consequence of the long-standing war between them. She saw Harriet's pregnancy as evidence of the girl's wickedness, not a desperate need to find love. Didn't this prove that she had bad blood in her veins?

Harriet found Joyce's disapproving scrutiny unnerving, quenching any lingering remnants of rebellion, but said nothing as she sat in the shelter of her grandmother's embrace. Nor did Joyce speak, as she restlessly paced to and fro, practically wringing her hands in anguish. After watching her stepmother take several more turns about the room, still cluttered with Joyce's personal belongings, Harriet could stand the ominous silence no longer.

'Look, I'll go. I'll not stay where I'm not wanted. I've no wish to cause you any further embarrassment.'

Rose protested. 'You'll stop here where you belong. This is still your home. It is as long as I'm alive, and own the deeds to this property.'

Joyce now directed her glare towards her mother, but her mind was whirling, thinking fast, considering ways to save her own good name and respectability. Perhaps she could put Harriet in a home for wayward girls. Did they still exist, she wondered? It was a pity they didn't have a maiden aunt in some far-flung rural backwater where the girl could wait out her time and then have the baby adopted without a soul being any the wiser. Unfortunately Joyce had no aunts, maiden or otherwise, no family but Rose, who wasn't the slightest use. But then the answer came to her, clear and simple.

Fortunately, Irma was no longer residing in Harriet's old room. Having achieved a satisfactory improvement in Rose's condition, the other woman had thankfully packed her bags and moved back home, much to Joyce's relief. And for once Joyce felt equally relieved that she had in fact failed to persuade Joe to move in, despite all her best efforts, for in the circumstances that would have been a total disaster. Discretion was now vital.

Joyce folded her arms. 'Right, we'll talk more of this in the morning. Meanwhile, you'd best get some sleep.'

Harriet kissed her grandmother a fond goodnight, then wearily climbed the stairs to her old attic bedroom. It felt strange, as if she were stepping back in time. She had a sudden longing to be with Vinny, to feel his arms round her, welcoming and loving.

Joyce fetched a pile of clean linen, dumped it on the bed and told Harriet to make it up. 'You stop in here, away from prying eyes till you're fit to be seen.'

Harriet frowned, feeling a sharp pang of concern. 'What do you mean "fit to be seen"? I'm only six months gone. I can't stay in my bedroom for three whole months!'

'You can and you will.'

Harriet gave a half laugh. 'You can't be serious?'

'You'll be allowed use of the bathroom at set times of the day, otherwise you'll stop in here.' Joyce went to the window and tugged the curtains closed, as if she could already sense prying eyes.

'Fortunately your room looks out over the back street, so no one is likely to spot you up in the attic here. Just make sure they don't. That young girl who brought you, Shelley somebody-or-other, assured me she'd keep her gob shut and not tell a soul. Good thing too. I want no gossip flying round the market over this. You'll stop in this room till it's all over and we've disposed of the evidence.'

Harriet gasped, looking at her stepmother in horrified bewilderment. 'Disposed of . . . I'm sorry, I don't understand what you're saying.'

'I'm saying, when your time comes, Mother and I will see to

you, then we'll get the child adopted. I'll make a few private enquiries through the church. I'm sure Father Dimmock will help, and respect the delicate nature of the situation. Confidentiality is vital.'

Joyce was at the door, her fidgety fingers now titivating her hair as if wishing to make sure she hadn't in some way soiled herself by coming into contact with this transgressor of all right and proper moral values. 'I'll fetch you up a bit of supper later, till then, get some rest, you look as if you need it.'

Only when Harriet heard the key turn in the lock did she appreciate her stepmother's full purpose.

Harriet lay on her bed and stared, dry-eyed at the ceiling. She was in total shock. She'd made up the bed, automatically obeying Joyce's instructions since she had to sleep somewhere. Then for want of something better to do, she laid down upon it to try to make some sense of all of this. Harriet felt overwhelmed by tiredness, the child she carried suddenly weighing heavy.

What on earth had brought her to this pretty pass? What was she even doing here, back in her stepmother's house, the very same from which she'd been booted out only a few short months before? It wasn't as if Joyce wanted her home, she'd made that very clear. Harriet was an embarrassment to her, a possible source of scandal to be hushed up and kept quiet at all costs.

She couldn't stay. She must escape. Vinny would be wondering what on earth had happened to her. He'd be worried sick and— This line of reasoning died unfinished in her head. No, he wouldn't. He was probably even now in bed with Shelley, and, kind as her friend had been to save her from almost certain death, she'd have no compunction in agreeing. Where was the harm in a bit of rough and tumble? they would say. It's just sex!

One lone tear slid from the corner of her eye and ran down on to Harriet's pillow. What a fool she'd been! What a complete and utter fool. She'd hung on to Vinny's coat-tails, believing he cared for her when he simply took such adoration for granted. He'd grown used to girls clamouring for his autograph, wanting to touch him, even begging for a kiss. He wouldn't even notice she was gone, let alone miss her.

And no one else knew she was even here.

It was the longest night of Harriet's life. It seemed to crawl by at a snail's pace, so that it was almost a relief when the first pale light of dawn found her perched on the narrow windowsill, arms wrapped tight about her knees.

Harriet watched a cat stretch itself and stroll nonchalantly across the tiles of a nearby roof, wishing she could do the same. From her eyrie she could trace a myriad of roofs over privies and ash pits, back kitchens and coal sheds. Immediately below her own attic window, the slate roof sloped precipitously downward. Even if she could push up the sash window, which hadn't been shifted in years, and try walking along the tiles like the cat, she'd end up sliding down it and crashing twenty feet or more into the yard below. Not a prospect she was prepared to risk.

Harriet saw no hope of rescue, or escape.

She went back to bed, shivering slightly as she pulled the blankets over her head, telling herself to stop being so melodramatic. Her nan was in the room below. Rose would never tolerate her favourite grandchild being held a virtual prisoner in her own home. When Nan woke up, she would let her out right away.

Harriet lay in breathless anticipation, expecting any moment to hear the key turn in the lock and Nan calling her to come on down for her breakfast. And then she remembered her grandmother's bad leg. Could she even get up the stairs? Probably not. She'd use the old lavvy down the yard and the little kitchenette behind the salon to wash herself.

A cold chill settled round her heart as she wondered what was going to happen to her.

She could smell bacon frying, which reminded her of how hungry she was, having hardly eaten a thing for twenty-four hours, worrying too much about Vinny, and not enough about herself and her child. This was surely the worst possible situation to be in. Wasn't being pregnant difficult enough without the added burden of being locked up like a criminal? The baby seemed to be pressing on her bladder and Harriet realised she wanted to pee, really quite urgently. She felt a surge of irritation towards her stepmother. Surely she didn't expect a pregnant woman to go for much longer without relieving herself? She certainly had no intention of using the chamber-pot Joyce had pointedly left in full view.

Harriet went to the bedroom door and hammered upon it. 'Hey! Joyce, can you hear me? Nan, are you up?' I need the lavatory. It's rather urgent.'

No reply. By the time Joyce finally came, twenty minutes later, Harriet was sitting curled up by the door in some distress and agony.

'Why didn't you use the chamber-pot?' Joyce scolded.

'I'm not a child! I insist you let me out of here. Now!' and Harriet marched along the landing to the bathroom which Joyce herself had had installed only a few years ago. Before then, they'd only had the privy at the end of the yard, but Joyce had wanted the house to be smart and modern, so she'd put in a proper bathroom as well as a new gas fire in the living room so they no longer had to carry coal upstairs.

'We could allus keep the coal in the bath,' Nan had joked at the time, which had earned her a freezing glare.

Now, Harriet ran herself a bath and made a vow to spend as much time in there as possible, and she would refuse absolutely to return to her room until bed time.

It didn't work out that way. By the time she emerged, fresh and clean and feeling much better both physically and emotionally, it was to find Grant lounging at the door. He stood, arms folded, blocking her exit to the stairs. Harriet looked at him, considered an attempt to charge past his square, bulky body, but then smoothed a cautionary hand over her round tummy. Perhaps not. She decided to try charm instead.

'Are you going to allow me to go downstairs and eat my breakfast in a civilised fashion?'

He shook his head. 'You're to go back into your room, and I'll fetch it up on a tray.'

Harriet took a breath, steeling herself for an argument. 'I don't want you coming to my room. If I must be confined, I'd rather Nan brought me my food, or Joyce.'

'Nan isn't fit enough to climb up and down these stairs, and Mam is busy with her first client in the salon.'

Harriet took a breath, feeling increasingly trapped in some sort of horror movie. 'And you're at a loose end, as usual?'

'Actually, I've just got back from work. I drive for Catlow's during the nights and early mornings now. I'm on me way to bed, as a matter of fact, so I'm doing you a favour fetching you your grub. Do you want it or not, it's no skin off my nose if you choose to go hungry.'

As he said all of this he was edging her backwards along the landing until Harriet was standing by her bedroom door. He held it open for her and she could tell by the triumphant glow in his small nasty eyes what pleasure he took from seeing her caged up like this, the revenge he'd always longed for.

Harriet remembered how he'd once stalked her, had seemed ready to actually assault her, his own half-sister. It chilled her a little to find herself at his mercy, but was determined not to show it.

Nevertheless, she had no alternative but to go back into her prison. Five minutes later Grant brought up a bacon sandwich and mug of tea which he placed on her desk with a sardonic grin. 'Make it last. You'll get nowt else till dinner time around twelvish.'

The key was already turning in the lock before Harriet thought to chase after him, and hammer again on the door. 'You won't forget to let me out to go to the lav every hour, will you? I'm *pregnant* for God's sake!'

She could hear her half-brother's laugh echoing back along the landing as he walked away.

33

Joyce

Joyce could hear them giggling together, laughing at *her* no doubt. How she hated them! Was it a crime, she wondered, to wish her husband and best friend dead? Yet she did, with all her heart. The fury and hatred she felt towards her one-time friend and husband was hard to control, threatening to erupt into incandescent rage at any second. It blurred her vision, roared in her ears whenever she saw them together, kissing and canoodling, Stan fussing over Eileen and the other woman casting her glances of utter triumph.

Most of the time Stan was away, and she and Eileen were left to rub along as best they could, with Rose acting as some sort of referee. It was far from ideal.

Joyce did her utmost to ignore Eileen, barely speaking to her, concentrating on finishing her hairdressing course, on planning a future for herself and her son. The house they rented, near the old mill behind Blossom Street in Ancoats, was a spacious terraced house with two living rooms as well as a back kitchen and three bedrooms, but it seemed to have shrunk now that Eileen had moved in with all her stuff. Not to mention her endless wailing and complaining.

The young woman seemed to be constantly throwing up, was finicky about her food, stuffing herself with chips instead of the good fruit and vegetables Joyce provided, and she would burst into tears over the slightest thing. She was driving Joyce to distraction, and because she was pregnant, seemed to imagine she needn't lift a finger. The stream of letters which came from Stan asking how Eileen was, and urging his precious sweetheart not to exert herself, didn't help either.

'Anyone would think he no longer had a wife. He rarely bothers to even ask how *I* am?' Joyce would bitterly complain. 'And I'm quite sure I didn't make as much fuss as this when I was pregnant.'

Rose judged it wise not to comment.

Joyce found it an absolute agony to long for another baby so much, yet be forced to accept that it was her husband's mistress who carried his child. Her stomach would churn and she'd feel physically sick. To add insult to injury she was obliged to care for the other woman throughout her pregnancy, surely more than any wife should be expected to tolerate.

The rage building up inside her was an absolute torment, a dark whirlpool of pent-up resentment and frustration.

The only consolation was that once her condition became obvious Eileen willingly confined herself to the house. She might constantly moan and complain but she clearly had no wish to present herself in public as an object of scandal and gossip. This was a huge relief to Joyce that her own respectability and good name would not be tarnished, a decision which made the whole experience at least endurable.

'I think it would be best if I stayed home too,' Joyce decided.

Rose frowned. 'Why?'

Joyce's answer, as always, was brusque, not wishing to discuss her private decisions with her mother. 'I just do. For one thing, I want to make sure Eileen stays put and doesn't create any unnecessary problems. For another, I've finished my hairdressing course and intend to start up a little business of my own, but not yet, not till this baby is born. We can surely manage for a month or two without my money coming in, since we have Stan's pay arriving regular. I need a rest, and time to think.'

The weeks dragged by, tempers were frequently frayed but somehow Joyce managed to tend to the health and care of her husband's pregnant mistress, while secretly making her plans.

Finally, one morning before dawn in late November 1941, Eileen went into labour.

She started screaming and shouting, gasping and grunting, obviously in considerable pain. Joyce very nearly panicked and called a doctor or midwife to assist, but was still undecided when it suddenly became plain that the baby would be born at any moment. Rose calmly took charge. She held the girl's hands and with a quiet firmness urged her to stop shouting, and to bear down and push.

'Come on, love, stop your fussing and get on with the job. It's hard work and you've got to concentrate. Give it all you've got.'

It was all over surprisingly quickly. Harriet came into the world without making the least trouble for anyone, even her own mother. It turned out to be the swiftest, easiest birth for suddenly there she was, a scrap of new life lying in Rose's capable hands. The child was perfect in every way, a beautiful, healthy baby girl.

Joyce's heart turned over. Why couldn't this have been her daughter? Why wasn't she the one lying in that bed having this easy birth, providing Stan with the child he so craved? Never, in all her life, had she wanted anything more.

As Joyce wrapped the infant in a towel and cradled her in her arms, all of those secret dreams and schemes of the last weeks seemed to crystallize in her mind. If Eileen would simply leave, or disappear off the face of the earth, then she might yet be able to salvage her marriage.

Now, locking up the salon at the end of a difficult day, Joyce congratulated herself that at least she'd provided a home for the child, for which the girl had shown precious little gratitude. No longer would she allow herself to be used and put upon, as she had been in the past by a selfish husband, and by his foolish mistress. Neither of them had given a moment's consideration to her own feelings, or to the sensitivity of the situation. It had been left to Joyce to sort everything out, to smooth over the cracks of her marriage, move house in order to avoid the malice of local gossip, in order to save them all from the wicked treachery of their betrayal without the least thanks from anyone.

Joyce certainly had no intention of allowing that child, Harriet herself, to ruin everything by shaming them before the entire street.

The very thought of Winnie Holmes gossiping with Irma Southworth, her hated rival, was more than any human being should be asked to bear. This was her home, her sanctuary.

No one seemed to appreciate what she'd had to put up with over the years. And if Joyce had found it impossible to love the child, was that her fault? Would it all have been happy families if she'd forgiven her husband for his betrayal? Joyce very much doubted it. Forgiveness was not a part of her nature. The bitterness brought on by a bad marriage had never left her, some might say it had destroyed her. Her mother certainly thought so, but then she wasn't the one who'd been forced to endure it.

And this girl, this love-child of Stan's, had turned out to be every bit as depraved as her whore of a mother. She deserved to suffer, Joyce decided, and she'd make damn sure that she did.

Rose had little appetite for breakfast the next morning. She pushed aside the porridge which Joyce had painstakingly made for her, and carried down to her on a tray. All Rose could think of was her precious granddaughter locked in that room.

'Go on, get it off your chest, whatever it is that's bothering you,' Joyce challenged. 'I can see that you're clearly working yourself up for a flaming row.'

'How can you keep our Harriet locked up? It's inhuman, cruel. How is she supposed to go to the lavvy if she wants to?'

'She's in the bathroom at this precise moment, as a matter of fact,' Joyce informed her mother, in clipped tones. 'Grant will take her some breakfast then fetch her some books from the library, magazines from the shop, whatever she fancies. She'll be fine.'

Rose snorted her derision. 'If she has to rely on our Grant to look after her, she'll be in a right pickle. The lass needs fresh air and exercise, and she should see a doctor. She's pregnant for heavens' sake.'

Joyce remained unmoved. 'That's *her* problem. She should've kept herself respectable, shown more sense in the first place instead of going off with that no-good Vinny Turner.'

'Oh, for goodness' sake, Joyce! What choice did she have? You'd kicked her out of her own home, if you recall. Your own *daughter*!'

'She's not . . .'

'Don't say it, don't ever say that again. *You* chose to keep her. No one twisted your arm.' Rose was wagging a furious finger, going red in the face with fury, which alarmed Joyce as it did no good at all for her mother's blood pressure. The last thing she wanted was for her to suffer another stroke.

'Mother, will you please keep your voice down. Half the neighbours will be able to hear you. Be calm, I beg you.'

But Rose wasn't listening. 'I don't care if they do hear me, I'm well past calm. You wanted that babby from the minute she was born, maybe even before, only it didn't work out quite as you'd hoped, did it? You couldn't ever forget that she was Eileen's child and not yours, or forgive Stan for his transgression, taunting him with it even when he came back from the war a cripple. No wonder Harriet became her father's girl, all because of your wicked jealousy. You've made that poor lass's life a living hell, picking on her the whole time for summat that wasn't her fault. How often have I needed to step in and protect her over the years? You should be ashamed of yerself, you should really.'

Joyce had gone white to the lips during this tirade, but now turned to leave.

'Don't you walk away when I'm talking to you. What sort of woman takes on a child and then refuses to love it? Ask yourself that.'

Stan arrived home a few days after the birth, having been granted compassionate leave although he'd told a lie in order to get it, somehow failing to mention it was his mistress who was giving birth and letting everyone assume it to be his wife.

He was delighted, thrilled with the baby, even though she was not the son he'd most wanted. And to her great surprise, Joyce discovered that he showed little interest in Eileen. Admittedly she was no longer the glamorous figure Stan had fallen in love with. She'd let herself go badly, piled on the pounds as she'd lazed about doing very little throughout her pregnancy. Now, he simply pecked a kiss on to her forehead before devoting his entire time and attention to the child.

Stan did have the decency to express his gratitude to Joyce for helping to look after Eileen, and for caring for this new baby.

'You wanted a child of your own, now you've got one, thanks to Eileen,' Joyce caustically remarked.

'You deserve credit too. Since her parents turned her out, Eileen wouldn't have been capable of coping on her own. I'm grateful for your generosity, Joyce. It was very – forgiving of you.'

Joyce had never felt less forgiving in her life, but she let the remark pass.

He appeared so grateful that he not only asked if he might join his wife in her bed that night, but was particularly loving towards her. He seemed to feel the need to celebrate this joyous event. Joyce was elated. It felt almost like a return to their old passion. Almost.

Yet she knew it was the child he loved most, and not her.

Stan was enraptured by Harriet, completely captivated. Maybe Joyce should have recognised the seeds of jealousy within which set down roots in those first few days. Too dazzled by her night of love, by the attention her husband was at last paying to her rather than to his mistress, she fooled herself into thinking that Eileen's task had been completed, that she was no longer relevant or of any concern to him. Joyce could almost believe that she was the one who'd given him this precious baby, and basked in his praise.

'You've done a tremendous job, Joyce. Look at her, isn't she wonderful? See how she grasps my fingers, so firm, so strong. You don't know what this means to me, to hold my own child in my arms.'

'She is indeed a lovely baby.' Joyce's heart ached that she hadn't been the one to provide her husband with the child he'd always wanted. There seemed no way to get round that fact. 'It breaks my heart to think how you and I were once so desperately in love, how we seemed so well suited at first, and yet our marriage has been a total disaster, through no fault of our own. All because I suffered that rape. It's so sad.'

Stan looked at her, considering her words with such care that Joyce's heart did a little flip. Was it possible that she could persuade him to forgive her, even now, for not being entirely honest with him over that?

'If I could turn back the clock . . .' she began, but he flapped a hand at her.

'We'd all like to do that.'

'Would you?'

'Of course.'

'And what would you do differently, if you could?'

He paused, looking deeply into her eyes, and then down at the child before answering. 'Maybe show a bit more understanding and patience, a little more compassion.'

'I should think this war destroys compassion.'

He nodded. 'Such emotions feel like weakness, and weakness in war is something a man can't afford. I've heard so many terrible stories among my comrades, seen so much heartbreak. My best mate's wife cheated on him with a local pacifist, would you believe? Another was left standing at the altar looking a right proper Charlie, and then was shot to pieces only weeks later. She could at least have made what miserable life he had left happy. He started taking stupid risks, I think, not caring whether he lived or died. There are loads of stories of guys being dumped by their girl-friends for someone else, despite the fact they are facing death and danger every day of their lives. You get so's you can't trust anyone. I assumed you were spinning me a yarn, about the rape.'

It was the first time they'd talked as reasonable adults in months.

'But now you've surpassed yourself, Joyce, looking after Eileen, and this wonderful baby.'

They both looked at the child, cradled in Stan's arms, her intense gaze seeming to consider them with a remarkable intelligence, as if wondering what they were going to do about her, now that she'd arrived.

Encouraged by Stan's more mellow attitude, Joyce took her courage in both hands. 'We could always adopt her.'

'Adopt?'

'You want the best for her, I suppose?' Joyce stroked the baby's soft cheek, smiled into those baby blue eyes which were already showing signs of darkening to a beautiful slate grey.

'Of course.'

'Well, I doubt you could prove you had any rights at all to her, not as things stand, since you and Eileen aren't married, even though we both know that she is indeed your child. Eileen could simply up-sticks and leave and marry someone else, and you couldn't stop her.'

Stan frowned, his hold on the baby tightening slightly.

'But you and I are man and wife,' Joyce went on, her voice perfectly calm and reasonable. 'Eileen isn't in a good position to bring up an illegitimate child. And, as I say, you have an equal right to her, a better claim, in a way, since your name will be on her birth certificate as her legal father, and you're in a good position to provide her with a stable home. We could adopt . . . legitimise her.'

'You mean officially, signing papers and such?'

Joyce looked him straight in the eye. 'Or simply pretend she's ours, let people assume that I was the one who gave birth.'

Stan puffed out his cheeks and was thoughtful for several long minutes. 'Well, I'll admit I let my commanding officer make such an assumption. It seemed easier that way. But we'd surely never get away with it, not here. Did no one attend the birth, no doctor or midwife?'

Joyce shook her head. 'It all happened so quickly there wasn't time to call one. Rose attended to her, and she'll keep quiet if I tell her to. For all anyone knows, it could have been me giving birth.'

Stan frowned. 'But you weren't the one looking pregnant all these last months, Eileen was. How would you get around that?'

'Actually, that isn't such a problem. Eileen had the good sense to stay indoors, out of the gaze of public censure, as she'd no wish to create a scandal. Once I realised this was her intention, some sort of instinct kicked in and I did the same. Neither of us has been out of the house for months. Mother did all the shopping, told people I wasn't feeling too well if anyone enquired. No one would be in the least surprised if I suddenly emerged with a baby. Many women prefer a quiet pregnancy, particularly if they've suffered a miscarriage, as I have.'

Stan was staring at his wife in wonder and disbelief. 'You've worked this all out, haven't you?'

'I've thought about it, yes.'

'And you'd do this for me? You'd forgive my – indiscretion – my affair with Eileen and accept this child, *my* child, as your own?'

Joyce lifted her chin and agreed that she would. 'I'm perfectly willing to give our marriage another go, if you are.' If he said no, if he chose instead to walk out the door with the baby *and* Eileen, what would she do then? It didn't bear thinking about. But if keeping this child meant she could also have Stan, then she would do it, at whatever cost to her pride.

There was another short silence and then Stan nodded. It was the smallest of gestures and yet made a world of difference. Joyce's hopes soared, and she actually smiled.

'Why don't you speak to Eileen, Stan? The suggestion would come better from you. See how she reacts. She might well be grateful for her baby to be given a bright, new, respectable future.'

The creases between his brow deepened as Stan thought through all the implications, perhaps wondering if they really could pull it off. But Joyce could tell that he was already hooked on the idea. She could see it in the softness of his gaze as he looked down upon his precious daughter cradled so lovingly in his arms. He would be a good father, Joyce thought.

The only question which remained was, could she be a good mother to this unexpected, alien child? But why should she not be? The baby might be the very thing to bring them together.

34

Harriet

The days passed in an absolute agony, each one torturously long so that Harriet was compelled to utilise the chamber-pot, much against her better judgement. She hadn't used such a thing since she was three years old when she'd been too afraid to go down the yard in the dark, particularly with the possibility of an air-raid siren going off at any moment. Now she felt as if she'd slipped back to those grim days of war.

Each day, as promised, Grant would bring her midday meal: a Spam or fish-paste sandwich, mug of tea or coffee, which she always ate simply because she seemed to be constantly famished. Maybe it was because she was eating for two. Rebelliously going on a hunger strike, she decided, wouldn't help her baby in the least, and probably give Joyce enormous satisfaction.

Grant would then allow her use of the bathroom where she would wash out the chamber-pot with hot water and Dettol, and take as long as possible over her ablutions. He always waited outside until she was finished, studiously marshalling the procedure so that there was no hope of escape.

Harriet was very often near to tears. How would she survive three months of this? It was horrendous! Inhuman! Was Grant going to act as her jailor throughout? Dear lord, it was outrageous. There must be some way out.

He also brought her some library books, which she leafed through in a perfunctory fashion. She started on a John Creasey detective story but couldn't quite engage her mind on the plot. Then she tried *Gone with the Wind*, a favourite which she'd read

many times. But not even Scarlett O'Hara's troubles could take
Harriet's mind off her own.

Very sensibly, Harriet lay down every afternoon to take a rest,
for the sake of the baby, as well as to ease her back and legs
which ached from constantly pacing back and forth in the small
confined space. More often than not she lay staring at the ceiling,
worrying and plotting over hopeless plans of escape, but occasionally she would sleep, if only out of exhaustion.

One such afternoon she woke feeling surprisingly refreshed.
Even though it was still light outside, it being June, there was
that slight change in the air which told her that the afternoon
was over and evening had come.

And Harriet again wanted to empty her bladder.

Irritated that Grant was once more late in allowing her to visit
the bathroom, Harriet hammered on the door loud enough to
bring the entire street running. Although not, apparently, loud
enough to bring her half-brother, or to disturb Joyce. Harriet felt
again that terrible sensation of being trapped. She was locked in
this room without anyone knowing where she was, and her stepmother held the key. It could have been some soppy fairy tale
had it not been so deadly serious.

And then she saw the note. Someone had pushed it under the
door. She picked it up and experienced a sudden spurt of hope
when she saw the familiar scrawl of handwriting. It was from
Vinny.

Oh, my goodness. Had he come looking for her? Was he missing
her already? She felt touched that Vinny should care enough
about her to take the trouble to come back to Champion Street
and deliver this letter by hand. But then it occurred to Harriet
that Shelley had probably been the one to pop it through the
letter-box, and not Vinny at all. She sighed with regret. If only
he'd turned out to be reliable and supportive, instead of wild and
selfish.

Her thoughts were interrupted by a tap on the door. 'Are you
all right, love?'

Harriet ran to press herself against it. 'Nan, thank heavens it's you. I've missed you so much. Can you let me out?'

'Sorry, love, I don't have a key. Are you all right?' The old woman sounded anxious, and slightly out of breath, as if climbing the stairs had taxed her energy.

'How long is she going to keep me here?'

'I wish I knew, love, and before you ask, no, I've no idea where the key is but I mean to get my hands on one just as soon as I can. We'll have you out of there in two shakes of a lamb's tail. Grant must have it. I'll appeal to his better nature and persuade him to lend it to me.'

Harriet's heart plummeted, knowing Nan had little hope of success as Grant didn't have a better nature. 'Please do,' was all she said, not wanting her grandmother to realise how upset she was.

'Eeh, love, what a pickle we're in.'

'Was it you who brought up Vinny's letter?'

'Aye, and I didn't let on to Joyce, so you're quite safe. I come upstairs last night on me hands and knees while they were all abed. You'd have laughed if you'd seen me. I must've looked a right tuckle with me nightie tucked up round me waist showing all me bloomers.'

Harriet couldn't help but laugh. Her Nan was a real case. What would she do without her? 'He says he's been promised a recording contract and wants me to go to London with him.'

'Will you go?'

Harriet shook her head, even though her grandmother couldn't see her through the bedroom door. 'I'm pleased for him. Maybe he'll get himself together now he has the chance to be a real success. But it's over between us as far as I'm concerned. I was stupid to get involved with him in the first place.'

'I hope you mean that.'

'I do.'

'I'm relieved to hear it. He's trouble is that one.'

Harriet neither agreed nor disagreed with her grandmother's opinion. She looked down at the letter in her hand. 'I'll write and wish him luck. Will you see that he gets it?'

'Aye, course I will, somehow.' Letters, Rose thought, weren't they the bane of her life?

Her grandmother came often after that first time, whenever Joyce was occupied with her customers in the salon, or out with Joe Southworth. Harriet would hear her fetch a chair from the neighbouring bedroom she used to occupy, the creak of the cane seat as she sat herself on it. Then Harriet would slide down to the floor, resting her back against the varnished wood panels so that they could talk.

Today, she wrapped her arms about her knees and asked the one question that haunted her. 'Tell me about my mother. Who *is* she? I know nothing about her, and my head is teeming with questions.'

Silence, followed by a heavy sigh. When Rose spoke again, her voice was tense and barely above a whisper. 'If I tell, you're not to mention this conversation to Joyce, not a word, you understand?'

'I won't, I swear it.'

'She'd have me roasted on a platter if she knew I'd been interfering again, spilling the beans, as it were.'

'I won't say a word, but you haven't told me anything yet,' Harriet reminded her, desperate for information.

The whisper was barely audible through the thick wooden panels, nevertheless Harriet heard every word, clear as a bell. 'She was a friend of your mother's, of Joyce's, I mean. Best friends. Joyce and Stan weren't getting on as they should, for whatever reason.'

Rose paused here as if choosing her words carefully, which in fact she was. She was deliberating over whether to mention the doubt over Grant's parentage. It was the sort of information that could be dynamite for the young lass if she let anything slip in an unguarded moment. She'd mebbe come to that later.

'I'm sure he were a good man at heart, your pa, but he had his faults, they both did. Stan were badly damaged by the war, in his head as well as in his legs. But then the war messed up a lot of folk in this street. Anyway, Eileen, that were her name, and Stan, they had a bit of a fling like, and you were the result.'

'I think I'd gathered that,' Harriet said.

'Aye, well, I know very little about Eileen, to be honest, but Joyce and Stan were like chalk and cheese, oil and water, at daggers drawn, like a red rag to a bull, however you like to put it, they never did get on.'

'Don't I know it,' Harriet responded with feeling.

'It were like that right from the start. The marriage might have had a chance if either of them had been prepared to offer a modicum of forgiveness to the other, but they never did, and trust was alien to them both.'

'But why, if they loved each enough to marry?'

'It were a bit of a rush job, because of the war, tha' knows, but Joyce did love him at first, that's true. Then it all went wrong.'

'But why? I don't understand.'

Another short pause, and then, 'You must keep your word not to let on that you know, not to anyone.'

'I promise.'

It all came out then about the rape, of Joyce being pregnant with another man's child, a stranger's child, at the time of their marriage. 'She didn't know his name,' Rose explained. 'And even if he were only a drunken sailor out for a good time and not some stranger up a back street, that were no excuse for such dreadful behaviour.'

Harriet was aghast. It made her see Joyce in quite a different light. 'What a terrible thing to happen! So Grant isn't Stan's son?' Harriet too was whispering, unable to quite take it all in.

'No, I don't who the lad's father was.'

'Does Grant himself know any of this?'

'No.'

'And Joyce didn't even tell Dad?'

'Not until after they were wed. She was too afraid she might lose him. He guessed the truth though when he came home and found the babe-in-arms he'd expected to see practically walking.'

'Oh, goodness, how awful!' Harriet was silent for a moment, sifting through this shocking information in her mind, trying to make sense of it. 'So that's why Stan never really got on with Grant?'

'I dare say. The fact that Joyce lied built up a deep resentment in him.'

'And that's why he had the affair, out of revenge because Grant wasn't his son?'

'I reckon so.'

For the first time in her life Harriet felt pity for her half-brother. He too was a pawn in this dreadful marriage, a victim of their parents' need to punish each other for the misfortunes life had dealt them. 'But why didn't *my* mother want me? Why did Eileen let Joyce and Stan keep me when Joyce clearly resented my very existence?'

'Nay, you'd have to ask her that.'

'If only the dead could talk.'

'Aye, if only they could.'

Eileen made it abundantly clear to them both that on no account was she prepared to surrender her child to anyone, particularly not to Stan who now seemed to have become quite cool and distant towards her. 'I won't do it, not simply to avoid stupid scandal and gossip, or even to see her legitimised, or whatever fancy name you might use for this so-called adoption, not at any price. Harriet is *mine!*'

'And how do you propose to survive? How will you provide for her?' Joyce gently enquired, as Stan stood silently by, apparently dumbfounded by this violent reaction to his generous offer.

'I'll cope somehow.'

'You don't even have a home to go to, a job or any money. Would your parents take you in?'

Eileen mumbled something incoherent, which obviously meant the answer was in the negative.

'So, what would you do? Where would you go? I've fed and kept you throughout this pregnancy, without even charging you board and lodging beyond your ration book. I'm still feeding you, *and* the baby, now. How could you possibly manage? If you were found starving on the streets, or put in some mother and baby home, she'd be taken away from you anyway. Besides which, she isn't simply your child, she's Stan's too, and as her father he has as much right as you to decide how she is raised.'

'I know what your little scheme is,' Eileen screamed. 'You want to steal Harriet from me. Well, I won't let you do that, do you hear? She's *mine*! *My* child, not *yours*, and you're not having her.'

Stan took her by the shoulders, trying to calm her. 'Look, it's nonsense to accuse us of trying to steal her from you. We aren't doing any such thing. You could still be involved in her upbringing, see her any time you like. You could become a favourite aunt. Wouldn't you like that? All the fun and none of the work. Don't get yourself into a state, Eileen. We want only to do what's right, what's best for the baby.'

She turned on him then like a spitting cat, making the baby cry as she still held her tightly in her arms. 'No you *don't*! You want to take her from me. Well, you're not having her, do you hear? I'm leaving *now*, and taking Harriet with me. You can't stop me!'

'You're upsetting the child,' Stan quietly reminded her, taking the baby from her and putting her safely in her crib. Eileen's gaze remained fixed on the infant, her fear and longing all too evident.

Joyce adopted a more placatory tone, while making sure she blocked the exit in case the other woman should decide to make a run for it. 'Don't be foolish, Eileen. Look outside, it's late November. It's cold and raining, and you have nowhere to go. Stop talking nonsense and start thinking about this child instead of yourself for a change.'

But Eileen wasn't willing to listen to anyone, certainly not Joyce. She launched herself at Stan. 'You said you'd marry me. You swore it. You promised me that you'd divorce her and marry me, then you and I could bring Harriet up as man and wife. You *promised*! Why can't we do that?'

'Because . . .' Joyce calmly interposed . . . 'Stan has no grounds for divorce. I'm not the one who has enjoyed, if that's the right word, an extra-marital affair. And for another, he's a Catholic and believes in the sanctity of marriage. Did he fail to mention that small fact to you?' Turning to her husband, Joyce quietly asked, '*Did* you promise her marriage?'

Stan looked uncomfortable, clearly regretting it if he ever had. 'I may have said something of the sort, I can't remember.'

'Can't remember?' Eileen screamed as she pummelled at his chest with her clenched fists. Joyce grabbed hold of her, desperately trying to calm the woman, and there was an undignified tussle between the pair of them as Eileen fought to reach Stan, sharp talons outstretched, eager to claw his eyes out for this apparent defection.

Joyce shouted at her, although words were having little effect. 'Stop this, Eileen. Stop it! Stan is going, this minute, to register the birth, naming ourselves, as a married couple, as the baby's parents. Your name won't even appear on the birth certificate. You will have no rights over her whatsoever.'

Eileen stopped crying upon the instant to stare at Joyce wide eyed with horror, and then she let out a high, piercing wail before putting her hands to her head and falling to her knees in fresh hysterics.

Even Joyce began to panic and, turning to Stan, ordered him to leave. 'Quickly! For God's sake, *go*! Get the child's birth registered and leave this to me. I'll give her something to calm her, and make her sleep. Go on. *Go!*'

Stan didn't hang around to argue. Enjoying a bit of fun with the woman was one thing, dealing with an hysterical female quite another matter entirely.

As he hurried out of the house, Eileen scrambled to her feet and ran after him, continuing to sob and rail, to scream and rage, but Joyce caught her at the door before she could escape. Once Stan had left, she gave her erstwhile friend a violent shake then slapped her sharply across the face, stunning her at last into silence.

'Now listen to me, you little *whore*! Stan is *my* husband, understand? And this baby is *his* child. You are just some two-bit tart he happened to pick up and play with for a while. He's a sailor, fighting a war. I don't suppose you were the first girl in port he's taken to his bed, and I very much doubt you'll be the last, but that's *my* problem. You should be deeply grateful that I didn't chuck you out on the streets the first time you set your grubby little toes over my threshold.

'I remember only too well that you and I used to be good friends, once upon a time. But then you invited me to that flipping party, one of your so-called mates raped me and my life was left in ruins, as you are only too aware. Your solution to this disaster was to steal my husband. So yes, Eileen dear, now *I* am going to steal your child, and there's absolutely nothing you can do to stop me. I'll swear in any court of law that she's mine, that I was the one who gave birth.'

'You'll never get away with it,' Eileen hissed. 'They could examine you, prove you hadn't given birth recently.'

'Ah, but I have. I had a miscarriage just a few months ago if you recall. So how could they tell? And why would they even need to check? What makes better sense if I decided, having suffered those recent disappointments, that I take especial care with this pregnancy and stay in bed throughout. You never saw a doctor, did you?'

Eileen shook her head, her expression dazed and bewildered. 'You said not to. You didn't want a scandal.'

'Quite, nor are we going to have one now.'

'But Rose was present at the birth too. She'll say what really happened.'

'She'll keep her mouth shut, if I tell her to do so. No one will question it, I do assure you. I shall take myself to bed now, to welcome visitors for my lying in, and *you* won't even be here. We'll see you're well provided for, find you a room to rent somewhere, and give you a sum of money to tide you over. You can go and mess up some other woman's life for all I care, but you'll leave my husband alone. Got that? So don't bother to try anything. The word of some jealous tart, who seduced my foolish husband and then complained when he abandoned her, isn't going to be believed by anyone. They'd see you as a woman spurned, simply out for revenge.

'And I would be very angry indeed if you did that, because it would ruin my good name, something I won't tolerate at any price.'

'I can't stay here,' Harriet railed, as the endless monotony continued day after day. 'I won't be locked up in my own bedroom for weeks or months on end. It's ridiculous, impossible, totally unfair. I won't put up with it.'

'So what do you intend to do about it?' Grant smirked, unmoved by her panic.

Harriet was making her feelings known as once more her half-brother presented her with breakfast on a tray. She'd quite lost track of time but she must have been locked up for over a week now, ten days, maybe twelve? They went through this same routine every morning, the well guarded trip to the bathroom, the break-fast accompanied by the usual taunting and caustic remarks. Then the sound of the key in the lock as she'd be left alone for several more long and lonely hours.

'I'll climb out of the window and over the roof, if necessary.'

Grant laughed. 'I'd like to see you try. You'd be smashed to smithereens in the back yard, which might save us all a lot of bother in the long run.'

As he set the tray down on her bedside table, Harriet made as if she were about to vomit. 'Oh, God, I'm going to be sick.'

Harriet lurched towards him, as if she was about to throw up all over him, and Grant instinctively backed off. 'Hey, don't chuck up over me. All right, all right, go on.' Instinctively, he stepped out of her way to let her rush to the toilet, one hand clapped to her mouth.

But she didn't go into the bathroom. Instead, Harriet ran to the stairs. She was almost half way down before Grant realised he'd been tricked. He rushed after her, crashing down the stairs in her wake, shouting for her to stop. Unfortunately, in her panic to escape, and encumbered by her pregnancy, Harriet lost her footing. With a cry of dismay she fell, tumbling down the last few stairs to lie unmoving at the bottom.

35

Harriet

Harriet was lying on the old couch in the living room since Joyce had decided it would not be necessary to call out the doctor. The last thing she wanted was for Doc Mitchell to come poking his nose in where it wasn't wanted. 'You've given yourself a bit of a shaking, but I reckon there's no real harm done beyond this sprained ankle.' She was wrapping the injured foot in a cold wet crêpe bandage as she briskly issued these unsympathetic comments.

Harriet was crying, worried about her baby, but Joyce had little patience for tears.

'Stop your snivelling, crying won't do no good. What were you doing, letting her run down the stairs?' she accused her son. 'You couldn't have been keeping a proper eye on her.'

'She was about to puke all over me,' Grant informed his mother in injured tones.

'Oh, for goodness' sake, give me strength. Why am I surrounded by fools and idiots? It was a trick, you moron.'

Grant looked suitably contrite, as he always did when his mother was berating him. 'I'll take her back upstairs then, shall I?'

'No! I'm not going,' Harriet cried. 'I absolutely refuse.' She intended to resist to her very last breath rather than spend her days incarcerated in that room. 'Look, you and I both know this isn't an argument about an illegitimate baby. This is about something which happened in the past, something that doesn't even concern me, except that maybe I'm a pawn in some stupid game or other. Did you agree to keep me out of some twisted need for revenge against this girl Dad got pregnant? If so, then I refuse to be a part of it. I have the right to live my own life, not to be manipulated by you any longer. You don't give a toss about me, or my child. You never have.'

'I care about my reputation.'

'True, I accept that, and I don't want any trouble, or scandal, any more than you do. If I promise not to do a runner, to stay in the house, will you at least leave the bedroom door unlocked?'

Joyce snorted her derision at the idea. 'How could I trust you? You've run away once, and could again. Besides, folk come in and out of here all the time. It's a hairdressing salon, for God's sake! They'd be sure to realise someone was upstairs and that it's likely to be you, even if your grandmother weren't blabbing her mouth off all over the place.'

'But there has to be a better way to deal with this.'

Joyce sat herself down on the chair opposite with a weary sigh. Harriet had never seen her look so worn out, haggard almost, with bags under her eyes. 'Such as what? There's only one solution. This child must be adopted. On no account will I have it here.'

Harriet lifted her chin and there was a firmness in her tone. 'I've already told you a thousand times that I'm keeping it. I'm not sure how I'll manage, but I'll work something out when the time comes. I'm sorry if my condition causes you embarrassment, but there's nothing I can do about that but agree to stay in the house. If that doesn't suit, don't you have any relatives who could hide me away in the country for the next two or three months?'

After several moments of consideration, Joyce said, 'I could speak to Father Dimmock, ask him to recommend a Mother and Baby Home. If you won't stay quietly here, then that seems the best solution.'

'Nay,' Rose interjected, unable to keep quiet any longer. 'You mustn't put her in one of them places. They're wicked! Look what they did to young Dena Dobson, and little Trudy, and that lot were Methodists. The nuns are much worse. We must steer well clear of them.'

Joyce got to her feet, key in hand. 'You either stay in that room, or go into a home where at least you'd have some company. Or I might just send you into a Home for Wayward Girls instead, which might never let you out. It's what you deserve. The choice is yours. Either way, you're not foisting that bastard child on me.'

Harriet put her head in her hands and wept.

Ever since Steve learned that Harriet was married he'd realised that he had no alternative but to do exactly as she'd instructed him to do, that is, forget all about her. He'd started dating a 'nice' girl, one of whom his mother entirely approved.

Caroline was petite and blonde, and rather pretty in a girly sort of way. A fellow student, she'd made it plain from the first week that she fancied him, and he'd really grown quite fond of her. They got along great and she'd persuaded him to join the chess club and film society, although the movies seemed a bit arty or French to Steve, not really to his taste.

He preferred a good laugh, like Jack Lemmon in *The Apartment* which they'd gone to see the other night. Caro had been less impressed, saying how awful it was to loan out an apartment in order to allow someone to commit adultery.

'That's the joke, how he comes to be in this mess because of his soft heart, and then he falls for the girl. It's just a story,' Steve had reminded her, but Caro's sense of humour didn't quite stretch that far.

This was only one of many drawbacks he'd noticed about her. She wasn't a great listener, and loved to organise him. More often than not she was the one who decided where they went on a Saturday night, leaving him very little say in the matter. Not that Steve cared. He seemed to have lost interest in most things along with losing Harriet, but he was starting to feel concerned about Caro. They had very little in common. She liked opera and he preferred rock music. Steve would much rather listen even to The Scrapyard Kids than some dire woman screeching on the high notes. He liked to read detective novels and Caro resented any time when he wasn't able to talk to her, or rather listen to her talking.

The other problem was his mother.

Caro had come home with him on numerous occasions for tea or Sunday lunch, and although her parents were only humble shopkeepers, the very fact she was training to be a teacher, as he was, meant that his mother was utterly captivated by her. Steve was beginning to feel quite incidental, as if this whole relationship with Caro was being engineered by his mother. The pair of them had become bosom pals – to such an extent that before he'd realised what was happening, he'd found himself agreeing to an engagement before he returned to college in the autumn.

Caroline was an attractive girl, and good company, so it seemed easier to go along with her plans when he wasn't in a frame of mind to see any alternative hope for happiness in his life. But fond as he was of her, he wasn't certain if what he felt was true love. Was Caro *the* one? How could she be when he still couldn't get Harriet out of his mind? And the idea of actually marrying the girl sent a shiver down his spine. He felt as if he was being manipulated into something he wasn't yet ready for.

He knew he would never even have looked at Caroline Lawson if Harriet had still been around. The mere thought of his lovely sweet Harriet being married to Vinny Turner was doing his head in. What had come over her?

All right, he could understood that because of the foul mood she was in, this bitter resentment she was holding against Joyce, against life in general, she'd probably slept with the guy. But that was no reason to tie herself down to the idiot, who would surely make both their lives a complete misery. Although, judging by his wild behaviour it's doubtful it would be a long life.

Steve hated himself for thinking such horrible thoughts, and he really must try harder to put Harriet out of his mind. Caro didn't even like him to mention her and had got quite touchy on the subject. And Harriet herself had made it very clear to him that her future was with Vinny. So what choice did he have? What did it really matter who he married if it couldn't be Harriet?

★

As the summer term, and his first year at college, came to an end, Steve returned home alone, without Caroline. He'd decided he needed time to think things through in peace and quiet, to be sure in his own mind that he wanted this friendship to progress to something more permanent. His mother was full of questions as to why he hadn't brought her with him.

'I thought you two couldn't bear to be apart?' she challenged him, a sentimental smile on her face.

'I never said that,' her son insisted, 'you did.' He felt a familiar nudge of panic, knowing that what had started as an innocent friendship was quickly escalating out of control. Steve guessed his mother would be practically putting the finishing touches to the engagement party she intended to hold to celebrate what would clearly be the social event of the season. And she was constantly expressing how keen she was to meet dear Caro's parents. If he didn't watch out, she'd be nagging him to put down a deposit on a nice little semi and starting to plan the wedding.

'There's no reason why I can't enjoy a bit of time alone, is there? She isn't my fiancée, let alone my wife.'

'Not yet! But the date of your coming engagement is marked in my diary,' Margaret teased, a knowing twinkle in her eye.

Steve began to feel quite hot under the collar. How he'd mired himself into a commitment of such magnitude, he couldn't quite understand. 'Even so, it doesn't mean I plan to rush into marriage. I've just got through school practice, which was tough enough, and there's still one more year of training to do, with my thesis and finals to face. With the long vac coming up I need some time to myself, to think, and to catch up on my studies. I also need to earn some money. I'm going to ask Barry Holmes if he'll take me back on the fruit and veg stall. I've neither the time nor the means to even consider taking a wife at the moment.'

'Of course not, dear, no one is suggesting you should,' Margaret Blackstock purred. 'But the months rush by, and before you know it your training will be over, and with it the opportunity to find yourself a nice girl.'

'Rubbish!' Steve retorted. 'There's plenty of time. Anyway,

I'm thinking that maybe I should date a few more girls, just to be sure.'

His mother looked horrified by the very idea of such a betrayal, and wagged an admonitory finger at her son. 'You would live to regret it if you lost her. She's a lovely girl and would make anyone a fine wife.'

'There are plenty of other fish in the sea.'

'Indeed there are,' his father murmured from behind his paper.

Margaret looked daggers at her husband, but managed to restrain herself and say nothing more, largely because of the warning glance he gave her in return. She confined herself to giving one of her disapproving sniffs, and Steve escaped, before the interrogation entered a more dangerous phase.

Steve went straight over to the market to speak to Barry Holmes, who was more than happy to provide him with work for the summer vacation. Steve was delighted, and said so. This particular evening, Winnie was also present, assisting her husband in packing away the fruit and veg into boxes. They exchanged a few pleasantries as they loaded up the van, and then Winnie said, 'Have you seen Harriet lately?'

Steve shook his head. 'Not for a while, no. Have you?'

Winnie glanced around, in that secretive way she had when she was in possession of a titbit of gossip. 'No, I haven't, but reliable sources inform me that she's back home.'

Steve's jaw dropped open. 'Back home? How can she be? What happened to her husband?'

Winnie frowned. 'What husband? Oh, you mean that Vinny Turner? Nay, I wouldn't know owt about that, but – my friend – my source, hasn't said anything about no wedding. I'm sure I would've heard if she were wed. The poor girl's er – general health – however, is another matter,' and Winnie tapped the side of her nose indicating she was allowed to say no more on the subject.

Steve went white to the lips. Harriet not married? She was still free, like him? 'Are you sure, Winnie?'

'Absolutely positive. Not much slips past me, lad.'

'No, indeed,' he agreed.

Left alone with her injured foot propped up on cushions, Harriet woke from her snooze to become conscious of raised voices below. She'd been half aware that someone had come in a little while ago but had presumed it to be a late customer; now she realised it was Steve, and to her horror they were talking about her, something about adoption.

By the time Harriet had struggled up from the couch and limped to the top of the stairs where she could hear better, Steve was saying, 'But it's not the baby's fault this has happened, is it? It must surely be the victim in all of this.' Steve rather thought Harriet was a victim too, of Joyce's harsh treatment of her, but didn't say as much.

He'd been badly shaken by the news but had done his best not to show it. Steve wished the baby was his, but even though it wasn't, his first instinct was one of joy that Harriet was still free, and he couldn't help wondering if she'd still have him. Although what his mother would have to say if he dumped Caro practically on the eve of their engagement and married Harriet, an unmarried mother, he had no wish to even consider at this juncture.

Despite these seemingly impossible obstacles, Steve asked if he could see her. He was filled with anxiety over Harriet's state of mind, longed to take her in his arms and console her, to tell her all that was in his heart.

Joyce instantly dismissed the idea. 'She's not receiving visitors at the moment. In any case, didn't I hear on the grapevine you were seeing someone? A pretty young blonde.'

Steve fidgeted with discomfort. 'I do have a new girlfriend, that's true.'

'Harriet will be sorry to hear that, in the circumstances.'

At the head of the stairs, crouched in a corner, Harriet put her hands over her face as her cheeks burned. Dear Lord, surely Joyce wasn't hinting that Steve should marry her? She felt humiliated enough that he should have learned of her shame, let alone that Joyce should even consider he might help her out of this mess.

And who was this pretty blonde? Was she the same blonde that Steve danced with that night when she'd first gone with Vinny?

Steve was thinking that all he wanted to do was rush upstairs to talk to Harriet. Joyce, on the other hand, was determined to stop him by physically blocking his path, and was now throwing every insult she could think of at her adopted daughter, even though Harriet wasn't present to defend herself.

'She's a foolish, wayward girl who's reaping the rewards of her own wantonness. She certainly won't want to see *you*, not now you've got yourself a fiancée all lined up.'

Harriet's cheeks burned all the more as she caught some of this tirade, but didn't hear Steve quietly suggest that this was perhaps for Harriet to decide.

'Don't imagine for one minute that she still loves *you*,' Joyce hissed at the young man through gritted teeth. 'The silly tart might well go back to Vinny Turner and marry him in the end. Who knows? I wouldn't put anything past that girl.'

Harriet nibbled anxiously on her thumbnail as she strained to hear the hushed, angry voices. What on earth were they saying now? Something about Vinny?

There was more mumbled conversation which she couldn't quite catch and then her stepmother's voice rang out, loud and clear.

'You're right to be cautious and make other plans, lad. A marriage for the sake of propriety rarely works, even if you were once fond of the girl,' Joyce announced, her tone growing increasingly strident, almost as if she wanted Harriet to hear. 'Anyroad, you're not the father so it isn't your responsibility, and taking on another man's child is always a disaster. You'd find that you quickly came to resent it, may well turn away from it altogether when you have a child of your own, as my husband did.'

Harriet closed her eyes in agony. She would never, ever, agree to marrying Steve, for that very reason. It was good that he'd taken her at her word and found himself a new girlfriend. She felt happy that he, at least, had a chance at happiness. Even if he hadn't found someone else, Harriet would never inflict herself upon him. This wasn't *his* child, *his* problem. Hadn't a similar situation destroyed Joyce and Stan's marriage? She certainly had no intention of making the same mistake.

Harriet could bear to hear no more and slipped quietly to her room where she began to pack her few belongings, which meant that she missed Steve's fervent response.

'I don't believe I would feel any resentment against the child. I would love it simply because it was Harriet's. Why would I not? I see no reason why a marriage between us couldn't work. Pardon me for saying so, but just because your own marriage was a disaster, Mrs Ashton, doesn't mean ours would be.'

Joyce's pale cheeks lit with twin spots of furious crimson, and Steve was suddenly filled with anxiety, realising he might well have overstepped the bounds of decency. But having gone this far, he couldn't stop now.

He took a breath and spoke calmly and quietly, with as much patience as he could muster. 'I love her, is that so difficult to understand? Can't you see that I always will? We were meant to be together, and, begging your pardon, I believe she still loves me. Where is she, Joyce? If you don't tell me I'll make your life a complete hell. You have my word on that. Is she upstairs?'

Spitting with fury, Joyce attempted once more to block him but Steve had had enough and patiently set her to one side. 'I'm going up. I want to see her. It's for Harriet to make these decisions on her own life, not you.'

There was no one in the upstairs living room, not even Rose or Grant. The old woman was probably asleep and the lad would no doubt be out drinking. Joyce was right behind him hissing her fury at him, ordering him to leave, but Steve kept on going.

He quickly sprinted up the short flight which led to the attic bedrooms, calling her name. But when he reached Harriet's bedroom it was only to find that empty too. If she'd ever been here, and he sensed by the mingled look of shock and relief on

Joyce's face that she had, then she certainly wasn't here now. The bird had flown.

Outside, in the alley, having hidden in the bathroom and then slipped down the stairs and out of the back door unobserved, Harriet didn't pause to reconsider her decision, but hobbled away as quickly as her sprained ankle would allow. If she felt adrift and alone in a big, unfriendly world with nowhere to go, it was no doubt the fate she deserved for being so wicked.

36

Joyce

His leave over, Stan was back on board ship and bound for South Africa. They both knew that he was in for the long haul this time. Stan didn't expect to be home for months, possibly years. But they felt strangely reconciled, closer than they had been throughout their marriage, and united in their decision to keep Harriet.

It was a better outcome than Joyce could ever have dreamed of.

After he'd gone, she wasted no time in seeing her husband's mistress off the premises. Within days of his departure, she packed Eileen's suitcase and pushed the girl, still weeping, out the door. Eileen did all she could to resist. She clung to the doorjamb with her fingers, desperately trying to fight off Joyce's hands, which held her in a vicious grip. But she'd only recently given birth and Joyce was both taller and stronger than she at the best of times. Eileen lost her footing and fell sprawling in the gutter.

Joyce smirked. 'And that's exactly where you belong.' Then she tossed out a brown leather suitcase and the girl's coat after her. The suitcase burst open, spilling clothes everywhere. Eileen ignored it as she dragged herself to her feet, rubbing the blood from two cut knees.

Joyce was unmoved by her plight, too busy issuing yet another stern warning for her to keep her mouth shut if she knew what was good for her. And she took great pains to remind her that the baby belonged entirely to them now, to herself and Stan, waving the birth certificate under her nose to prove it.

'You should be grateful that we're prepared to give this illegitimate child a decent home. Now go on, be off with you. You're free as air, so take your money and go find yourself some other paramour.'

'I'll see you in hell before I let you keep her,' Eileen hissed through gritted teeth.

Joyce laughed, as if she'd said something highly amusing. 'I reckon I've already been to hell and back, with clogs on, thanks to you. Now I'm just fine and dandy and laughing all the way to paradise.'

'Where's she off to?' Rose asked, rushing over when she spotted a plump and breathless Eileen chasing her personal and private belongings all over the cobbles. Snatching them up the young woman was stuffing them any how into a brown suitcase while Joyce tossed out yet more bags and baggage on to the pavement.

Rose was well aware of the rows that had been going on in the house over the past few days, but hadn't paid too much attention to the details. Generally she managed to keep her nose out of it by electing instead to take refuge at the Edinburgh Castle pub with her mates. There was only so much she could take of her daughter's temper.

Now Joyce was smiling, not out of joy but with a kind of warped triumph, if Rose was any judge.

'Eileen has decided to go and live with relatives, haven't you, dear?'

Her unfortunate friend made no reply as she pulled on her coat and began to button it with frantic fingers against a biting wind. She merely looked over at Rose with a plea for pity out of eyes puffy and swollen from copious weeping.

'And where's the babby?' Rose asked her daughter. She was beginning to get an inkling of what was going on and didn't much care for her suspicions.

'Harriet is staying here. She belongs to Stan, don't forget. And now to me too.'

Eileen stood frozen and forlorn on the pavement, her head in her hands, and began to sob as if her heart was breaking. 'I never meant this to happen, Joyce. You have to believe me. Stan thought we'd just have a bit of fun to make you jealous, to make you sorry for not being honest with him about Grant. Then I fell in love. I couldn't help it, he's lovely is your Stan. He was so kind to me. No man has ever been so kind.'

'I'm not interested in your sob story, just get out of my sight. Get the hell out of here.' Joyce tossed out a brown paper carrier-bag full of clothes which rolled into a puddle. 'And don't think I'll soften, or change my mind and take you back, because I won't. You've got money in your pocket, and somewhere to stay, that's all I'm prepared to do for you. It's more than generous considering you've stolen my husband.'

'But you've just stolen my child!'

'It's a fair swap then,' Joyce snapped and closed the door. She felt very much like slamming it but had no wish to further alarm the neighbours. They'd made enough of a spectacle of themselves already. Fortunately, in this street, neighbours knew better than to interfere with other folk's business because it might be them sounding off next week. The sooner she got out of here for good, the better.

'Cup of tea, Mother?' Joyce cheerily offered, before going off to make a brew as if she hadn't a care in the world.

Harriet was once again on the road. Her first instinct was to break her promise to Nan and seek out Vinny and Shelley, and the rest of the band. They would at least feed her and provide her with shelter, might even welcome her back into the fold. But she could find no sign of them in any of their usual haunts, and then she remembered the letter Vinny had sent, telling her that they were off to London to seek their fortunes in the capital. He'd suggested Harriet meet him at London Road Station if she wanted to join them, giving the exact time and date. This, of course, was an appointment she hadn't kept.

Not that she regretted her decision. There was no future for her with Vinny. Harriet had thrown the letter away in the end without even answering it, which was probably the right thing to have done. What was the point in bothering to reply when she hadn't the first idea where to send it? And what was there to say?

So now she was all alone.

At least it's summer, Harriet thought, as she settled down that first night under one of the canal bridges with the old lags. One or two gave her funny looks, clearly wondering what a good-looking, very pregnant girl was doing dossing down with the dregs of society. They watched with interest as she went on a hunt for cardboard, but once they saw how she made herself a makeshift bed with the ease of long practice, they left her to her own devices. It was the accepted code in this community. Never interfere.

Even though the summer days were long, darkness had already fallen and a cool breeze wafted over the water. Harriet curled up in a protective foetal position, hugging her swollen body, feeling her baby kick, and she worried how they would both survive.

She hadn't even seen a doctor, thanks to Joyce's determination to keep her locked up and not create a scandal. And how she would manage when her time came, Harriet didn't care to think. Tears slid unchecked down her face but they were silent tears. Not for the world would she let anyone see the depths of her fear and distress. She had her pride at least, even if she'd lost everything else.

Joyce did not find caring for a baby easy. It made her acutely aware of her own failings, that she wasn't a natural mother. The child cried constantly, didn't sleep well and was an obstinately picky eater, very like her mother. Joyce felt obliged to call in the health visitor on more than one occasion, concerned by the child's fretfulness.

'Are you a new mother, Mrs Ashton?' the nurse kindly enquired, but then seeing Grant she'd smiled and said perhaps it seemed more difficult this time because Harriet was a tiny little girl and not a robust young man like her big brother.

'Perhaps your own anxiety is upsetting her. Stay calm and happy, and you'll have a happy baby.'

It didn't seem to work for Joyce. She would frequently be in despair as no matter what she did the baby would scream and fret and work herself into a lather till she was overheated and red in the face.

Then Rose would take her and she would stop crying almost at once. It was infuriating.

Yet in general terms, Joyce was pleased with the way things had worked out. She had the child in her possession, the means of keeping Stan by her side. She'd done what was necessary to save her marriage. When next he came home on leave they'd be a proper family, just as they should be. Even in the days immediately following her suggestion to keep Harriet, his attitude towards Grant had changed noticeably. It was going to be all right, she was sure of it. And she would at last have him all to herself.

If only she could get Eileen off her tail.

Joyce might have thrown Eileen physically from the house, but it was less easy to banish her from her life. Whenever she walked out with the baby in the pram, she was aware of the woman following her, a persistent shadow trailing after her everywhere she went.

Eileen would be sitting on the doorstep when she came out of a morning to pick up the milk bottles. Or Joyce would see her standing across the road watching the house for hour upon hour. She'd find herself drawing the curtains in the afternoon, even when it was still light, in order to shut out the image of her.

And Joyce never dared to leave the baby alone, even for a moment.

Rose was deeply distressed and finally broke her silence, filled with compassion by the sight of this desperate mother. 'Eeh, heck, are you sure this is right? It does seem a bit draconian. Are you certain you're allowed to keep that babby, Joyce?'

It had been raining for almost a week and still Eileen came, day after day, to stand in the empty street, shivering with cold but otherwise oblivious to the fact she was getting soaked to the skin. She made no move to seek protection from the downpour.

Nor did the girl possess an umbrella, at least she never brought one with her, and looked utterly wretched, her face a picture of misery.

Joyce continued with her daily routine, giving no indication of being in the least moved by the sight of her one-time friend. This afternoon she set the usual tray of silver teapot and jug down upon the table sharp at four and began to pour tea into delicate china cups.

'I'm absolutely certain that no one is in a position to dispute my claim, which is, in any case, in the child's best interest.' Joyce's icy tone brooked no argument, and, to prove her point, she went to the bureau and took out the birth certificate, which she handed to her mother. 'Harriet is mine now. Stan registered the birth, as the child's father, and I get to keep the baby as recompense for all that woman has put me through. Which means I get to keep Stan too, thanks to my generosity in this delicate matter.'

'Generosity? But – you'd be living a lie. You'd be telling a wicked lie to that innocent child over who her real mother was.' Rose looked aghast, not quite able to take in all the implications.

'What Harriet doesn't know can't hurt her.'

'I'm not too sure about that. No good will come of this. No good at all. Anyroad, you'll never get away with it. You're the one who allus frets about what folk will think. What will they think about this?'

'They'll never hear the truth from me, Mother, nor from you. And certainly not from Eileen either, not if she wants to continue receiving her allowance. If you recall, I had a dreadful pregnancy and was obliged to stay in bed almost the entire time. I had a doctor call on me from out of town, a specialist gynaecologist, rather than the local GP. No one will ever find out any different. And after that difficult birth I endured with Grant, and my last disappointment, is it any wonder? Just remember those simple facts and you won't go far wrong.'

Joyce twitched the lace curtain aside and peeped out. 'Ah good, she's seen sense and gone at last. I thought she'd soon grow bored with her vigil and move some place else, no doubt find herself a new paramour, as I suggested. That will be the last we hear of her.'

'I wouldn't be too sure,' Rose murmured. 'It'll end in tears will all of this business. Mark my words. Honesty is always the best policy . . .'

Rose might have gone on in this vein for some time but right then the air-raid siren sounded and both women wearily set their cups aside and started to gather up their belongings, coats, warm woollies and gas masks. Rose rushed into the kitchen to snatch up a heel of bread and cheese, wondering if she had time to boil some water for a flask of tea before the bombs started dropping. Joyce hurried upstairs to collect Harriet and grab the new pink frock she'd bought only that morning. Even in an air-raid shelter she mustn't be seen looking anything less than her best.

'No one will find me neglecting my wifely duty, or that any child of mine will want for a thing.'

'Nay, it won't,' Rose muttered to herself. 'It'll want for nowt but love.'

37

Rose

Summer dragged by, hot and sticky and busy as ever on the market. Mothers bought their children ice cream from Bertalones' old cart which had stood on the Champion Street Market for decades, and then sighed with relief when September came and they went back to school. For the first time in their lives they watched the Olympics take place on their own television screens in their own living rooms. A miracle of modern science, they thought, even if the poor competitors were sweltering in the heat.

On Champion Street Market the children jumped over skipping ropes, galloped imaginary horses and boxed with extra fervour at Barry Holmes's Lads' Club, imitating their heroes, pretending they were Cassius Clay or Lester Piggott.

It had seemed like the longest summer of her life for Rose as she stopped one morning to buy herself a quarter of coconut macaroons from Lizzie Pringle's Chocolate Cabin. She couldn't stop worrying about Harriet, even though the girl was now grown up and about to have a child of her own. Where had she vanished to this time? Surely she hadn't gone back to Vinny Turner, when she'd faithfully promised it was all over between them? Rose prayed not.

But if she wasn't with him, then where was she? She could hardly get herself a job with that bump she was carrying, and Rose wasn't even certain she had any money left. By heck, but the lass was a worry.

Rose's main task for the morning was to buy herself a new

hat from Clara Higginson's stall, something smart to wear when she attended a most important meeting with the City Council. She felt it was vital to look her best, but couldn't keep her mind on the task in hand.

'Didn't you say you wanted navy, to match your coat?' Patsy gently enquired. 'Only, you've just picked up a brown felt, which would look entirely wrong.'

'Eeh, heck, I don't know whether I'm coming or going,' Rose mourned. Things seemed to be going from bad to worse, and for the life of her Rose didn't dare to imagine what might happen next. The tea leaves had been right, both about the visitor and the tears. But then hadn't she predicted from the start that this would all end in tears?

Her lovely Harriet could be living on scraps left over from market stalls for all Rose knew. At least she wasn't in one of them Homes with wicked nuns beating moral virtue into her. But where on earth would she have her baby, and who would be with her to hold her hand when the moment came? It didn't bear thinking about. Childbirth wasn't summat to face on your own.

'Maybe this one?' Patsy suggested, setting a hat in crushed burgundy velvet with a curvy brim atop Rose's tight curls. 'That should brighten up your navy outfit beautifully. A lovely autumn shade, don't you think?'

'Aye, you're right. I quite like this one. I'll take it. It'll give me just the confidence I need to face them councillors. It's not going to be easy,' Rose warned. 'They'll run rings round us if they can, do their level best not to hand over a penny unless it's surgically removed or squeezed out of them by force.'

The market committee was in serious conflict over how best to handle the campaign. Many more people had been persuaded into accepting the developers' offer, and things were looking increasingly bleak, although several residents remained determined to stand firm.

Only last week the surveyors had arrived, moving around with their special equipment, taking measurements and sight lines, making notes on where the new flats would be built once the damp old Victorian houses had been cleared away and the market hall razed to the ground.

'They'll have to get up early to outface you, Rose. You're always ready to stand up for what's right. Never let us down yet.'

Rose looked at the younger woman with a bleakness in her tired old face. 'There have been times, in the past, when I haven't done what's right, when I've kept quiet and wished later that I'd spoken up. Mebbe that's why I've let meself get involved in this business. I felt it were about time I started making me voice heard.' Rose frowned. 'Happen it's time I did in other respects too, if it's not too late.'

There was an uneasy silence as Patsy wrapped the hat in tissue paper and stowed it carefully into a box. 'We've every faith in you, Rose, so just you follow your instincts. They've never let you down yet.'

Rose looked at the girl, startled. Wasn't that what the cards had said, all those months ago? But if her main instinct was to protect Harriet, how would telling her the whole truth achieve that when it would be bound to bring fresh pain? All supposing Rose could find her, which she hadn't so far managed to do, despite trailing over half the city searching for the poor lass.

Jerking herself back to the present, Rose handed over the money for her hat and offered up an encouraging, if rather stiff, smile. 'Anyroad, they'll not chuck us out of this street, demolish our fine old houses or deprive us of our livelihoods without due compensation, or better still an alternative location, not if I've any say in the matter.'

'Atta girl!' Patsy laughed. 'A woman after my own heart.' Then she put her arms about the old woman and hugged her close as she whispered words of comfort in her ear. 'Don't worry too much about your Harriet. She's a real chip off the old block, and has got her head screwed on too. She'll sort herself out, don't you fret.'

'How, that's the question?' Rose wiped a tear from her eye as she walked away, carrying her hatbox with care.

But although rumours were flying around Champion Street

Market like confetti, being exchanged along with slices of polony on Jimmy Ramsay's stall, or with every length of curtain net on Winnie's, not another word on the subject of her granddaughter would cross Rose's lips. Let them make what they will of the lass's latest disappearance, they'd not hear owt from her lips.

Harriet was at that precise moment sitting by a smoky fire which gave off very little heat, eating a chicken sandwich she'd found in the rubbish dump behind one of the new supermarkets.

Through a long, hot, dusty summer, she'd discovered these to be a good source of food, as were baker's shops when they threw away stale items. Sometimes, if she had a penny or two, she'd be able to buy herself a barm cake for a treat. The shop assistant might take pity on her and add a scraping of marg. Passers-by tossed her a coin or two occasionally, out of pity, as she sat huddled in her layers of grubby clothes, no doubt resembling a bundle of rags.

For some reason Harriet felt demeaned by this, even though it meant she could provide herself with a hot bath, or a decent lunch for a change. Even a simple mug of tea was welcome.

On the days when she didn't even have a penny in her pocket, Harriet had become an expert at picking out the good bits from rotten apples, scraping mould from old cheese and even eating raw cabbage leaves. Once, she made herself very ill by spit-roasting a piece of pork she really should have left in the dump.

She'd lost weight, naturally, her hair was badly in need of a good combing, and she smelt, for all she made a point of going to the public baths for a bath or shower whenever she had a copper or two to spare. No matter how much she scrubbed herself with the srong lye soap they provided, she never felt clean. The dirt from the streets, and from the weight of the sin she carried, seemed ingrained in her, on view for all to see.

Shame and humiliation ate at her soul. She'd brought herself to this pitiful state by running off with Vinny Turner and sleeping with him. Had she hoped to change him? Had she imagined that he would forsake the comfort of cannabis for her sake? If so, then she'd been stupidly naïve. It had all seemed like a silly game, a daring escape. Now reality had set in. Was this the price of freedom, this terrible sense of hopelessness and guilt?

She watched other young mothers walk by, proudly wheeling their newborn babies in fancy high prams, and she envied them their contentment and their security. Why couldn't her life be as uncomplicated as theirs? Why couldn't Joyce have loved her as other adoptive mothers do?

And why had she stupidly run away instead of staying and fighting for her rights?

Because she had felt unwanted. Because there had been no place for her, not even with Steve. And she certainly wasn't going to go to him now, as some sort of charity case.

There were times when Harriet blamed herself for everything. On other days, when she was cold and wet and hungry, she would rail against fate, against Joyce, or even against her much-loved, late departed father. If Stan hadn't foolishly embroiled himself in an affair because he refused to believe his wife's story about the rape, all their lives could have been so very different. The pair of them had wanted only to punish each other but it was Harriet, and Grant too, who had suffered the most. Their children were the ones paying the price now.

Harriet sighed, desperately trying to shake herself free of this melancholy, which did her no good at all. The baby was still moving, still kicking, surely that was all that mattered?

And when it was time for it to be born . . . ? Harriet instantly shut off the thought. The prospect of childbirth terrified her. All she knew about the subject was what she'd learned from scraps of girlish gossip at school, none of it much use. When she was ten she'd imagined a baby came out through your belly button, by means of some miracle or other created by the Virgin Mary. Now she might know the correct place, but not the means, nor what would be required of her to bring this baby safely out. And there was certainly no one to ask, so she banished the worry from her mind.

She'd deal with it later, when the time came.

Once, finding a penny in her pocket, she'd slipped into a Catholic church and lit a candle and said a prayer for her unborn child. The act had given her some sort of comfort and strength, but then a cleaner had arrived and shooed her out into the street as if she were vermin.

Harriet's mind remained a defensive blank on many issues concerning the future. She determined to cross each bridge as and when she came to it. On one matter though, she was absolutely certain. She had no intention of spending her pregnancy being locked up by Joyce for months on end, either in her own attic bedroom or in a Home for Wayward Girls, as Joyce had threatened. Nor would she allow Steve to ruin his life by feeling obliged to marry her. None of this was his fault.

Harriet had no desire to be found. To make sure her family didn't find her and drag her back to one or other of these fates, she never stayed in one place for too long.

One day she spotted Nan standing at a bus stop. That was when she'd been trailing the streets of Ancoats. Rose was chatting to the other women in the queue, and some instinct told Harriet that she was asking them if they'd seen a pregnant girl hanging around street corners, as they were all shaking their heads and looking concerned. She'd left Ancoats that same day and gone back to Salford.

This was her favoured spot, an old bomb site by the River Irwell near St Simon Street. No one she knew from Champion Street would think to look for her here. Today, with the cool nights of autumn approaching, Harriet remained at the bomb site for only one more night, sharing her pitiful food with old Tom, a tramp she'd become acquainted with. She even wore fingerless gloves now, and had newspaper stuffed into her shoes, just like a real old lag.

As dawn came up over the city, lightening the sky with streaks of pink and yellow, she rolled up the old rug she'd brought with her and prepared to move on.

'Go home,' old Tom told her in his usual toneless voice, as he had done a thousand times before. 'Go home to yer mam.'

Harriet merely smiled and told him to take care of his chest, then set off in the direction of an old air-raid shelter that she used regularly. She thought this might be a good place for the birth, which must come soon, as she would at least be out of the rain.

The trouble was, the shelter was some distance away and her pace of progress was slow these days. Inhibited by her cumbersome size and loaded down with her entire worldly possessions, she hobbled along like an old woman. Even old Tom was fitter than she was, for all he was three times her age.

But then Harriet had been bothered with cramps in her belly for over a day now, and an aching back. All part of the joys of pregnancy, Harriet supposed. And she was suffering from an even greater urgency to pee. An hour later, though it was still barely five in the morning, Harriet was grateful to find some public lavatories and went inside to relieve herself. She sipped some water from a rusty tap and washed her face and hands. The wash freshened her and she felt better, but then the pains started in earnest, and Harriet realised it hadn't been cramp at all, but labour pains.

Rose sat in her meeting, fast losing patience with the obstinacy of councillors. Belle Garside had put forward their case and robustly defended it, all to no avail.

'We can't be seen to be holding up progress,' reiterated one pompous councillor, who sat with sausage fingers steepled over a bloated stomach, revelling in his own self-importance. 'Manchester has to move forward and embrace the modern world.'

Rose stubbornly repeated what Belle had already told them. 'We accept that some of these houses in Champion Street would be best pulled down, the old Victorian slums by the fish market certainly, and maybe the row by the old horse trough. But the top half of the street is perfectly respectable, the row where Clara Higginson and Molly Poulson live. Why knock down houses which are still in good shape? Does this so-called modernisation have to be quite so drastic? What is to be gained by destroying a happy and worthwhile community? And why demolish a market hall which you only recently granted us permission to extend and improve?'

She might as well have been speaking in a foreign language for all the good her words did.

'We can't be seen to be holding up progress . . .'

Round and round they went in an ever-decreasing circle of pointless argument.

'So what about an alternative home?' If the councillors could be stubborn, then so could she. She was in just the right mood for an argument.

'Everyone will be rehoused in brand-new modern flats,' the chairman in charge of this particular project informed her with little evidence of sympathy.

'What if folk don't fancy looking down on the world from a high-rise monstrosity?' Joe Southworth asked.

The councillor adopted a patronising tone. 'I'm sure people will be only too grateful when they realise they can escape the dreadful conditions they've been forced to endure all these years.'

'Clara Higginson isn't enduring dreadful conditions. Her house is as neat as a new pin, as smart as yours any day,' Rose snapped.

This comment was met with a gimlet glare. 'Nevertheless she'd be very foolish to refuse, very foolish indeed. The new flats will be fully equipped, with washing machines and everything. We mustn't be seen to . . .'

'. . . be holding up progress, I know,' Rose said, barely managing to disguise her irritation.

Belle Garside intervened, 'And what about the market traders who have their livelihoods to think of? Where can they go to make a living while you're bull-dozing the street around their ears?'

'Aye, we should be paid due compensation for the disruption and loss of trade,' added Jimmy Ramsay, thinking of his own butcher's business.

'And found an alternative site,' Rose finished.

The sound of indrawn breath was unnerving to hear as all the councillors glanced sideways at each other, then became suddenly absorbed with their jotting pads and engagement diaries, refusing to meet the eye of the delegates from Champion Street Market.

'I'm afraid finding an alternative site has to be your responsibility. I'm not sure the funds are in place to allow for such things as relocation or compensation.'

'Then put them in place.'

'What you have to appreciate, Mrs Ibbotson, is we mustn't be seen . . .'

Rose closed her ears. She wanted to tell the lot of them to shut up, to slap their silly, arrogant faces, to drag their attention out of their own fat pockets, lined by rich developers no doubt, and think about the effect of their actions on the residents themselves. Many people would shortly be turned out of perfectly respectable homes which they loved, a community which had become a part of their lives over a fair number of years, and for what? Another block of modern flats.

'Surely there's room for compromise, for a half-way course?' Belle was saying.

It would seem not, and while everyone did their utmost to support their Market Superintendent by putting forward a sound argument for a reprieve, it was all too apparent that their hopes for success were rapidly fading.

As one, the four delegates got to their feet and prepared to leave, the generous frame of the butcher seeming to dominate the small stuffy council office. 'You haven't heard the last of this,' Jimmy warned.

'No,' Joe Southworth added. 'We're not satisfied with the treatment we're getting. We're not done yet.'

'Quite right,' Rose added her two pennyworth. 'We'll start looking for another site, as you suggest, and you can speak to the developers about footing the bill for the cost of the move. It'll be peanuts to them.'

'And surely far better than open confrontation and bad publicity in the national press,' Belle reminded him.

The chairman began to stutter with rage, his face turning a

dull purple. 'Is that some sort of threat? Because if you are attempting to blackmail this project committee into . . . ?'

Belle flashed her beautiful violet eyes, thickly fringed by long mascara-coated lashes. 'We're attempting to achieve justice, a word you gentlemen don't seem familiar with. You can't just chuck folk aside, rob them of their homes and their livelihoods without so much as a by-your-leave, without a care for how they will survive.'

'You'll be hearing from us,' Rose darkly threatened as they swept out of the room, a small yet determined figure in her best navy coat, new burgundy velvet hat, and trademark dangly earrings.

If she stayed in that office a second longer, she'd clock him one, she would really. And for all this was an important matter, at the back of her mind Rose was still haunted by a far more serious problem.

38

Harriet

Harriet was sitting with her feet braced against the lavatory pan, her back against the door, panting and gasping, too frightened even to cry. Never had she known such pain. She felt as if she were being ripped apart. Weren't first babies supposed to take their time? Harriet was sure she'd read that somewhere, yet this one seemed to be in a tearing hurry, clawing itself from her flesh. But then she'd probably been in labour for days, without even realising it.

She'd already flooded the floor with water that had gushed out of her of its own volition. She'd tried to mop it up with toilet paper but given up the task as hopeless. Now Harriet looked down and was transfixed by the sight of a small head emerging from between her legs. It seemed to be blue and streaked with blood. Terror engulfed her. Was the baby dead even before it was born? Pain swamped her, stopped her from thinking or fretting for several long moments which felt like hours, enveloping her totally. She let out a terrified scream, half hoping someone might hear and come to help. Not that many people were around at this time in the morning.

But maybe it was better if they didn't find her. The last thing she needed was for some busybody to start calling the police, or worse, Joyce. She bit down hard on her lower lip so that she didn't make a sound, so hard that she tasted blood.

There was a brief respite as the pain momentarily ebbed away but then it came again, overwhelming her, as if *it*, and not herself, was in control of her body. For one horrifying moment Harriet thought she might faint but then the baby slithered from her in a slippy mess of blood and liquid, a long wiggly cord attached to its belly. Harriet stared at the infant lying between her legs. Shouldn't it be crying? She picked it up, anxious suddenly as she thumbed away the mucus from its eyes and nose. The baby opened its mouth and howled.

'Oh, clever you. That's a good girl. There, there.'

Harriet gathered her baby to her breast, smiling down into her tiny furious face, overwhelmed by wonder. She was perfect. Utterly perfect! How could such a wonderful creature have survived through all of this torment and neglect, the lack of sleep and good food, the misery and upset that Harriet had endured? She counted fingers and toes, complete with shell pink fingernails, smoothed the damp blond curls and smiled into a pair of baby blue eyes, fringed with amazingly beautiful, long dark lashes. Then she carefully tied and cut the cord, using a bit of string and small penknife she'd learned to keep handy among other useful bits and bobs in her pocket.

'Welcome to the world, baby, although there's a bit more to it than this lavatory stall. Outside the sun will be shining, and you'll discover that you have a whole wonderful life to look forward to.'

It was in that moment, with this thought uppermost in her mind, as Harriet fell in love with the miracle that was her own child, that she realised she couldn't possibly keep her.

What kind of life would she be able to offer? How could she provide for and care for this baby? Did she want her daughter to eat scraps out of dustbins? How would she keep her warm through the endless cold nights of winter as they slept beneath the railway arches or down by the canal? Even the old deserted warehouse, which had seemed like a fun place to be when the band was filling its emptiness with music, was no place to bring up a baby.

And what was the alternative? Supposing Harriet was able to look clean and respectable enough to get herself a job, where would she live? And who would look after the baby while she earned the money to keep them both?

Great fat tears rolled silently down her cheeks and a pain worse even than childbirth clenched her heart in an iron fist. It would be quite impossible. Much as she loved this baby and wanted to keep her, Harriet knew that it was impossible. What kind of mother would want such a life for her precious child?

She felt very sore and her stomach was aching. Harriet instinctively kneaded her belly, to at least ease the physical pain, and brought forth the afterbirth. She stared at the resulting mess on the floor of the stall for a long time, then dumped it down the pan. It could well block the entire system, but what did she care?

Then she wrapped the baby in the one towel she'd brought with her, and in a warm woollen sweater. When she'd cleaned the stall floor as best she could with what remained of the roll of toilet paper, she lay the baby down in a place where she would easily be found, the moment someone came in to use the lavatory. Then with tears streaming down her face, Harriet picked up her bag and walked away.

Rose was not in a good mood. She'd come home, hung up her coat, changed out of her best clothes, stowing the new hat away in its box on the top shelf of a wardrobe, still fuming over the way they'd been treated. The councillors didn't even seem willing to discuss how the demolition would be carried out, whether temporary accommodation would be provided for the residents, let alone compensation for lack of trade or a proposal for an alternative site for the market.

Eeh, but she was fair worn out with all that argufying. She was glad to be back in her own home, looking forward to a brew and an Eccles cake. She next took down the jewellery box where she kept her pension book and a wad of money, before slipping off her earrings and tucking them inside.

For once, Rose knew exactly how much there should be in the box, as she'd checked it after going to the post office to collect her pension only yesterday. Something made her count the notes again, and she frowned. It was ten pounds short. And this wasn't the first time this had happened. Was she losing her mind? Had she got in a muddle, what with the stroke and moving her things into Stan's old room? No, she'd counted the notes three times just to make sure, since she'd been puzzling for some time over missing money.

Rose lay down on her bed, in dire need of a nap after all the trauma of the morning. Not that she had much hope of one as her mind was buzzing, in far too much of a turmoil to rest. She was worrying about the campaign to save the market which still seemed very much alive, then there was the anxiety she felt over Harriet, and now this. Who would steal money out of her box? Who could pick the lock and be able to get into it without leaving a mark?

The answer was obvious, coming to her in a flash. Grant.

Rose felt sick. Oh, but could that be right? Surely the lad wouldn't steal money from his own grandmother? Yet she knew that he had. Rose was only too aware that during her illness a great deal of money had gone missing. She'd said nothing about it at the time, being focused on getting well, but she'd known even then, even when she'd been unable to articulate the words, that someone was stealing from her. And it certainly wasn't her friend Irma, who'd spoiled her rotten, practically saved her life, and was as honest as the day.

Later that afternoon when the old woman had gathered her strength, she went upstairs to the living room and confronted her grandson, arms folded across her corseted chest. Rose had fought one battle today, now she would fight another, if she must, this time against her own kith and kin. 'Where is it then?'

Grant looked at her, shoulders hunched defensively, round face puckered into a picture of manufactured innocence. 'Where's what?'

'All that money what you stole from me? Where's it gone? What did you do with it? Lost it on the gee-gees, I shouldn't wonder.'

It was Joyce who answered. She came rushing out of the kitchen with a face like thunder. 'Are you accusing my son of being a thief?'

'If the cap fits.'

There followed the most almighty row, the worst they'd ever had, with Joyce vehemently defending her son and Grant letting his mother get on with it, while he sat in the corner smirking in that self-satisfied way he had.

'You can't prove any of this,' Joyce yelled. 'You're a suspicious old goat, blaming the boy for your own stupid carelessness.'

Grant mocked his grandmother with his laughter. 'Most of the time you don't even know what day of the week it is, let alone how much money you have in that box.'

Rose's head snapped up. 'Oh, so you admit you do know where I keep it then?'

Joyce looked slightly discomfited by this but instantly rallied. 'We all know you keep your precious bits and pieces in that old jewellery box. You should put it in the bank as sensible people do.'

'This is my weekly pension I'm talking about here, not me life savings. I'm surely entitled to think it's safe in me own wardrobe? But you're right, I can't prove it. What I can do is make sure he gets nowt else. I'll be more careful where I stow it in future, and in case you don't know I've already cut you out of my will, even if you are me only daughter, so put that in your pipe and smoke it.'

Joyce went white to the lips. 'B-b – but what about the salon? You'll be leaving me that, surely? It's my home!'

'It's *my* home, actually, legally speaking,' Rose reminded her. 'Not that you've ever made me feel welcome in it. But I hold the deeds, thanks to the careful provision my Ronnie made for me. You never thought owt of your poor dear father, never thought him worthy of your love and attention, your respect. Yet he were a good man, even if he was only a dustman.'

'Oh, for goodness' sake, Mother. You aren't dragging up all that old history, surely.'

'Why not, you're the one who lives in the past, not me. Obsessed by summat that happened years ago. Just because it ruined *your* life you're now allowing it to ruin that of your children. You've certainly ruined young Harriet's, and all because of something that wasn't her fault. When are you going to own up and tell her that it was *you* what destroyed her mother?'

White faced, Joyce flew at Rose, yelling and screaming at the top of her voice. '*That's a lie!* And you know it. I never wanted . . . I didn't . . .'

'. . . lift a finger to help, don't I know it. I was there, remember, so you can't lie to me. When Eileen needed you most, you just . . .'

'That's enough, Mother! You've said more than enough.'

'Naw, go on,' Grant said. 'I'm interested in this.'

Rose turned on her grandson. 'And if you're nurturing any fond hopes of inheriting when I die, you can think again too. I've left everything to our Harriet. She's the only one in this family who deserves it, the only one who's ever shown me the slightest bit of love and attention.'

'*What?*'

'Think yerself fortunate I haven't called in the police. You're getting off lightly, lad.'

Ignoring the look of shock and fury that came over his face, Rose turned back to her daughter. 'Your thief of a son might have found it easy to rob an old woman blind, particularly when I was lying paralysed in me bed from a stroke, but that's all he's getting out of me. I might be old but I'm not stupid. He's a greedy little tyke and you're a cold, hard, unfeeling woman, too wrapped up in your own self-pity to find it in your frozen heart to love that lass. But you'll be the greater loser, not her.

'As for the salon, I doubt it'll be here for much longer anyroad, but whatever compensation I manage to wring out of that parsimonious local council or them greedy developers, will go in *my* pocket, save for what's due for your hairdressing business, not yours.

'I sussed the pair of you two long since and when Judgement Day comes, you'll get your just deserts. In the meantime, Harriet will get the cash. Happen you'll then learn to be nice to her, cos you'll be dependent upon her for help and a home, instead of the other way round.'

★

It wasn't until she'd been walking for a full twenty-five minutes that it came to Harriet what she had done. *She'd abandoned her own child!* She stood stock still in the middle of Liverpool Street. Dear lord, what was she thinking of?

What if someone wicked found her? What if they didn't hand her over to the hospital authorities at all? What if they took her and kept her, hurt the baby or even killed her? Supposing some stupid kids thought she was merely a doll and chucked her in the River Irwell? A thousand fears rushed through Harriet's head. What if nobody found her and she perished slowly of starvation and cold?

Spinning on her heel she began to run. She ran as fast as she could, her heart racing.

What kind of mother was she to treat her child in such a way? She was worse even than Joyce.

Harriet was breathless by the time she reached the block of public lavatories where she'd given birth. Blood was running down her legs and she felt sick with exhaustion, but she didn't care. 'Oh, let her still be there. Please let her still be there,' Harriet sobbed as she pushed open the door and ran inside.

39

Joyce

Steve arrived at the hair salon just before five that Friday evening to find Joyce creating some sort of balloon with Dena Dobson's hair. Bits of it were standing up in all directions as if she'd been hit by an electric shock, and he watched in mystified silence as Joyce jabbed and teased at the hair, brushing it in what seemed to Steve to be entirely the wrong direction, then smoothing the piece down to join up with the rest of the balloon.

Seeing the expression on his face, Dena laughed at him. 'Don't look so alarmed, Steve, it's called back-combing. I've got a fashion show this evening, so need to look my best. This is the latest style from America, it's called a beehive.'

'Right.' Steve took off his glasses and began to polish them on his clean handkerchief, quite unable to think of anything else to say except where were the bees? Hair salons were embarrassing places for a chap. He sat patiently waiting while Joyce sprayed the resulting pile with half a can of hair lacquer. What did he know about hair, or women, for that matter? They were an increasing mystery to him.

He'd expected Caro to be furious with him when he'd called off their engagement. Instead, after weeping copious tears all over his shoulder, she'd quickly rallied and bravely claimed that it was all her fault that he was getting cold feet, because she'd rushed him into having an engagement. And she really didn't mind if it was called off for a while. She could always wear the dress she'd bought specially for the party on some other occasion.

'I can wait until you feel ready,' Caro assured him, all teary-eyed. 'I'll wait forever, so long as I don't lose you.'

'I don't expect you to wait forever,' Steve had assured her, his heart softening with pity at this evidence of her love for him, quite unable to extricate himself from its cloying demands.

'Didn't you? Oh, Steve, I'm so glad. I can't imagine facing life without you.'

Steve had felt such a rat that he'd mopped up her tears, kissed her better and before he knew it they were standing in the jeweller's shop actually choosing the ring. He still couldn't work out how that had come about. Her excitement and eager hugs and kisses afterwards made him feel like a real hero, big and strong, loved and wanted, almost happy, carried along on a blissful tide of hopes and dreams. But then the enormity of what he'd done hit home.

Perhaps reality struck when his mother had shrieked her delight and instantly launched into organising the Party of the Year.

Dena tapped him on the shoulder on her way out of the salon. 'Cheer up, Stevey boy, it might never happen.'

'It already has,' Steve grumbled.

It still hurt badly that Harriet should run away rather than speak to him. He understood that she might have been embarrassed, even filled with shame for having got herself into this situation, but why couldn't she trust him? Didn't she know that he would never judge her? His love for Harriet was bigger than that. Yes, he'd been shocked to hear of her predicament, but these things happened; it didn't make her any less lovable, not in Steve's eyes.

When he'd chased through the house looking for her, only to find she'd gone, Joyce had taken great pleasure in informing him that she'd been quietly sitting on the couch only moments before.

Now he repeated the question he asked every weekend when he called. 'Is she here?'

Joyce shook her head, looking irritated, as always.

At that moment Rose rushed in, looking deeply troubled. Before she'd even caught her breath to speak, Joyce turned on her mother.

'What now? I've no time for any more arguments. I'm off out with Joe.'

'That was the telephone. It's the hospital. They've got Harriet in there, and she's had her baby. They think we should go right over.'

'Why?' Joyce snapped. 'She certainly won't want me there.'

'Apparently she does.' Rose put a hand to her chest, as if she felt a sudden pain. Steve was instantly on the alert. 'Let me take you, Mrs Ibbotson, and Mrs Ashton. I've got my car outside. It's a bit beat up, but will get us there in one piece.'

Joyce glanced across at Grant, whom Steve hadn't noticed until now, sitting sulking in a corner, and then returned her glare to her mother. 'Have you changed your mind about that matter concerning money we were discussing earlier?'

'Not a bit of it. Nor will I, not while you keep that heart of yours encased in a block of ice, and your son has itchy fingers. Are you coming to see our Harriet, or not? I need to know if that baby's all right, and if Harriet is well.'

Joyce gave a loud sniff and her lip curled. 'I don't think so. I reckon she's your responsibility now, Mother.'

Rose sucked in her breath. 'I reckon she allus has been.' She turned to Steve. 'Come on, lad, let's go.'

Steve was left kicking his heels in the waiting room while Rose hurried in to the maternity ward. She seemed to take forever, and he almost gave up hope of them ever allowing him in.

This was the moment, he realised, to put those high-sounding ideals of his into practice. What would he feel when he came face to face with Vinny Turner's child? Jealous? Bitter? Resentful? He hoped none of these things, that it wouldn't even matter to him who the father was. But it was hard to assess how he might react, when faced with the reality.

A nurse came over to him. 'Are you the father?'

Steve shook his head, suddenly filled with an attack of shyness. 'I – I'm a friend, her best friend.'

The nurse smiled at him. 'You're Steve. She was delighted to hear that you'd come. Follow me.'

His heart lifted and he followed the nurse to the ward, bracing himself for whatever he might find there.

His first sight of Harriet shocked him to the core. She looked pale and ill, and so very thin. Yet he also felt a great rush of love for her and hurried over to grasp her hands in his. 'How are you? You look as beautiful as ever.'

She laughed. 'I look like death warmed up.'

Steve pecked a kiss on her cheek, wishing he dare gather her in his arms and kiss her properly, but sternly warned himself to be cautious. 'You always look beautiful to me.'

'That's all right then.'

Harriet could tell that he was valiantly trying to disguise his shock at seeing her in this state. The expression on his face said everything, but then Steve had always possessed the kind of open, boyish face in which his emotions were clearly shown. And living on the streets had done nothing for her complexion, she thought wryly.

Rose, who was seated beside the bed, tapped him on the arm. 'What about saying hello to Junior here.'

Steve looked down into a pair of wide blue eyes. He'd always thought that new babies were supposed to be red and wrinkled and ugly. This one was certainly tiny, but the skin was smooth, almost translucent, and it had a crown of red-gold hair, just like Harriet's. The baby seemed to be wrapped up in some sort of swaddling sheet but those beautiful eyes looked bright and alert, weighing him up as if wondering who he was. And they didn't remind him of Vinny Turner at all, only of Harriet.

'Would you like to hold her?' Rose asked, and Steve felt a surge of panic.

'I'm not good with babies.'

Rose chuckled. 'I should hope not, but she doesn't bite,' and, loosening the sheet, she placed the baby carefully in Steve's arms, showing him how to support her head.

'It's a girl then?' For some reason he was delighted about this, perhaps because a boy would more likely resemble the father. 'What are you going to call her?' he asked, trying to disguise the silly grin he felt creeping over his face as the baby grasped his finger in a fierce grip.

'I haven't decided yet.' Harriet looked a bit sheepish about this, as if it were a form of neglect, but she hadn't wanted to personalise this unknown baby until she was absolutely certain she could keep her. Even now there were doubts, but at least she was safe. Harriet had been so relieved to find her still warmly wrapped in the towel in the lavatory stall.

She'd then set out to walk all the way to the hospital, realising the baby at least should be checked over, when a woman in the street noticed she was bleeding and insisted on calling an ambulance. So she'd arrived in style and both mother and baby had been thoroughly examined. What happened now, Harriet had no idea.

After much badgering from Rose, Joyce agreed to visit Harriet the next day. She sat in the straight-backed chair beside the hospital bed, her spine as rigid and unbending as her manner, and asked Harriet if she was well. Her tone of voice seemed to indicate complete indifference whether she was or not.

Wasting no further words on trivialities such as health, or why her stepdaughter had felt it necessary to live rough on the streets, she swiftly came to the point of her visit.

'I've spoken to Father Dimmock. A good Catholic family will be found to take the child.'

'I thought I explained that—'

'Arrangements have been made, Harriet, so don't make any more difficulties.'

Joyce remained adamant that the baby be adopted, but after all Harriet had been through she was even more determined to keep her. She'd loved her from the moment of her birth, even in the lavatory stall. In those very first seconds despite the mess, the pain and the fear, she'd been swamped with love for her child. Amazingly, regardless of the lack of pre-natal care, and the difficult circumstances of her birth, she was a fine, healthy baby. A little miracle, the nurses were calling her.

'I've already told you that I intend to keep this baby.'

'Don't be ridiculous! How can you possibly care for a child? You don't even have a job.'

'I'll get one. Don't worry, I'll cope. It's *my* choice, not yours.'

Joyce barely glanced at the child, concerned only with keeping scandal from her door, at whatever cost. 'I'm still your legal guardian, if no longer your mother, and you'll do as I say.'

Harriet hung on to her patience with difficulty, determined to fight for her child. 'You can't bear for me to be happy, can you, or for your carefully constructed respectability to be destroyed?'

Joyce ignored her. 'Arrangements are being put in place for the adoption, and you'll either do as I say, or go back to living out of dustbins.' Having made her announcement, Joyce left, stalking off with her head high. Harriet chewed on her lip and felt deeply afraid.

Later that same afternoon, Harriet was surprised to be visited by Father Dimmock who informed her, in that kindly, caring voice that only a priest can adopt, that he'd come to tell her he'd solved her little problem.

'And what "little problem" would that be, Father?'

He half glanced at the crib, but didn't approach it to take a closer look at the baby. 'I've found a good, middle-class couple in need of a child. Desperate, in fact, since the wife cannot have one of her own. And the fact it's a girl makes it easier to place.'

'She's called Michelle, and you address her as she, Father, not *it*.'

He looked momentarily discomfited by this remark but scowled as he hurried on. 'Quite so, quite so. Anyway, Harriet, your troubles are over. I've come to take the problem off your hands. All you need do is sign this form, right here.' He handed her a pen and smoothed a paper out on her lap.

The words swam before her eyes. If she wrote her name on this piece of paper then Michelle's future would be assured. She would never have to suffer the ignominy of being called a bastard, of people gossiping behind her back, shutting her out or refusing to allow her to play with their more respectable children. She'd be loved and cherished, spoiled rotten no doubt by this couple desperate for a child.

Ignoring the pen, Harriet pushed the form away. 'A baby isn't something you give away, like a present you don't want or can't afford to keep. Even if she doesn't have a father, she has me. I'm her mother. Nothing can change that.'

'In the eyes of God, Harriet, she is base born, a child born out of sin.'

'Then I'm glad my God is a kinder God than yours, Father. I'm afraid this couple will have to look elsewhere for a child, they can't have mine.'

Father Dimmock did not look pleased by her decision. In fact, he looked extremely annoyed, and marched away muttering darkly about speaking to her mother, to see what she had to say on the matter.

'If you mean my *real* mother then don't waste your time, she's dead,' Harriet called after him, before bursting into tears.

40

Harriet

Seeing Harriet look so frail and weary after her terrible experiences, yet so full of love for her child, somehow filled Steve with fresh hope. She was back in his life again. She'd smiled at him and let him hold her hand. She hadn't pushed him away. She'd even allowed him to kiss her cheek. Best of all, Vinny Turner was nowhere in evidence.

Steve was quite convinced that Harriet still loved him, that all he had to do was get her to admit it.

He could hardly wait to visit her again, his mind spinning with unlikely possibilities. Following his visit to the hospital he'd gone home as if walking on air, filled with joy and hope for the future, a sensation that had quickly evaporated as reality had once more kicked in.

How could he even begin to dream of them getting back together when he was already engaged to someone else? The college week seemed to drag by and always there was Caro at his side, a rude reminder of the cruel trick fate had played on him. He'd only taken up with her in an attempt to banish Harriet from his mind, and because Harriet herself had urged him to forget her. He'd believed she was about to marry Vinny Turner but that hadn't happened. She'd obviously seen sense in the end, and walked out on him. Now it was too late. He was no longer free because he'd lumbered himself with a girl he didn't love.

Yet one word to Caro and he could be free.

He certainly couldn't go on like this. It would be entirely wrong. No matter how painful, he should be honest with her. Even if he failed to win Harriet back, it was unfair to Caro when really he felt nothing more than friendship towards the girl. All he had to do was explain his mistake, and ask her to release him from his promise.

He thought of her tears when he'd tried to postpone their engagement, which had resulted in his going off with her the very next day to buy the ring. He must tread more carefully this time, exercise tact and diplomacy yet remain firm, or she'd have him at the altar in no time. It was not going to be easy.

They'd spent the afternoon sitting in his study bedroom working on their respective theses. Caro wasn't an easy companion as she tended to chatter all the time, which rather spoiled his concentration. Steve had barely listened to a word she'd said as his thoughts were elsewhere, still wrapped up in Harriet and her predicament, which was undoubtedly serious. If Joyce had her way, she'd have that baby adopted, using fair means or foul.

Steve suddenly became aware that Caro had raised her voice, demanding his attention. 'You aren't even listening to me,' she complained. 'You don't seem interested in your own wedding.'

Steve's eyebrows climbed in surprise. 'Wedding? Who said anything about a wedding?'

Caroline pushed his books away and slid on to his knee. 'Don't be silly, when people get engaged there's always a wedding shortly afterwards.'

'We're still at college. How can we even think of getting married?'

'Silly boy, we'll be leaving in just a few months. By next May or early June, we'll be free as air. Our finals will be behind us and we can do as we please. A June wedding would be lovely, don't you think? Should we have the bridesmaids in ice blue or cerise? What do you think? Then a honeymoon in Paris or Rome, and your mother suggests that we put a deposit down on one of those nice new houses in Chorlton.'

Steve leapt to his feet so that she fell off his lap, too startled by the sheer intricacy of her plans to remember his intention to exercise tact and diplomacy. 'There isn't going to be any wedding.

I'm sorry, Caro, but this farce has gone on long enough. I blame myself entirely for allowing the situation to go this far, but I can't marry you. I don't love you.'

Looking back Steve could hardly bear to recall the scene. Caroline had cried a great deal, sobbing and begging him to change his mind, flying about the room in a rage one minute and flinging herself on to his bed in hysterics the next. She saw through his excuses at once and bitterly accused him of two-timing her with Harriet, which he'd strongly denied. Finally, when she'd realised that her tears were pointless, she'd slapped his face, flung her ring at him and stormed off. Steve felt nothing but relief.

'Taking on another man's child is bound to lead to disaster,' Joyce had sneeringly informed him, when he'd battled with her to allow him upstairs to speak to Harriet.

His mates said very much the same thing, all insisting he was completely mad when he confided his intentions to them, which he supposed he was. But if this was madness, then he welcomed it. He knew that it was Harriet he wanted, and he would allow no one to stand in his way. Not Vinny Turner, not Joyce, not his mother, and certainly not convention. Stuff convention. He loved her.

The only person who could prevent him from achieving his dream was Harriet herself. She'd naturally be nervous that any marriage between them might turn out to be a replica of Joyce and Stan's, and who could blame her?

All he had to do was persuade her to set aside these fears, along with her pride and stubbornness, and admit that she'd never stopped loving him. Steve rather thought preventing the lean on the Tower of Pisa might be easier to accomplish, nevertheless he was definitely going to give it his best shot.

The day after Harriet had sent Father Dimmock away in some-thing of a temper, Rose came again to see Harriet, and Steve came too. He turned up just ten minutes into visiting, and for some reason her grandmother instantly remembered an urgent appointment she must keep that very moment.

'I'll pop in later this evening, as usual, but I've got to dash now. Steve'll keep you company for a bit, won't you, lad?' Seconds later she was rushing out the door, not having stayed long enough to even remove her hat and coat. Harriet felt very slightly offended.

Equally embarrassed, Steve smiled awkwardly down at Harriet. She looked tired but freshly washed, much better today. There was some colour in her cheeks and the beginnings of what might be contentment in her smile. She was wearing a new blue quilted bed jacket over a matching nightdress which Rose must have bought for her, and looked so beautiful he felt a lump come into his throat. Suddenly at a loss, he said the first thing which came into his head.

'I expect Mrs Ibbotson knows I shouldn't even be here. By rights I should be at college, but I rang in sick.'

Harriet couldn't help but chuckle. 'Playing truant, eh? I'm glad you are here though. As you can see, I'm in need of a friend right now.'

'That's what I thought.' Steve's mind went blank again, and he couldn't think what to do with his hands so he took a peep at the baby, snuggled in a cosy blanket in her crib at the foot of the bed.

Harriet said, 'I thought I might call her Michelle, as that means gift from God, which this child surely must be to have survived such an inauspicious start in life.'

'Michelle. I like that. It's a lovely name.' He thrust his hands into his pockets, so that they wouldn't do anything crazy of their own accord, like snatch her into his arms. Rushing her could ruin everything. 'Does he know? Vinny, I mean. Sorry, that's a daft question. Of course he must know. Has he called to see her, to see you?' Steve could feel his heart pounding as he waited for her answer.

'You must be joking. To be fair I haven't even told him yet of Michelle's birth, but then I'm not quite sure where he is, somewhere in London, I believe.'

He glanced down at the fingers of her left hand, to make sure it was still bare of any ring. 'I assume he wasn't prepared to marry you then, and that's how you came to be homeless and wandering the streets?'

Harriet shifted uncomfortably in the bed, not quite meeting his eye. 'You presume correctly, although there were other factors involved.'

He came to sit on the edge of the bed, quite against the rules, and took her hand in his. 'I realise how difficult it must have been for you, Harriet, and I'm sorry. I know you loved him.'

'I *thought* I loved him, but that's not quite the same thing, is it? It seemed fun at the time, swept along in a madcap whirl of decadence and freedom.' She gave a bitter little laugh. 'But he didn't really care for me at all, or I him, for that matter. I was just confused.' She blinked back the tears in her eyes which pride wouldn't permit her to let fall.

Steve thought of Caro when last he'd seen her, her eyes wild with fury, and nodded. He understood about that sort of confusion, of being swept along by events.

As if reading his thoughts, Harriet asked in a pseudo-bright voice, 'So, what about this girl you're seeing? Are you about to get engaged or anything? Doesn't she mind your being here?'

'Caroline?' Embarrassed, Steve took off his spectacles and rooted in his pocket for a clean handkerchief. Unable to find one, he gave them a quick rub on the end of his tie, then put them back on again. 'Actually, it's over. It wasn't going anywhere. I went with Caro on the rebound, because I'd lost you. Got myself tied up in something I never wanted, just as you did. To be honest, it was all a bit of a mess.'

There was a small silence in which they both looked at the baby, at the grey clouds scudding past the window, anywhere but at each other. After a moment, Steve took a breath and said, 'So, what do you intend to do now?'

Harriet spoke with a determined fierceness. 'I intend to keep her, no matter what the gossip-mongers of Champion Street say, or what the priest says, or whatever Joyce tries to do.'

Steve smiled. 'Good for you.' He looked at her hand, still nestled in both of his, than tenderly kissed each fingertip as he'd used to do in that other time when the love between them had been freely expressed, a vital part of both their lives.

Harriet closed her eyes, as if in pain. 'Please don't . . .'

'Why not? I still have feelings for you. I've never stopped loving you, Harriet.'

'Oh, Steve . . .'

'No, please don't stop me. I've been wanting to say this to you for so long. I know I made a mess of things, not supporting you when you needed me to, always saying the wrong thing, putting my foot in my mouth, then struggling to apologise. And I understand there was a lot going on, a lot of problems in your life, and that's why – well, why you went a bit wild and behaved as you did. But I need you to know that I never stopped loving you, and if you still care a little for me, then . . . Well, it's not too late, is it? I mean . . . Dammit, what I'm trying to say is, that I still want to marry you.'

Harriet looked at him aghast. 'Stop it, Steve, you don't know what you're saying.'

'I most certainly do.' All embarrassment had gone from him now, his resolve to win her outweighing any awkwardness. 'I know it won't be easy for us, after all that's happened, but I'm still potty about you. I can't seem to get you out of my head. Not that I want to. That's where you belong: in my head, in my life, in my arms. I don't care if little Michelle is another man's child, I shall love her because she's yours. I hope you don't still have feelings for Vinny Turner . . .'

'I don't.'

'Good, because I want to take care of you. I want you to be my wife.'

Harriet gently tugged her hand away and wrapped her arms tightly about herself, as if for protection. 'I would never do that to you. It wouldn't be right. Joyce did something similar when she married my dad. They loved each other too, at first, but it wasn't enough to get over the fact she was carrying another man's child. The marriage was a disaster from start to finish, so no, it simply wouldn't work. Thanks, but no thanks.' She put up a hand as he was about to speak. 'No, don't argue with me, I've made up my mind. I'll cope somehow. I'm certainly not prepared to ruin your life as well as my own.'

'Do I take it from that convoluted refusal that you do still care for me a little?'

Harriet turned away, her cheeks flushed. 'That's not the point.'

'I think it's very much the point. I love you, Harriet. Maybe I haven't said that enough recently, but I do still love you. You're the only girl for me, and always will be.'

She looked at him then, her eyes swimming with tears. 'Oh, Steve, what can I say? I'm so afraid of making the wrong decision, of making a mess of things just as Joyce did, of making you unhappy and regret ever having known me.'

He wiped away a tear from her cheek with one finger. 'I could never do that. We're not Stan and Joyce. We're us! I've loved you forever, ever since I used to pull your plaits in junior school, and will continue to do so for as long as I live. I know things aren't easy at home, and if Joyce really is set on having this baby adopted, of making things difficult for you, then why don't you come and stay at mine for a while? At least give yourself time to think properly about what you want to do.'

Steve made the offer without even considering how his mother might react to this invitation, without even caring. He still had to explain to her about ending his engagement with Caroline.

Harriet considered her though. 'And what about your mother?'

'She'll be fine about it, once I've explained things properly to her. Besides, Mother likes babies.'

'Oh, Steve, I don't know. Everything is stacked against us, how can we be sure we'd survive?'

'We can't, we can only love each other and hope for the best.'

'If I accept your kind offer, to stay at your house, I mean, it's on the strict understanding that it's only temporary. I do need time to think, you're right about that, but the last thing I want to do is to rush headlong into another disaster.'

'That's fine. Take as long as you need.' At least he would have her close by, which would give him the opportunity he needed to convince her of his sincerity. 'When do they let you out of this place?'

Harriet gave a rueful smile. 'Next Sunday.'

'Right, tell me the exact time and I'll be here with my car to take you home. All I want is for you and this little one to be safe.' He kissed her then, just as he used to, long and deep, proving the sincerity of his feelings far more than words ever could.

Harriet didn't find it easy to settle in with the Blackstocks, almost instantly regretting her decision the moment she arrived. Steve's mother showed her to a small guest room, right at the top of the house, with a face like thunder.

'I – I really do appreciate this,' Harriet stuttered, in an attempt to placate her. Didn't she get enough disapproval from Joyce, without this woman on her case as well? 'I do assure you, it's only temporary, till I have time to make more permanent arrangements.'

'Yes, I can see you would want something more permanent,' Margaret Blackstock acidly replied.

'Don't worry, I've no intention of doing anything silly, well, even more silly than I've done already, I mean.' Harriet found herself blushing. 'I want you to know that I'm not out to trap Steve into marriage. Michelle isn't even his child.'

'I'm aware of that,' his mother interrupted in a voice like ice. 'And of course he did have a new girlfriend, until you appeared back on the scene. Caroline was a lovely girl, quite delightful. You'll find clean towels in the bathroom next door. If you need anything else, please let me know.' Whereupon she marched off and left Harriet to her own devices.

Mention of Steve's new girlfriend unnerved Harriet slightly. Mrs Blackstock clearly was not pleased that Steve had finished with her. Harriet told herself it probably would have ended anyway and tried not to think about it, or hope for too much as she unpacked her few possessions and tended to Michelle.

Since collecting Harriet from the hospital and moving her in to his home, Steve had rushed back to college, promising to return the following weekend when they'd have more time to talk.

Relations with his mother did not improve over the following days but Harriet did her best to cope. The atmosphere remained chilly and she opted to stay in her room, only venturing out for an hour or two each afternoon to take Michelle for a walk in the small, soft-bodied pram Steve had bought for her.

'I've not much money, living as I do on a student grant, but I've a bit put by from a summer working for Barry on the fruit and veg stall,' Steve had informed her.

'I don't want to take your money.' Harriet had valiantly attempted to resist but Steve very reasonably pointed out that she couldn't carry the baby everywhere, and that she'd need other things too: nappies, nightdresses, vests and stuff.

'You'll have to tell me what's needed.'

His kindness filled her with fresh guilt, but it was Rose who came to the rescue, taking Harriet shopping and buying all that was necessary for the baby, apart from the pram which Steve insisted on paying for.

'Joyce might not be prepared to provide you with a home, but you're still my granddaughter, and this little one is my great-granddaughter, so I'll see we do right by her.'

To Harriet's great surprise and gratitude, Mr Blackstock made enquiries about a maternity allowance and made sure she got it. It wasn't a fortune but it would give Harriet a modicum of independence until she found herself a job and a place of her own. Steve didn't want her to do any such thing, of course, but Harriet had no intention of being dependent on anyone, or rushing into marriage for the wrong reasons, as Joyce had clearly done.

In her heart she knew she still loved Steve as much as she ever had, if not more. And she believed him when he told her that he still loved her. But was love enough? Her experiences of that particular emotion thus far in her short life was that it was largely an unreliable commodity.

41

Harriet

Margaret Blackstock watched her young guest with close attention. Steve had confessed to her his defection over Caroline. They'd had quite an argument on the subject, Margaret actually accusing her own son of toying with the girl's emotions. She was most disappointed in him and secretly appalled at the idea of welcoming this young hussy into her house.

Nevertheless, Margaret was nothing if not the perfect hostess, no matter what her private opinion on the moral standards of her guest might be. She provided Harriet with a MIRROMatic de luxe electric kettle which would allow her to make herself a cup of tea or coffee whenever she should want one. The girl also had her own bathroom up there on the second floor.

'You may come down to the kitchen to prepare yourself a meal at any time, and there is a washing machine for Baby's nappies. You only have to say, and so long as I am not using it, it is all yours.'

Margaret certainly had no intention of waiting on the girl. It was, in any case, time Harriet learned some sense of responsibility. Margaret would sit in her small parlour doing her tapestry work or listening to *Woman's Hour*, half an ear cocked for any sound from above. Not that there ever was any sound. She might still have been alone in the house all day for all the noise the girl and her baby made.

Margaret had to admit she seemed to be a very good baby, with hardly a peep out of her. A part of her almost regretted this. She might well have welcomed an opportunity to dash upstairs once in a while on the pretext of offering help and advice, if only to see this child close to. Margaret had to admit she was curious, and she did rather like babies. She would have liked more than one of her own, but no more had come after Steve.

Sometimes when Harriet came downstairs at three o'clock, as she did every afternoon to put little Michelle in her pram which stood in the hall, Margaret would jump to her feet and rush out to make some comment or other.

'It's rather cold outside, have you made sure she is well wrapped up?'

'Oh, yes, Nan bought her a warm matinée jacket.'

'Don't stay out too long though, it looks like rain. Young babies are very prone to catching a chill.'

Harriet would smile and go on her way.

'How is she sleeping?' Margaret politely enquired as Harriet returned to the house one afternoon.

Surprised by the interest, Harriet answered with equal politeness. 'She's doing very well, thank you.'

'And how long can she go between feeds?'

'About four hours.'

'Oh, that's good for such a small baby. What weight was she when she was born?'

'Six pounds two ounces.'

'She is doing well then.'

'Yes,' Harriet agreed, 'she is. Thank you.'

That evening as Margaret sat with her husband listening to a concert on the Third Programme, she commented thoughtfully, 'I believe this girl could shape up to make quite a good mother.' Mr Blackstock gave a non-committal grunt from behind his evening paper.

'There's an air of common sense about her which is really quite surprising, considering her background. Of course she will need help,' Margaret mused. 'Babies can be tricky creatures.'

She glanced across at her inattentive husband, and the empty chair where her son used to sit before he'd gone off to college. 'Not that you would either know or care. Men don't understand such things,' she finished rather quietly to herself, and went to put the kettle on.

Harriet made a point of expressing her gratitude for Mrs Blackstock's interest, even for the advice the woman offered, such as not to pile on too many blankets which could overheat the baby, and never to use a pillow.

'And don't rely too much upon a dummy,' Margaret firmly instructed. 'If a baby is crying there is generally a good reason for it.'

'Yes, Mrs Blackstock.'

Yet, surprisingly, her comments didn't make Harriet feel inadequate in any way, rather it made her feel less alone in this difficult situation, perhaps because she was also equally ready to offer praise, such as her frequent remarks about what good progress Michelle was making, and how well she must be sleeping.

Generally though, Harriet did her best to keep out of the Blackstocks' way. She took careful note of their mealtimes and adjusted her own eating plan so that she didn't intrude upon them. Harriet found it preferable, in the circumstances, to avoid much cooking altogether, and got by largely on bread and cheese, fruit and cold meat sandwiches. Sometimes she would treat herself to a hot pie from Big Molly's stall, or fish and chips from Frankie's. Her one consideration was for Michelle. So long as the baby was well and happy, nothing else mattered.

Best of all she loved her afternoons when she would walk round the market, proudly showing off her child. Harriet refused to be concerned if some people did indeed gossip about her behind their hands, whispering that she was still unwed and her child illegitimate. Michelle was still beautiful, and very healthy despite her poor start in life. A baby to be proud of.

Joyce never came near but Rose was a constant visitor, calling in most days to dangle this new addition to the family on her knee.

'The cards told me I was to find a new love in my life. Not that I imagined for a minute they meant a babby, getting the wrong end of the stick entirely,' Rose chortled. 'But they were absolutely right, as always, and here she is, a real little love. Isn't she a treasure?'

'Does Joyce ever ask after her?' Harriet ventured to enquire, and her grandmother's face darkened.

'Don't expect too much from our Joyce, chuck.'

'But she'll miss so much if she refuses to even get to know Michelle.'

Rose shook her head in despair. 'Don't dwell on it, Harriet love. We are as we are, and my daughter isn't going to change at this late stage in her sad life.'

To be fair to Margaret Blackstock, unlike Joyce, she didn't take out her disapproval upon the baby. One rainy afternoon, seeing Harriet struggling to put the hood down on the pram, she quietly took Michelle and held her while Harriet unloaded her shopping and carried the bags upstairs. When she came back down again, only moments later, Mrs Blackstock was sitting in the kitchen with the baby on her knee, making *coochee-coochee* sounds and pretending to tickle the baby's tummy.

'She's a little darling.'

Harriet smiled with relief. '*I* think so.'

'Of course you do. And what does your mother think of her?'

'Joyce, you mean?'

'Ah, I was forgetting for a moment. Yes, what does Joyce think of her?'

'She thinks I should sweep her under a carpet, or, failing that, have her adopted.'

The other woman looked slightly stunned by this robust response. 'You always were very direct, Harriet. And are you going to have her adopted?'

Harriet shook her head. 'Would you have given Steve away?'

A small silence, and then Steve's mother asked the inevitable question. 'And you think you can manage to bring her up on your own, do you?'

'I'll do my best.'

'Hmm!'

Still she didn't hand over the baby, but at that moment the kettle on the Aga started to whistle. 'I thought we might have a cup of tea. Why don't you make it while I change her nappy? I see there's one in her little bag here.'

Harriet could scarcely believe her eyes as Steve's mother efficiently changed Michelle's nappy, talking and smiling to her all the while, then sat to sip her tea, still with the baby on her knee.

'I take it the father is not going to be of any help.'

'No,' Harriet replied, rather shortly. She had no intention of discussing Vinny with Mrs Blackstock.

'Babies can be very demanding.' She jiggled Michelle in her arms to keep the baby content as she began to grizzle and suck her little fist. 'They deprive you of sleep, suffer from colic, need constant attention and feeding, and cry for no reason, or so it seems at times.'

'Nan has given me lots of advice.'

'I'm sure she has.'

Michelle started to whimper and Harriet leapt to her feet. 'It's nearly time for her next feed, I'd best take her upstairs and get her bottle ready.'

'Aren't you feeding her yourself?' Margaret lay the baby against her shoulder and gently rubbed her back. Michelle instantly stopped crying, although her little mouth was still searching for food.

'I don't have enough milk. Sister said it was because I was malnourished when I had her. It's all right, I get the National Dried Milk from the clinic, along with her orange juice and cod liver oil, and she seems to be thriving on it. That's what counts.'

Margaret considered Harriet with all seriousness. 'You must take great care of her. My Stephen suffered from jaundice shortly after he was born, which was partly due to some feeding difficulties he was having, and a consequent shortage of fluids. Quite common with small babies, I believe, but nonetheless worrying.'

'I will take the very greatest care of her.'

Margaret looked the girl straight in the eye. 'I rather believe you will. And what about you? Are you taking proper care of yourself? I don't see you operating my cooker very often. What are you eating?'

'I'm fine.'

'Hmm!' said Margaret Blackstock again as she handed the baby over. 'Well, no one shall remain malnourished in *my* house. And if you are to be of any use as a mother to this baby, then you must eat properly too. We have dinner at six as a rule, but we can put it back an hour until after you've settled her, then you may join us. Don't argue, I won't take no for an answer.'

'Thank you, Mrs Blackstock, I appreciate it.' Harriet was appalled by the prospect of dinner alone each night with the Blackstocks, without even Steve there for support, but she could hardly refuse when they'd opened their doors to her, however unwillingly. And at least the woman thought Michelle was a little darling.

Steve came home every weekend and it soon became clear that they were getting along as well as ever, happy just to be in each other's company.

'You might even fall in love with me all over again,' he teased as he helped fold Michelle's clean nappies and stow them away in a cupboard.

Harriet rewarded him with an impish smile. 'I just might, you never know.'

Steve was less astonished to find his mother entirely captivated by the baby than Harriet was, being only too aware that her bark was far worse than her bite. But he *was* amazed to find himself equally enraptured. He'd never ever given a thought to babies until now, but this one was indeed a darling, a sweet little baby who took her feed without a murmur, slept soundly, and surely that was a smile just now when he'd tickled her under her chin?

'Let me feed her,' he would say, as she tuned up with the first opening cries of hunger, and Harriet would laugh.

'All right, softie, but make sure you burp her properly.'

Steve watched how Harriet did things, and took great care to follow her lead. She was a natural mother, and his admiration and love for her grew with each moment he spent with her.

And when the baby was tucked up for the night, they would sit together in the lamplight and talk, not about anything in particular, not about Harriet's uncertain future, which he knew was of great concern to her. They would stick to more general topics, perhaps chewing over the day's news from her transistor radio. Whether Kennedy would make a good president now that he'd scraped into office, or the fact that for the first time in cricket history, a test match had ended in a draw despite Australia needing only six to win with three wickets left.

'A catch dropped, a run out, five frantic runs, then finally a fantastic throw from Joe Solomon,' Steve cried. 'What a game!'

Not understanding a word, Harriet smiled fondly at him.

They might talk about whether or not Yul Brynner should have shaved his hair off again for *The Magnificent Seven*, or the new star Albert Finney in *Saturday Night and Sunday Morning*, but they went to see neither of these films. For one thing they didn't have any money, and for another they were quite content to light a fire in the small Victorian grate in Harriet's room and toast crumpets. Then she might let him kiss her a little, which was adorable, although Steve made sure that he kept his emotions in check.

Sometimes, when he reluctantly left her to go to his own bed, he couldn't remember what they'd talked about at all.

It was a week or two after Christmas when Harriet got the shock of her life. She was just giving Michelle her morning bath when there came a tap on the door and Margaret Blackstock popped her head round it, for once not smiling when she saw the naked pink baby kicking her little legs in the bath.

'Ah, I thought you might be busy. You have a visitor. Two, actually.'

Harriet could tell by the tightness in the other woman's face that this wasn't a welcome visitor, and her heart skipped a beat. 'Who?'

'It's him, your young man.' Margaret Blackstock nodded coldly in the direction of the baby, in case Harriet had forgotten the identity of the baby's father already.

'He isn't – my young man,' Harriet said in her quietest voice. 'What does he want?'

Margaret considered Harriet's ash-pale face and her heart softened a little. It was very clear that her son was desperately in love with this girl, a fact which had at first alarmed and displeased her. Now her opinion was gradually changing. She wasn't in fact a bad lot at all, as she had at first assumed. A bit silly and rebellious perhaps, but who wasn't in their teens? Margaret preferred not to recall how close she had come to making a similar mistake herself. And with Joyce for a mother, or stepmother, was it any wonder? 'There's a girl with him, quite pretty.'

'Shelley. She's the singer in the band.'

'Ah!' There was an awkward moment while Margaret waited for Harriet to say something more. When no further response came, she continued in a softer tone, 'You don't have to see him, if you don't want to. I could take a message, or ask him to leave, if you prefer.'

Harriet looked into the older woman's face, momentarily startled by the sympathy she found there, and took less than a second to decide. 'Yes. Yes, please do that. Thank him for calling and ask him to leave.'

Margaret nodded. 'A good decision.'

She returned ten minutes later with a cup of coffee for each for them, and two slices of jam sponge. 'There, a little treat for us. I baked it only this morning so we must eat it while it's at its very best. May I take her for a moment?'

Moved by the woman's unexpected generosity, Harriet happily handed Michelle over. After a moment, in which she praised the lightness of the sponge, she asked, 'Has Vinny gone?' She felt the need to use his name, to prove to herself she could say it without any ill effects, and was pleased to find that she could.

'Indeed he has. He asked me to tell you that the band is back in Manchester. Things apparently didn't go too well in London and he'd be happy for you to join them, if you're interested. But it's now or never, apparently. You must make up your mind once and for all, because if you aren't available to work for them as before, then he'll have to find somebody else.' Margaret glanced at the girl, gauging her reaction.

A slight pause, and then Harriet said, 'Did he ask about the baby, whether I'd had a boy or a girl, for instance?'

Margaret shook her head, watching the girl closely from over the rim of her cup as she sipped her coffee. 'He did say that you were welcome to bring the baby, no strings attached. He seemed to imply you were well aware of his need for freedom.'

'I am.'

'And will you be joining him?'

'No, I won't.'

'I see. No regrets?'

'About not accepting his offer? No, none at all.'

Harriet managed to smile even though she was silently fuming inside. She felt angry towards Vinny for not caring if he'd fathered a boy or a girl, for not even bothering to ask how Harriet was coping on her own, or if she needed any money. Not that she would take it, she told herself, but it was the principle that mattered. He could at least offer.

And how had he known she was here? Had Joyce told him she was living with the Blackstocks? Most significant of all, he still had Shelley with him. Nothing had changed then.

Well, he was gone now, thank goodness. They both were, and Harriet doubted they'd be back.

It was true what she'd just said, she didn't feel any regrets, except for having met him in the first place. She reached over to tickle her baby's chin. 'I have Michelle, I don't need Vinny Turner. He is indeed trouble with a capital T.'

'Good girl,' Margaret said, without the slightest hint of being patronising. 'And what about our little treasure then? She seems to be growing daily, before our very eyes. What a little beauty you are going to be,' Margaret said, placing a raspberry kiss on the baby's bare tummy. Michelle chuckled and both women burst out laughing. 'Do you think that was a laugh or simply wind?' Margaret asked, surprised.

Harriet shook her head in delight. 'I've no idea, but it sounded lovely, didn't it?'

'It did indeed!' And the two women contentedly played with the baby while they enjoyed Margaret's excellent coffee and jam sponge.

42

Joyce

The market was in turmoil with the arrival of bulldozers and JCBs. Homes were within days of being razed to the ground, the hairdresser's salon included, and Joyce was frantically packing up to leave. She'd found them a house to rent in Quay Street, just a short distance away, but hadn't yet found alternative accommodation for the salon.

Joyce was filled with fury over the situation, angry with her mother for not having accepted the generous offer from the developers. At least then they could relocate her business somewhere decent. Many people had already done so, the rest were beginning to ask if it was worth going on with the fight?

All except for one or two stalwarts, her mother included. Rose was still calling the newspapers and trying to drum up support for this fruitless campaign.

The folk who lived at the bottom end of Champion Street were, of course, delighted at the prospect of being rehoused in a posh new flat, thrilled to escape the damp overcrowding, the peeling wallpaper and the invasion of cockroaches in the dark of night. But those in the top half of the street took a different view.

The Poulsons were still holding out, as were Winnie and Barry Holmes; Dena Dobson too was hoping either for a last-minute reprieve or word that the developers or the city council had found them a new home and were willing to relocate the market. Patsy Bowman, now Patsy Bertalone, was likewise hanging on, having persuaded Clara Higginson not to accept the developers' offer either. It was a dangerous game they were playing.

Amy and Chris George had already sold up and gone, as had Sam Beckett. His ex-wife, Judy, was standing very much behind the campaign to save the market, and the fact she'd recently won full custody of her children made her even more determined to win. She was also reputed to be back with Leo Catlow, although not in a hurry to remarry. The world's morals, Joyce thought, rather hypocritically, were rapidly disappearing.

Terry, Alec's son, was steadfastly hanging on to Hall's Music Shop in the Market Hall, opening his door for business every morning irrespective of the dust and disruption in the street. He was assisted by his wife Lynda when she wasn't doing her stint working for her mum Betty Hemley on the flower stall. Betty was another stubborn soul not prepared to be bullied by any tinpot building firm, a somewhat ungenerous description of one of Manchester's largest developers.

'This isn't simply about folk's homes,' Rose reminded her daughter. 'Or whether they will be given the opportunity to live in one of the new flats, once they're built. It's about people's livelihoods. Champion Street Market has a long tradition going back hundreds of years and to see it dismantled with all the attendant community spirit lost for ever, would be criminal.'

'I do see that, Mother, but where are we supposed to live, if they tear down our house? Tell me that.'

'And it would be little short of a tragedy if the wonderful Victorian Market Hall with its new extension was demolished,' Rose continued, as if Joyce hadn't interrupted her.

'Are you listening to me?'

Rose was far too busy painting posters for the final demonstration in the campaign to listen to anyone. Who was listening? Nobody, in Joyce's estimation. Nobody ever had. They were all too wrapped up in their own concerns, too busy to care if she was happy. What was she supposed to do if she lost this business? Where was she supposed to go? She'd poured years of hard work and toil into this place.

★

Joyce had quickly grown bored of being stuck at home with a baby and come to a decision. She would go back to work. They needed the money, in any case, if she was to continue paying Eileen her allowance, as Stan insisted they should, and which even Joyce felt obliged to do, at least for a while. In six months or so she'd fully intended to gradually reduce the amount paid, then stop it altogether. Stan would still have been away at sea and none the wiser.

Joyce had longed to start her own business. Rose would have to come too, of course, to help look after them during the day, but at least they'd be away from Ancoats, and from Eileen.

She'd soon found and taken on the lease of this shop in Champion Street, which was perfect. There was the flat above, although when she'd first seen it, this had been occupied by an elderly couple. Given time and the right inducements, Joyce had persuaded them out of it, and she'd moved in with the children and Rose, eager to start afresh and put the past behind her.

Despite the perfidy of fate, everything had seemed to be working out for them at last.

Now, her own mother had betrayed her, refusing to sign the property over into Joyce's name, and all because of that flaming child she'd stupidly adopted. Taking Harriet on had been the biggest mistake of her life. She'd succeeded only in landing herself with a great deal of trouble and responsibility. Her noble act of generosity hadn't saved her marriage in the end. Nothing had.

Stan had come home at the end of the war a damaged man, both physically and psychologically. He'd blamed Joyce for everything that had gone wrong since he went away, and proved himself deaf to her complaints for their entire married life.

If she'd disagreed with any decision he made regarding Harriet, he would ignore her, making it very clear that she had no say over the girl's welfare, that his word was final. Stan had been far too soft with the girl, and always shut Joyce out. He'd allowed her to wear make-up far too young, and to go out with boys, that Steve Blackstock for one. She might well have behaved far more responsibly if Joyce had been allowed to exercise a bit more discipline over her.

Stan's answer to everything was to shower the child with soppy love and affection, give her pointless cuddles and thoroughly spoil her. Was it any wonder if Joyce had come to hate her? Just like her tart of a mother, she'd stolen Stan's affection from her.

But what would her husband think of his beloved daughter now? Shacked up with one lad after giving birth to the child of another. What effect did that have upon a decent girl's reputation? Joyce sincerely hoped such wanton behaviour would reap its just rewards in the end. The lass really didn't deserve to be happy.

Harriet had been staying with the Blackstocks for almost six months now and was still obstinately refusing Steve's frequent and increasingly persistent offers of marriage. Summer was upon them, his finals were over and done with and a teaching certificate was in his hand. He even had an offer of an excellent post teaching mathematics at a nearby secondary school.

'So what's the problem?' he asked her, times without number. 'You know very well that you love me.'

Yes, it was true, she did love him. And yes, she knew that he loved her, but where did that get them? Joyce had loved Stan once upon a time, and Stan had loved Joyce, apparently. But Harriet's father, fine man that he still was in her eyes, had found it quite impossible to live with the fact that Grant was not his child. And from that moment on, the pair of them had resolutely set out to destroy their marriage and each other.

No matter how many times Steve insisted they weren't Stan and Joyce, Harriet remained adamant. 'Maybe later, after you've settled into your new job and had time to think straight. We have to be sure.'

Even Margaret was beginning to ask if there was something wrong with her son. She'd surprised herself by warming towards the girl during the months she'd lived in their home. She admired her courage, her resolve to be independent and not be a bother to anyone. She'd even got herself a part-time job working mornings for Lizzie Pringle making sweets and chocolates, but even then Margaret had had a hard task persuading Harriet to allow her to mind the baby.

'Nan has offered to look after her.'

'Yes, but I thought I could perhaps share the load. Looking after a baby is quite tiring and your grandmother is not as young as she was. Perhaps I could have Michelle for a couple of mornings a week at least?'

'I – I'm not sure. I don't want to be a nuisance.'

'If you were a nuisance, dear girl, we would tell you.' This was from Mr Blackstock, who briefly put down his paper to put an end to a discussion which threatened to go on all night and quite ruin his hopes of listening to the football.

'I know Rose is also fully engrossed in this campaign to save the market. Would you object if I spoke with her, discussed the situation and see what she proposes would be a suitable routine?' And with a resigned sigh Harriet conceded she would have no objection to this. She was stunned by this change of heart on Mrs Blackstock's part, and nervous of relying too heavily upon her good will, in case it should fill her son with hopes she might not, in the end, feel able to fulfil.

Rose was indeed agreeable to Mrs Blackstock minding Michelle for two or even three mornings a week. The two women happily agreed to share the task as they were both utterly besotted with the child.

'And of course if Harriet and Steve should marry, in the end, then I will be Michelle's grandmother too,' Margaret reminded Rose, with a secretive little smile.

Rose frowned. 'Do you reckon they will marry? They've one or two obstacles to overcome first, and that lass of mine has a stubborn streak.'

'Obstacles surely can be overcome if love is strong enough,' Margaret said, almost waxing lyrical.

'I take it you'd have no objection then?'

'We want only what's best for Stephen, but I can see Harriet is not quite the harlot that folk have made her out to be. Misguided perhaps, and rather foolish, but by no means wicked.'

Rose was glad to see that Steve's mother had grown less intractable, won over by the charms of young Michelle, no doubt. Unfortunately, Harriet herself had grown more cynical about life, and seemed to have lost all faith in love. She was like a lost soul searching for the truth, and finding it might hurt her even more. Yet sometimes risks had to be taken.

Watching the way her granddaughter was behaving, and afraid the silly lass might be about to throw away all chance of happiness with her stubbornness, Rose decided once again to listen to the wisdom of the cards and act on her instincts.

She went to a secret place in her old room, one which even Grant knew nothing of, lifted a floorboard and took out an envelope. It was time the past was finally put to rest, so that sound decisions could be made about the future. She took the letter to the Blackstocks' house in St John's Place and posted it through the letter box. Tomorrow she would call and see what Harriet felt about it.

Mrs Blackstock brought the letter up to Harriet just before supper. She quickly read it through, not realising at first what it was, then sat staring at it in a state of total disbelief. If she hadn't been holding this paper in her own hands she wouldn't have believed it even existed. It wasn't a note from Nan, as she'd expected when she'd recognised the handwriting on the envelope, it was from her mother. Not Joyce, but her *real* mother. Nor was it a long letter, no more than a few lines of print in an unformed, shaky hand.

Rose tells me you know now that Joyce isn't your mother, and that she has thrown you out on the streets, just as she did with me many years ago. She also tells me that you've been asking after me. I expect you are angry for my having abandoned you, but there were good reasons why I kept out of your life. I will agree to see you now, if that is what you want. Think carefully before you decide.

Your loving mother.

It was dated about a year ago, at a time when Harriet was trailing around the streets with Vinny and the band, sleeping rough under the canal bridges, and then in that old warehouse as they made their way in the music business. She'd thought herself all alone in the world, and yet she did have a mother, after all.

For this letter must mean only one thing: that she wasn't dead at all. She was very much alive.

Harriet pressed the letter to her lips in wonder, almost as if she wanted to smell the imprint of her in the writing. Her mother's own hand had touched this paper. Her *real* mother! She could hardly believe it. All these years of silence, and now, because of the callous way Joyce had treated her, she suddenly decides to reveal herself and make contact.

But why, for goodness' sake? What on earth was going on? Harriet's mind was teeming with questions. Where had her mother been living all this time? Why had she neglected to get in touch for all these years and allowed them all to think she was dead? Why had she gone away in the first place?

Did she feel angry that this woman had abandoned her as a young child? What sort of mother could do that? Yet there must have been a good reason, as she says in the letter. In the main, Harriet blamed Joyce.

Whenever she thought of what her stepmother had done to her, she felt filled with resentment. Joyce was surely the one responsible for this mess and no one else. Just by the way she'd callously packed Harriet's bag that night and told her to leave, didn't bear thinking of. She hadn't given the slightest thought to Harriet's well-being, or to the dangers she would inevitably face in the streets.

As things had turned out, Harriet had felt safer living rough with her tramp friends than at the mercy of a woman who hated her.

And who had told her mother of these recent events? Could
it be Rose? Had her grandmother been holding on to this letter
for months, while she was agonising over whether or not she
should stay with Vinny? If so, why?

It was long past time someone properly explained to her what
this was all about, what exactly had happened during the war to
drive her mother away.

Rose came over the next day and Margaret showed her straight
up to her granddaughter's room. She suspected at once there
was some emergency or problem when Rose refused her offer
of a cup of tea and a slice of her best fruit cake. Rose was never
one to miss a treat.

'Perhaps later then,' Margaret said with a smile. 'When you've
had your chat.' She tapped on Harriet's door and when it
opened, she could see at once that the girl had been crying.
Even after Rose had thanked her and closed the door, Margaret
did not immediately return downstairs. She remained where she
was at the top of the stairs, secretly listening, concerned over
whatever drama was about to unfold and whether it would
concern her son.

She could hear Harriet sobbing and Rose offering soothing
words that Margaret couldn't quite catch, and wished Steve was
here. Unfortunately, he was away on a school geography trip and
wouldn't be back until the morning.

Then Harriet said, 'Will you take me? I need to make this visit.
I surely deserve a full and proper explanation. I need to understand what's going on, how I feel about things, before I can make
any definite decisions about my future. But I can't face this alone.
Will you come with me?'

'Course I will, but it won't be easy for either of you after all
this time. It took me a while to decide whether it was the right
thing to do to even give you this letter.'

'I dare say, but I have all this love inside of me still waiting to
be expressed.'

'You mustn't decide too quickly, chuck. There's a lot at stake,

Harriet. Give yourself a few days to think about it. If you still feel the same at the end of the week, then I'll support you in whatever you decide.'

Having heard enough, Margaret crept quietly downstairs and put the kettle on.

43

Rose

The following morning, and with little thought of the consequences of such an action, Rose rather foolishly admitted
to Joyce what she had done. She confessed that she'd given Harriet
a letter from her mother.

Joyce gazed at Rose stunned, utterly lost for words.

'I let her think about it for several days but she's still of the
same mind, so I've agreed to arrange a visit for next Sunday.'
Rose wanted Joyce to realise that it was time to let go of this war
she had waged for half a lifetime against an innocent child. 'I
think the time is right, don't you?'

Sadly, her daughter didn't see things in quite the same light.
Furious that the truth was about to come out, Joyce was outraged,
and firmly resolved there and then that whatever the cost, her
mother's interference would have quite the opposite effect to what
she intended. The last thing Joyce wanted was for Harriet to meet
with Eileen, or for her to learn the details of what had gone on
all those years ago. The past was the past and best forgotten.

Nor was Joyce pleased that after all her years of hard work, her
livelihood seemed to be dissolving before her very eyes, about to
be bulldozed out of existence. While Rose was doing everything
she could to save the market, the home Joyce had believed would
one day be hers, was now to be handed over to Stan's by-blow,
as if she were the one with a better right to it. The very idea was
execrable to her. Even her darling son was to be disinherited, just
because he'd borrowed a few quid from his grandmother occasionally, without asking.

Joyce had absolutely no intention of allowing that girl to dis-inherit her. She needed Harriet out of her life once and for all. Hadn't she suffered enough from her blasted father over the years?

She was only too bitterly aware that whenever she went out and about round the market, folk were talking about her behind their hands. To her horror, Joyce realised she'd become an object of scorn and pity, all because of that hussy. Having destroyed her carefully nurtured respectability, Harriet really had no right at all to be happy.

Joyce wished the girl would run away again with her junky boyfriend. But if she wouldn't disappear, then the baby must. Surely she deserved some peace in her life, some retribution for all she had suffered? A lifetime of seeking revenge had left her without any facility for forgiveness.

There was no reason at all why she couldn't hand over the baby to Father Dimmock and the good Christian family he had found to care for it. It was but six months old and would soon forget its real mother. She'd been right all along. Adoption was the only solution. Perhaps then, when the child was gone, Harriet would leave too, this time for good.

It took no time at all to put her plans in place, then she went over to St John's Place and found, to her delight, that Margaret Blackstock was alone with the baby. Harriet was at work this morning, and, as luck would have it, Steve was away too on a geography field trip.

'Perhaps I might be allowed to take my grandchild for a walk?' Joyce asked, smiling confidently at the other woman. 'I could take little Michelle to meet her mother on her way home from Pringle's.'

Of course, neither Pringle's Chocolate Cabin, nor the work-shop where the sweets and chocolates were made, was her goal this morning. Joyce had already arranged an appointment with Father Dimmock.

'Oh, I'm sure she would like that,' Margaret agreed, all unsus-pecting. 'I'll just get her little matinée coat, there's a chill wind out today.'

Steve arrived about an hour later and headed straight to the bathroom, Margaret chasing after him. She chided him for never being here when he was needed and told him there was no time for showers or unpacking. 'A matter of great importance has come up, which you need to be told about forthwith, whether you like it or not.'

'And what is so important it can't wait for an hour or two? I'm filthy, Mother, and could do with a cup of tea, if you're putting the kettle on.'

'Harriet has had a letter, from Vinny.'

Steve looked stunned. She'd promised him faithfully that the relationship was over. 'She can't have.'

'The letter was delivered by hand via her own grandmother. Rose actually called in yesterday to speak to her about it, and I just happened to hear a snippet of their conversation.'

Margaret's cheeks were slightly flushed as she admitted this while Steve's blazed to a bright crimson. 'You were eavesdropping? What did you do, put your ear to the keyhole?'

'Don't be ridiculous! Anyway, there isn't a keyhole on that bedroom door. And no, I didn't put my ear to the panel of the door either, but I could hear what was said, quite clearly – well, reasonably clearly.'

Steve gave his mother a withering look. 'I don't want to know what they said.' He turned away in disgust, still heading for the bathroom, but Margaret snatched at his arm to prevent him.

'Yes, you do, Stephen. Harriet asked her grandmother if she would go with her. She said, and I quote: "I surely deserve a full and proper explanation. I need to understand what's going on, how I feel about things before I can make any definite decisions about my future." And when Rose attempted to caution her against doing anything in a hurry, she said, "I have all this love inside of me still waiting to be expressed." Who else could she be referring to but Vinny Turner?'

'Oh, God!' Steve said. 'Will we never be free of that man? Where is Harriet?'

'Working. Joyce has gone to meet her with the child. She

may well be seeing him now, today, this very minute, for all we know.'

'We'll just have to wait till she gets back, and ask her.'

Margaret said no more, obliged to accept her son's decision.

But when Harriet returned to the house around lunchtime, she was alone. Steve met her at the door, his expression cold and condemning. He didn't say hello, or ask how her morning had gone as he normally did. Instead he launched right in with, 'I hear you've had a letter.'

Harriet had been about to run into his arms, but seeing his set face and hearing the ice in his tone, she paused and frowned up at him. 'Where did you hear that?'

'Mother tells me Rose delivered it, by hand.'

'Ah, I see. Then I'm sure you'll understand how delighted I was to receive it.'

'I'm surprised, I must say. I assume you've agreed to go?' He meant back to join the band, with Vinny, but Harriet didn't understand what he was suggesting, picking up only on his first words.

'*You're* surprised?' She laughed. '*I* was absolutely stunned, and so *thrilled*! I expect I should be angry, by rights, but I'm not at all.' She went to hug him then in her excitement but felt him flinch away from her. 'What is it? What's wrong? You look so worried, and there's really no reason to be.'

Steve almost snarled at her. 'Why should anything be wrong? You get a letter from your old boyfriend and instantly want to dash off into his arms. Why should I be worried about that?'

'My old boyfriend, what are you talking about?'

'I'm talking about that letter,' Steve crisply informed her, folding his arms across his chest so that his hands wouldn't be tempted to reach for her.

Harriet began to laugh. 'Is that what you thought?'

'I don't see anything funny about it.'

Her laughter instantly faded. 'No, you're quite right, it isn't funny at all. What you're saying is that you still don't trust me. A letter is delivered to the house, by hand, and without any proof whatsoever you assume it to be from Vinny. Now why would that be? Because you're still haunted by the thought of him, of the time I spent with him, the fact I slept in his bed and that he is Michelle's father. And you wonder why I still won't agree to marry you?'

Harriet was fuming as she spun on her heel and headed for the stairs, desperately upset. She wanted only to be alone where she could weep in private. Why did everyone always let her down in the end? Why was love so useless and unreliable?

Steve took a sideways step to block her way.

'Please get out of my way.'

Ignoring her, Steve remained where he was, now looking deeply troubled and very contrite. 'Look, I'm sorry if we jumped to the wrong conclusion but . . .'

'We?'

He glanced away, not wishing to meet her condemning gaze. 'Mother overheard some of the conversation between you and Rose last evening, and she rather thought you were talking about Vinny.'

Now Harriet was even more angry. 'Well, she was wrong. If you want to know the truth that letter was from my *mother*, my *real* mother, who apparently isn't dead and wants to see me, after all these years. She's the one I'm desperate to see. Now do you understand why I'm so thrilled?'

'Oh, my God! But Mother thought . . .'

'Well, she thought wrong. Serve her right for eavesdropping on a private conversation. Please, it's been a long morning and I wish to see my child.' Pushing Steve out of the way Harriet started up the stairs, unshed tears already marring her vision.

'She isn't there,' Steve called after her retreating figure, puzzled by the comment.

'What?'

'Michelle isn't there. Joyce collected her earlier. She was supposed to be meeting you after work.'

'Oh, lord! Joyce has stolen my baby? Why didn't you tell me?' Harriet flew down the stairs and out of the house, and, after a moment of stunned paralysis, Steve ran after her.

★

The stallholders of Champion Street were attempting to go about their business as normally as possible, despite the presence of bulldozers at one end of the street, lined up like an army waiting to invade. Men in hard hats stood about making notes on their clipboards, engaged in endless discussions. They seemed to be blocking off the street with barriers, erecting scaffolding here and there, putting up warning signs.

'Are they going to start work today?' Jimmy Ramsay was asking, as a group of them stood huddled together in the rain, worrying over what to do next.

'Since they've given us only till the end of the week to move out, it's bound to be soon, that's for sure,' Patsy agreed. 'Then what? Do we meekly leave, or stay and fight?'

Rose was livid that all their efforts seemed to be coming to nought. 'We stay and fight. We ring all of the newspapers again, the nationals this time, not just the local lot.'

'And the television people,' Papa Bertalone raged, shaking his fist. 'We should make them take pictures to show the world how these developers mean to take down perfectly good houses and destroy our market.'

'You're absolutely right,' Belle agreed. 'I'll get on to it this very minute. We need to show everyone that we haven't given up yet, that we remain strong.'

Jimmy Ramsay turned to Rose. 'It's time you and me paid another visit to them flippin' councillors, tried one more time to get them on our side and persuade these people to at least meet us half way.'

'Let's march on them right now and chase them dozers off our street,' Winnie Holmes shouted, and a roar of approval went up.

It was at this moment that Harriet come running across the cobbles towards them, quite out of breath and her face ashen, a picture of distress. Steve, looking equally concerned, was by her side. He half supported her as she skidded to a halt and instantly burst into tears.

It took a moment for Rose to get any sense out of her, the

entire gathering of stallholders and residents listening agog to the tale. It seemed that out of some long-held desire for revenge, Joyce had stolen little Michelle and clearly meant the baby harm.

'She would,' Frankie Morris agreed. 'That sounds very like Joyce. She's been out for revenge all her life.'

'But why take it out on an innocent babby?' Winnie Holmes wanted to know.

'Because she's a paranoiac and has lost all sense of reason and logic. She were raped when she were young,' Frankie bluntly told them, suddenly tired of secrets. 'By my brother, as it turned out, though she didn't know that at the time. I've kept quiet to protect him 'cos he was nobbut a lad, a young sailor the worse for drink at a party and really hadn't the first idea what he was doing, or that she was unwilling. Unfortunately, he left Joyce pregnant with Grant and she's tried to cover it up with lies ever since. The bitterness of that tragedy ruined her marriage and warped her mind. But now isn't the time to talk about the rights and wrongs of the case. We have to find that baby.'

The campaign to save the market was instantly put on hold. A baby's life was at stake, which was surely far more important.

Everyone began to search and the police were called in to help. Only the men driving the bulldozers carried on working, perhaps glad to be free to get on with the job.

They could find no trace of her. Harriet was distraught, and accused Grant of aiding and abetting his mother to steal Michelle. He denied all knowledge of her plan, and for once he looked so earnest that Harriet felt obliged to believe him.

Grant did, however, agree to help search for the baby, while privately thinking that if he found the child first, he would indeed help Joyce to dispose of the little bastard, any way he thought fit. He also felt aggrieved at being disinherited, which seemed to encapsulate all the neglect he imagined he'd been subjected to over the years.

He knew all about the rape now, that his father was some young drunken sailor, apparently Frankie Morris's useless younger brother and not a rich businessman at all. It was too much, serving only to fuel his resentment and anger.

Unaware of these thoughts, Harriet frantically hammered on door after door, working her way down the street, terrified her child might have been hidden in a house about to bulldozed out of existence. She kept screaming at someone to stop the men from working, but nobody took any notice, perhaps couldn't even hear her above the din.

She felt as if her life were crumbling to ashes before her eyes. She'd come to trust Margaret, then the woman blatantly eavesdrops on a private conversation and jumps to entirely the wrong conclusion. Steve too had instantly assumed that she'd be eager to rush back to Vinny at a moment's notice. Could she trust no one? Did nobody believe in her, or listen to a word she said?

Now her precious child was missing. What more could go wrong?

And why would Joyce suddenly take it into her head to run off with the baby? She'd largely ignored them both for months, barely speaking to Harriet and only then when out in public in a rather embarrassing pretence of family unity for the benefit of the neighbours. Surely she wasn't still trying to prove that Harriet was an unfit mother, or angling to have the child adopted?

It came to Harriet in that moment where Joyce might have taken the baby. To Father Dimmock and that Christian middle-class family who were so desperate for a child. The priest lived at the top of the street, opposite Leo Catlow, right next to the church.

Harriet began to run. She didn't wait for Steve or anyone else to join her, she just flew up the street in search of her child. Nor, when she reached the presbytery, did she pause to knock or ask politely if she might come in. Harriet thrust open the door and marched right in.

Joyce was sitting in the Priest's private office. Father Dimmock was seated at his desk and opposite him sat a middle-aged couple who glanced up with a welcoming smile as Harriet charged in. There was no sign of Michelle.

'Where is she? What have you done with her?'

'Ah, Harriet,' Father Dimmock said, getting up to go to her. 'Do come in. I'm so pleased that you've changed your mind about having the baby adopted. We have the papers here, all signed. The new adoptive parents in this very private adoption are absolutely delighted. Well done, Harriet, for doing the right thing. I'm sure you won't ever regret it.'

Harriet could think of no response as she stared at them all, numb with shock. In that moment of utter horror she felt as if she had lost everything. Whatever problems she'd had to contend with were as nothing compared with losing her child.

She'd been forced to accept the fact that her beloved father wasn't quite the hero she'd imagined him to be. He had flaws, as everybody did, never finding it in his heart to believe his wife's explanation of being raped, growing to hate her for failing to mention her pregnancy at the time of their marriage. Harriet could understand his attitude but a lifetime was a long time to carry a grudge.

Joyce though, was even worse. Having lied and tricked him, hoping to miraculously pass off Grant as Stan's own son, why would she be surprised when he cheated on her? The pair of them, once so deeply in love, should have exercised a little more forgiveness, something they consistently failed to do.

But Joyce's need for revenge hadn't died with her husband. Instead she'd redirected her venom on Harriet, his love child.

'Why?' Harriet flew at her stepmother, ignoring the hands which attempted to restrain her as rage roared through her veins like liquid fire. Father Dimmock made a grab for her, anxiously attempting to calm tempers all round. Harriet shook him off to confront her stepmother. 'Just tell me the truth for once. The whole truth, and not some fabricated, sanitised version. What happened between you and my real mother back in 1941 when I was born?'

'All right,' Joyce said, folding her hands calmly in her lap. 'I'll tell you.'

44

Joyce

Joyce would never know what woke her. She'd given Harriet her last feed at ten o'clock, put her to bed as usual, and must have fallen asleep while reading in the armchair. She hadn't bothered to light a fire but switched on the electric heater instead, the warmth of which had obviously lulled her off to sleep. But something must have disturbed her. She sat up, all senses alert, ears straining for any sound, the light in the room gloomy with only a small table lamp lit and the black-out curtains firmly drawn.

Was it an air raid? Had the siren sounded? She could hear nothing, not even a whimper from the baby. After listening for some long moments, she tucked her legs under her and went back to her book when once more her senses were alerted. Something was definitely wrong, she was sure of it.

A strange prickling awareness crawled down her spine. Was that a creak on the stairs? Someone was in the house. Joyce got up from the chair and padded to the door in her bare feet. Wrenching it open, heart pounding with fear, she was confronted by the sight of her hated rival. Eileen was standing frozen half way down the stairs, and in her arms was Harriet.

'How the hell did you get in?' Joyce was appalled, livid that this woman, this *harlot* had somehow invaded her privacy.

'She's mine!' Eileen said, and ran the rest of the way down the stairs. Before she had a chance to reach the front door, Joyce grabbed hold of her, shouting for her to hand over the baby.

'Give her to me, give her to me!' Joyce yelled, tugging at her coat as the other woman struggled to free herself. Joyce hit out, striking her across the head. Eileen yelped, then struck back, clawing at Joyce's face with her nails. Joyce screamed, then retaliated by grasping the other woman by the hair and shaking her like a dog.

Eileen squealed in desperation. 'Let go of me! Let go! She's *my* baby, she's *mine*! Stop it, you'll hurt her.'

'It's *you* I want to hurt, not the baby! Give her to me or I swear I'll kill you!'

They fought like mad women, Harriet screaming at the top of her lungs as Joyce frantically struggled to rip her from her mother's arms, Eileen desperately clinging to her child. Somehow, as they thrashed about, punched and clawed at each other, they were no longer in the hall but in the living room. Joyce snatched off Eileen's scarf and flung it across the room. It landed on the electric fire that stood by Joyce's chair and soon began to smoulder. Neither woman paid it the slightest attention, their focus being entirely on the tug-of-war over the child.

Joyce punched Eileen in the mouth, knocking the other woman to her knees which sent the electric fire spinning across the shiny linoleum floor to the window. The draught of its journey caused the already smouldering scarf, still caught on the bars of the fire, to burst into flames which in turn set the long black-out curtains alight. Yet still Eileen kept a tight hold of the baby, not even noticing.

The two women fought like tigers, each determined to take possession of that baby, at whatever cost. In her fury, Joyce's vision began to grow blurred. She felt a tightness in her chest and started to cough, yet she didn't give up, not for an instant. Once again she lunged at Eileen, kicking her legs from under her as she made a grab for the child.

It was then, as Eileen managed to right herself, attempting to escape Joyce's grasp that they heard the ominous crackle and at last noticed the flames. The fire had leapt from the window curtains to the wing chair, blackening the curled pages of Joyce's abandoned book, and was now swallowing the cushion in a hungry tongue of flame.

In that horrifying moment, time seemed to stand still, and Joyce realised her coughing and choking was due to the wreaths of smoke swirling around them both. Sparks leaped like livid fire-flies all about the room, even the carpet beneath her feet was beginning to crackle and sizzle with the heat.

'What have you done?' Joyce could hear herself yelling at the top of her voice, shouting over the increasing roar of the flames.

'It wasn't me, it was *you*! You must have thrown my scarf on to the fire, then knocked it over, you stupid woman.'

'If you'd never broken into my house in the first place and tried to steal Harriet from me, this would never have happened!'

'*You* stole her from *me*,' Eileen screamed right back.

As they swore and yelled and screamed at each other, the fire continued to grow and make steady progress round them. They might well have continued with this pointless argument for several more dangerous moments, even fallen to fighting again, had they not heard a cry. Rushing out into the hall, both women saw Rose poised at the head of the stairs.

Dressed in her cosy tartan dressing-gown, hair in curling pins, she stood with a look of dazed horror on her face. The old woman was coughing and gasping, looking as if she were about to tumble downstairs. Smoke was billowing all around, pouring out of the door of the room below, which was by this time a furnace. Before Joyce had time to move, Eileen rushed up the stairs to grab her, still with the crying baby held in her arms, Harriet's tiny face pressed into her shoulder to protect her from the smoke.

'Quickly, quickly, but don't fall.'

'Never mind about me,' Rose cried. 'Save that baby.'

Eileen tucked Harriet under her coat. 'There, she'll be fine. Come with me, Rose, come on. Take my hand. That's right, don't panic. I didn't start this fire, I swear it. I just wanted to take my child back! It was an accident,' Eileen was sobbing as she helped the older woman safely down the stairs.

Watching them, Joyce was filled with a sudden rage. This woman, this *strumpet* who had already stolen her husband was the one responsible for this horror. If she'd only accepted the allowance they'd generously provided, and got on with her life, instead of obstinately stalking them and now breaking into the house to get Harriet back, this tragedy would never have occurred.

What happened next could never afterwards be accurately explained. Joyce, having failed to wrest the child out of her rival's arms and with the fire rapidly growing out of control, was anxious to call for help and get them all out of the house, so she opened the front door. It was perhaps the worst thing she could have done.

Just as Rose and Eileen reached the foot of the stairs, a blast of hot air rushed past them and flames suddenly seemed to engulf the tiny hallway. Paint blistered and part of the banister collapsed, strips of lath and plaster fell everywhere, and the living-room door fell off its hinges, almost blocking their exit.

It seemed impossible that anyone could survive this inferno but then the two women emerged through the haze of smoke and flame, arms wrapped about each other. Eileen's hair was starting to burn, flames lighting her head like a halo yet she continued to assist the older woman towards the open front door. And the baby, tucked under Eileen's coat, was now ominously quiet.

Consumed with fury every bit as terrible as the fire that raged all round them, Joyce wrestled Harriet from the other woman's arms and then hit her hard across the face.

'You *bitch*! *This is your fault, you whore!* You could have had us all *killed.*'

Caught unawares, Eileen failed to defend herself and fell backwards into the flames, just as part of the ceiling fell down.

The baby was taken straight to hospital. Fortunately there wasn't a scratch on her, and no sign of any burns, but they gave her oxygen and kept baby Harriet in for observation, fearful of damage to her tiny lungs. Rose too was obliged to remain in hospital for a night or two, having suffered some minor burns, mainly to her hands and arms, but the doctors assured the old woman that there would be no long-lasting ill effects. Both herself, and the baby, would make a full recovery. Rose put her remarkable salvation entirely down to Eileen's timely rescue.

'She saved my life,' Rose announced to Joyce.

Her daughter's lip curled. 'She deserves to be dead for trying to steal Harriet and very nearly getting us all killed.'

'You stole Harriet from *her*, Joyce, if you remember. Eileen is the child's mother, and, understandably, wanted her back.'

'She has no right to her, none at all. First she steals my husband, now she takes Stan's child. And she's *my* child too now, by law! Let her sue me. Let her take me to court if she wants to. I'll fight her all the way and win my case, just you see if I don't. She's a harlot, a *whore*! Not fit to bring up a child.'

'I don't reckon the poor lass will be in any position to face any court for a long time to come,' Rose sadly commented. 'She might even wish that she were dead, poor girl.'

At these grim words even Joyce fell silent.

Her erstwhile friend was even now being treated for severe burns. It was a miracle, the doctors said, that the fire officers had got her out alive. She would never, however, be the woman she once was. All her hair had gone and her once pretty face was a mass of burns, much of the skin having bubbled and melted. Her arms and legs too were badly affected and it would be some weeks before they could even be certain that she would survive.

Her condition was being carefully monitored and, once they were sure that she was stable, Eileen would be sent to one of the specialist hospitals set up to treat pilots shot down in dog fights. A great deal was being learned about the treatment of burns, and in the use of plastic surgery to reconstruct damaged faces, but it was early days so far as Eileen was concerned. She faced a long, hard road of pain and suffering ahead.

Rose was staring at her daughter, her usually forgiving eyes quite cold. 'Why did you do it?'

'What?'

'Why did you hit her just then, right in the midst of that hell-hole? You'd finally wrestled Harriet out of her arms, so why hit her? And just when the lass had risked her own life to bring me down them burning stairs. Why couldn't you wait till we were all safely outside before having another go at her?'

Joyce looked at her mother askance. 'You think I care about *her*?'

'She's a human being.'

'I've told you, she stole my *husband*! She ruined my marriage.'

Rose sank back against the pillows of her hospital bed with a weary sigh and sadly shook her head. 'Nay, lass. You did that all by yourself. Your marriage never stood a chance. You can't live life based on a lie. It never works. And you can't keep that child and pretend she's yours, that too is a lie.'

'Who else would care for her now? Not Eileen. So would you rather I tell the truth and let Harriet go into an orphanage? Is that what you want? Would that solve anything? And she's still Stan's child, remember. So far as I am concerned, Eileen has only herself to blame. She brought this catastrophe upon herself.'

'You both did, I'm sorry to say.' Rose was feeling poorly and deeply agitated, not knowing what was the right and proper way to deal with this disaster. 'So what do we tell the authorities when they start asking questions about this tragedy? What do you tell Stan?'

Joyce drew in a sharp breath, remaining thoughtful for some long seconds. 'That it was an accident.'

'Caused by you and Eileen fighting over a child. You say you flung her scarf and it landed on the fire, then you knocked it over while you were fighting. How will you explain that to the firemen?'

'I'll say the fire was caused by a stray incendiary bomb. There was an air raid tonight.'

'Not before the fire, there wasn't.'

'No, but the timing surely won't matter, not in all the confusion of war. Will the fire brigade have time to properly investigate how it started? I don't think so. They're already off on some other mission, saving other poor souls from the conflagration. With luck, this accident will be put down to an act of war.'

'But that's another lie.'

Joyce sounded irritated. 'For goodness' sake, what does it matter anyway? Do you want us both to be carted off to prison for causing an affray, or trying to burn down the street, as well as being nearly roasted alive? As for Eileen, she deserves to be punished. Serve her right for not staying away like she was told.'

Rose was lost for words. 'By heck, Joyce love, how did you get to be this hard? You *slapped* her. You knocked her backwards into them flames. And when the ceiling came down you did nowt to save her.'

'I saved Harriet, didn't I? Who do you think was more important? Besides, it seems like justice to me that Eileen should be the one burned alive, and not us.'

Rose gave up and said no more.

45

Rose

Manchester has a long history of markets, going right back to 1066 when William the Conqueror conferred the manor, together with the privilege of holding fairs and markets, to celebrate his victory at Hastings. Yet despite this, Champion Street Market was about to be closed down, and, much to Rose's annoyance, no alternative site had yet been offered or found.

Rose had never thought of herself as a rebel, preferring to leave all of that to the younger generation, to her granddaughter and grandson who had more than enough rebellion in their blood for one family. Nevertheless, she wasn't going to stand back and witness the loss of her beloved street, and her home, without a fight.

Belle had rallied numerous members of the press, both local and national, and she and Rose were even now holding court and giving interviews, while keeping half an eye on what was happening at the bottom end of the street. Rose could hear the bulldozers grumbling and groaning and grinding their gears; heard the thunderous crash as a great metal ball swung through the air and smacked right into the sides of the old Victorian houses behind the fish market.

'All we are saying,' Rose shouted at the young reporter, lifting her voice above the din, 'is that while some of Champion Street may well need demolishing and rebuilding, that doesn't apply to all of it. And the market shouldn't be affected at all. Why can't it stay here even when the new flats are built?'

'Since no one has paid any heed to these arguments so far, what do you think your next move should be?' he asked.

It was a good question, one to which Rose had no answer. She was at her wits' end, her mind a complete blank, yet her fighting spirit, her fury at being treated in such a cavalier fashion was as strong as ever.

'We're going to carry on fighting,' yelled Jimmy Ramsay, waving his home-made banner in the young man's face.

Cheers went up all round as a gathering of fifty or more people prepared to march on the bulldozers. Big Molly Poulson had barricaded herself and her husband Ozzy in the house, swearing they'd have to knock it down round her ears before she left it. Most of the stallholders were more circumspect, but they were all fired up with anger.

The street was in chaos with television camera crews very much in evidence, men with microphones finding the prettiest girls to talk to for their opinions on the loss of this traditional market. Where would they go for their gossip and their bargains now?

Papa Bertalone was there with his entire family gathered about him, including Gina and Luc, declaring this draconian decision reminded him very much of Hitler. The Bertalone children had decorated both the parlour and the old ice-cream cart with home-made streamers and posters. SAVE OUR MARKET, these proclaimed in slightly drunken, bright red, blue and yellow letters.

Barry Holmes had collected together a box of rotten toma-toes, ready to throw at the bulldozer drivers if they came anywhere near the top end of the street. Not that that would stop them, but rotten fruit and veg were the only weapons he had to hand.

Clara Higginson, together with all her friends from the church, were quietly forming a protective chain in front of her house where they were singing 'Onward Christian Soldiers' as if they too were about to go into battle. Clara had escaped from the Nazis in Paris during the war, so had no intention of being fazed by a few bulldozers.

Lizzie Pringle was there too with her husband Charlie, along with Aunty Dot pushing a pram with the usual group of children in tow including Joey, Beth and Alan. The actual sweet-making took place elsewhere but they'd be sorry to lose Pringle's Chocolate Cabin, which had been the inspiration for the entire business. Lizzie was determined to stand firm with her friends.

Betty Hemley and her daughter Lynda stood arm in arm, together with her son Jake, and Lynda's husband Terry ready to withstand all-comers to save both Hall's Music Shop and Betty's flower stall. Dena Dobson was with them, stoutly assisted by her new doctor friend Adam, and, of course, little Trudy. Dena could, if necessary, set up her fashion business elsewhere, but she loved this market, this street, and had no intention of leaving it while one house, one wall, one *brick* remained in place.

The unlikely trio of Irma and Joe Southworth with Belle Garside, as chairman of the committee and market superintendent respectively, placed themselves in the centre of the street, right outside the main doors of the iron-framed market hall, as if they meant to guard it with their lives if necessary.

The crowds were growing, everyone who'd ever had any affection for the market had come along, ready to defend it. Joan Chapman and her sewing circle. Constable Nuttall and Miss Rogers, the sour-faced social worker, the whiskers on her chin seeming to bristle with anger. The old men who spent their days mulling over their betting slips by the old horse trough. Young Spider, who'd been taught to box by Barry Holmes at his Lads' Club, showing he was more than ready for a punch up with these so-called developers.

Benny was handing out free hot potatoes from his cart, to keep everyone's strength up, and even Chris and Amy George were present, despite them having now left Champion Street. If the market was saved, Chris thought he might open a bread stall, supplying it from the baker's shop he'd opened nearby on Deansgate. Everyone was shouting and jeering, preparing to begin their march and ignoring the line of police waiting for them at the end of the street.

'All we need is for the chairman of our local council to get behind us, that's all,' Rose mourned. 'We need him to see sense, to realise that Manchester can have its fancy new blocks of flats but they shouldn't let developers walk all over them and destroy perfectly good houses. Their power and greed should be restrained. If only somebody would be on our side!'

'I've just been talking to Leo Catlow,' Jimmy Ramsay said, rushing up, 'I thought, since he's an important businessman living on the corner of our street and well in with the council, he might put in a word and help us at the eleventh hour.'

Rose set her jaw into a grim line. 'No matter how long it takes, we're not moving an inch.' So saying, she sat down in the middle of the road, and, following her lead, so did several dozen others.

Right at the top of the street, in the house next to the church, an almighty row was taking place. Harriet was screaming at Joyce, and had resorted even to shouting at the priest, insisting that she had definitely *not* given her permission for this adoption, nor had she signed any papers. If he had such documents in his possession then they were fraudulent, possibly forged by her stepmother.

He didn't believe her, urging the girl to calm herself, so that 'this little matter could be satisfactorily sorted out'. Father Dimmock could see no wrong in Joyce. She was a stalwart, loyal member of his congregation and, in his opinion, would never stoop so low as to tell a lie or forge a signature. Her foolish daughter, on the other hand, who'd run off with an itinerant musician and given birth to his illegitimate baby was an entirely different matter. An unreliable witness, if ever there was one.

'Stop fighting, Harriet,' he warned her. 'This is by far the best solution for your baby. Be grateful that she is to go to such a fine, morally upstanding couple who will give her the kind of upbringing you can't.'

'But I'm her *mother!*' Harriet sobbed, quite beside herself with anguish. 'Doesn't that count for anything?'

'You are a very foolish, silly girl. A wanton little hussy who should beg the Holy Virgin for forgiveness for your sins. Have you even attempted to make confession?'

Steve stepped forward. 'Hold on a minute, that's putting it a bit rich. I'll not have you speak to Harriet in that way. Anyway,

I'm hoping to persuade Harriet to marry me soon, perhaps when my probationary year is over, then the baby will have everything she needs, a proper home with loving parents.'

Joyce interrupted, her mouth twisted with bitterness. 'It's too late for that. The deed is done. The papers are all signed.'

'And *you* signed them,' Harriet yelled. '*I* certainly didn't.'

'I am still your guardian. You'll do as I say.'

'Never!'

And while they argued, while Harriet wept and railed and the priest and her stepmother refused to listen, the proposed adoptive parents anxiously waited to take possession of their child.

Eventually, Father Dimmock forced Harriet into a chair and ordered her to calm down and stop being hysterical or he would be obliged to take more stringent methods to make her do so. 'Go and bring the child,' he gently instructed Joyce. 'Let us put an end to this nonsense.'

Joyce disappeared into the back kitchen where she'd apparently left little Michelle sleeping in her pram, while Harriet again jumped to her feet to batter her clenched fists against the priest's chest. Despite his warning, and even if it was a mortal sin to lay a hand on his sacred cassock, she was past caring. Harriet was overwhelmed by fear, terrified she was about to lose her child. And then Joyce burst through the door, breathless.

'She's not there. The baby's gone. Someone has taken her!'

The roar of bulldozers grew louder as the huge machines began to make their cumbersome progress along the street, moving ever closer to the demonstrators. The work's boss had evidently grown fed up of all the bad press and attention he was getting, and resolved to put an end to it as swiftly as possible.

'He's coming for us now, heading for the top of the street here,' Clara Higginson pointed out.

'By heck,' Rose cried. 'He's going for Big Molly's house first. Right, we'll show him.'

As one, the stallholders and residents, their numbers swelled by an increasing band of loyal customers, surged towards the machines. Rose lay herself down on the cobbles right outside Molly Poulson's house. Big Molly's anxious face could be seen peeping through the lace curtain, yet she stayed put, as did Rose.

It was at this precise moment that Harriet and Steve emerged from the presbytery. Harriet looked rather like a zombie as she walked somewhat unsteadily towards the assembled crowd, Steve supporting her as best he could with one arm about her waist.

Rose sat up, wary of leaving her post but concerned for her granddaughter. 'What's wrong, love? Where's our Michelle?'

Harriet shook her head, quite unable to answer. Steve quietly told the old woman that there was a problem. Swiftly, he explained what had taken place in the priest's office. Rose's jaw dropped open, the campaign for saving the market instantly forgotten.

Scrambling to her feet, Rose turned on her daughter. 'What have you done now?'

'I've done what's right, what's best for that child,' Joyce announced, her mouth firming into its customary tight, forbidding line.

'You've done what's best for *you*, as you always do, because you don't understand the meaning of mother love. Never have.'

'I will not have my reputation ruined.'

Rose gave a bitter laugh. 'If your reputation was ruined, then you'd have no one to blame but yourself. You've been sleeping with my best friend's husband for months, if not years. Why is it that you think yourself above the basic moral issues you freely impose upon others?'

'How dare you!' Joyce's cheeks flamed, acutely aware of the gossiping crowd gathered about her, smirking behind their hands, agog at this very public display of dirty linen. 'Drat you and your interfering ways, Mother. Somehow you always manage to set yourself against me.'

'Someone has to. I might be a bit blunt and rough but I don't hurt childer, as you seem to enjoy doing. I don't treat people with contempt, or waste my entire life on some misguided mission of revenge. Love and affection seem to be strangers to you, and truth something you manipulate to suit yourself, so is it any wonder if your husband came to hate the sight of you? And what did you do when he sought comfort elsewhere? Almost burned to death the lovely girl he'd fallen in love with, then stole her child.'

Whatever Joyce might have been about to say by way of response to this very public revelation of her darkest secrets, was lost in a terrified scream from Harriet.

All eyes turned as one towards the bulldozers. 'Oh, dear Lord, it's Grant,' Harriet cried. 'Look what he's doing. He's putting Michelle down on the cobbles, right in the path of the bulldozer.'

'*Murderer*!' Rose screamed, but her voice was lost in the hubbub as everyone moved at once, surging forward instinctively to rescue the baby.

Despite her disability and age, the old woman very nearly got there in time, shouting at the driver and ineffectually setting her shoulder against the huge machine as if she could single-handedly stop it.

Surprisingly, it was Joyce who reached the pair first. Flinging herself in front of the bulldozer, she pushed her son out of the way, but just as she reached for the baby she somehow lost her footing, slipped on the wet cobbles and fell.

46

Harriet

Whether it was the baby she was trying to save or, more likely, her beloved son, they would never know, but she failed to save herself. Joyce was dead, crushed beneath the giant caterpillar tracks.

By a miracle, her last act was to save the baby she'd resented so much. Despite a lifetime of seeking revenge in the pursuit of her good name, even Joyce, cold and hard as she undoubtedly was, could not commit murder. As she fell beneath the great yellow machine, she performed the one heroic deed of her life. She pushed the baby, warmly and securely wrapped in a blanket, along the ground, so that it slid across the slippery cobbles and came to rest, unharmed, at Harriet's feet.

Harriet instantly snatched up her child and held her safe to her breast, sobbing with relief. She was indeed a miracle child, a gift from God.

And Joyce had become a most unlikely heroine.

Steve wrapped his arms about them both and held them close. 'You're safe now, Harriet. No one will ever hurt either of you again, not without going through me first.'

It seemed that while the arrangements for the adoption were being made in the priest's office, Grant had simply picked up the baby and walked off with it. Not, apparently, with any firm idea in his head about what he intended to do with it. As he confessed to Constable Nuttall on their way to the station in the police car, hands securely handcuffed, he simply wanted 'to upset Harriet'. A disturbingly familiar motive for mischief.

Grant claimed that he'd expected the driver of the bulldozer to see the baby in good time, and stop. 'I only wanted to frighten her, to make her suffer as she has made me suffer by always being the favourite, both with Stan and with my grandmother, and for being the only one who'll benefit from Nan's will. I hate her, and her blasted child.'

'Well, let's see if you like the men who'll be sharing a cell with you in prison any better,' Constable Nuttall drily remarked.

Rose came home from hospital with her arm in a sling. She'd broken it in two places in her ineffectual and bravado attempt to stop the machine.

'At least this little babby is alive and well,' she said, giving her granddaughter and great-granddaughter a one-armed cuddle. 'Nowt else matters. And it could have been much worse. Tough as old boots, that's me. I'll not be much good at knitting for a while, that's all, but then I never were.'

They agreed to wait until Rose was better, and her arm out of plaster, before making their planned visit to Harriet's mother. Harriet didn't mind the delay, as there was so much going on right now, and they all needed a respite to recover from the trauma.

The market did indeed earn a reprieve in the eleventh hour, not simply because all work was stopped for the day due to the accident, but because the council had called a halt to the project. Leo Catlow had apparently been negotiating with the developers for some time, and the efforts of Rose and Belle Garside, Jimmy Ramsay, Joe Southworth and the rest of the committee, had also made them think twice.

New meetings were held and it was agreed that demolition would continue on the lower half of the street, the damp old Victorian houses would be replaced with modern flats, but the better houses at the top end would be spared. In view of this change, new plans needed to be drawn up. The flats would not in fact be high-rise, but a range of two-storey maisonettes and apartments, more in keeping with the remainder of Champion Street.

The historic, iron-framed market hall would be retained, along with its new extension. Champion Street Market was to be re-located to nearby streets, by permission of the council, until all building work was completed, at which point it could return and continue to operate for the next hundred years, if the committee so wished.

The stallholders held a street party to celebrate, attended by the likes of Big Molly and Clara Higginson, the Bertalones, Dena, and Winnie and Barry Holmes, Amy and Chris George, Betty Hemley, Terry and Lynda, Patsy and Marc, Lizzie Pringle and Charlie, not forgetting Aunty Dot and the children, with everyone overjoyed that their beloved Champion Street Market was to be saved and their homes spared from the wrecking ball.

Joyce was given a proper and dignified funeral, as she would have expected. Father Dimmock gave the eulogy and spoke movingly of her complete selflessness which she'd amply demonstrated in her last moments. Harriet and Rose didn't trust themselves to even glance at each other as he spoke these touching words.

Later, at the wake, which Irma organised for them in the salon, Harriet took the opportunity for a private word with Father Dimmock. He accepted that whether or not Joyce had forged the papers, Harriet, as the baby's mother, had the right to refuse permission. The adoption would not now go ahead.

'Perhaps,' Harriet asked the old priest, with a twinkle in her eye, 'you'd be willing to marry us now that Steve has qualified?'

Father Dimmock smiled kindly at her. 'I'd be proud to. Delighted, in fact.'

Steve whooped his delight. 'If that's a proposal, I accept,' and laughing he hugged and kissed Harriet right there in front of the priest, with Joyce not even cold in the ground.

Joyce's hair salon was also to be spared from demolition and Harriet thought she might take the shop over herself. She'd learnt quite a bit already watching her stepmother work, and could take a course in hair styling to learn the rest. She and Steve would live in the flat above, once they were married, and Rose could continue to live in Stan's old room at the back.

It felt like a new beginning, fresh hope for the future.

But it all seemed such a dreadful waste, of a life and of the love Joyce might have shared with Stan if only things had not gone so badly wrong for them. How much happier Joyce would have been if she'd been able to forgive the silly drunken sailor who'd first taken advantage of her, and if she'd been honest and open with Stan. How very different all their lives would have been with a little love and forgiveness all round.

'But I might not then have been born,' Harriet said to Steve, as she explained all this to him.

'And that would've been the worst disaster of all,' he agreed, kissing her tenderly, not in the least embarrassed by people watching and smiling fondly at this clear evidence of their love.

Harriet laughed. 'I'm grateful to Dad for that at least, even if he wasn't quite the hero I'd imagined him to be.' She was also anxious to meet the woman who'd given birth to her.

Later, when everyone had gone home, and Harriet was alone with Rose in the flat above the salon, her grandmother explained how she'd kept in constant touch with Eileen over the years.

'I paid her regular visits, at least once every month. She saved my life, after all, and she weren't at all a harlot as Joyce made out. I want you to know that she's doing remarkably well, considering what she's been through.'

It seemed Eileen lived in the wing of a special hospital which housed military personnel and civilians who had suffered badly from burns and bomb damage during the war. She was too afraid, too embarrassed by her appearance, to go out and about, or to see anyone. In spite of all the operations she'd endured, the painstaking plastic surgery, she was nervous of what her young daughter might think of her.

'Don't get me wrong, she's longing to see you, thrilled to pieces that you want to see her. I've kept her up to date with what you've been doing over the years, and she has an album full of photos of you. Your baby pictures and school photos,

holiday snaps when we went to Blackpool, that time when you were Harvest Queen, she has them all. And she loves you to bits, believe me.'

Harriet held her grandmother's hands. 'Then why should her appearance matter? You don't mind what she looks like, Nan, so why should I? Take me to see her soon, please. It's time I found out what mother love really feels like.'